DEMON FARE

BY
CORY DALE

Demon Fare

ISBN-13: 978-0692342633

Cover art and design by Duvall Design at
www.duvalldesign.wordpress.com
Interior layout, design and formatting by Duvall Design at
www.duvalldesign.wordpress.com

Published by Karen Duvall
www.karenduvallauthor.com

Printed in the United States of America.

Books by Karen Duvall include:

Desert Guardian

Knight's Curse

Darkest Knight

'Til The World Ends (Sun Storm)

"Tell me about this gang you used to belong to."

Henry nearly choked on his haggis. He gulped some water and cleared his throat. "My father —my human father—threw me out of the house when I started showing signs of being Hellspawn. I had nowhere to go, no friends, no family, so I lived on the streets of Brooklyn, eating out of trash cans and stealing dog food from people's yards."

Wanda wrinkled her nose. "It sickens me to think how many Hellspawn have been abandoned by their families. It was like that in Kentucky, too."

"Yeah, but the city's a lot tougher than a mining town. Hellspawn kids grouped together to survive, to protect themselves from humans who wanted us dead. Jasper saved my life."

She set down her sandwich. "How?"

The memory didn't hurt as much as it used to. It was true about time healing all wounds. Well, most of them. "A group of men tied me to a fence. They ripped off my shirt and started peeling the scales from my back. Claimed they were *curing* me."

Wanda held her hand over her mouth. "Oh, my God. They were torturing you?"

Oh, yeah. They sure as Hell were. "I'm none the worse for it. My scales grew back."

Dedicated to my grandchildren:
Kai, Nehlani,
Zach, Cheyenne, Aiden, Bella,
Adam and Andrew

The author wishes to thank...

...The Alpha Critique group from Rocky Mountain Fiction Writers for their insightful feedback. My agent, Elizabeth Winick Rubenstein, for being such a terrific story editor and helping me iron out the plot kinks. Thank you, dear beta readers, Alan Larson, Shannon Baker and Jim Ciaramitaro, for your excellent comments, corrections and suggestions. Thank you, Margaret Bailey, for being my copyeditor, and my heartfelt thanks to Chris Devlin for a thorough proof reading that uncovered the errors I missed. Big hugs all around!

It does indeed take a village to produce a book. I couldn't have done it without you.

CHAPTER ONE

Clouds of steam billowed through manhole covers and sewer grates, making it extra hard for Henry to see while driving in the dark. The taxi's smudged headlamps didn't help. He opened the throttle and the twenty-first century Model T barely sped up. "Mystic, can't you go any faster?"

Lights blinked on the possessed taxi's dashboard and the tuner flickered through a dozen stations before finding what it wanted. A Victrola horn protruding from the dash blared a few chosen words from the airwaves: "Need... water... for steam."

"Dammit." Henry would rather not be late for tonight's pick-up. Levi was his best friend, but the man had no patience when it came to business. He'd lock Hell's Gate just to keep Henry from getting what he needed.

The radio sputtered so he reached outside the cab's window to give the antenna a twist. The static cleared and a sultry melody of band music hummed through the cab. Henry shook his head. After a century and a half of recovery from The Great Earthquake, you'd think the industrial world would be caught up by now. But no. Not even a freaking radio worked right.

He patted Mystic's steering wheel and shifted in the seat, his cramped knees hitting the dashboard. Releasing the lever on his back-up water supply, he said, "Full steam ahead."

"I'm... on it."

The taxi lurched forward and the sudden force shoved the hair back from Henry's face. That's more like it. They sped over the Brooklyn Bridge, suspension cables strobing by on either side, the cab's spindled wheels thrumming over bumpy pavement. The radio cycled to a new station. A barbershop quartet crooned a catchy harmony until it came to the chorus, where it repeated two words over and over.

"*Call the police coz you've stolen my heart... the police... the police... the police...*"

A police steam car sidled up beside them on the driver's side. A cop stared in through the window of the cab.

Henry leaned forward, relaxed arms folded across the dashboard, though his heart hammered against his ribs. The last thing he wanted was to get rousted by the cops for speeding.

Hoping to come off as friendly, he called out the window, "Evening, Officer!"

Eyes wide enough to show their whites, the cop flushed crimson. He looked madder than a mule chewing bumblebees.

"Hands on the wheel, mister! Pull over!"

Crap. "Better do as the man says," Henry muttered.

Mystic slowed down and steered to the curb. At three in the morning, the streets weren't nearly as congested as they'd been during the day. The cab angled into a deserted alley. "*Ticket,*" Mystic said through the radio. "*Traffic... Ticket.*"

Not if Henry had anything to say about it. One more ticket and he'd lose his hack license and would no longer be allowed to operate his taxi business. Legally, anyway.

The police car parked behind them, and its driver stayed in the car while his red-faced partner lunged from the vehicle as if launched by a slingshot. He slammed the door behind him and stomped up to the cab.

"This your rig?" The cop jabbed the brim of his police-issued derby back from his forehead. The act of aggression made the scales on Henry's spine stiffen in response.

"Yes, sir." Just be polite. Nothing to get worked up about. He might still be able to talk his way out of this and *only* talk. None of the tricky stuff like he used to do. Those days were over.

"Did you know you were speeding?"

Technically, *he* wasn't speeding. Mystic was. "It didn't feel like I was speeding."

"Are you being a smart ass?" The cop pulled his face into a scowl tight enough to burst a blood vessel.

"No, sir."

"Ten miles over the speed limit." The cop huffed in and out like a bellows. He acted angry, but Henry smelled fear strong as rancid seawater off a Manhattan pier. A scared man was a dangerous man. He knew that from experience.

Henry held his hands up in a pose of surrender. "My mistake. It won't happen again."

"Cut the crap." The cop gritted his teeth. "License and registration."

Henry nodded at the wooden glove box set into the lacquered dash. "Help yourself."

"Get it! Now!" The officer jabbed his thumb backward over his shoulder. "Out of the cab."

Henry tugged his bowler down to cover his pointed ears. The gray scales running down both sides of his neck might rile up the cop even more. Though Hellspawn were grudgingly accepted in the city, some humans weren't so keen about it. Henry had a feeling this cop might be one of them. He couldn't afford a confrontation, not with Hell's Gate expecting him at any minute.

Henry leaned sideways to grab his license and registration from the glove box. Tossing his head to make his longish hair fall forward over his scales, he climbed from the cab.

He stood slowly, knowing the cop's eyes followed every inch of his seven-foot height as he straightened his back and legs. Mr. Policeman's eyes widened and his face blanched while his hand rushed to the gun on his hip.

Well, shit. Henry could let the man shoot him for all the good it would do. His wounds would heal while the cop watched. At the age of a hundred and fifty, but looking like a man in his mid-twenties, Henry had been shot, stabbed, strangled, and beaten enough times to prove just how sturdy he was.

The cop's hand shook as he pointed the gun. "You're Hellspawn." He waved his weapon at the cab. "And I bet that's one of your demon pets possessing your cab."

Mystic was much more than a pet. She was a friend. Henry snorted and crossed his arms over his chest. He should have gone into acting because he didn't feel nearly as confident as he pretended to be. "What's your point?"

Not letting Henry out of his sight, the cop stepped sideways toward his car. "Mac? Mac, get out here. I got me a big one."

His partner slid out of the car, knees bent in a slight crouch. Every movement he made shouted his intention to bolt at the first sign of trouble. "What's he done?"

"Nothing," Henry said.

"Shut up." The first cop circled Henry in slow, measured steps. "Who said you could talk, Spawnster?"

Henry winced at the nickname.

"Don't like being called a Spawnster, huh? Well, word's out that a big ole *Spawnster* robbed a corner market in Brooklyn tonight. You match the description." The cop jerked his chin at Mac. "Get me the brine gun."

"That's goin' a bit far, ain't it, Ned?"

"Bullets won't hardly stop him." Ned stood in front of Henry again. "But I know what won't heal so fast." Mac returned carrying what looked like a rifle with a tank the size of a small fire extinguisher attached to the stock. He handed it to Ned.

Sweat beaded on Henry's forehead. He gritted his teeth, steeling himself for what was to come. He could stand it. Wouldn't be the first time he got salt-burned. Let 'em have their fun so he could move on. It was better than the alternative; Henry rather not hurt anyone.

"You recognize this, do ya?" Ned grinned, showing a silver tooth that glinted in the light of a street lamp. "These squirters come in mighty handy on nights like this. You never know when you're gonna meet up with a trouble-making Spawnster."

Henry shifted uneasily on his feet. This could end badly. He'd never known a cop to be this paranoid. "I'm not a thief—"

"I told you to shut up!" Ned lifted the gun and aimed it at Henry's chest.

Henry sucked in a breath. Salt water would burn clean through his half-demon skin, but he'd heal. He always did. If they wanted to take him into custody, fine. His nephew would bail him out within the hour.

"No sense getting your monkey up, Officer. You want to arrest me? I'll come in peaceful. No trouble." Arms held above his head, Henry waited for the cop to put the gun down.

"Arrest you? Where's the fun in that?" Ned pumped the gun and re-aimed it at Henry. A breeze blew dried leaves around their feet, the raspy sound like a crackle of electricity inside Henry's head. Then came a click, loud as a mallet to a nail, when Ned's finger squeezed the trigger.

Henry dodged a stream of salt water from the gun's muzzle and shielded his face with one hand. The water sizzled over his skin, steam rising from the scorched flesh. Exquisite pain shot through his fingers.

Ned laughed.

Henry struggled to hold his temper. Jaw muscles flexing in time with his heartbeat, he stared at the cop with eyes he knew glowed red with barely contained rage.

"Woo-ee, we got us a feisty one." Ned chuckled and aimed his gun at Henry again.

Mac stepped forward to grab his partner's arm. "Don't be stupid. He's Hellspawn, Ned! You don't know what you're messin' with."

Ned jerked away. "The Hell I don't." The shit-eating grin dropped from the cop's face.

This wasn't just an act of bigotry. The cop behaved like he was on a mission and Henry was it. Come to think of it, Henry wouldn't put it past his ex-business partner to hire a cop to do his dirty work for him. Out of hundreds of Hellspawn in New York City, why pick on Henry? Because Jasper Clark, kingpin of the Hellspawn underground, held one hell of a grudge.

Blisters formed on Henry's hand, the bubbled flesh already leaking warm, sticky fluid down his upraised arm. He had no choice now. Time to shut it down. "Put the gun away."

"Ain't happenin', friend." Ned lifted the gun higher, setting his sights squarely between Henry's eyes. Blindness was a deal-breaker for Henry. He wouldn't hold back this time.

Henry sucked in a breath, the pressure behind his eyes building and flooding his brain with heat. He focused on Ned, seeking the other man's will, braicing his own will around it like strands in a rope. Ned stiffened and lowered the gun.

"Good boy," Henry said as the heat in his eyes intensified. "You're starting to forget why you picked up the gun in the first place."

Ned's eyes glazed over. "Forget."

"That's right. You and your partner never saw me or my cab on the street—"

"Hey!" Mac put his hand on Ned's shoulder and narrowed his eyes at Henry. "You're doin' one of those mind-whammy things. You hypnotized my partner!"

Henry nodded. He wasn't too concerned about anxious Mac, who was obviously unhappy with the whole situation. "You gonna try to stop me?"

Mac swallowed. "No." His shoulders slouched. "Sometimes Ned doesn't show a lick of sense. I knew goin' after you would be a mistake."

"It sure was." Henry slid his gaze to Mac, then refocused on Ned so as not to lose the connection. His powers were limited. He couldn't influence more than one person at a time. "But he'll be fine. Just take him home and put him to bed. By morning he won't remember a thing."

Ned's body began to shake. He resisted. A slow trickle of blood dripped from his nose.

"What are you doing to him?" Mac sounded frantic.

Henry kept his focus, mild pain thumping at his temples. "Ned's in denial, that's all. Just hurry and get him out of here. The sooner he's away from me, the faster he'll recover."

Mac grabbed hold of Ned's shoulders to steer him toward the police car.

"Oh, and Mac?"

Mac turned to look at him.

Henry glared at the cop. "This stays between you and me."

Eyes round as aviator goggles, Mac nodded and quickened his steps with Ned stumbling alongside him.

Tension eased from Henry's shoulders as he watched the two cops drive away. That had been close. Too close. There was a time in his youth when he had thrived on altercations just like that one. Back then, he'd had no qualms over controlling the will of others, making them bleed from the nose, eyes and ears, often to the point of passing out. He hadn't cared who he hurt, but that had been over fifty years ago. Times had changed. *He* had changed. The day his human descendants found him and accepted him into their lives, he had stopped hating humans. His life had purpose now: To be with his family and keep them safe.

Thoughts of Jasper Clark nagged at him. If his ex-partner wanted to take Henry down, what would stop him from going after his family, too? Humans were no match for an enraged Spawnster with a thirst for vengeance. Henry would have to take extra precautions for the safety of his human kin.

Henry stretched his neck, feeling the vertebrae pop with released stress, and marched toward Mystic. He had a new batch of demon arrivals to retrieve. Hell's pets made life easier for everyone, including humans, and Henry had a job to do.

He would make sure his demons had a safe place to go.

He slid onto the front seat of his taxi. "To Hell's Gate, Mystic, and make it snappy."

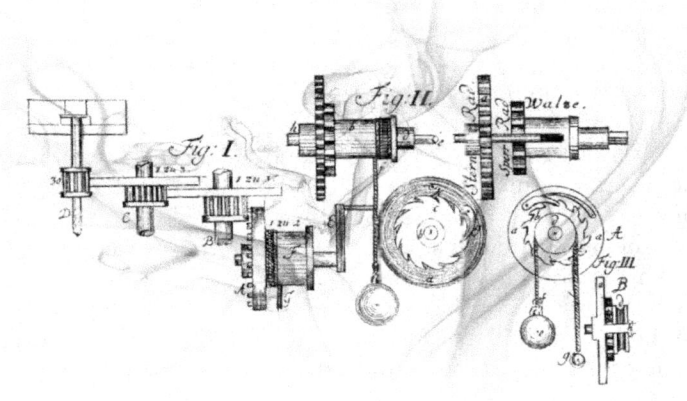

CHAPTER TWO

Wanda Snow fastened a row of buttons on her coat. Damn, it was colder than a banker's heart out here. She studied the park across the street, watching leafless branches waggle their twiggy fingers in the fog. Drawing back a sleeve, she checked her watch, its large, visible gears a weight around her wrist. Four in the morning. Two hours until sun-up.

Leaning against a lamppost, she gazed up the street, her senses tuned in to the demon energy flowing through the city. She sensed a Bringer coming her way.

Unclasping the tin choker from around her neck, she opened it just wide enough to let the voices in. Eyes closed, she focused on the whispered thoughts of a hundred demons that confirmed the identity of the Hellspawn she waited for. He was the Bringer, and although he didn't know it yet, he would help her stop the evil that conspired to take over New York City.

"How doin'?" A real voice came from the foggy dark, the words sounding burned as if by coal dust. She knew that sound. The raspy voices of coal-digging Spawnsters had filled the patch towns of her Kentucky home. She still heard them in her sleep. "Spare a dime for a man down on his luck?"

Wondering if she'd been followed, she turned to face him, her spine stiff and booted legs poised to kick what would hurt most. Wanda welcomed some trouble if it would warm her up. But the half-breed was a head shorter than her six feet, and his top hat had no top, his gloves had no fingers. The only threat he posed was the stink coming off him in waves strong enough to choke a skunk. Her gaze raked him up and down as she said, "I'm poor as you, mister. You won't hear no coins clinkin' in my pocket."

"I be a pig's uncle. You's a woman, ain't ya?"

"Last I looked."

He chuckled. "You dressed too manly to be one of Hell's Belles. What you doin' out in Central Park all by your lonesome?"

"Waitin' for someone. How 'bout you?"

His brown-toothed smile spread his mouth wider than normal for a human. He was a Spawnster, all right. And a drunk one at that. "Makin' new friends." He took a swig from a bottle wrapped in a paper bag and held it out for Wanda. "Wanna be my friend?"

She grimaced at the smell of rancid olive oil that was like a hundred proof grain alcohol to a Spawnster. Pushing the bottle away, she shook her head. "I'll pass, thanks anyway."

He frowned, his dark eyes starting to glow. Just her luck. A drunk Spawnster with a temper.

"I'm sure you're a nice guy and all, but I ain't interested. Share your oil with someone who can enjoy it, 'kay?" She turned toward the street.

"Fuckin' human." Venom deepened his voice. "You think you're better 'an me?"

Strong fingers gripped her arm above the elbow and tried to spin her around, but she didn't budge. The drunk yanked again and she took her time turning to face him. "You *don't* wanna do this."

He swung back a fist, aiming his scaly knuckles at her face, but she stopped the blow with one open palm.

Wanda slapped him hard in the face and he staggered backward, eyes wide. "Did no one ever teach you manners?" She slapped him again. "It ain't nice to beat up on a lady." A solid punch to his left temple dropped him face down in the gutter.

"Not that I'm a lady, you understand, but you still shouldn't go 'round beatin' up on people. It ain't polite." She smiled down at the unconscious Spawnster who was too dumb to be a spy. Even if he were, she'd left a clear message for whomever he worked for. His hat lay in the street about ten feet away. She picked it up, dusted it off with the sleeve of her coat, and set it on the ground beside him. He didn't move. "Have a nice night."

As she crossed over into the park, twin headlamps from an

oncoming car forced her into the shadows.

⚉ ⚉

Henry steered Mystic toward the PT Subway station in Central Park. "Noxious fog's too damn thick. Brighten your lights so I can see."

Mystic did as she was told and her lights reflected off the polluted mist to make it appear twice as dense. A shadow darted into the trees behind the station. "*Hmph.* Another homeless skell. They're like an epidemic around here." Henry pulled the cab to the curb and cut the engine. He glanced at the gear clock embedded in the dash and whistled. "Crap. Half-hour late. Levi's not gonna be happy."

The cab's radio found a talk show and snatched a bite of laughter from the studio audience.

"You think it's funny? You're not the one who has to go in there." Henry blew out a breath. He loved Levi like a brother, but isolation had shortened his friend's temper and after what Henry had just been through, he was in no mood for attitude. "I won't be long."

He stepped from the cab and the cold air enveloped him like an icy blanket, making him tug his trench coat tight against his body. Henry hated winter. At this time of year, his nose always ran and his toes went numb. He envied the coal-digging Hellspawn who got to live in the heated coal pits all year long. He'd chosen to freeze his scales off in the city because... Oh, yeah. Because his human family needed him. That was a good thing, right?

There were a couple hours left before the station would get busy with the day's urban travelers. Henry used a key to open the door to a stairwell leading to tunnels underground. The walls were made of ancient brick on the verge of crumbling, and dirt sifted from the low ceiling as his hat brushed up against it. Once beneath the main tube line, where capsule-like cars would soon get sucked throughout the city's subterranean tunnels by a vacuum, he approached a copper rectangle the size and shape of a door. This was the entrance to Levi's underground home. It also led to Hell's Gate.

Calling it a door was misleading because there was no keyhole, no lever or knob to twist or turn. Gaining entry was unnatural, and Henry would be damned if he'd ever get used to it. He shrugged out of his coat and pushed up his shirtsleeves. A string of black diamond-shaped tattoos lined the underside of his forearms, and he pressed the branded flesh to the door's surface. He had to admit the cold metal felt good against the blister on his hand. A slight tingle like an electric shock skittered over his arms, and then the door began to soften. He slipped a finger into the liquefied metal, thinking it should come out coated with copper. It came out clean.

No matter how many times he passed through this entrance, it never failed to unnerve him. What if he inhaled the copper and it suffocated him? Or what if it seeped beneath his eyelids to make him blind? The illusion worked so well that his mind had trouble comprehending the glamour spell that replaced the metal.

Henry sucked in a breath and stepped through.

He heard the whoosh of thrown darts before he saw them. Five copper needles thick as porcupine quills stopped a fraction of an inch from his face.

"You're late," came a graveled voice from across the room. "You know I hate waiting."

Henry touched the hovering dart aimed between his eyes. The sharp prick left a dot of blood on his fingertip. "I get your point." He slid sideways and all five darts dropped to the ground. "You can be so dramatic." Levi would never hurt him badly, but he'd pulled some painful surprises on Henry in the past. His moods were unpredictable. "It's not like I'm late on purpose."

"Then why *are* you late?"

"Can I come in first?"

Levi nodded, the mask of leather that covered his disfigured face bobbing like a doll head on a spring. The mask clashed with his velvet frock coat and crisply ironed slacks. White lace peeked from beneath the cuffs.

Levi stepped around Henry to approach a long couch inside an old wooden subway car. The car's capsule-like roof was gone, the doors missing, and it served nicely as Levi's parlor within a dank and dusty tunnel. The lacquered wood gleamed and ornate copper scrollwork lined the seams that joined each wall inside the car. Lush carpet patterned with lilies and roses lay at Levi's feet. He gestured for Henry to join him.

"Cops got me," Henry said as he leaned back against the

velvet cushions. He held up his blistered hand. "One of them did this."

Henry couldn't see Levi's face, but his friend stiffened. Levi empathized, though it hadn't been a policeman who dipped Levi headfirst into a barrel of seawater when he was a boy. The dipper had been Levi's older human brother.

Henry recited the entire story, from when he and Mystic were stopped on the street to when he had "shoved" the cop's mind into doing what he wanted. When he finished, Levi said, "At least you made the asshole bleed."

Henry winced. Hurting the cop hadn't been his intention, but his friend didn't need to know that. Levi cared little for humans, but accepted them as necessary. He needed their money.

"So what will you do about the cops?" Levi asked.

Henry shrugged. "Nothing. What would be the point?"

"They saw your face."

"Only one will remember me, and he was more scared than a rat in a flooded sewer." He thought back to Mac's frightened eyes, his cowering posture. Nope, he'd never see that cop again. Henry suspected the other one was on the take, an instrument for his enemy Jasper Clark, but he had no way to prove it.

Levi's mask tilted and Henry felt the gravity of his friend's eyes studying him. "If you need help getting rid of—"

Henry shook his head. "I'll take care of it."

"Suit yourself."

Enough about the cops. "So tell me about this new batch of demons I'm here to pick up."

Levi's shoulders squared and he said with enthusiasm, "They're Vox, just like your Mystic."

Henry frowned. "Mystic isn't a *pet* like the others. And she's not a beast of burden."

"A century ago, she possessed your horse and pulled your hansom cab, as I recall."

That was a very long time ago. Mystic had changed since then. She had... matured.

As if hearing Henry's thoughts, Levi said, "Vox learn quickly. They evolve." He nodded like he agreed with himself. "Our demon cousins are drawn to natural leaders like you. They thrive on dominance and direction from their betters, which is why Mystic has stayed with you for so long."

Placing two gloved hands over the mounds of his knees, Levi pushed himself to stand. "Since The Healing, our demon brethren have been sifting up from the Earth's core like sprouting seeds."

Henry cocked an eyebrow. Demons were harmless for the most part, and eager to please within reason. They liked being used. "Is there anything special I need to know about the new *sprouts* I'm here to collect?"

"These Vox are curious about working with humans and they expect compensation for their help." He couldn't see Levi's smile, but Henry heard the amusement in his friend's voice.

Henry knew the cost was small and most folks had no problem paying. He shrugged. "Of course. Companionship and sunlight."

"And don't forget domination." Levi stepped beyond the doorway of his parlor, the heel of his boot scuffing over the threshold. "A lesser demon's purpose is to follow. If no one leads them—"

"Trouble follows." Henry's jaw tightened. A free demon was an unruly demon, and an unruly demon got angry. He'd had encounters with a cranky demon or two in the past and it wasn't an experience he wanted to repeat.

Levi snapped his fingers and a Tiffany lamp hanging from the ceiling suddenly burst with light.

"Snit demon?" Henry asked.

Levi grunted. "No. Imp. They're not so demanding of sunlight. And since I have none to offer, it's a fair arrangement."

He followed Levi to an iron grate that covered a hole in the ground. Crimson light glowed from its depths. A fissure. And a deep one. It ran all the way to The Source.

"I have five demons for you." Levi knelt and lifted the grate. He peeled the glove from his right hand, flexing the scarred fingers that looked like raw meat in the glow of light streaming up from below. "They're volunteers. If these Vox enjoy their visit and decide to stay, they'll encourage others to join them."

Henry crouched on the ground beside Levi and reached for one of the redwood boxes stacked low on a shelf. A Chinese sorcerer in Chinatown used redwood blessed by Buddhist monks to build these boxes that held like iron. Henry handed the four-inch cube to Levi.

Levi slid the lid open and hovered his ungloved hand over

the hole. A thick mist rose to collect between his fingers and twined around them like wispy threads from a spider's web. He made a scooping motion, then dropped the luminous tendril into the box. The lid closed with a snap.

"You can mark it now," he told Henry.

Henry lifted a thumb to his mouth and ran it across one sharp canine. The tang of blood shocked his tongue. He pushed the pad of his thumb to the box and whispered, "My brand. My will. And so you are bound." The bond was temporary, just until he could turn the demons over to his nephew Vernon.

Four more boxes were filled and marked before the job was done. Henry blotted his thumb with his handkerchief, though the bleeding had already stopped and the cut nearly healed.

"Are these Vox for your human nephew?" Levi asked, a sour note in his voice.

"They are. Vernon pays good money." His nephew stood to make a bundle on this special batch of demons, but Vernon was always generous with his profits. "He's created some amazing inventions for the Vox to operate. We're making history."

"Just don't let him know the demons come from me," Levi said. "I expect no thanks or glory, Henry. Cash money is all that matters."

"Do you need me to bring you anything besides the money?" Henry glanced around the dark room and found the usual sparse furnishings, everything clean and in perfect order. "How are you set for food and clothing?"

"I'm fine, but thanks for asking." He pulled at the lace on his cuffs to make both sleeves even. "You know Claire takes good care of me."

"Of course." Claire was Levi's lover. She was Hellspawn, though signs of her demon side were hardly noticeable unless she took off her gloves or shoes. The woman's limbs were covered in shimmering turquoise scales. Lovely from a Hellspawn's perspective, but disturbing to most humans.

Henry glanced at his watch. It would be light within the hour and the station would soon be teeming with people. "I better run."

Levi nodded, handing him a gunnysack that contained the five redwood boxes. Henry slipped through the fake copper door and into the adjoining tunnel that led the way out.

The fog was still thick outside, but light crept along the

edge of a distant horizon. Enormous turbine generators hummed below the city, causing swirls of steam to seep up through manhole covers in the street. A haze of mist floated around Mystic like a cloud.

"Pop the trunk," Henry called to his cab and slung the sack of demon boxes over his shoulder.

But instead of the trunk's lid popping up, Mystic's horn began beeping.

Not what Henry was expecting. The noise would attract the attention of every skell in the park, and they'd be sure to come begging. Or worse. Henry turned his brisk walk into a trot. "I didn't say beep your horn, I said pop the trunk."

The horn kept beeping.

Henry muttered a curse and grabbed the latch on the trunk to give it a tug. That's when he heard the rapid tap of footsteps coming up behind him.

Before he could turn around, a sharp pain hit him between the shoulder blades, then another hit him in the temple. He went down like a felled tree. Flashes of light sparked behind his eyes. He blinked against the invading darkness, and from his vantage point behind Mystic's rear tire, he saw two slim-booted feet jog beside the cab.

His sack of boxes... It was gone.

Mystic's back door swung open and slammed into Henry's assailant, knocking him off his feet. He landed on his back with a grunt, but scrambled quickly to his knees.

The park wavered in front of Henry's eyes and the ground seemed to wobble once he gained his feet. He touched the back of his head and his fingers came away bloody. "Hey!" he yelled at the thief.

The man staggered, the sack clutched in greedy fists. His hat slipped off his head and...

A long braid of blonde hair tumbled free. The guy who had conked him on the noggin was a woman!

"Hey!" Henry called again and rushed forward, but his stomach lurched and his eyes crossed. Mystic started her engine and flung open the driver's side door for him to get in. He grabbed for it, but slid clumsily to his knees. Too dizzy. And the woman was getting away.

She sprinted across the street while tossing a look back over her shoulder. Her pale eyes stared with defiance. She'd succeeded in taking what she wanted and was making sure to rub it in.

The long braid loosened and blonde hair trailed free behind her. A single tress glowed a vibrant green that lit up the fog like a beacon. She was no ordinary human woman and would be easy to find.

"Hold off on that victory dance, little missy," Henry muttered to the shrinking form in the distance. He plucked her fallen cap from the street and gave it a sniff. "You're mine."

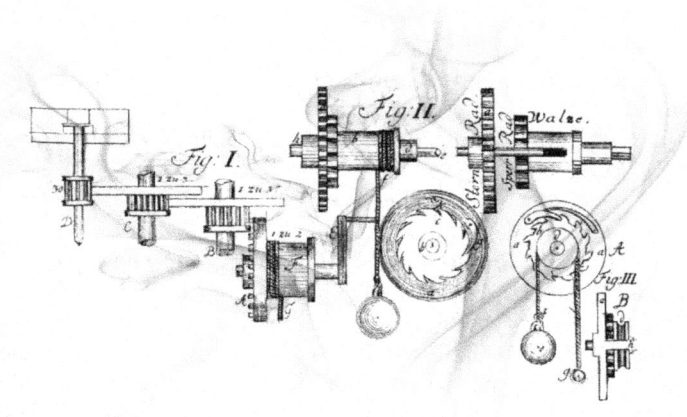

CHAPTER THREE

Wanda screamed in frustration and threw the wooden box against the basement wall. A chunk of plaster tumbled from the hole it made.

"Wanda, dear, you need to calm yourself," said a woman's voice from the stairs. "You'll upset the neighbors."

Breathing hard, Wanda stomped on the box and it skittered across the basement floor, stopping beneath a shelf cluttered with old toys, bedding, and stacks of ancient dishes. Why wouldn't the damn thing break?

She blew a wisp of hair from her forehead. "Aunt Alva, I can't open these boxes. It's like they're made of iron."

The middle-aged woman sat on the bottom step and shrugged. "Then you'll have to return them."

"No." Wanda retrieved the perfectly intact redwood box and turned it over to stare at the thumbprint branded on its lid. "Okay, maybe. I still need to think on it some."

"It looks like the Bringer placed his mark on those demons. You can't send them back to The Source without setting them free first." Alva sighed. "And you can't set them free without *him*."

Wanda nodded. "At least I have somethin' to bargain with. He has to hear me out."

"You'll charm him into it." Alva beamed at her niece. "You did well tonight, Wanda. Your great grandmother would have been proud."

A half-hearted smile tugged up the corners of Wanda's mouth as she remembered the Hellspawn woman who had set her on her path. "She'd always said the lesser demons would come to no good someday. Grandma Lacy had been vague on how, but I don't think that matters. A prophecy is a prophecy."

Alva stood and approached her niece to give her a hug. She wasn't tall enough to reach Wanda's shoulders, so she wrapped her arm around Wanda's waist instead. "You'll work it out. Now that you have his boxes, you're sittin' in the catbird's seat."

Wanda gathered up the wooden cubes and dropped them back in the sack. She'd tried everything to crack them open, had even thrown them in the furnace, but they wouldn't burn.

She used her booted foot to shove away the sheet of plywood covering the narrow hole in the basement floor. The rift glowed red, and hot, and hungry. It wanted its demons back. If the fissure mouth were bigger, she'd drop the boxes in whole.

"Wanda, honey," Alva said. "I'm so happy you're finally here. I've missed you."

Wanda smiled. "I missed you, too. The big city's different from what I'm used to, but I'm learnin' to like it okay."

Alva laughed. "Getting out of Kentucky now and then will do you good. It did me." She headed back to the stairs. "Come on up and I'll make you some breakfast."

Wanda closed her eyes, feeling exhaustion seep into her bones. She needed rest. Her energy level was a lot lower than it should be and if she didn't recharge her batteries, she couldn't do what she'd come to the city for.

"You can look for your Spawnster later," Alva added.

"He's not *my* Spawnster." Wanda wiped the back of her hand across her forehead, her fingers coming away damp with sweat. The furnace down here was baking her alive. "I don't want nothin' to do with him."

"Of course you don't, dear," her aunt said, a sly tone to her voice. "It's just that you haven't stopped talking about him since you got home."

That wasn't true. She didn't know him from Adam's housecat, but damn, he was a tall half-breed. And broad across the shoulders. And he swaggered when he walked. Arrogant Spawnster, and a tough one, too. She'd socked him hard enough to knock him into next week, but he got right back up, madder than spit on a griddle. Her smile spread a little wider.

"Get those stars out of your eyes, girl, and go on upstairs to take a bath." Alva gave her a playful pat on the rump. "I won't have no gutter rat dirtying up my kitchen chairs."

"Yes'm." Still grinning, Wanda trotted up the steps. Hot

water of a different sort was exactly what she wanted to get into.

⚙ ⚙

Henry opened one eye, then the other, and rolled onto his stomach. "Make it stop," he mumbled into the pillow.

The radio played a Big Band tune, and instead of stopping, it played louder.

"Stop!" he shouted.

The radio fell silent.

"Thank you." He drifted off again, and just as quickly, the radio switched back on.

"All right, all right! I'm up." The radio went instantly dead. Squinting against the muted daylight through his bedroom window, Henry sat upright. "*Cawwfeeee*," he yawned.

The sound of a percolator burbled from the kitchen, followed by the rich aroma of coffee.

"Eggs. Scrambled. Toast, and not burnt this time." He blinked and looked at the gear-covered clock taking up half his nightstand. Four in the afternoon. Ugh, it was too early, but he had a job to do and a thieving wench to lynch. "Make it five eggs and don't scrimp on the hot sauce."

The heavy four-poster bed creaked as he swung his legs over the side. He felt around with his toes for his slippers. The hardwood floor was cold as cement. Shivering, he said, "I need some heat here. What are you trying to do, freeze me to death?"

A large copper disk the size of Mystic's hubcaps rose up on spindly metal legs and crab walked closer to Henry. He snapped his fingers and it skittered faster, stopping a foot away. The rim began to glow red and Henry moaned with satisfaction as welcome heat flowed around his feet. "Much better. You know, I think you're probably the best invention Vernon's come up with yet."

The disk tapped one metal leg on the floor two times, which meant "thanks" in Imp-speak. Also Snit-speak. The lesser demons had a limited vocabulary.

Henry pulled on a pair of canvas trousers and trudged to the kitchen for his breakfast. Next item in Vernon's automated kitchen should be a butler robot. That would be keen. Then Henry wouldn't have to leave his bed at all.

He stretched and took the filled mug of coffee from the percolator's dispenser. The robotic arm on the wood-paneled refrigerator reached for the skillet on the stove and slid a mound of steaming scrambled eggs onto a plate. Henry plucked a slice of burnt toast—they'd never get it right—from the toast rack.

Easing into a chair by the window, he started on his breakfast. Halfway through his meal, he noticed an exceptionally tall woman pacing along the crowded sidewalk below. His flat was three stories above the street and he could see the top of the woman's head. It was barely above freezing out there, yet whoever this was had chosen not to wear a hat.

He reached for the coat rack and grabbed the driver's cap worn by last night's thief. "Scout," he called to the air, and a shiny red pinwheel fluttered down from the top shelf of a bookcase. It landed on the table beside his half-eaten breakfast. He picked up the Scout and set it on the cap. "Take a good whiff," he told the flying toy he'd bought at a curio shop last year. "Fly down to the sidewalk and let me know if anyone down there smells like this."

Henry opened the window just enough for the Imp to sail through. A blast of frigid air hit him in the face and he slammed the window shut. Damn winter weather. The Scout spun like a top and twirled just above the tall figure, whose face was hidden behind a turned up lapel. He looked for a lock of green hair, but saw only a blonde bun. Maybe it wasn't her.

When the Imp returned, Henry asked, "Well?" He shut the window against a gust of icy air. "Is that her?"

The Imp bobbed its pinwheel wings.

Henry smiled, amused by what was obviously no coincidence. What had she come to take from him this time? He clenched his fists and glanced at his Imp-powered heater. Over his dead body.

He looked out the window. The woman was gone.

"Cuss The Source," he growled. Now he'd have to chase after her. He snatched his coat from the rack before jerking open the front door to his apartment.

And there she stood.

The sight of her up close caught him off-guard. She was less than a foot shorter than he, and her enormous eyes were like blue marbles that she blinked and then narrowed to study him. She didn't appear a bit worried, but in fact seemed to grow a few inches taller while squaring her shoulders and resting a hand on one hip.

"This yours?" she asked, thrusting a redwood box in his face. *One* redwood box.

He didn't flinch. "What about the others?" His voice sounded gruff, but he had good reason to be upset.

"May I come in?"

"No." He grabbed for the box and she yanked it out of reach, holding it behind her back.

Henry crossed his arms and glared at her. One of his neighbors stuck her head out of her apartment to stare at them, then quickly disappeared back inside.

The thief raised an eyebrow. "You sure you won't invite me in?" She tossed the box in the air, and he caught it. Her wide smile showed an even line of snowy white teeth. "I thought you wanted your other four boxes back."

Henry gazed down the hall one way, then the other. Mr. Harris from 314 stepped out of his apartment and gave him a crusty look. The old man never had liked him. Henry was the only Hellspawn in the building, but he owned the building. The other tenants liked Henry just fine. "May I help you with something, Mr. Harris?" he asked, trying not to clench his teeth.

The old man vanished back inside and slammed the door.

"Your neighbors don't seem to like you very much." She hadn't stopped smiling.

The word "neighbors" sounded like "naybehs." A Southern girl. Henry sighed and backed his way into the apartment, sweeping out his hand to welcome her in.

"Thank you," she said and stepped inside.

The woman had guts, he gave her that, but he questioned her intelligence. He outweighed her by a good hundred pounds, though that hadn't stopped her last night. The bruise on the back of his head was gone, but not the memory of how it got there. She obviously wanted something else from him and he was curious to know what it was.

"I'd offer you coffee, but I'm fresh out," he lied, inhaling the luscious scent of his morning brew.

"I prefer chicory." She gazed around the apartment, not bothering to take off her coat, which meant she didn't intend to stay. Good. But she did unbutton it and flapped the lapels to fan herself. "You keep it mighty hot in here."

"My kind like the heat."

She nodded as if she understood. "Nice kitchen, though

that's the oddest-lookin' refrigerator I've ever seen."

The robotic arm on the fridge unfurled from its side, two eggs clutched in its steel-clawed hand. It angled as if to throw them straight at the woman's head.

Henry stepped in the way and scowled at the fridge. It seemed to know more about her than he did. "What is it that you want, uh..."

"Wanda. Wanda Snow." She stretched her fingers to grab the pinwheel on the table and it flew out of reach, twirling up to the top of the bookcase. "Your little spy is a nice touch, Mr. Paine."

"How do you know my name?"

"The cab company where I traced your possessed steam car told me you lived in this building. But no one would give me your apartment number. Thanks to your spy—" she glanced up at the bookcase —"I knew just where to look."

Wanda stared down at his copper heater and it scuttled underneath the bed. It was scared of her. Why?

"Lady—"

"The name's Wanda."

"Whatever. Look, you're upsetting my machines and you stole my demons last night. I've been patient, but if you don't tell me where my boxes are right now, I'll—"

"You'll what?" She didn't sound so pleasant now. A thick strand of hair braided into her bun began to glow a vibrant shade of green. "Please tell me, Mr. Paine. What will you do?"

He didn't know anything about this woman, but his demon intuition told him she was dangerous. She was up to something, and it had to do with the demons she'd stolen.

He locked eyes with her, his will funneling through him like water through a rain spout. He poured it directly into Wanda.

Her smile faltered and she scowled. "What are you doing?"

"I only want to make you happy, Wanda." His eyes sizzled in their sockets. "And you won't be happy until you tell me where you stashed my boxes."

"Can't." She swallowed and in a choked voice added, "Must send them back to Hell."

"But they're here to help people." He meant every word, though his intention was to soothe whatever had aggravated her into taking his Vox to begin with. "They *want* to be here."

She shook her head. "They can't understand. It's not

right."

It was Henry's turn to scowl. "What's not right?"

A thin line of blood trailed from one of Wanda's nostrils. That wasn't good. She had to stop resisting him.

It was vital she tell him where his Vox were. Those boxes held the future. They represented progress for the modern world. And most of all, they were tied to his family's livelihood.

Wanda launched herself at him and he caught her by the elbows. Her right hand pressed against his chest, fingers splayed over his heart. "Stop," she whispered.

"I will. Just as soon as you—"

There was a tugging sensation beneath his skin, then beneath his rib cage. His heart pounded, the muscle cramping and then opening, as if to release something from inside. Part of him felt compelled to return to the Earth's center and the molten core where the source of his being still lived. It hungered for half of him, his demon half, pulling at one part of his soul while the other part clutched desperately at his humanity.

He gasped. "No!"

They stood locked together in a stalemate of power. If he didn't release her, she'd die. If she didn't release him, his demon half would leave him forever. And he'd surely die without it.

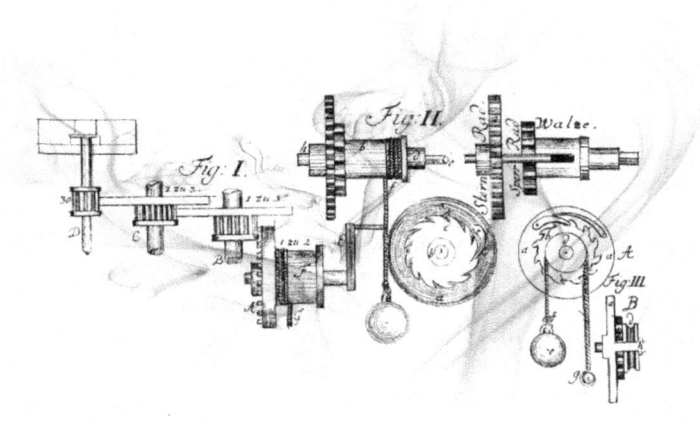

CHAPTER FOUR

Wanda wobbled on her feet, darkness seeping over her like an icy blanket, but she never lost her grip on Henry. It felt like she melted into him, seeking, finding...

"Music!" Henry yelled.

A sudden blast of sound from the radio startled Wanda and she jerked away from him. She staggered, her feet shuffling for purchase on the slick hardwood floor. She backed up against a wall to steady her legs. Where was she? Oh, yes. She'd made the idiot move of tracking Henry to this apartment building without first learning what kind of power he had.

"Brain damage is a higher price than I'm willin' to pay for your services, Mr. Paine," she said, scowling at Henry.

Henry tossed a thankful look at his radio. He clutched his chest with a meaty hand big enough to palm a small pumpkin. "What the Hell did you do to me?"

She blinked and looked away. "Real sorry about that, but it was self-defense."

"Like Hell it was. You nearly killed me!"

Wanda shook her head. "Nope. You'd only be half-dead. Spawnsters can't die all the way from exorcism. Just their demon parts... depart." She grinned.

He stared at her, horrified.

"Never met a bonafide exorcist before?"

"Can't say I've had the displeasure." Henry took an uneasy step backward, then braced his legs a shoulder's width apart. "I want you out of my home. Right now."

"But don't you want your demon boxes back?" She blinked at him, turning on the charm and feigning innocence. "They must be important to you, considerin' you branded them and all."

"Oh, now I get it." Henry's stick-straight posture relaxed, or at least his shoulders did. "You need me to free the Vox so you can exorcise them back to Hell. Well, I won't. They have a job to do and I aim to help them do it."

Wanda bit her lip. Vox. They were the smartest of the lesser demons. "They're all creatures with the potential for evil, Mr. Paine. The demons will destroy this world, and I mean to see them stopped before they do."

Henry laughed. He laughed so hard he started coughing and his eyes watered. In the kitchen, a mechanical arm covered in rivets and hinged by steel cables sprang up through a hole beside the sink. It filled a glass with water from the faucet. Henry grabbed the glass and downed the coffee in two gulps.

Impressed by the gadget, Wanda pretended to watch with detached interest.

Henry wiped a tear from his eye and shook his head. "These demons you want to *exorcise* are harmless as puppies."

"Even lap dogs can go rabid, Mr. Paine.' Her gaze roamed the room, scoping it out, looking for his little *creature* comforts. She touched the tin band around her neck to make sure it was clasped tight. The demon energy in here was strong.

They stood glaring at each other in silence.

Henry Paine could almost pass for human. He was brutishly handsome, his features youthful though his terminal scowl had etched a severe dent between his eyebrows. His dark hair was long enough to touch his collar, and his hairline met a patch of delicate scales that spotted the highest part of his forehead. There were lines of gray scales on both sides of his neck, and the bit of chest peeking from the open neck of his shirt showed the same fine pattern of scales as those at his hairline. Very nice.

"What are *you* looking at?" He wasn't smiling anymore. "Hellspawn aren't as alike as you humans think, Miss Snow. Each of us is unique. Does that surprise you?"

She shook her head. "Of course not. Many of my relatives are Spawnsters. In fact, my great-grandmother was Hellspawn. It takes a few drops of demon blood for a human to be an exorcist."

He huffed. "So I've heard. And how does your great grandmother feel about what you are?"

"Not that it's any of your business, but if she were still alive, she'd be very proud." Wanda wasn't offended by his question. She wanted him to know everything about her and why she'd come to New York. That was the only way to convince him to get involved and help her stop the prophecy from being fulfilled.

"Hellspawn don't die easy." He appeared to try masking his sympathy with disdain, but she saw through it. He was a caring man. "She must have been murdered."

"No." Wanda swallowed a small lump of pain. "She killed herself." She heaved in a breath and pushed off the wall, angling for the window. Staring down at the darkening street below, she said, "Grandma Lacy wasn't quite right in the head. Her prophecies, her visions, had been takin' their toll for decades. She got depressed and drank a quart of salt water that burned a hole straight through her gut. Never did heal and she bled out. Her death was slow and painful."

"I'm sorry."

Wanda shrugged. "She was clairvoyant. She knew there'd be a day in the future when the world would fight demon-possessed machines for survival, and it would start here. In this city." She slid her gaze to Henry. "Isn't that your business? Bringin' in demons to possess machines?"

"I don't think my toast rack has what it takes to be a killer."

Smart ass. He didn't get it. He had no idea what the future held.

Henry lifted his chin. "My demons are gentle, and they're here to help people, not hurt them. Why would they want to kill anyone? It's their nature to serve."

"The *why* doesn't matter." She shifted her eyes back to the window. "What matters is that they *will* kill. And my great grandmother set me on the path to stop it."

"So you've come here to rid the city of its demons."

Nodding, she turned to face him. "Yes." Sliding a folded sheet of yellowing paper from her coat pocket, she cleared her throat. "Grandma Lacy has her prophecy written down and you're gonna hear it."

He scowled and dipped his chin in a short nod. "Get on with it."

Wanda licked her lips and read: *"Seven score and ten years from The Great Earthquake there will be creatures of metal, wood and coal.*

Unseen demons live among the humans to usurp New Amsterdam. A Bringer will cleanse the city to lay ground for a new order and only exorcism can free Amsterdam from its bonds. If Amsterdam falls, the civilized world will be next."

Henry quirked a half-smile. "Mumbo... jumbo."

Wanda lifted her head in surprise. "I beg your pardon?"

"New York hasn't been New Amsterdam for hundreds of years, and everyone knows machines are naturally possessed. No big deal. That's how my demon cousins serve humans. And a new order for what?" He shook his head. "Free the city from its *bonds*? What bonds? Give me a break."

"My great grandmother's predictions were never wrong."

"That may be, but the hooey you just read makes no sense. And you want me to *help* you?"

She tilted her head to one side. "Will that be a problem?"

"Lady, I think your corset's laced too tight." He snapped his fingers and three lamps instantly switched on to chase away the twilight shadows. "Or maybe I caused you some brain damage after all."

Why had she thought this would be easy? "I'll make you a deal."

"What kind of deal?" The scowl was back, even deeper than before.

"If you let me show you a bad demon that's tryin' to kill someone, I'll give you the rest of your demon boxes. That is, if you still want 'em afterward." She was really hoping she could convince him to take her side. Partnering with a Bringer would make winning the coming war a lot easier.

Henry looked skeptical. "Wait a minute. I thought you said you needed my help."

"You're a Bringer. You call demons to you and bond 'em with your thumbprint. The demon I'm fixin' to introduce you to was bonded to a man who's dead now, which means it's stuck where it is. It's mighty ticked off about it, too. I can't exorcise it till its bond is broke. I need you to free it."

"But it doesn't belong to me."

"Don't matter." She swept out her hand and motioned toward the kitchen. "None of these were yours neither, am I right? They came to you, like metal sucked to a magnet." It puzzled her that he seemed not to know what he was capable of. Had she made a mistake? "Don't tell me this talent of yours is news to you."

He looked worried for a second, then lifted his biggety chin again. "Of course not. I'm a demon magnet. I knew that." He pinched his chin between thumb and forefinger, looking thoughtful. "You've got a deal."

⚕ ⚕

Mystic slammed the passenger side door a second time. Then locked it.

"What's with you, Mystic?" Henry grabbed the taxi's door handle and gave it yank. It didn't budge.

"I don't think it likes me much," Wanda said as she leaned against a lamppost to watch. "It's not goin' to let me in."

"Mystic is a *she*, not an *it*." He gave the cab's hood an affectionate pat. "You hurt her feelings."

Wanda snorted. "Feelin's? Who you tryin' to kid? That *machine* feels about as much as this here lamppost."

"You're wrong," Henry said. Mystic was afraid of Wanda, and he didn't blame her. The exorcist could easily pull Mystic's demon soul right out of the cab and send it straight to Hell, or worse. Mystic didn't belong in Hell. She belonged with Henry.

"It ain't happenin', friend. We might as well take the tube." Wanda pushed away from the lamppost and started down the sidewalk, joining the other pedestrians who made up the late afternoon rush. Henry couldn't tell which were human and which were not because everyone was bundled in wool coats and scarves of dull, dark colors that made them resemble lumps of dirt. Ah, there was a thin, hairless tail peeking out from beneath a woman's knee-length frock. Other than the tail, the rest differed only in weight and stature, and wore the requisite gas masks to protect against the city's noxious fog. Hellspawn breathed the air with impunity.

When Henry started to follow after Wanda, both the taxi's front doors flew open. A few passersby stopped to give the cab a startled look. Eyes narrowed with bewilderment, they quickly moved on.

Henry grinned. "It looks like she changed her mind."

"Uh huh." Wanda slinked back to the curb. She obviously wasn't eager to get in. Bending over to peer at the interior, she said, "Is it clean?"

The door swung shut and Wanda leapt back.

"For Pete's sake! Can we call a truce?" Henry slid onto the driver's seat. "Either that or I'm taking the tube. What'll it be, Mystic?"

The engine started and the radio dial spun in circles until it found what it was looking for. "*Bitch*," it said, snatching the word from one of the more provocative talk shows.

Wanda gasped. "What did you call me?"

The passenger door creaked slowly open, as if unsure it wanted to open at all.

"At least you acknowledged her as a living being," he said as he snapped the latch on his seat belt. "Get in and close the door. I'm freezing my scales off."

Wanda hesitated before sliding in, her face tight. Her lip peeled back and Henry saw that she gritted her teeth.

"Relax. She's just a car." Henry checked his side view mirror and eased out onto the street to merge with the flow of traffic. Steam billowed from behind every car, curling through a thick mist of burning coal fumes that clogged the city's air. "You've ridden in a steam car before, haven't you?"

"Not a possessed one," Wanda said, sucking in a breath when Mystic hit a bump. "It did that on purpose."

Henry sighed. This was going to be a long drive.

She directed him to the neighborhood where this alleged rogue demon was wreaking havoc. Henry didn't doubt there was a problem. Demons needed to be dominated, and if there was no one around to do it and they weren't free to find someone who would, things could get ugly. Did that mean it schemed to take over the world? Henry smiled to himself. Hardly.

If the demon was branded by its dead owner, Henry worried about his ability to put things right. Wanda had been correct that free demons were attracted to him, but it was because they knew he'd treat them right. A bonded demon was a different matter. He'd never tried freeing one that wasn't his to begin with. His spell-casting was rudimentary at best, and there was nothing in his limited repertoire that included breaking a demon bond. That was more up Levi's alley than his. But if he didn't break it, he'd lose his Vox to Wicked Wanda.

He steered Mystic on to Springfield Boulevard in Queens and she checked the numbers on apartment buildings he drove by.

"Right there," Wanda said, pointing to a brick structure

surrounded by chaos.

Flashes of light brightened a window on the fourth floor. It was clearly the site of the disturbance because all the other windows were dark. Power outage? The underground generator hummed beneath the street, so the building's power supply was fine. Someone, or something, had put the lights out.

Henry parked Mystic at the curb. "Can you answer a question for me?"

"Don't know until you ask." Wanda studied him, one eyebrow raised. "So ask."

"Why do you think I'm a... that I can..."

"That you're a Bringer?" She touched the metal around her neck, the center of it dotted with copper rivets. "The voices told me." Without waiting for him to respond, she pushed open the door and stepped out onto the sidewalk. "Damn. It's colder than a well-digger's ass out here."

He stood from the cab and faced her. "Did you say voices?"

She nodded, but didn't look at him. "Comes with the job."

"Of being an exorcist?"

"Yep. They're not literal voices because demons don't have mouths to talk with, but they can think. They think all the time. And I get their thoughts inside my head, which is why I wear this pretty necklace I got on." She touched the collar again. "It keeps 'em quiet until I'm ready to listen."

Wanda Snow had to be the strangest woman Henry had ever met. And though she was tall, her face was that of a girl barely out of her teens. She couldn't have been more than twenty, and yet this *child* had almost snatched his soul right out of his body. Or half his soul. It would take awhile to wrap his mind around that one.

"I tried to capture the demon myself yesterday and it about singed my eyebrows off," Wanda said while smoothing her bangs over her forehead. "I couldn't cut its bond and that made it mad."

"What's it possessing?" Henry asked.

"The kitchen oven."

"Where's its master?"

"Like I already told you, it doesn't have one. The possessed oven is with the new tenant in the dead master's apartment."

"A tenant who obviously doesn't know how to handle a demon."

"Obviously."

"Maybe if I just explained how to dominate a demon—"

"The new tenant is too scared. He wants it out of there and so do I." Wanda narrowed her eyes at Henry. "That's why *you're* here, remember?"

A crowd had gathered in the building's courtyard, everyone chattering and pointing in the direction of the disturbance. Henry gazed up at the apartment as a flame abruptly blew the window out. Glittering shards of glass rained down onto the scattering group of neighbors.

"You're not taking that out of my deposit!" someone on the ground yelled. It was a middle-aged man wearing canvas trousers and a tattered coat that hung off one shoulder. On second glance, it wasn't tattered. It was burned. "That oven tried to kill me!"

Folks were used to having a couple of Imps or Snits hanging around, and most unbonded demons wouldn't stay where they weren't wanted. The miserable creature up there had no choice.

"What a cruel way to treat a demon," Henry muttered. Bondage was meant to protect, not enslave. Its dead master had been an irresponsible bastard, probably a mage who put himself above all living things, including demons.

"Okay, Miss Snow, let's get on with it. What's your plan?"

Wanda pulled a small oval basket out of her coat pocket. "Put it in here."

He took it from her and inspected the basket from all angles. Fairly ordinary, except for the green strands of hair woven through strips of bark that held the basket together. "This your hair?"

"From my skunk stripe." Wanda tapped her bun and poked it with her finger. "It ain't showin' now, is it?"

"No." The basket had a lid, but it didn't close very tight. Not like the redwood boxes Levi used. "This won't hold." He handed it back.

"Yeah, it will. My hair will keep the demon from gettin' out. I promise."

So all he had to do was free the poor thing. Not caring how he'd get it done, Henry shrugged and headed for the building, Wanda at his heels.

It was an old building, built sometime after The Great Earthquake that had brought the world to its knees over a hundred and fifty years ago. If the building were any older, it wouldn't still be standing. Not many structures from that time were.

The crowd had moved to a small park across the street. There were reporters scribbling in notepads and a photographer snapping pictures. Henry assumed most of the people gathered were tenants, many of them human, but also some Hellspawn. He called out to the group, "Is anyone here a mage?"

People looked at each other until one young man wearing a grey driver's cap held up his hand and said, "I'm a mage's apprentice. Does that count?"

Henry approached the guy, who wasn't even as tall as Wanda. Towering over the man, Henry asked, "What's your name?"

"Hiram. Hiram Foss." He gazed up at Henry and grinned. "Is there something I can do for you?"

"Have any graveyard dirt?" It would help if it came from the dead master's grave, but there wasn't time for that.

"Sure," Hiram said. "Local or European?"

"Local's fine. And I'll need oil. What kind you got?"

"Cinnamon, sesame, rose, sweet pea—"

"Rose and sweet pea will work." Demons loved flowers because they were made of sunlight, a delicacy since sunlight didn't exist where they came from. Sunshine made them happy. The flower oils would calm the demon, and Henry hoped that burning the grave dirt would break its bond with the dead master. "Do you have them with you?"

"You're in luck. I just got out of a spell-casting class at the college." Hiram handed Henry two small vials stopped with corks, and a small fabric bag. "Keep 'em. I have lots more."

"That's very generous. Thank you." He smiled and turned away.

As Wanda walked beside him toward the building's entrance, she said, "I already tried burnin' grave dirt, you know."

Damn. "Didn't work?"

"What do you think?"

I think you're a cocky little bitch. Not that he'd say it outright. At least not until after he got his Vox back. "You probably did it wrong."

Looking indignant, she said, "The Hell you say."

"The Hell I do." He walked ahead of her up the stairs and from her heavy footfalls behind him, he imagined her in a temper. Good. Let her stew.

When he reached the fourth floor, he spotted a flashing line of light from underneath one apartment door. This had to be the place.

Henry knocked and the flashing stopped. That was a good sign. He waited a full minute before turning the knob and slowly pushing his way inside. He'd barely stepped across the threshold when a fireball erupted from across the room and hurtled straight for him.

It exploded in a wall of flame that covered Henry from head to toe. The heat felt good after the frigid conditions outside. Hellspawn were impervious to fire.

"Hey, that was nice. Can I have another?"

The oven sat in silent darkness, pouting.

"Look, buster, you gotta get a grip. I understand, okay? You need a new master, someone to tell you what to do. And I'll find you one."

Wanda cleared her throat.

Henry kept talking. "Or maybe it would be better if you return home for a while. See the old neighborhood in Hell. Catch up with the family."

The oven shook and began to glow. Henry took that as a no.

"You want to go free, right?" he asked the demon.

The oven's door flapped open and shut. Henry took that as a yes. From its behavior, he could tell this demon was a Snit, slightly more aggressive and less playful than an Imp.

"I have something to help calm your nerves." He stalked up to the oven, removed the cork tops on both vials, and dribbled their contents over the stove top.

It began to glow again, and not in a happy way. Smoke puffed out of its burner plates.

"What'd you do?" Wanda asked from the safety of the doorway.

Henry was confused. The demon should be calmed by the flower oils. He sniffed both vials. One was definitely rose, but the other...

"Pepper oil." Henry tossed the vial to Wanda so she could smell it for herself. "That mage's apprentice gave me the wrong one."

Flames licked out from the dials on the stove and stretched like fiery fingers for the kitchen walls. The room was about to light up like a torch.

"Now what?" Wanda asked, her voice tense.

Henry saw her eyebrows slant with worry. It was a good look on her. Softened her sharp edges.

"We burn the dirt."

"I told you I already tried that." Her annoyed tone made the scales on his neck stand up. "It won't work."

The flames from the oven grew brighter and smoke spewed from its open door. A fireball was growing inside.

Henry opened the tiny bag of grave dirt. "This is from your dead master's grave," he yelled above the roar of flames coming from the oven. He was lying about where it came from, but the demon didn't know that. "When I burn it, your bond will break."

But before throwing the bag into the flames, he bit his thumb and held the bleeding wound over the dirt. Having no idea if it would work, he doubted it could make things any worse. He squeezed out a few generous drops, then closed up the bag and tossed it through the oven's open door.

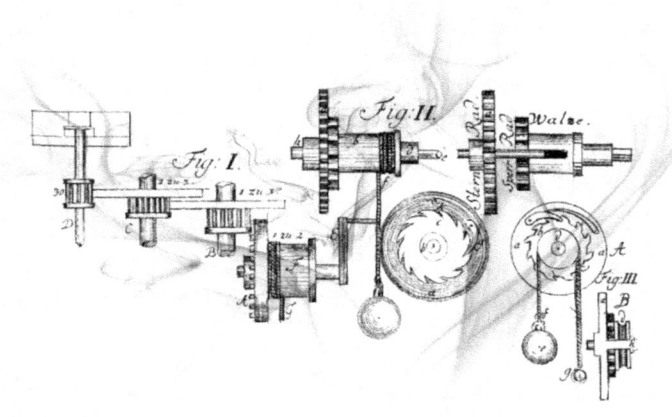

CHAPTER FIVE

It was like someone blew out a candle.

The flames died and the kitchen went dark again. A glowing blue mist swirled out the oven door and drifted toward Henry.

Wanda shoved the basket at him. "Now catch it."

Henry stared down at the basket, reluctant to capture the demon. It had made it clear it didn't want to return to Hell. What if it was an old one from The Healing? Those were valuable because they hardly had to be trained. They already understood the human world and its ways.

"If you don't scoop it up, it'll escape," Wanda whispered, a frantic edge to her voice. "I thought we had a deal."

"It won't escape." The mist twirled around his legs and rubbed up against him like a contented cat. It just needed a companion, a master. It wasn't a bad demon, just a desperate one.

"Mr. Paine, if you want your Vox—"

"Shut up." He held out the basket and the rogue demon coiled itself inside. He shut the lid and shoved the basket at Wanda. "Happy now?"

"As a pig in mud." She grabbed the basket and stuffed it in her coat pocket. "You'll thank me for this someday."

Henry's mood took a dive. "I don't think so."

She tugged on his sleeve and turned to leave. "Come on. Our dealin' ain't done yet. I got myself a promise to keep."

Wanda held the basket in her lap, her fingers wrapped around the braided rows of willow bark. She tried to get a sense of what the demon could be feeling, but there was nothing there. How could there be? You wouldn't expect your lamp to be sad, or your vacuum cleaner to be lonely, or your lawn mower to be scared. They were machines, and a demon just helped them work better.

"How come you're not talkin'?" Wanda asked Henry.

His eyes stared at the road straight ahead, his big hands making Mystic's steering wheel look like a child's toy. "Because I have nothing to say."

He left off the last part, *to you*, but she still heard it in his tone. Not that it should matter. Henry Paine was only a means to an end, and if he didn't like her, so what? She'd have to figure out a way to make him believe Grandma Lacy's prophecy. Wanda couldn't stop the city's destruction if he didn't join in the fray.

He pulled up to the curb in front of her aunt's Brooklyn apartment building. "I'll wait here."

"Ah, come on, Mr. Paine. Won't you come inside? My Aunt Alva is a fantastic cook, and she knows how to cook for Spawnsters since half our family is Hellspawn." She'd rather him not come in, but how else would she win him over? "You ain't even hungry?"

"I'm fine. Just get me my demon boxes and I'll leave."

"You sure? My belly's so empty I'm fartin' cobwebs."

He gave her a horrified look. "You eat with that mouth?"

She rolled her eyes. No sense of humor. "I'm gonna have my supper before I fetch your boxes, so come in or stay out in the cold. Up to you."

He shivered and switched off the engine.

"Great!" Wanda smiled and pushed at the cab's door, which opened so fast it swung her out onto the sidewalk with her still holding the handle. She landed flat on her ass.

"Mystic, cut it out. We're almost done with this... this..." He waved a hand at Wanda as if unsure what to call her.

She glared at Henry, silently daring him to laugh as she mustered what little grace she had left to regain her feet. Brushing dirt from the back of her skirt and pretending not to feel humiliated, Wanda said, "Is there something I can do for your, uh, Mystic? Bless her heart."

Henry gave her a sardonic grin. "Nice try."

He followed her inside the building and up the stairs to her aunt's apartment. Wanda used her key to let them in and called out, "Aunt Alva? We got company. Set an extra plate."

Her aunt appeared from around a corner, wiping her hands on an apron. Wanda had told Alva beforehand that she would try getting Henry to stay for supper, so her aunt had planned a salt-free meal loaded with Spawnster favorites. Wanda had calluses in her stomach from years of eating spicy food hot enough to burn holes through a human's teeth.

"Aunt Alva, this is Henry Paine."

"Nice to meet you, Henry," Alva said, her smile wide enough to split her face clean in half. She held out her hand and Henry gave it a brief shake. "You stayin' for supper?"

"No, ma'am. I have a late shift with my cab."

Wanda couldn't understand why he bothered driving a taxi. Based on her research, she knew for a fact the man had more money than God.

"What a shame," Alva said, her mouth turning down in a pout. "I got a pot roast with enough horseradish to set the entire state of Kentucky on fire."

Looking sheepish, he said, "That's very kind, but I'm on a special diet—"

"If you're worried about salt, don't be. We're a salt-free family. Too much salt is bad for the blood pressure."

Henry closed his eyes as if praying for rescue.

"Never mind, Aunt Alva," Wanda said. "He's probably not even a drinkin' man so that rosemary-jalapeno oil you put up last month won't interest him one iota."

He blinked. "Rosemary *and* jalapeno?"

Wanda smiled. "Aunt Alva grows the rosemary herself, and Mr. Sanchez down the hall gave her a bushel of jalapeno peppers to pay her for rechargin' a talisman that lost its juice. The oil's got some kick. Fried eggs in it just this mornin'."

If she wasn't mistaken, she thought she saw a drop of drool glisten at the corner of Henry's mouth.

"Maybe one drink," he said.

Which quickly turned into a sit-down with a full plate of pot roast under an inch of horseradish and pickled jalapeno peppers on the side. Hot cinnamon apples for dessert.

"I'm stuffed," Henry announced, leaning back in his chair with a mitt of a hand covering his stomach. "I haven't eaten like that in... Well, it's been so long I don't remember."

"I'm happy you enjoyed it," Alva said. She reached for his

cleaned plate. "More cinnamon apples?"

He shook his head, eyes drooping with heavy lids.

"Before you pass out from over-eatin', I better get you what you came for." Wanda scooted her chair back from the table and made tracks for the door. She took the basket holding the rogue demon along with her.

In the basement, she stood over the brightly lit crack in the dirt floor and gazed deep into the Earth's core. Hell lay thousands of miles down, yet it felt much closer. Her collar helped block the whispered thoughts of demons from below, not that she always understood what they meant. Sometimes they were clear as a bell tone, and other times just a jumbled mess of static that gave her chill bumps. She wanted to know what was down there, what Hell was like, but the demons wouldn't or couldn't say.

She held the open-lidded basket over the fissure and felt a tug from below. That's how it worked, like a siphon drawing from her, but it wasn't her it wanted. It wanted the demon Henry had caught. The blue snake of mist didn't want to go, and its resistance made the basket shake in her hands. However, it was no match for The Source, and the demon vanished down the glowing hole.

Wanda wasn't heartless. She could kill a demon with her bare hands just by crushing it to smoke, but it was rare for her to go to such extremes. She would only kill one if it threatened a human life, and that almost never happened. At least not so far. Banishing a demon back to Hell was usually enough.

She nudged the plank of plywood over the hole, then topped it with a box of Alva's gardening tools. Her Aunt Alva was an Appalachian mountain witch and because of the prophecy, she'd known a direct line to The Source would be needed someday. Alva's divining rod had led her to this apartment building when she first moved to New York City twenty-odd years ago. Alva had known Wanda would grow up to be an exorcist and come here to live with her. Grandma Lacy had foretold it all a century ago.

Time for Wanda to head back upstairs, but first she had to get Henry his stash of demons. As much as she hated doing it, a promise was a promise. She'd work on a way to steal them back later.

Wanda dug through the cardboard boxes on the other

side of the basement, where she'd hidden Henry's sack. At the time, she thought it would be ironic to hide it with Aunt Alva's Christmas decorations. But as she pawed through the holiday stockings, dough ornaments, and a knotted string of Christmas lights, she didn't see the bag.

Relief flooded her chest when she spotted a corner of burlap sticking out from underneath a paper mache snowman. It was the first time she'd ever seen this particular holiday figure among her aunt's stuff. Maybe it belonged to the Browns, a family who had moved into the building last week. She lifted it up and the sack with its boxes tumbled out the bottom. Someone had tried to hide it. She looked inside the sack and counted three boxes. Wait a minute. Minus the one she'd already given Henry, there should be four. What happened to the fourth box?

Her heart played her ribs like a xylophone. Henry would get more than a little cranky over this. Maybe he'd forgotten how many boxes he'd had to begin with. Three, four, what's the difference? He can always get another Vox demon.

She couldn't give up that easily. The fourth one must be around here somewhere.

Wanda poked and prodded every corner, and upended almost every cardboard box in the basement, but the Vox box was gone. Whoever had hidden the sack inside the snowman had obviously taken it. She'd have to question all the neighbors tomorrow. In the mean time, she had some explaining to do.

She left the basement and locked the door behind her. When she turned around, there was Henry, sitting on the bottom step of the basement stairs looking dark and broody.

"Miss me?" she asked brightly.

He didn't smile back. "No. I'm late for my shift." He held his hand out for the sack. "If you don't mind?"

"Of course not. Here you go." She handed it to him.

Without a thank you or see ya later, he stood and tromped up the stairs. So that was that. And lucky for her he hadn't bothered to look inside the sack. But he would eventually, and when he did—

He came barreling back down the stairs and nearly collided with her on her way up. "There's a box missing."

"Is there?" She frowned as if confused. "Are you sure?"

"There are only three in here."

"Don't forget I returned one of 'em already."

"There were five to begin with, Wanda. I know how to count." He stared down at her, his eyes starting to glow.

"Don't go there, Henry. Remember what happened the last time."

He closed his eyes and his jaw clenched, his cheek muscles twitching. "I don't know what you're trying to pull, but that Vox demon is mine. The box is branded with my bond."

"No kiddin'?" Wanda folded her arms and glared at him. "That's what started all this trouble. If you hadn't bonded them, we wouldn't be havin' this conversation. You'd never have known who I was if I hadn't found you first."

"That's a load of crap. I had your scent. I was on my way to you when you showed up at my door."

Exasperated, she pressed her palm against her forehead. "No point standin' here arguin' 'bout somethin' that never happened. I know a box is missin' and I looked everywhere for it, but it's scarce as bird shit in a cuckoo clock."

Henry stood there getting madder by the second. If smoke started pouring from his ears she wouldn't have been surprised.

"Go on off to work," she told him, making a shooing motion with her hands. "It's my fault, okay? I'll make it right and find your damn Vox. I never go back on a promise."

He set his jaw. "I don't believe you."

"That's because you don't know me. Now get. I got a plan. I'll have your box for you by tomorrow."

Looking somewhat mollified, he nodded and trudged out the building's front door, his shoulders hunched against the cold.

Henry slid into the cab, which started up the second his butt hit the seat. Mystic blasted the heater for him. He felt blessed to have such a good friend.

"That woman is a piece of work," Henry told the cab. "But I'm afraid we're not done with her yet."

Mystic puffed steam out her grill and it made a groaning sound.

Henry grunted. "I agree." He set the sack of boxes on the seat beside him and checked the clock on the dash. The flickers in the theater district should be letting out soon and there'd be folks needing rides. A few chatty fares were just what he needed to help get his mind off his troubles. Then he'd stop in to see his nephew and deliver the bad news. A missing demon. He hated to disappoint family.

He pulled out onto the quiet street and headed for Manhattan. The fog was thick but traffic was light. Midnight approached and anyone still on the streets would be eager to get home. The PT Subway had already shut down for the night, so trollies and cabs were the only transportation options left to people in the city.

Henry kept an eye out for the other cabs in his fleet. He owned his own cab company, and though his fleet was small, he did a decent business. Being an equal opportunity employer, he had a diverse group of drivers from humans of every ethnicity to Hellspawn of all ages, including those born of The Healing Waters soon after The Great Earthquake. If anyone were to ask if his drivers were specialized, he'd have to say they excelled at discretion. They knew how to keep a secret, and they knew the importance of privacy.

Thinking of which, he decided to put a driver on surveillance duty tomorrow to monitor Wanda Snow. She said she had a plan to get his Vox back, but Henry didn't believe her. She was obviously scheming something and he wanted to know what it was.

He turned onto Forty-Seventh Street, skirting around a horse-drawn bobtail car that was picking up a small group coming out of The Strand. Henry glanced up at the neon-lit marquee to see what flicker played this month. Healing Waters, a docudrama. He'd been wanting to see that one. It was a reenactment of events after The Great Earthquake and The Healing that followed. Most folks had their own interpretation of events, human and Hellspawn, and this flicker supposedly showed an unbiased representation of the facts. He really should see it, and maybe take his seventy-five-year-old niece along. It was something Eunice would enjoy.

A trolley filled to capacity with theater-goers drove by, and Henry knew there had to be a few folks left behind who needed a ride. Sure enough, a couple stood huddled on the corner beneath a streetlamp. The second the man saw Mystic, he waved Henry over.

"Where to?" Henry asked, as the two crawled into the

back seat. The man wore a tailored coat and brocade vest, and though his companion had on a black flannel coat that covered her from neck to toe, a train of green velvet peeked beyond the hem. These people had money.

"The Upper East Side," the man said, and gave Henry an address on Park Avenue. Yep. They most definitely had money.

Henry tugged self-consciously on his bowler to hide his pointed ears.

The man in back said, "Julia, he's Hellspawn!" And he sounded delighted about it, too.

The woman named Julia wore an elaborate felt hat trimmed in fur with netting that drooped to cover one eye. She leaned forward and Henry watched her in his rear view mirror. Her uncovered eye appeared bright with excitement. "And look, Gerald, he's installed a radio in his car. That's the latest thing! See the Victrola horn? Oh, do turn on some music Mr.—" She peered at the ID clipped to his dash. "Mr. Paine."

"You heard the lady, Mystic." He nodded at the radio and it began its cycle through the stations, landing on one that played a jazz tune with lots of trumpet and sax.

Julia gasped. "Did you hear that? The radio is voice-activated." She grabbed her companion's hand. "We must have one for our steamer."

Henry chuckled. "These radios are hard to come by, ma'am. Only one manufacturer I'm aware of, and he's my nephew."

"Is he Hellspawn as well?" Gerald asked.

"No. Just your average human genius."

"May we have his card?"

Henry passed one back to the couple. Vernon had been working on a new car radio operated by a Snit that was having trouble choosing appropriate music stations. Mystic, on the other hand, had no problem figuring it out. She made an excellent demo model for the product.

The couple spoke in low whispers so Henry couldn't hear their conversation, but he could guess the topic. They were interested. "My nephew has a showroom."

"Really?" Julia asked.

Henry nodded. "But visitors are accepted by appointment only. His products are exclusive."

Gerald squinted at his wife and said, "I'm guessing the technology is... experimental."

But not secret. "Demonetics," Henry offered.

Julia gasped again.

"Does that surprise you?"

"Not at all," she said, and gave her husband a coy look. "One of my neighbors is blessed with a Snit that operates a coffee maker in her kitchen. She's had it for years. It used to belong to her mother."

"Is it bonded?" Henry asked, now cautious about older machines after his experience with the oven.

She frowned. "I don't know. Anyway, she calls it Mia. Isn't that sweet? It's Italian for *mine*."

Vernon may just have a couple new customers.

"Tell me about the flicker you just saw," Henry said. "Was it any good?"

"Excellent," the gentleman said. "I think it cleared up a lot of questions."

"Oh?" Henry had a lot of questions of his own, considering The Healing was responsible for his birth. "Like what?"

"Like confirming what had turned The Healing Waters red," Julia said. "I'm afraid I can't say it in mixed company."

"I can," Gerald said, and Henry saw the man grin in the rear view mirror. "It was sperm."

"Hush." Julia sat back and tugged the netting down over her face to hide her blush, though it wasn't lost on Henry.

Henry knew the sperm hypothesis must be true. His existence was proof positive of that. After the great quake, all the hot springs in the world had turned red as blood. Christian evangelists believed it was the Bible's book of Revelation: *The rivers became blood.* But that wasn't entirely accurate. And it most certainly wasn't Armageddon. Divine creation would be more like it.

"If you don't mind me asking," Julia said, a coy tilt to her chin, "when were you born?"

"The summer of 1861."

Gerald slapped his knee. "Marvelous!"

Voice halting, Julia asked, "So your mother...?"

"Had enjoyed soaking in the hot springs at Saratoga in Albany," he answered, putting a smile in his voice. "That's where I was conceived."

"Do you know your father?"

"My real father?" Henry shrugged. "No. But my dad, the

one who raised me, didn't care for me much." In fact, he'd kicked Henry out of the house the moment he hit puberty, which was when his scales started to show.

"We're sorry, Mr. Paine," Gerald said in a low voice. "We didn't mean to pry."

Henry waved it off. "No problem. I like talking about it. How else can the world know the truth if we don't get it out in the open? That flicker you saw tonight has valuable information for the public. Hellspawn are not monsters."

"Absolutely not," Julia said, sounding offended. "And your poor mother. Did the waters cure her?"

Henry nodded. "She and my father had been injured in the quake. My mother had broken both her legs and my father's spine had shattered. The Healing Waters of the hot springs fixed them up good as new. With a little added bonus." He jabbed a thumb at himself. "One bouncing baby Hellspawn boy nine months later." And whose species went unnoticed for the first twelve to thirteen years of life.

"Oh, my." Julia pointed at the street up ahead. A police steamer idled with lights flashing, and a crowd of people gathered. "That's our building."

"It sure is," Gerald said. "What's going on?"

The sight of the police steamer made Henry's blood pressure spike. But there were thousands of cops in the city. What were the odds of these being the same guys from last night?

One of the officers turned around and looked directly at Henry.

Apparently the odds were pretty darn good.

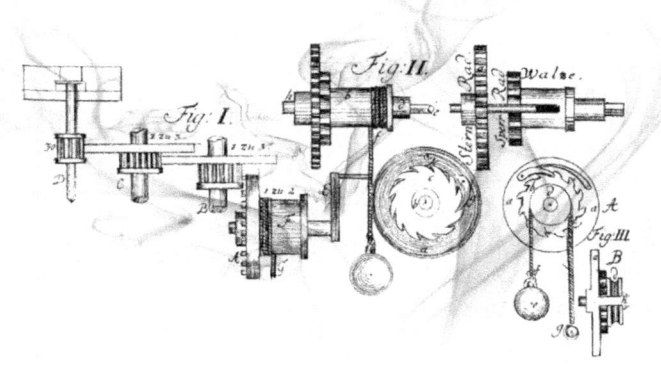

CHAPTER SIX

"Is everything okay, Mr. Paine?" Gerald asked. "It's probably nothing more than another drunk passed out on the stoop."

"Maybe you should roll down your window to get some air," Julia suggested.

Mystic did the honors and a brisk rush of winter air dried the sweat beaded on Henry's forehead.

"Did you see that?" Gerald pointed at the window. "He didn't touch the lever. Is that an automated feature as well?"

"Uh..." Henry's throat went dry. "It's, uh, my cab. It's possessed by a Vox demon."

Julia and Gerald went silent.

"Okay, then." Henry swallowed. "Have a nice night."

Gerald left the cab and paid the fare, adding a generous tip. "Thank you, Mr. Paine. And we'll be calling your nephew soon."

When Julia joined Gerald on the sidewalk, she gazed into the crowd and her eyes widened. She yelled, "Trudy? Trudy! Are you all right?"

A woman wearing a long, camel hair coat and a woolen scarf tied around her head shuffled over to Julia, her oversized house slippers scuffing across the pavement. Her face looked haggard and her eyes bloodshot. "Oh, my God, Julia. It's Mia!"

"What about Mia?" Julia wrapped an arm around her friend and pulled her close. The woman named Trudy was visibly shaking.

Trudy shook her head. "If I'd known she would react this way, I never would have..." Her voice dissolved into sobs.

Henry heaved a sigh and switched off Mystic's engine.

Julia had said her neighbor had a demon named Mia. Another demon causing trouble on the same night? This was no coincidence. Something was up and he wondered if similar incidences could be cropping up elsewhere in the city.

Henry stepped out of the cab. "Maybe there's something I can do to help." He strode to the sidewalk and stood beside Gerald. "I have a way with demons. It's my nature." He smiled and Julia smiled back.

"I'm beside myself, and the police are absolutely useless." Trudy gazed at Henry with pleading eyes. "I thought Mia and I were friends, but when I brought home a new coffee percolator, she got really upset."

"Jealous?" Henry asked.

Trudy frowned. "I don't think so. I told her it was hers to operate, but she refused. She stubbornly stayed inside the old one."

Henry waited for her to go on. After a long pause, he asked, "So what happened?"

"I punished her for disobeying me."

Punishment was a good thing when it came to disciplining demons. They liked being punished. "How?"

"I put the old percolator in a box and stuck it in the pantry."

Which meant poor Mia was without sunlight. "For how long?"

"About a week."

No wonder the demon was upset. But upset enough to cause the kind of trouble that would bring the cops? "And then what did you do?"

"I brought the box out of the pantry and told Mia I was giving her another chance. She set fire to the box. Then she got inside the new percolator and broke it."

He still didn't see why the cops were involved. Henry gave Trudy a questioning look and the woman broke down into tears again.

"I want to help you," he said, "but I need to know—"

She pulled back the scarf to show him several long gashes in her right cheek. They were deep enough to need stitches. Voice shaking, Trudy said, "Mia has never been violent. She belonged to my grandmother, then to my mother, and now me. I've always known her to be a gentle and helpful demon to my family. But tonight she took the screws and rivets from the new

coffee percolator and shot them at me like bullets from a gun."
She tugged the scarf back over her face. "So I called the police.
I didn't know what else to do."

Mia could easily have put her master's eye out, or if the
screws had been aimed at Trudy's jugular, Trudy wouldn't be
standing there talking to him right now. "Is Mia bonded to
you?"

Trudy looked confused. "Of course not. Why?"

"Never mind," Henry said. "Let me help. I'll take Mia away
with me."

The woman's eyes filled with tears again. "What will you
do with her?"

He wasn't sure. This demon was dangerous. He immediately
thought of Wanda. "I'll make sure she's taken care of. It's no
longer safe for you to keep her."

Trudy held a bloody towel up to her cheek and nodded.

Julia gave her a gentle hug. "Come along, dear. You can stay
with Gerald and me tonight." She gave Henry an apologetic
look. "I'm a nurse. I'll stitch her up. Thank you, Mr. Paine, for
all your help."

"I know where Trudy's apartment is," Gerald said to Henry.
"I'll take you up."

"No one's takin' no one anywhere," said an angry voice.

Ned swaggered up to them, one hand resting easily on the
gun at his hip.

Henry stiffened. Ned shouldn't remember anything from
the night before, but if Mac had talked...

"He's a friend of the family," Gerald explained, though his
voice raised an octave when he said it. A clear indication of a
lie, and if Henry noticed, so could Ned.

"Family friend, huh? He just *happen* to drive a taxi? Just
happen to be dropping you and the missus off right when all
Hell's breakin' loose in your building?" Ned narrowed his eyes
at Henry. "Big old Spawnster like you wouldn't be tryin' to
fleece these nice folks, would ya? Spawnster?"

There was no recognition in his eyes, just bigoted hatred.
Here we go again. "No, sir."

"Well, I think you are. You're a filthy, greedy—"

"Excuse me, officer, but that's my friend you're insulting."
Gerald squared his shoulders and shot his cuffs. "And even
if he wasn't, this man has rights. It's my job to defend those

rights." He handed Ned a calling card. "Gerald Amos Lawrence, Attorney at Law."

Ned looked mad enough to chew glass. His mouth clamped shut and he spun on his heel to head for his steam car, calling for his partner along the way. "Let's go, Mac. We're not needed here."

Ned stopped in the street to look over his shoulder at Henry. "I'll be seein' you around, Spawnster. I'd watch myself if I was you." Then he got in his car with Mac and took off.

"What an unpleasant man," Julia said.

Henry jutted his chin at Mystic, who switched off her headlights. "Okay, Mr. Lawrence. Lead the way."

By the time they reached Trudy's floor, a few neighbors had crowded around the door to what Henry assumed was her apartment.

"What's going on?" Gerald asked them.

"Not sure," said an elderly man wearing a maroon bathrobe with a matching woolen hat. "Kind of noisy though."

The group separated when Henry approached, which made him self-conscious. He hoped it was his size that intimidated them and not that he was Hellspawn, but it was more likely the latter.

There was the sound of breaking glass, then loud thuds as if furniture were being knocked over. Odd behavior for a lesser demon, but Henry supposed if it had the mechanical means, like something bigger than a coffee pot, it could manage.

"Should we go in?" Gerald asked, holding up the key Trudy had given him.

"Just keep your head down."

Gerald opened the door and sparks flickered around the doorframe. Trudy must have wards, which was smart since she appeared to live alone. The wards deactivated when Gerald used her key.

The two of them rushed into the apartment, bodies crouched low and arms held over their heads, but no missiles hurled in their direction. The noises came from the kitchen.

Mia must have possessed a carpet sweeper at some point and rammed it into the dining room table and chairs. The chairs lay on their sides and the table sat askew. A vegetable sprayer attached to a hose in the sink was now waving in the air like a snake, slamming into cupboards and sweeping through stacks of dishes on a double row of shelves on the wall. Broken glass and china lay in a shattered jumble on the hardwood floor and granite counter tops.

Nothing made a mess quite like a cranky demon on the warpath.

"Stay here," Henry told Gerald.

"But what if you~?"

"It can't hurt me. And if it does, I'll heal." However, despite his body's ability to swiftly mend itself, he was *not* resistant to pain.

Henry had an inspiration. "Gerald, would you mind going into the powder room to find me some perfume?"

Gerald frowned. "What for?"

"The scent of flowers. It helps calm an agitated demon."

While Gerald went in search of perfume, Henry stepped quietly to the kitchen doorway and peered around the corner. "Mia?" he called gently.

The vegetable sprayer coiled like a cobra and sprang at him, but the hose wasn't long enough to reach.

"It's time for you to leave this home. You've caused pain and destruction, and you're no longer welcome here."

It sprayed him. Henry blinked and wiped a hand down his face to clear water from his eyes. "You can come with me. Don't you want to go to a place where you'll be welcome?" He wasn't lying. Hell always welcomed back its former residents. At least that's what Levi had told him.

He spotted the old percolator on the counter, its copper surface dented, the hinged lid bent, the delicate scrollwork on the feet tarnished with age. He wanted Mia to get back inside that machine.

Henry felt a tap on his shoulder and turned to see Gerald holding a small atomizer bottle. He grabbed it and squeezed the bulb to release a fine mist into the air. It smelled exotic. Coconut and orchids? It reminded him of those fruity drinks human women liked so much.

The hose with the vegetable sprayer swayed from side to side, its energy waning. The scent appeared to be working. It started to retreat back to its hole beside the sink when it stiffened as if something had caught its attention.

Henry glanced behind him and saw Gerald standing out in the open.

Shit.

Henry whirled back around just as the sprayer swiped at a butcher knife on the counter. It flipped it up and batted it like a baseball. The knife shot through the air, going straight for Gerald's head. Henry tried to block its path but was impaled through the chest. Man, that hurt.

Henry grunted, Gerald gasped, and the sprayer retreated in a flash to its hole.

"You malicious little Snit." Henry was really ticked off now. He grabbed the old percolator and flipped up its lid. Eyes hot, he directed his will at the unruly demon, and within seconds a thin blue mist swirled up from the hole beside the sink. It drifted lazily to the coffee maker and disappeared inside. Henry snapped the lid shut, wiped his thumb across his chest where the knife still protruded, and jabbed it onto the machine to leave his mark.

"My brand. My will. And so you are bound."

"Shouldn't you tie it up or something?" Gerald asked Henry, while Julia stitched up his knife wound.

Henry shook his head and hissed air in through his teeth.

"Sorry." Julia dabbed antiseptic on the wound, her eyes lingering on his chest with more than professional interest. It made Henry uncomfortable. "Don't want any infection now, do we?"

What was it with medical people and the word "we?" She wasn't the one getting skewered with a needle and thread.

"Honestly, Henry, that thing makes me nervous." Gerald prodded at the percolator with his foot. "I might have an old strong box in the closet you could put it in."

"Not necessary." Henry grimaced as Julia pulled another stitch through his flesh. "It's bonded. It can't go anywhere or hurt anyone, I promise."

When Julia was done bandaging him up, Henry thanked her for her doctoring, took the murderous Snit, and left.

Once outside the building, the coffee maker tucked under one arm, he said to the demon, "You're in a heap of trouble."

The Snit didn't answer, not that it could. But Henry felt

compelled to let it know where it stood. "I could leave you with my nephew Vernon, seeing as how you're already trained to serve. But considering you tried to kill your master, me, *and* an innocent bystander, I'm inclined to hand you over to an exorcist I know."

When he and Mystic left the upper crust neighborhood, they headed to Manhattan's East River, and to the lab where his nephew worked with demonetics to create his inventions. So far, he'd produced mostly test models, the majority of which were in Henry's apartment. It would soon be time to introduce Vernon's innovative machines to the open market. People like Gerald and Julia Lawrence would be the perfect customers, however after what had just happened to their friend Trudy, Henry wasn't so sure anymore.

He parked Mystic in front of a line of old counting houses on Water Street. A century and a half ago, the four-story buildings had been a mound of rubble, but now they resembled the original nineteenth century architecture. Vernon's operation took up all four floors of his counting house, and like Henry, the inventor worked mostly at night.

Henry grabbed his sack of Vox demons and left the Snit behind in the cab. He let himself inside the building with his own key and went straight to Vernon's office on the second floor.

Vernon sat behind a drafting table, where unrolled scrolls of plans covered every inch of visible surface. He didn't look up when Henry knocked on the door frame and said, "Have a minute?"

The gray-haired man, stooped over his plans and figures, raised one finger in the air. Henry waited.

Vernon turned in his chair and sighed. He plucked his wire-framed glasses from his face and said, "What do you want, Uncle Henry?"

Vernon wasn't usually so snappish. Henry scowled. "Okay if I come in?"

His nephew looked thirty years older than Henry but was actually close to a hundred years younger. Vernon closed his eyes and massaged his temples. "I'm being rude. Sorry. It's the stress."

Henry stepped into the office and grabbed a stack of papers and file folders from a chair to set them on the floor so he could sit down. "Stress? I thought you were excited about a breakthrough on a new gadget you're working on. That's why you wanted these." He held up the potato sack.

Vernon heaved out a sigh. "There are a few problems."

"Oh?"

"Not with *that* project, which is going fine, but some others aren't going so well." He tilted his head from side to side, popping his neck bones. "It's like something's wrong with the Snits. They're not following directions, they're forgetting what they've learned, and they're goofing off."

Henry sucked in a breath. Whatever was happening to the Snits seemed to be spreading. "There could be an epidemic of bad demon behavior. I've come across it myself tonight. Twice."

His nephew's brows bunched together. "Were they *my* machines?"

Henry shook his head. "No, untrained demons."

Vernon's dark eyes looked glazed, the sclera pink with fatigue. "Is there anyone in your circle of Hellspawn who might know what's going on?"

Henry thought of Wanda and her great-grandmother's prophecy, but decided to keep it to himself for now. It was all speculation anyway and his nephew was upset enough as it was. "I'll ask around."

Vernon nodded. "We've invested almost every penny in this business, Uncle Henry. I can't lose it now."

"We're not going to lose anything." His nephew was usually such an optimist. Henry didn't understand how a few unruly demons could upset him this much. It wasn't *that* big a deal. "We'll figure it out. Maybe Max knows something. Have you talked to him?"

"That's part of the problem. Max's telepathy isn't working so well lately. We think he's lost communication with the Snits." Vernon stood and ran his hands down the front of his dirty lab coat, patting the ink-stained pockets as if looking for something. He obviously had a lot on his mind. "Let's go find him. He can tell you himself."

Vernon was tall for a human, not as tall as Henry, but close. They were four generations apart so the resemblance between them was weak. Their eyes, which were shaped like giant almonds with long, thick lashes any woman would envy, were the only tell-tale sign they were related.

Vernon hunched a bit when he walked, and Henry guessed it was from years of slouching over worktables and drafting boards. His skin was pale from being indoors all the time, his thick gray hair tousled as if left uncombed for days. The man needed a wife.

They passed a room filled with copper disk heaters like the kind Henry used in his flat. Another room contained metal boxes with a clamp that held tin food cans while a curved blade bit into the top and the demon inside rotated the can to saw it open. Henry didn't have one of those. They were mainly for people who cooked, which Henry didn't do. Though his refrigerator had robotic claws and arms for preparing meals, it only made the simple stuff: eggs, grilled cheese, fried possum burgers, beaver steak. Nothing that required contents from a can.

They rounded a corner into a hall lined with doors. Most were storage units filled with materials Vernon used to manufacture his inventions.

"Max must be in his office," Vernon said. "He had a headache earlier and I told him to lie down and rest."

When they opened the door to Max's office, the Hellspawn teen lay on a green couch on his back, his legs kicking and a metal hose from a vegetable sprayer twined around his neck like a noose.

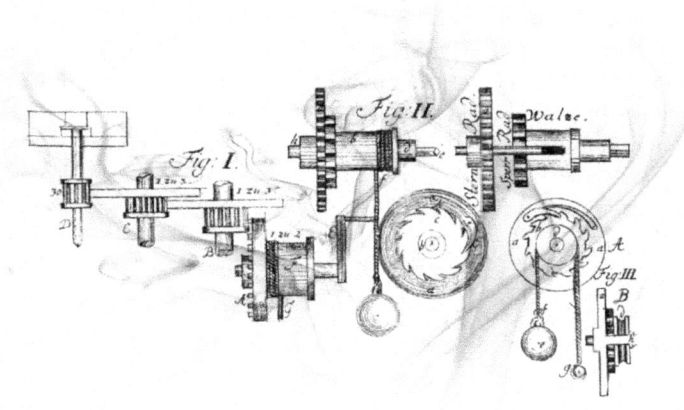

CHAPTER SEVEN

"What is it with these things?" Henry shouted, and rushed to grab the metal hose from around Max's neck. He tugged at the thing, which was coiled tight. Max's oversized head was turning blue. "This is the second hose I've wrestled tonight."

"At least it's not one of *my* inventions." Vernon took hold of the sprayer's head and gave it a twist. If it had been a snake, it would be dead by now. But it was a demon-possessed machine that didn't need its head to keep working.

Max's eyes started to bulge. He was Hellspawn, so Henry knew strangulation wouldn't kill him, but if the hose managed to break his neck, that would do it. And it was trying damn hard to do just that.

Henry stopped struggling with the thing and focused on using his will to make it stop. The hose loosened and he unwrapped it from around Max's neck. He gripped both ends hard enough to crimp the openings shut. He didn't want what was inside to escape and hurt someone else.

Vernon was breathing almost as heavily as Max. "How did this happen, son?"

Max coughed while trying to catch his breath. "It sneaked up on me while I was asleep."

"Had you done something to make it angry?" Henry asked.

The younger and smaller Hellspawn shook his big head, long hanks of thin, ash-colored hair flopping over his pointed ears. Max had more obvious demon features than Henry. His ears were longer and stuck out from his head like horns.

"I'll get you some water," Vernon said, and left the room.

"It tried to take my head off." Max touched the front of his throat and drew back his hand to see blood on his fingers. He swayed on the couch.

Henry grabbed him by the shoulders. "Easy there. You're okay."

Max swallowed. "I get queasy at the sight of blood, especially my own."

"So what's this about not being able to mind-chat with your demon trainees?" Henry asked.

"Bad news travels fast."

Vernon returned with a glass of water and handed it to Max.

"Thanks, Dad." Max took a sip and cleared his throat. "I'm getting no mental impressions whatsoever from the Snits."

Like human sign language, Max read symbols and images from demon thought transmissions. Imps and Snits understood the spoken word, they just didn't have the ability to speak.

Henry held up the sprayer hose.

"That's the first Snit to turn violent," Max said.

Henry slung the crimped hose over his shoulder and told Vernon and Max what had happened earlier that night. He left out the part about Wanda, her special talent for exorcism, and her reason for coming to New York. One problem at a time.

"If the Imps aren't affected by whatever's getting to the Snits, maybe I can still roll out my new Imp line of machines." Vernon's eyes brightened with hope.

"I advise against it. Let's keep a low profile, at least until we know what the problem is. If there is one," Henry told him.

His nephew's defeated expression reminded Henry of when Vernon was a boy and had his chemistry set taken away. His experiments had made his mother nervous. "And the Vox?"

Henry looked at Max, who shrugged and said, "So far, so good. We've only ever had a handful of Vox to work with, and we only use them for machines that require problem solving. They're doing fine."

"Max, why don't you go on home." Vernon placed a fatherly hand on Max's shoulder and gave it a squeeze. "Henry and I will lock up."

Max smiled and stood from the couch. He wiped the front of his neck with a handkerchief, but there was no need. The damage done by the metal snake had already healed. "Thanks, Dad," he said to Vernon.

When Max turned to leave, the back of his lab coat tented from the stubby tail he couldn't completely hide.

Once the boy was out of earshot, Henry asked, "Is Max still having nightmares?"

Vernon stared at the floor and nodded. "But not as frequent."

"Does he call out for his mother any more?"

Vernon looked so pained that Henry felt badly for asking. "It's only been two years since she died, but I think for him it's like it happened yesterday, poor kid. He feels responsible, and I can't convince him it wasn't his fault."

This was a familiar story for families of mixed demon blood. Max's birthfather murdered his mother and then himself soon after Max turned sixteen, which was when his Hellspawn features had fully formed. He was eighteen now. Vernon had adopted him from the city's Hellspawn Sanctuary for Indigent Youth, a home for unwanted Hellspawn adolescents. Vernon wanted to adopt more kids, but laws regarding Hellspawn adoption were strict. Only one per single-parent family.

"The boy's smart, Vernon. He'll be okay."

"I'm not so sure." Vernon shook his head. "We just found out his mother had bathed in the Alleghany Mountain hot springs to *cure* her infertility. She'd known The Healing Waters were guaranteed to make her pregnant."

Henry winced. Which meant she'd known all along that her baby would be Hellspawn.

"Just because access to the hot springs is illegal doesn't mean a woman desperate for a child won't break the law. "

A woman like that would do almost anything to conceive. The Healing Waters were just the answer. "His human father never knew, huh?"

"Not a clue. He'd thought Max was his own flesh and blood." Vernon scratched his chin in thought. "He should have known from the start that Max wasn't his. That boy's too damn bright to have had such a narrow-minded father."

And like so many men with Hellspawn children, Max's dad had refused to acknowledge him as his son. Same as Henry's own father had done. At least his dad-in-name-only hadn't murdered his mother. There'd been no Hellspawn Sanctuary for Indigent Youth back when Henry was a kid, only gangs, and it hadn't taken him long to join the toughest one.

Henry held up his potato sack of Vox boxes. "So what will you do with these?"

Vernon's eyebrows curved up into his hairline. "Good question. Come on, I want to show you something."

Henry followed him down the hall and up the stairs to the third floor.

The space was devoted to research and development: a wall-to-wall workshop of about 4000 square feet. Giant gears from one end of the room to the other turned cogs and belts, the engine in perpetual motion as it ran everything from a tea pot to an assembly line for machine parts. It was the heart of Vernon's entire operation.

The clanking of gears should have been loud, but Henry heard hardly a whisper of sound. Tons of wood and metal pounded the steel-girded floor, though the only evidence of the machine's operation was a mild vibration Henry felt through the soles of his boots.

Vernon stopped and swept his hand toward a steel table holding a beautiful piece of kinetic art.

"Nice looking machine," Henry said. "But what does it do?"

Vernon frowned. "Can't you tell? It's a Long Distance Communication Device. See the typewriter at the center?"

Henry peered at the round keys lined up in rows, each with a letter or number stamped on the top. "So it is."

Vernon quirked an eyebrow. "You *have* used a typewriter, haven't you?"

Henry made a pecking motion with both index fingers.

Giving him an exaggerated eye roll, Vernon jerked a nod at the machine. "It's powered by a demon so I call it demon mail. Or D-mail for short. You talk into this horn and your words are transposed as type onto a roll of paper that feeds around the carriage." He indicated a black cylinder and a ribbon of white paper held in place with a clip. "The Vox demon inside this one telepathically communicates your message to a demon in a similar device at a different location."

Henry wasn't sure about the appeal of such a contraption. "Can it cook?"

"No, it can't cook."

"Then it's no good to me."

"Uncle Henry, this invention will revolutionize the way

people communicate." Vernon folded his arms and looked defensive.

Another glance at the gizmo didn't change Henry's mind. It was keen to look at if you were into kinetic art, but it was still a hunk of junk.

Henry yawned and slid back the sleeve on his coat. According to his watch, daylight was only a couple hours away. He needed to stop by his company garage and leave surveillance instructions for one of his drivers before heading home to get some sleep. He wanted to be well-rested for his confrontation with Wanda later.

"There are five Vox in there?" Vernon asked, pointing at the sack bunched up in Henry's fist.

"Four."

"You'd told me there would be five."

Henry shrugged. "There will be. I'm picking up the fifth one later." He chose a box from the bag and showed Vernon his thumb print. "They're all bonded so they're not going anywhere. We'll leave them as is until we're sure it's safe to let them out." Holding up the metal hose that contained the murderous Snit, he added, "I'll take this guy with me."

"What will you do with it?"

Give it to Wanda. "Send it home."

Jasper Clark gazed out his window at a street shrouded in perpetual darkness. The avenue outside would never again see the light of day because daylight didn't exist there anymore. Jasper lived in the city *below* the city, his special Hell on Earth, and he liked it that way. It reminded him of his roots.

"It's a peaceful night," he said to the woman sitting beside the window. "We should go out."

"It's not night, it's day." She drank something thick and yellow from a cocktail glass. "And as much as I'd love to go out with you, I already have a date."

Jasper chuckled. "Well done, Claire. I've been meaning to ask you about that. So the boy fell for it?"

She grinned. "Like a hormone-crazed teenager. Oh, wait. He *is* a hormone-crazed teenager."

"And who better than a Hell's Belle to introduce him to the mysterious and wondrous ways of carnal demon love."

She gulped the rest of her drink and plunked the empty glass on the table. Sounding less than sincere, she said, "I can hardly wait."

Jasper slid her a sideways glance and saw her lower lip plump in a pout. Did she regret her plan to spend time with that big-headed Spawnster brat? He hoped so, because Claire belonged to him, though he did loan her to Levi now and then. Jasper pretended not to care. He didn't want her thinking he was a soft-hearted buffoon. "It must be exciting for you to break in a young stallion."

She shrugged and leveled him with a predatory gaze. "I can think of far more exciting things to do with my talents."

He held back a moan. She was certainly right about that. "How about another drink?"

She stood and approached the bar, her long skirt fluttering just above the ankles of her buttoned up boots. Such a shame to hide those lovely turquoise scales that covered her from toe to thigh. Her red leather corset was cinched tight around her waist, accenting her round hips, and the sight of them made Jasper's tailored slacks tighten in the crotch.

"What's your pleasure?" she asked.

As if she didn't know, but he'd settle for a cocktail. "Olive oil, and go light on the vinegar. Drop in a couple pickled chili peppers, would you? There's a jar in the ice box."

"He's a smart one, that boy you call Max." Claire dropped two bright red peppers into Jasper's oil. "You said he's an inventor?"

"His father is." Jasper smoothed a hand over his bald pate, feeling for stubble. He liked showing off the natural pattern of color on his scalp, a pattern that his demon feathers used to cover up before he plucked them all out. He had other plans for his plumage.

Claire brought him his drink and sat at the table. "Max." She breathed out the boy's name like a sigh. Jasper felt a twinge of jealousy. "I think that Spawnster got a double dose of whatever made us."

She referred to Max's obvious demon features and again Jasper felt a twinge, but it was envy this time. Had he made a mistake by including the boy in his scheme? No, Claire offered only sex to bribe Max for the skills Jasper needed to succeed with his plan. Yet Max had no idea what that entailed, and he wouldn't find out until Jasper was ready for him to.

"Don't forget about Levi," he told her. "I promised him he could have you tonight."

Claire's eyes twinkled when she said, "I'm looking forward to that, too."

Their banter wasn't fun anymore. Talking about Max had disturbed Jasper and he wasn't even sure why. His anxiety made him uneasy and he needed the comfort of his city around him, a city that would soon grow to rival the one above ground. That was his dream and he aimed to have it, even if it meant losing Claire. And if he did lose her, he'd make sure to get her back. "I'm going out for some air."

"Was it something I said?"

"Of course not. Have another drink. I'll be back in a bit." He shrugged on his coat and left the house.

Out on the street, darkness thick as coal dust permeated every building, and the cracked sidewalk crumbled beneath his feet. He gazed up at what should have been sky, but saw the underside of the street above instead. The dim gas lamps on street corners revealed a sky made of dirt, exposed pipe, and dangling tree roots. This section of Manhattan had been swallowed whole in 1859, but the Earth's gaping wound had since healed as new buildings were built above the old. The old ones suited Jasper just fine. He ruled this piece of the city. He was its mayor.

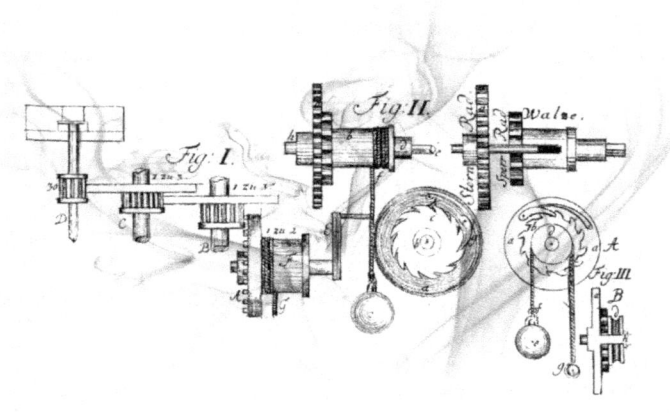

CHAPTER EIGHT

It was noon by the time Wanda got out of bed. Polluted fog drifted thick outside her bedroom window, and clouds of it plump as clotted mist formed a few familiar shapes: mashed potatoes, cotton candy, a scoop of vanilla ice cream.... It made her hungry.

When she sat down at the kitchen table, her aunt dropped a folded newspaper in front of her. "Thought you might like to see page five."

Wanda opened the paper to see a photograph of a crowd outside an apartment building. Henry towered over everyone as he talked to the college kid who'd given him the flower oils. She saw herself standing a little behind him, visible only in profile. "Well, don't that beat all."

"Read what it says," Alva said.

The headline was: Demon-Possessed Oven Turns On Human Master.

Wanda chuckled and shook her head. "The tenant wasn't its master because its master was dead! The guy livin' there didn't want the dang thing. Can't they get their facts straight?"

"Keep reading."

Wanda hadn't talked to any of the reporters there, not even the college student, so she knew her name wouldn't be mentioned in the story. That was good, because it wouldn't do for her to be exposed as an exorcist. There were Hellspawn in the city just waiting for the chance to put an exorcist to death.

Though the article had nothing to do with her or Henry, it had plenty to do with uppity lesser demons messing with folks in unhealthy ways.

Alva stood beside her, hands on hips. "Pancakes or waffles?"

Wanda didn't answer. She was too busy reading. The article wasn't a long one, but it mentioned a few demon-related incidents that had gone on in the city last night. It claimed more reports could be found in the police blotter. She'd known it would come to this someday, or rather, her great grandmother had known.

Now wasn't a good time for the city to start a panic over a possible demon uprising. That would only lead to chaos, which would in turn interfere with her goal. She wasn't ready for a full-on catastrophe and hoped to avoid one altogether, but if not, organizing a multi-demon exorcism would be like herding rabbits. Wanda had her work cut out for her.

"I could really use Henry's help," she said, taking a distracted sip of the brewed chicory her aunt had set by her elbow. "He calms the beasts, I destroy them."

"So you don't intend to send the demons back to Hell?"

Wanda shook her head. "Too many of 'em now. When they turn murderous, they can't be allowed to live. Demons ain't smart enough to repent. They can't feel emotions."

"Think Henry will go along with your plan?"

She shrugged. "Not sure, but he seems the decent sort. He's a Bringer. He'll do the right thing."

Taking a swig of the chicory that was already turning cold, Wanda left the table to get herself a refill. She stood at the kitchen counter and glanced out the window at a yellow taxi steam car that drove by. Her heart twitched. It might be Henry and she smiled in spite of herself. "That Spawnster spyin' on me?"

Alva joined her at the window. "Could be. That same taxi's been by a few times since I got up."

Wanda didn't mind. She had nothing to hide, though she guessed his interest had to do with her promise of finding that fifth Vox box. Time to canvas the building of a dozen neighbors. She was about to get busier than a stump-tailed cow in fly time.

She started with Mr. Sanchez in 301. He was a rudimentary magic user, apprentice level, and a recent immigrant from Mexico. He'd mentioned something once about wood magic and Wanda wondered if redwood, the material the boxes were made from, might be valuable to him.

"Redwood?" Mr. Sanchez asked when she questioned him. "No, no. Is not strong spiritual wood. If elder or hawthorne, maybe. Why you ask?"

She tilted her head to look past him into his apartment, but he stepped sideways to block her view. Feigning innocence, she said, "I had a sack of five redwood boxes in the basement and one of them is missing."

He frowned, his thin eyebrows forming a sharp V between his eyes. "You calling me a thief?"

She blinked. It did kind of sound that way. "No. Just wondering if you might have, you know, seen it around anywhere?"

Narrowing his eyes, he slammed the door in her face.

She doubted he'd be giving her and her aunt any more free jalapeno peppers.

Wanda continued to the next apartment, then the one after that, carefully wording her question so she wouldn't offend anyone. Nobody seemed to know anything about the missing box, or so they said. She visited nine apartments before coming to the last two on the first floor.

She stood outside the door of Mrs. Stravinsky's place. The old woman who lived there toted her bible everywhere and was always quick to spout scripture about the demon scourge invading the world. The woman hated Spawnsters. Her mind was about as open as a window painted shut. Mrs. Stravinsky walked with a cane and wore glasses that had lenses thick as cola bottle bottoms, and considering her religious affiliations, no way would she need redwood for spell-casting. Wanda doubted the woman could even make it down the stairs to the basement.

She hadn't completely dismissed Mr. Sanchez as a suspect, and Mrs. Stravinsky wasn't off the hook, either. Bible thumper or not, it's a guilty dog that barks the loudest.

Wanda knocked on the old bat's door. No answer. She wondered if Mrs. Stravinsky's hearing was as bad as her eyesight.

She knocked a little harder. "Mrs. Stravinsky? It's Wanda Snow, Alva Snow's niece. Can I talk to you for a minute?"

No answer.

The door to the apartment next door opened and a young woman Wanda didn't recognize poked her head out. "Gladys isn't home. Can I help you with something?"

"Yeah, um, I'm staying with your neighbor, Alva Snow. My name's Wanda, and Alva's my aunt. I need to talk to Mrs. Stravinsky."

The woman narrowed her eyes. "What about?"

Busybody. "Do you know when she'll be home?"

"She had to leave town for a family emergency." The woman was petite, her light-brown hair like a frilly cloud around her head. She was plain-looking, but not unattractive. No make-up, no hat, no jewelry. She cleared her throat and stepped out into the hall. "I'm Mrs. Stravinsky's granddaughter, Eloise. I'll be house-sitting for her while she's away."

Wanda gave her a questioning look and jutted her chin at the apartment Eloise just left.

The woman offered Wanda a tight-lipped smile. "It's vacant and the landlord gave me a key. I'm thinking about renting it so I can be closer to Gladys. To my grandmother."

She called her grandmother Gladys? Wanda wondered if it was common for folks in the city to refer to their grandparents by their first names. That was disrespectful if you asked her. "Then welcome to the neighborhood. My aunt and I live on the third floor. Feel free to stop by for a visit any time."

The woman ignored her. When Eloise walked past her to Mrs. Stravinsky's door, Wanda detected a very unpleasant odor, like rotted meat. She looked down at the woman's feet and noticed her scuffed and faded shoes. Talk about old, and old-fashioned. The shoes were like the lace-ups her grandmother used to wear. Wanda's gaze wandered up to Eloise's dress; an out-of-date frock with faded floral fabric and a frayed hem. Had the woman taken over her grandmother's wardrobe as well as her apartment?

"I'm lookin' for a redwood box I lost in the buildin's basement yesterday," Wanda said to the woman's back. "You haven't seen it, have you?"

"No." Eloise stepped inside Mrs. Stravinsky's apartment and Wanda caught a whiff of sulfur mixed with stale cooking odors. "I'll keep an eye out for it." She slammed the door shut.

"Rude bitch," Wanda said. "And what the Hell's she cookin' in there? Smells like spoiled onions and dog farts." She pinched her nostrils and marched down the hall to the stairs.

When she got back to her aunt's place, she asked about the vacant apartment next to Mrs. Stravinsky.

"It's been empty for a long time," Alva said. "I almost took it myself so I wouldn't have to climb stairs anymore, but after checking the place out, I changed my mind."

"What was wrong with it?"

Alva wrinkled her nose. "Stunk like old farts."

"Have you ever been inside Mrs. Stravinsky's apartment?"

"Once. I brought her mail that had found its way into my box." Alva smiled. "She was baking cookies and the whole apartment smelled like vanilla. She gave me a dozen as a thank you."

Well, it sure didn't smell like cookies now, unless dog turds had been mixed in the dough. "Did you know Mrs. Stravinsky's granddaughter is moving in?"

Her aunt frowned. "Gladys doesn't have a granddaughter. She was never married. She has no family, except for one sister."

Something very strange was going on in apartments 102 and 103. "Alva, is there some kind of magic that can make people younger?"

Alva gave her a puzzled look, then chuckled. "If there were, don't you think I'd be using it?"

She had a point.

Looking thoughtful, her aunt added, "There's a religious sect of youth-chasers that started up during The Healing. They thought The Healing Waters would make 'em young again, but when it didn't work, they started worshipping Hebe, the Greek goddess of youth."

"Did *that* work?"

"Yeah. But youth comes at a price. It requires human sacrifice and it can't be just *any* human. It has to be a blood relative." Alva's eyes brightened. "You know what? A Hebeite used to live in that apartment next door to Mrs. Stravinsky."

"Where's the Hebeite now?"

"Dead." Alva clucked her tongue. "Murdered by a member of her own family after they found out she'd killed her brother as a sacrifice to Hebe."

Humans could be the sickest kind of evil. Demons seemed like angels in comparison sometimes. "I think you've got a new Hebeite living in that same apartment on the first floor." Wanda told Alva about her run-in with Eloise. "I think she might have killed Mrs. Stravinsky."

There was a knock at the door and Alva went to answer it. Wanda jumped ahead of her and there stood Henry, his shoulders wide as the doorframe. He thrust an old copper coffee percolator at Wanda and said, "Don't say I never gave you anything."

Wanda frowned at the machine, then at Henry, bewilderment in her huge blue eyes.

He cleared his throat and shoved it closer. "Here. Take it."

"Why?"

Did he have to spell out everything? "Because it tried to kill me."

"Oh." Her brows tilted upward and she accepted the percolator. "Not sure what you expect me to do with a lethal coffee machine—"

"There's a Snit inside," he said slowly, as if talking to a child. "It stabbed me in the chest. It's bonded so it can't get out. You're safe."

"What about you? Are you all right?"

"What do you think?" He rubbed at the healed knife wound through his coat. It still itched a little. "Now give me my Vox."

She looked at him blankly.

"You don't have it."

She shook her head. "But I think I know where it is."

Backing into the hall, he said, "Then let's go get it."

Wanda looked at her aunt and asked, "Anythin' else you can tell me about those Hebeites?"

"Other than them being ruthless killers with the single-minded goal of staying young forever? No, can't say that I do."

"I'm familiar with that group," Henry said. "Goddess worshippers. You have some in your building?" The temperature inside his eyes heated up. "Did one of them take my Vox?"

"Calm down," Wanda said, handing the percolator to her aunt. "I don't know if she took it or not."

"So it's a woman." Figures. Women were at the root of most of his problems lately. "Not enough to make a deal with a goddess, she has to mess with an innocent demon, too?"

"Henry, I told you I don't know. I'm not even a hundred percent sure she's a Hebeite."

"Then let's find out." He spun on his heel and stomped down the hallway toward the stairs. The sound of clomping footsteps followed him. Wanda had the grace of a Clydesdale.

"We need a plan before we go barrelin' into a person's

home and accuse 'em of bein' a thief," Wanda said to his back.

"What's the apartment number?"

She didn't answer and he stopped on the bottom step. He glared up at her and asked more directly, "What's the number?"

She stood two steps above him and met him eye to eye. "I'm not tellin' you until we have a plan." She reached out as if to touch him, then pulled her hand back. "What's that around your neck?"

He touched the crimped end of the metal hose containing the Snit that tried to kill Max. "I almost forgot. This is yours, too. It tried to kill my nephew's son."

"My, but ain't I the lucky one," she said with a smirk. "So many gifts, and I didn't get you anythin'."

Running his thumb along the rough edge of the bent metal, Henry had an idea. "You *can* give me something. Like a chance to get my Vox away from that filthy Hebeite."

"But we don't know yet if that's what she is or even if she has—"

"Don't need to." He lifted the hose off his neck. "I have a plan. Now tell me the number."

Wanda gave him a dubious look and sighed. "102."

He strode down the hall and she galloped after him.

Stopping in front of the apartment door, he heaved in a breath and rapped his knuckles lightly against the wood.

"Who's there?" called a woman from the other side. Her tone wasn't friendly.

Henry thought for a second. The woman sounded young, which made sense if she was a Hebeite. And if her young skin was new, she'd be eager to show it off, or at least be vain about it. He looked down at Wanda and whispered, "What's her name?"

"Eloise," she whispered back.

"I have a flower delivery for Eloise," he said in a voice loud enough to be heard through the door.

A short hesitation before the expected question, "Who are they from?"

"The card says 'To Eloise from your secret admirer.'"

"Just set them outside the door and I'll get them later."

"Sorry, ma'am, I can't. You have to sign for them."

There was another pause before the door knob slowly turned. Henry kicked at it and the door flew open.

The young woman's eyes went wide, and she clutched a knitted shawl around her shoulders. Her voice shaking, she said, "I don't have any money. You better leave or I'll call the police!"

Henry stepped over the threshold with Wanda close at his back. "We don't want your money."

Wanda eased out from behind him, scowling as she stared hard at Eloise.

"You!" Eloise backed up, putting more space between them. "I told you I don't have your stupid box. Go away!"

"I know what you did," Wanda told her. "You killed your sister to make yourself young again."

The woman's jaw dropped open. "Are you insane?"

"No, but I bet you are." Henry knew something about Hebeites and the goddess herself. No one can be young again without help. Spirit help. It was a deadly bargain, a life for a life that allowed the spirits in Hebe's service to live again. The Hebeites pledged their souls to Hebe and were rewarded with a youthful body. The caveat was they had to share their body with a ghost.

Eloise looked genuinely frightened, but it didn't last more than a few seconds. Her expression went blank before cunning glazed her dark eyes, their pupils growing to fill the whites around them. "The goddess stands with me," said a deep, raspy voice that couldn't possibly belong to the fair Eloise.

"You sound so sure about that," Henry said, knowing he addressed the ghost that possessed Eloise and not the woman herself.

"Hebe gives me strength. I will crush you."

Wanda barked a laugh. "Dream on."

A hot wind blew around them, lifting Eloise's frizzy hair and sending stacks of unopened mail, newspapers and magazines flying around the room. The stench inside the apartment worsened and Henry lifted an arm to cover his nose with the sleeve of his coat.

This had gone far enough. "You live in a vomitorium, you know that? It's disgusting in here," he told Eloise, who had levitated a foot off the floor. "I want my box. Give it to me."

She laughed, deep and phlegmy.

"Okay, if that's how you want to play it." He held up the metal hose containing the Snit and snapped it in half. A blue stream of smoke snaked out of the broken hose and, unaffected by the hurricane-force wind that made Henry's eyes water, shot straight at Eloise. The woman opened her mouth to scream, but inhaled the homicidal Snit instead. She made a choking sound. The fetid wind stopped howling, and her body fell like a sack of rags to the floor.

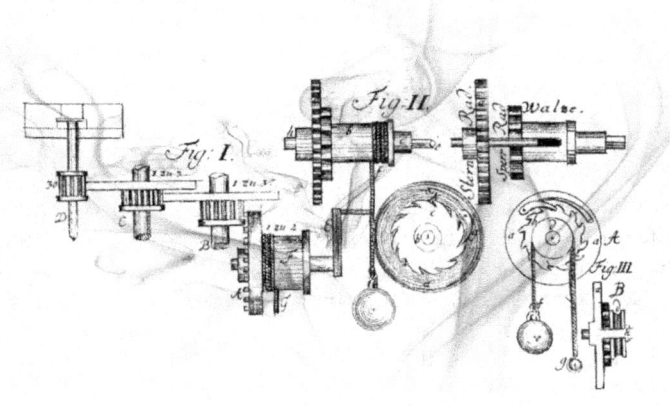

CHAPTER NINE

"Demons can't possess people!" Wanda sounded on the verge of panic.

"That's right, they can't." Henry watched the small woman on the floor writhe with convulsions, but he didn't try to help her. The battle waging inside her body was beyond help. "But demons have an appetite for ghosts, which is exactly what was possessing your friend here."

"She's *not* my friend," Wanda said flatly.

Semantics. "Ghosts are protected by the gods and goddesses they serve. But this one became vulnerable the moment it took over Eloise's body. The spirit went outside the goddess's circle of protection as soon as it got a host."

"How do you know so much about it?"

"When I was a kid, I ran with a gang of Hellspawn who liked to mess with Hebeites." He shrugged and tried to hide the horror at remembering what he once considered sport. "Their bodies do keen stuff when the invading spirit turns into demon chow. Watch."

The convulsions slowed, then the young Eloise began to shrivel, her skin puckering with age, her frizz of dark hair becoming more like white cotton. She gazed up at them with rheumy eyes filled with hate. "How could you?" she asked, her voice sounding normal again.

"Us?" Wanda's focus on Eloise was intense and her glare pure ice. "How could *you* kill your own sister?"

"She lived a worthless life and was dying anyway." Eloise threw up her shriveled hands and added, "At least her death wasn't in vain. You saw what it did for me before *you* and your Spawnster ruined everything."

The green stripe of hair peeking out of Wanda's blonde braid started to glow. Her gaze veered to a spot behind Eloise, who was now an old woman sitting cross-legged on the floor. Wanda stretched one arm out in front of her, palm out and fingers spread like a star.

A blue stream of mist undulated in the air and made a lazy trek toward Wanda's outstretched hand. It quivered, as if reluctant to meet her fingers, but it seemed to have no choice.

"What are you doing?" Henry asked, fascinated and revolted at the same time. "That demon just—"

"That demon just ate a ghost. Yeah, I saw." Wanda curled her fingers around the coiled mist in her palm. "You want me to give it a medal?"

"It deserves something," he said, feeling sick inside. "It was only following its instincts."

"And I'm following mine." She closed her fist around the demon and squeezed. A second later, gray smoke puffed from between her fingers and the demon was gone. "It was a killer, Henry. You told me it tried to kill someone in your family. It had to die."

Stunned, he stared at her closed fist. "You didn't have to kill it. You could have sent it back to Hell like you did the other one. You're a murderer."

"Correction, Henry. I'm an exorcist."

He gritted his teeth, his anger a metal taste in his mouth. "Even without a beating heart, a demon is still a living thing. You destroyed a life."

Wanda sighed. "I kill to *save* lives. *Human* lives."

Henry closed his eyes to quench the heat seething behind them. He knew the truth in her words, and even understood why she did what she did, but he didn't like it. Never would. He'd tolerate Wanda just long enough to get his Vox back, then the two of them could part company for good. "What about her?" He pointed at Eloise, who gazed up at them blankly. "Someone needs to call the cops."

Eloise raised her hand. "I'll do it."

"I just bet you would." Wanda snatched up the candlestick phone and handed the cone-shaped receiver to Henry. "You call 'em. I'm keepin' a low profile."

He shook his head. "Me and the cops don't get along too well these days. I think your aunt should do the honors."

Wanda nodded. "You're right." She looked down at Eloise, who gazed up at her innocently, a sweet little old lady victimized by a couple of roughneck burglars. "But right now we've got a problem."

"I can see that." Henry flicked a glance at Eloise, who had seen too much and knew too much. It's not like Wanda and Henry had been invited into Eloise's home. They'd broken in. The cops would listen to her story before they'd listen to theirs. "Stay with her while I check the apartment for her sister's body."

The bedroom and bathroom were clean. Well, not clean because both were filthy with dirty laundry, trash and plates of spoiled food. But he didn't find a body.

"Try the apartment next door," Wanda said, scooping a key off a counter in the kitchen. "I'm guessing she stashed it in there."

Eloise stood, wincing as she straightened her back and legs. "You won't find anything in there. I swear! I, uh, I killed her in the basement. Then I threw the body in the furnace."

"That's sick," Henry said, his lip curled. "And it's a lie. The whole building would smell like barbecued human if you'd done that."

Wanda wrinkled her nose and gagged.

He dared not tell her how the gang he once ran with would kill humans for food when they had nothing else to eat. Never having the stomach for it himself, he'd been told human flesh tasted a lot like pork. "I'll check out the apartment next door."

The smell inside 103 almost made him pass out. He held a handkerchief over his nose and within a few minutes located the dead sister's body. The woman lay supine in the bathtub with a gaping hole in her chest. On further inspection, he saw that her heart was missing.

"Found her," he announced when he returned to Wanda. "Most of her, anyway." He looked at Eloise, who now sat on a couch adorned with lace doilies. "She's missing a major organ."

Eloise had the good grace to look ashamed, but what came out of her mouth was anything but graceful. "I ate her heart."

Wanda paled. "You did what?"

"It's part of the Hebeite ritual," Eloise said. "The goddess demands it of her followers before she'll grant them eternal youth."

"How long were you planning to keep your sister in the

bath tub?" Henry asked.

"Only until I could dismember her and put her in the furnace." Eloise glanced away and focused on an unraveling piece of yarn from an afghan. "Now you know I wasn't lying about that, at least not completely. I figured one piece at a time over the course of several days wouldn't leave a strong smell."

Wanda made a choking sound.

Henry stared hard at Eloise, feeling that familiar fire build behind his eyes. It was time to give the lady some memory loss, and help her take a nap.

"You never saw us," he told her.

"Pardon me?" Eloise looked confused, then her thin, wrinkled lips turned up at the corners. "You're standing right in front of me. How wouldn't I see you?"

"Because we were never here," he added.

Wanda nodded at him and glanced at the gear-watch on her forearm. Henry didn't like being rushed. He didn't perform well under pressure.

Eloise's eyes glazed over. "You were never here."

"You don't remember us, and you don't remember having your Hebeite spirit taken away. You're still young and beautiful."

Her smile broadened and she ran her hands down her body, lingering over her breasts. "I'm young and beautiful again. I'm going to live forever."

"That's right." Henry funneled his will through hers, but didn't have to work very hard. She was extremely malleable and didn't fight him. "Now you're going to tell me where you hid my redwood box."

She frowned. "Box? I don't know anything about a box."

She told the truth. Damn. So where the Hell was it? Someone had taken it and Wanda was to blame. He slid her an accusing glare.

"I told you I was sorry." Wanda firmed her jaw and lifted her chin. "I'm doin' everythin' I can to find the damn thing."

He ignored her and focused on the old woman again. "It's been an exhausting day for you, Eloise. Time for a nap. Lie down on the couch and don't wake up until you hear someone say *Open up. Police!*"

"But I don't want—"

"Hush. Relax. You have a long and glorious life ahead of you." In prison, though it would be neither long nor glorious.

The electric chair would be waiting for her there. Convicted Hebeites usually met their end that way if the surviving members of their families didn't find them first.

Eloise pulled an afghan off a chair and settled it over her as she lay on the sofa. She was asleep within seconds.

Wanda stared at him without blinking.

"What's wrong?" he asked her.

"You do that so well."

He snorted. "I guess we both excel at what we do."

She dropped her gaze and stepped toward the door. "I'll have Alva make that call."

☙ ❧

"And here he is," Jasper said brightly, his arms open in welcome. "The young man I've heard so much about."

Max grinned, his big head looking ready to topple off his narrow shoulders. "It's nice to finally meet you, Mr. Clark." He offered his hand to shake.

Jasper wrapped his long fingers around Max's short ones and squeezed, gratified when the younger man winced. "My darling Claire has told me a lot about you, son. She's like a daughter to me, you know." Jasper dipped his chin and scowled as he continued to smile. "I trust you're treating her well?"

"Very well." Max glanced at the fair-skinned, dark-haired beauty with her arm linked in his. The admiring look she gave him was convincing. Too much so, as far as Jasper was concerned.

Jasper cleared his throat. "Can you excuse us for a few minutes, my dear? Man talk."

Claire lifted her delicate brows. "Of course. I'll wait in the parlor."

Jasper steered Max through a wide doorway that opened to his private den. A fire crackled in the marble fireplace, and the mantle above it held an ornate clock with a design of golden sheaves of corn. This was his favorite room in the house. "Did Claire tell you why I wanted to see you?"

"You have a job for me?" Max asked, sounding uncertain.

"I do indeed." Jasper slung a fatherly arm across Max's shoulders, the velvet sleeves of his frock coat making a *shooshing* sound against the canvas of Max's jacket. "You have a special gift, yes? Aside from being brilliant."

Max's face reddened. "I suppose so."

"You're being modest." Jasper chuckled. "It takes a special skill to communicate with our demon friends and train them to do whatever you want. That makes you very special."

Max shrugged. "I don't know about that, Mr. Clark. It's a natural ability. I'm sure you have one, too."

Nodding, Jasper said, "I can talk to demons just fine, make them do whatever I want, but I can't sense a response. I need a receiver for that and you're just the man for the job."

"My Uncle Henry can sort of do what you do, but I don't think it's a special power. Demons obey him because they like him." Max lit up with a proud grin.

"They like me, too," Jasper lied. In truth, they hated him. He could control them with his will and they had no choice but to obey. What set him apart from an exorcist was that he didn't have the power to kill a demon, or send it back to its maker. So unfair. "How is your Uncle Henry?"

"He's okay."

"Did you know he's an old friend of mine?"

Max's eyes brightened. "Really?"

"From back in the old days. We were pals as kids. Then his human descendants found him and, well..."

Max frowned. "You're still friends, right?"

Jasper motioned for Max to join him on a satin sofa by the picture window that looked out over Spawnstertown. The burgundy fabric glistened with reflected light from a Tiffany lamp on a corner table. "Your uncle and I haven't spoken for decades."

"Why not?"

Jasper shrugged. "Once Henry's family took him back, his Hellspawn friends didn't matter to him anymore. I think we embarrassed him."

"That doesn't sound like Uncle Henry."

Because that wasn't what happened. It was actually the other way around. "We were a dirty street gang of trouble-making youths. His new family had money and position. Us? We had the gutter and makeshift tents under the Brooklyn Bridge." That last part was true, but Henry's family had actually been dirt poor when they found him. It was Henry who made their money for them.

Max brooded quietly at his end of the sofa, his right hand

opening and closing into a fist.

"Is something wrong, Max?"

Max turned his head to give Jasper a wobbly smile. "Nothing's wrong. I'm just thinking."

"I hope I didn't say anything to upset you."

The younger man shook his head.

Jasper smiled. "Good. Because I'm none the worse for what happened between your uncle and me. Just look around you." He gestured at the rich furnishings, dark wood paneling, magnificent fireplace, and rich oriental carpets that covered a gleaming floor of polished maple. "I've done well for myself. It's been a good life."

"What do you do?"

"I'm an entrepreneur, just like your father." Jasper reached over and gave Max's knee a friendly pat. "I operate several profitable businesses that cater mostly to our Hellspawn brothers and sisters."

Max raised an eyebrow. "What kind of businesses?"

His list of illicit operations would curl Max's thin hair if he knew what they were. "Health care, which is unique to our species. And I'm a distiller of fine, savory oils for the most discriminating Spawnster palate."

"Spawnster?" Max stiffened. "I'm not comfortable with that word. It's a racial slur."

Jasper laughed. "It's not a slur, it's what we are. I'm proud of who I am, aren't you?"

Max shrugged. "I guess so."

The ghostly lyrics of a childhood taunt whispered between Jasper's ears: *Spawnster-monster, no one wanster, be around a Spawnster-monster.* Cruel little human shits. He hated them all.

"Did you say something?" Max asked.

He must have chanted the old ditty under his breath. Jasper blinked and clapped his hands once. "I asked if you wanted a drink. I stock my bar with only the best oil. I have a jalapeno oil that will set your teeth on fire."

"Sounds great. I'd love to try it."

"Then you shall." Jasper stood and called for Claire. "She's a marvelous bartender, and very creative. We're thinking about publishing a book of Hellspawn oil cocktail recipes."

Claire walked in and took their orders, lingering a bit longer than Jasper liked. She pressed her shoulder into Max and leaned her head on this shoulder.

"We're still discussing business, Claire. You can have Max back when we're done. Understand?"

She looked from one to the other, then gave Max a quick smile, her eyes bright with an emotion Jasper didn't recognize. She never looked at *him* that way.

The two men chatted about Max's father's inventions as they waited for their drinks. It was all Jasper could do to keep from yawning. Good grief, what a bore.

Claire reappeared minutes later with their cocktails.

"Thank you, dear," Jasper said.

Claire gave Max another one of her prize-winning smiles before leaving the room.

Max took a sip of his oily concoction and his eyes grew round. "Holy Toledo! This stuff packs a wallop."

"I'd like to show you something." Jasper set down his drink and stood. He gestured for Max to follow him down a narrow hallway. "I have a laboratory, too, though I'm sure it's nothing so elaborate as your father's."

He led the way to what looked like an enormous ballroom, which it had been a century-and-a-half earlier, when it was still part of the city above. The marble floor had been restored to its original luster, and a giant chandelier sparkled from the ceiling. At the center of the room stood a table with a hat stand.

"What's that?" Max asked, his voice echoing through the large room. "It looks like half a helmet."

"It does, doesn't it?" Jasper plucked the headgear from its stand. "Your father isn't the only inventor in the city."

"You're an inventor, too?"

Jasper tilted his head left to right. "In a way. This was my idea, but I didn't make it. I have a team of Spawnster scientists for that."

Max cringed at the word Spawnster and Jasper thought the boy had to get over himself. It was about time he embraced his species.

"See these feathers?" Jasper touched the multicolored feathers braided into the wire and cable that made up the head piece. He smoothed a hand over his bald head. "They used to be mine, but I thought using them in this amplification machine would make it more effective."

"What does it amplify?" Max asked as he ran his finger

down one of the braids.

"Reception."

"Reception of demon telepathy?"

"That's right." He reached out to slip the piece over Max's head, but the young man jerked away. "Something wrong?"

Max let out a breathy laugh. "Well, yeah. What will it do to me? It won't eat my brain, will it?"

Jasper chuckled. "You have quite the imagination, my boy. Of course it won't eat your brain. It only amplifies transmission from demons. Thoughts and pictures, both. Aren't you curious?"

"Have you tried it yourself?"

"Yes, but it did nothing to enhance my ability to receive. I still get nothing." Jasper ran his hand down the side of the piece, petting it like a kitten. The feathers were still soft. Still a part of him.

Looking unsure with his eyes slightly squinted, Max asked, "What's it like?"

"Are you asking if it hurts? I promise it won't hurt. It might make you a little dizzy at first until you get used to it. Here." Jasper retrieved two chairs from a group of several that lined one wall. He sat in one and shoved the other closer to Max. "Have a seat. Try it on, then tell me what you see."

Max sat and studied the gadget, turning it one way and then the other. Jasper had to admit it was a beautiful piece of work, especially with his multi-colored feathers woven through. Clockwork gears covered one side, and psychic energy from the wearer made them turn, which caused friction that amplified reception. Jasper didn't know precisely how it worked because he didn't have to. That's what his scientists were paid to do.

Finally, Max slipped the machine over his head and sat back in the chair. Within a few seconds, his expression changed. Surprised at first, then worried. "Damnation." Max swallowed. "They're sick. The Snits are infected with a virus."

Jasper felt almost giddy. It's just what he'd been hoping to hear.

CHAPTER TEN

"Mystic, do you trust her?" Henry asked the cab. "Should I count on Wanda to tell me the truth?"

Mystic hesitated, then her radio dial spun until it found the words she was looking for. "*Not... sure.*"

That's not what he wanted to hear. He started to worry. "She still hasn't found my box, or so she says. I wonder if she found a way to free the Vox inside and killed it without telling me."

"*Doubt it. She... not... that... smart.*"

Henry wasn't sure he agreed, but Mystic's words made him chuckle. "Still don't like her, huh?"

"*No.*"

"Jealous?"

Hesitation. "*Don't... flatter... yourself.*"

Cheeky automobile.

Four days had gone by since they had confronted the Hebeite. Wanda had not only killed the Snit that ate the ghost from inside Eloise, she also killed the one from Trudy's old percolator. He wasn't surprised by the exorcisms, just repulsed. Witnessing a murder, even a bloodless one, was never a pretty sight.

The result was still the same.

Henry was supposed to get more Vox from Levi tonight, but he'd cancelled their meeting. What was the point? He hadn't freed the first batch yet. Instead he would work the streets for a while, pick up some fares and listen to city gossip. There had been more chaotic incidents involving Snits since last weekend, and the cause was still a mystery. People were starting to worry and Henry couldn't blame them. He worried, too. The danger had escalated and even a few lives had been lost. As much as he loved his lesser demon cousins, there was no excuse for murder.

He had stayed in touch with Wanda, calling her every day to check on the progress of her search for his missing property. He'd called so often, in fact, that her aunt now screened her calls. Henry didn't like being ignored.

"You hate Wanda because she's an exorcist, don't you?" he asked Mystic.

"*Yes.*"

Henry nodded. "She was born that way, you know. It's not like she chose a life of killing demons."

Mystic had no response to that. Her silence spoke volumes.

"I don't fault her for what she is. Look at me. I'm no paragon of Hellspawn virtue."

"*You... are... good... person.*"

"I doubt Wanda thinks so. Have you seen how she looks at me? Like she'd try to kill me the minute my back was turned."

The laugh track from a studio audience chortled through the Victrola horn on Mystic's radio.

"What's so funny?"

"*Seen... her... when... your... back... turned. You... wrong.*"

"Yeah?" Now he was curious. "How so?"

"*Not... try... kill... you. Kiss... you.*"

Henry frowned. "I must have given you the wrong oil for your engine today. You've gone loony." But it did make him wonder. As lovely as Wanda was, he couldn't help thinking those full lips of hers might be deadly for someone like him. What if she sucked out his demon soul? Not a risk worth taking.

Silence from the cab.

Henry asked, "Do you think Wanda—?"

"*Shut... up.*"

Mystic had never told him to shut up before. He must have struck a nerve.

Just before midnight the weather turned nasty. What had started out as light and fluffy snow now included rain, which created a slushy mess on the streets. Mystic had some trouble gripping the road around corners, but she managed not to run into anything. Good thing, too, because a couple of guys with umbrellas jumped out in the street to flag them down.

Mystic slid to a stop and the two men slid into the cab. "Thanks!" one of them said. "Chinatown, Canal Street."

Henry was about to scold them for leaping into the path of an oncoming car, but decided not to bother. It would only get him a smaller tip, or no tip at all.

Both men were dressed entirely in black from head to toe, including shirt and bow tie. He recognized the silver logogram pinned on their lapels that identified them as members of an elite society of Chinese bankers.

"Nasty night," Henry said.

Both grunted their agreement, but had nothing to add. This would be a quiet trip.

Without thinking, Henry lifted his hair to scratch the side of his neck and one of the men asked him something in Chinese.

Henry didn't have to speak Chinese to recognize the words for Hellspawn. He shrugged. "That I am. You okay with that?"

Both men smiled and spoke a few words to each other in Chinese. "We speak English."

Maybe they could have a conversation after all. They seemed pleased he wasn't human, possibly because half of Chinatown's population were Hellspawn. Their women purposely bathed in the Healing Waters just to get pregnant. They felt honored and adored their Hellspawn offspring.

"Hey, does *Jau Sin* still have that tasty otter stir fry on the menu?" Henry asked.

He watched the men in the rearview mirror. Both nodded and the taller one said, "The restaurant added a spicy sauce just for Hellspawn. No salt. You should come try."

"Love to," Henry said. He really would, too. Chinatown was a favorite hangout for Hellspawn, almost as popular as Spawnstertown, where he'd lived for decades during his years in the gang. "Anything new happening in the neighborhood?"

The two men shrugged at the same time. "It is same. Nothing exciting ever happens in Chinatown."

Not if you lived under a rock. Henry could share a rowdy story or two, but not with these guys.

A few blocks later, Mystic turned onto Canal Street. Brightly lit shops and street vendors lined the sidewalks, and crowds of late-night shoppers bumped shoulders as they browsed and bargained for deals. The rain and snow had let up and sharp cooking smells filled with garlic and ginger wafted through Mystic's heat vents. Henry's belly rumbled. Rarely an hour went by when he wasn't hungry.

"*Dou!*" shouted one of the men from the back seat. He pointed out the window. "*Faan!* Isn't that Chen Hai?"

Henry knew Chen Hai owned the neighborhood rickshaw service. Chen Hai had at least a dozen carts, each rig operated by a Snit.

Chen lay in the gutter, where a crowd gathered near the corner. His head was cocked at an awkward angle. A rickshaw struggled to free itself from the hands of several people trying to hold it still. The robotic limbs in front of the vehicle were fashioned like bird legs that bent backwards at the knee, and the carriage balanced on an axle holding two spoked wheels.

Not even Chinatown was exempt from whatever plagued the city's Snits. The demons had gone completely mad.

Henry steered Mystic to the curb and his passengers hopped out. He followed them to where Chen lay, unmoving. On impulse, Henry touched the side of Chen's neck. His body was still warm but there was no pulse.

"His machine killed him," said a frantic woman on the sidewalk, her wide-brimmed hat shaking as much as her hands. "I saw it. It went crazy and knocked Mr. Chen down, then trampled him."

"What about the other rickshaws?" Henry asked the crowd.

They all looked at each other and shook their heads. The guilty rickshaw, with its dirty white bonnet flopping like a windblown flag, bucked and tugged against the arms holding it back.

Henry grabbed the out-of-control rickshaw, and it continued to struggle. He saw a brand on the side of its leg; a red Chinese character that was Chen's personal mark. The demon was bonded. Shit.

He could break the bond using Chen's blood, but the demon was crazy. It was a killer. And as much as he hated to do it, he had to call Wanda for help. Killing killers was her business.

"Can you hold onto it for a while longer?" he asked the men, whose arms shook with the effort to keep the rickshaw contained.

One man was Hellspawn, his Chinese heritage evident in his almond-shaped eyes. He wasn't as big as Henry, but he looked strong. "Can you do it?" Henry asked him.

The Hellspawn gritted his slightly pointed teeth. "Not for long. Where are you going?"

"To make a phone call."

Henry sprinted down the block toward a payphone. He yanked the wooden bi-fold door so hard it nearly popped from its hinges. Grabbing the cone-shaped receiver, he spun the rotary dial to call Wanda.

She answered on the first ring. "Henry?"

Henry frowned. "How'd you know it was me?"

"It's always you." She paused to swallow. "There's a vibe runnin' through the thoughts in the city's demon network. Somethin's terribly wrong."

He, too, had been feeling it build over the past few days. It was like a festering boil ready to burst. "I have a killer Snit in Chinatown I need you to take out." He gave her the address.

"I'm there." She hung up.

Henry left the phone booth, but by the time he made it halfway down the block, the restrained rickshaw had broken free of its captors. It looked like a headless ostrich galloping down the street.

It would be easier to free the Snit with its master's blood, so he whipped out a handkerchief from his vest pocket. "Anyone have a knife?" he asked the remaining few in the crowd. The others had scattered the second the rickshaw took off.

"Here." A teenage boy handed him a pocketknife.

Henry slit Chen's wrist and wiped up a smear of coagulating blood with his handkerchief. A collective gasp came from the onlookers. Each took a step back.

"I don't have time to explain," he told them, and tried to hand the bloody knife back to the boy, who refused to take it. He held the cloth up for emphasis. "This will help me break the bond so I can take the Snit out of the rickshaw!"

The group stared at him in confusion.

"Forget it." He left them to puzzle it out and ran back to Mystic. Once seated behind the wheel, he asked her, "Did you see where it went?"

"*Yes.*"

"Follow that rickshaw."

The engine hummed to life and Mystic's tires spun over the ice-slickened street.

"Here you go." Alva dangled a key in front of Wanda. "The throttle sticks sometimes, but the tires are still good."

Wanda's insides clenched and she gave the key a dubious look while locking her hands behind her back. "Can't."

Alva frowned. "Can't what?"

"Can't take your car." She cleared her throat. "I don't know how to drive."

"Then I'll drive you." Alva palmed the key. "Grab your coat."

"You can't come with me," Wanda said, her fear for her aunt's safety making her voice shake. "I gotta do this on my own."

Alva stood with both hands on her hips. "Then how will you get to Chinatown? The tube's shut down for the night. Do you have time to wait for a taxi?"

Wanda closed her eyes and blew out a frustrated sigh. "Damn. Okay, but just drop me off and leave, understand?"

"Don't tell *me* what to do, young lady," her aunt scolded. "I'll decide what's best for me after we get there."

"But Aunt Alva, it's dangerous. This Snit is a killer and I don't want you gettin' hurt."

"Stop treating me like I'm old and feeble. I'm more fit than most women half my age." Alva turned her back on her niece and stomped to the apartment's front door. "You coming? Or do I have to help Henry by myself?"

"Damn, you're stubborn."

"Runs in the family. Now get a move on."

The green fabric seats of Alva's old Doble steam car were faded and ripped in spots. She'd had the steam car for over twenty years, but there was less than five thousand miles on it. Alva hadn't taken very good care of it and often left the top down in inclement weather so the interior was ruined. At least the engine still worked.

When they arrived in Chinatown, Henry wasn't where he said he'd be. Alva stopped the car in front of a small group of people on a street corner. Wanda rolled down the window and stuck her head out. "You see a tall Spawnster guy drivin' a taxi?"

They all nodded, and a teenage boy ran up to her and said, "He followed a runaway rickshaw after it killed Mr. Chen Hai."

He pointed at the gutter where a dark circle of red stained the pavement.

"Where's the body?"

"Chen's family took it home with them," the boy said.

"Did anyone call the police?"

He shook his head. "Death is private in Chinatown. We take care of our own."

Wanda was glad to know the police wouldn't be involved. They'd only screw things up, turn it into a murder investigation, and start collecting suspects the way her aunt collected salt and pepper shakers. "Which way did he go?"

The boy pointed down the street. "The rickshaw turned on Mott Street, and the taxi was right behind."

"Thanks." She looked at her aunt. "You can drop me off here, Aunt Alva. I'll call you when it's over."

Alva stepped on the gas.

"Hey! Stop the car!"

"The boy said Mott, right?" Alva stared ahead as she concentrated on steering.

Dread pooled like molten lead in Wanda's belly. "You can't go with me."

"And I told you not to tell me what I can and cannot do. My car, my rules." The car slid as they made the turn. "Sit still. I'll let you out when we find Henry and not before."

Wanda felt like a child, which was not a horrible feeling. It was kind of nice to be cared for rather than the one always doing the caring, which is how it had been back home. But tonight she had to put her aunt first. The woman was out of her league and Wanda wasn't sure how she would protect her. "Really, Aunt Alva, please stop and let me out. You need to get yourself home."

"I don't see him anywhere." Alva ignored her as she crept the car along the icy street. She squinted and leaned forward, her face inches from the windshield.

With growing trepidation, Wanda grasped her collar and released the clasp. She pulled it away from her neck. A rush of whispering demon voices hit her like wind through a tightly slatted fence. The mental sounds morphed into whistles, creaks, and crackling static that bounced like echoes between her ears. She focused on the closest thoughts and weeded painfully through the mind-bending voices of hundreds. A few twisted together in howls of pain. She counted six. Panic amplified the emotions of one of them, and she knew it must belong to the Snit in the rickshaw Henry was chasing.

Gritting her teeth, she struggled to get a bead on the Snit's location. She sensed darkness, which wasn't new information since it was nearly two in the morning, but she also picked up its perception of tiny animals moving around. Rats scrabbled to get inside a dumpster. A nearby alley seemed the most likely place for the rickshaw to hide.

"Honey, you're sweating and you're pale as flour. You all right?" Alva's voice sounded miles away.

"I'm fine." Wanda's words sounded hoarse in her ears while mind-numbing thoughts from demons battered her brain. "Turn here." She motioned at a narrow opening between two buildings.

As Alva directed the car down the alley, the Snit's thoughts intensified, its panic like a knife inside Wanda's skull. It felt sick and confused. Having heard enough, she reclasped the protective metal band. "We're very close now."

Wanda searched for any lingering "alley bats," the prostitutes who favored dark alleys for selling their bodies. She watched a figure move at the far end of the paved passageway. There was no mistaking Henry's tall, broad-shouldered silhouette. "Stop the car."

When Alva stepped on the brake, Wanda opened the car door to climb out and gagged on the putrid odor of stale garbage. A black dumpster stood between her and Henry, and the rickshaw crouched beside it. Its carriage stuck out like a white hanky in a black suit pocket.

She didn't know why they were being quiet. It's not like the Snit didn't know they were there, and it was trapped between them. She crept closer to the dumpster, and so did Henry.

He held up a dark rag, and as he approached, Alva's headlights revealed blood on the rag. Henry must have taken it from the rickshaw's master.

"You ready? Because I'm about to light this hanky on fire to break its bond and set it free." Henry clasped a small flint lamp between his fingers and dangled the rag over it.

Wanda's skunk stripe pulsed against her scalp. She couldn't see it but she could feel it, and she knew it glowed like green neon. Holding out her hands, she let the force inside her pull at the air in search of demon energy. The rickshaw creaked as it turned to face her.

"Wait!" Henry's eyes started to glow red. "It's not alone. Can't you feel them?"

She did feel them. And behind Henry, through the open mouth of the alley, strutted five more rickshaws. They pulled their empty carriages behind them, the wheels crunching over pebbles and broken glass, their long ostrich legs casting elongated shadows against the building walls on either side. It was the first time Wanda had ever perceived a demon as sentient. Seeing a possessed machine walk like an animal sent a chill down her neck and made her heart shudder.

Sweat gathered beneath her arms despite the freezing rain that created slush around her feet. "I don't know if I can take on six all at once," she told Henry.

Henry's face appeared calm and confident, a lot more than she felt. "You can do it, Wanda. It's who you are."

Just hearing him say it drove home the truth in his words. A surge of strength shot through her limbs as she straightened her spine, and she jerked her chin in a hard nod. Henry lit the rag.

A tiny flame crawled up the fabric, growing as it devoured the blood. Henry's lips moved with an incantation Wanda couldn't hear. All six rickshaws went instantly still.

Her hands shook as she drew out the demons' energy. Her muscles tensed and bunched in her neck, her concentration so focused she thought her temples would bleed.

A small fire burst from the bonnet of one rickshaw carriage, then another, and another. As they burned, tendrils of blue mist twirled up from the two-legged machines attached to the front of each. One by one, they drifted through the air toward Wanda. She gathered five demons into the palms of her hands.

Where was the sixth?

All the rickshaws were engulfed in flames now, but one wasn't standing still anymore. It started to run. And it headed straight for Wanda.

She was about to dive to the ground when the flaming thing leaped over her and ran toward the alley's exit, where Alva had parked the car. The stubborn woman still sat inside.

Wanda closed her fists around the demons in her hands and crushed them to smoke. "Henry! My aunt's still in—"

But he was already running for the flaming rickshaw and closed in on it fast. Not fast enough. It tried to leap over the car, but its rear wheels caught on the front fender and the long legs of the machine crashed through the windshield. The canvas roof on the car erupted into flame.

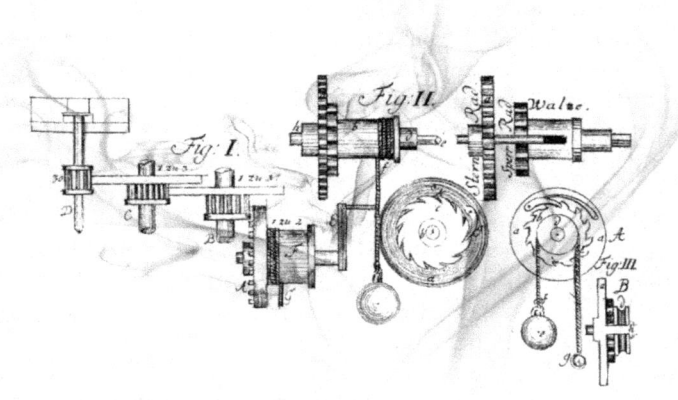

CHAPTER ELEVEN

Henry flung himself on the car's hood and shoved the struggling rickshaw onto the ground. He plunged his hands through the flames to search for Alva.

He found her within seconds and grabbed her by the shoulders to yank her up through the hole in the windshield. Hugging her to him, he rolled off the car's hood and onto the pavement, careful to brace the ground with his elbows so he wouldn't crush her with his weight. They landed in a splash of slush that turned into clouds of steam. Alva lay unmoving beneath him.

"Aunt Alva!" Wanda screamed.

Henry heard fast footsteps slosh through puddles as she rushed toward them.

"Oh, my God. Henry, is she okay?"

"Where's the last Snit?" Henry asked, still protecting Alva's body with his own.

"Dead." Wanda's voice shook.

Henry felt Alva's heart beating beneath him and heard her quick breaths. He eased up slowly and gazed down at her. Singed hair framed the woman's blistered face and her charred clothing crumbled around her. She didn't look good, but it could have been much, much worse.

Wanda knelt beside her. "Aunt Alva? Can you hear me?"

The woman moaned.

Wanda sighed and released a breathy laugh along with a few tears. "You're not dead."

"Not yet," Alva croaked. "I feel like something left on the barbecue too long."

Sirens screamed in the distance.

"Ambulance, fire truck and the cops," Henry said, his relief and anxiety taking bets on which was stronger. Relieved that help for Alva was on its way, his fractured nerves over another encounter with the law got the better of him. He should hightail it out of here, but he couldn't abandon Wanda and her aunt. Watching Wanda in action tonight convinced him how vital her role was as protector of this city. If someone had to go in for questioning, Henry was the expendable one.

"I'm going with Alva to the hospital," Wanda said.

He nodded and kicked at a burnt piece of wood from the rickshaw. "If they ask why you were here, just tell them your aunt took a wrong turn."

"What about you?" Her forehead crimped with worry. "Someone will be held liable for destroying the rickshaws. You can't take all the blame."

"I have to."

Her brows furrowed and he could almost see the thoughts working behind her eyes. "And take all the credit, too, huh?"

He smiled. "Nice try. You know there's no credit here, no good deeds. At least the cops won't think so. It's all about the law, the destruction of property, being a public nuisance, arson—"

"Arson?"

He shrugged. "There was a fire, wasn't there? And I'm Hellspawn, so..."

"Don't let yourself get caught."

"Why not?"

"Because I need you." Her eyes glistened in the flickering light from the fire still consuming her aunt's car. "You'll go to jail, or worse, and I can't save the city without your help."

Which was exactly why he had to give himself up. Or pretend to. "I have a plan, but you have to trust me. Act like you don't know me. Can you do that?"

"Wish fulfillment?" Her smile looked smug. "Sure, I can do that."

He hardly heard her over the blare of sirens as a fire truck and a cop steamer stopped behind Alva's burning car. The ambulance rolled up next.

Henry stepped deeper into the shadows and backed his way toward the dumpster to crouch behind it. Peering toward the other end of the dark alley, he saw Mystic. Her headlights stayed off as she awaited his signal.

Who should step out of the police steam car but Henry's favorite police officer. Taking no chances, Ned held his brine gun at the ready.

This was no coincidence. Someone had tipped off this guy. The cop held a grudge against demon half-breeds and he probably honed in on any incident that involved people like Henry.

The emergency medical crew from The New York Hospital quickly attended to Alva. Wanda remained quiet, tossing Henry a discreet glance now and then. Ned and Mac explored the burning car and the charred remains of the rickshaws.

"Anyone know what happened here?" Ned asked Wanda.

"I didn't see much," she told him, sounding unsure. And very believable if she did say so herself. "I was riding with my aunt and she made a wrong turn into this alley. A bunch of flaming machines ran at us and then..." Her voice cracked and she looked down at her aunt, who was now strapped to a backboard. The medical crew lifted her up and carried her toward the ambulance.

"One of the machines crashed through the windshield and caught the car on fire..." Wanda covered her mouth with her hand and closed her eyes. She made a choking sound.

Mac offered her a handkerchief.

"Thank you," she said and blew her nose.

Ned gave his partner a narrow-eyed look of annoyance. "Ma'am, did you see who started the fire in the rickshaws?"

She shook her head. "No. Excuse me, officers, but I need to be with my aunt now. I'm the only family she has."

"Sure," Mac said with a smile. "Just give us a phone number so we can reach you if we have more questions."

"I already told you everything." Her gaze jumped to the dumpster, then back to the ambulance. "Okay, here's the number for my aunt's place."

Ned watched her closely. Too closely. Henry noticed that Ned had seen her attention make a sudden shift. The cop approached the dumpster as the ambulance sped Alva and Wanda to the hospital. Henry knew he'd be found eventually, so he saved them all some time by stepping out into the light of

Mac's electric torch.

"You got me," Henry said, and raised his hands high above his head.

Ned laughed. "You're like a bad penny, Mr. Spawnster Man. This is the second time I've seen you in a week. What is it about crazy demons and their kin? Birds of a feather, right?"

It was actually the third time they'd seen each other, but who was counting? Ned had forgotten all about the first, and that was fine by Henry. He wished he could forget what a bigot the cop was.

Ned held up the brine gun and aimed. "Start talkin'."

"Not much to say," Henry said. "I like fire and thought I'd light a few. I wasn't expecting an audience."

"So you're a pyromaniac." Ned clucked his tongue. "Fuckin' Spawnster. What a waste of human genes."

Mac came up behind Ned and gave Henry a look that said *don't even think about it*. Controlling the cop's mind was out of the question. Mac remembered, and he wouldn't let it happen again. That left Henry with only one other option.

"Lucky for me I got an informant who tipped me off about you tonight. Says he's a friend of yours." Ned gave Henry a sly look. "Some friend."

When it came to old foes, Henry had plenty, but it didn't take long to figure out the rat who must have fingered him. Jasper, his gang's leader from decades ago. The anger between them still lingered. Anger was one letter short of danger, which Jasper would be in if he didn't butt out of Henry's business.

Henry turned to face the opposite end of the alley, his back to Ned. The scales on his neck stood up because he knew how vulnerable he was to Ned's gun. But he had to stand where Mystic could see his face.

"I'm ready, Officer." He held his hands behind his back to accept the cuffs. Staring at Mystic now, he mouthed the words, "Come get me."

Mystic's engine started, a low volume hum that echoed through the alley. Because Henry faced away from Ned, he couldn't see the cop's expression. His back tingled in anticipation of a blast of salt water searing his flesh.

Mystic angled into the alley, her headlamps blinding. Henry heard Ned curse behind him, then the click of the brine gun being cocked. The cab's front passenger door flew open and Henry raced down the alley to meet Mystic halfway. The sound of spewing water hitting pavement just inches from his heels encouraged Henry to run faster.

He had no idea what kind of range the gun had. A sudden burning sensation on his calf gave him the answer. The salt ate through his skin like acid through paper and he almost fell. He barely made it to Mystic's open door and dived inside. The taxi geared hard into reverse.

Gunshots echoed like cannon fire in the narrow alley. Mac must have had a regular gun to shoot at Mystic. She wasn't impervious to gunfire. A bullet blasted through her windshield, then another pinged her body. She jerked, but didn't stop.

They peeled backwards into the street, the rear tires burning rubber. Then Mystic shot forward down the avenue.

Henry breathed heavy, his leg sizzling with pain. He knew the cops would be on his tail at any minute. It was a struggle for him just to say, "Evasive action. Just get us to Vernon's."

"*You... got... it.*"

⤢ ⤣

Mystic zigzagged through alleys and side streets, and even made a pass through the depths of Spawnstertown. Henry finally believed he'd lost his pursuers. The cops had fallen behind after only a few blocks, but Henry told Mystic to keep going for the sake of caution.

His leg throbbed while sitting inside his cab within Vernon's underground garage. It was the secret entrance to his nephew's labs and also where Vernon stored myriad parts and equipment for his inventions. Plus he stocked a variety of magical implements used by the mages in his employ. Vernon wasn't a magic user himself, but he was open to whatever enhanced the workability of his machines. Magic spells could be an amazing resource.

"*You... all... right?*" Mystic asked.

"I'll heal," Henry said, though he knew it would take longer than usual for a salt burn.

"*Want... me to... honk... for... help?*"

"No, I don't want the wrong people to hear. I'm okay. I can walk." The leg of his canvas pants rubbed against the blistered skin. He ripped the fabric away to air out the burn so it could scab.

Henry used the freight elevator to reach the first floor. Limping out into the hall, he was happy to see Vernon standing outside his office. He couldn't stay on his feet much longer and needed to sit before he fell.

Vernon slid his glasses down his nose and looked over the top of them at Henry. "What happened to you?"

"Long story." Henry limped into Vernon's office. It was time to tell his nephew about Wanda Snow.

He relayed all the evening's events, beginning with Chen's broken body in a Chinatown gutter and ending with how he got sprayed with the cop's brine gun.

Vernon sat behind his desk and listened intently, but at the end of Henry's story, he said, "Back up a minute. You say this Wanda Snow is an exorcist?"

Henry nodded and said sheepishly, "She stole one of my Vox boxes."

Vernon stood. "She what?"

Making a leveling motion with his hands, Henry said, "Calm down. First she stole all five, and then—"

"How the Hell did she get *all five* boxes?"

"It doesn't matter. I got four of them back, but the fifth one disappeared." Henry cleared his throat. "Someone took it and she doesn't know who."

Incredulous now, Vernon placed both hands on top of his head. "You're dealing with an exorcist who kills demons. The very demons I use to operate my machines. The demons my business—*our* business—depends on."

"It's not about business anymore, Vernon." Henry leaned forward in his chair. "It's about people's lives. The Snits are turning into killers and we don't know why."

Vernon returned to his chair. He sagged into it, his expression defeated.

"I understand your stress. You have a son now, and your mother depends on you financially. She depends on both of us." Henry attempted a smile. "We still have the Imps. And I swear that little heater you designed will end up making us a fortune."

The corner of Vernon's mouth lifted in a half smile. Then his expression shifted, his brows tangling in a frown. "Wait a minute. I know why the Snits are so hostile."

"You knew and you didn't tell me?"

"I haven't seen you for a few days." Vernon picked up a notebook from his desk and flipped to a page. "It was Max who told me. He said the Snits have a virus."

Henry had wondered if it might be a plague of some kind, though it didn't seem possible. Demons didn't have physical bodies so they weren't prone to disease or infection. "Is it a psychic illness?"

"Apparently. But Max says he has no idea how they got it, or how it can be cured." Vernon stared at the notebook a second longer before snapping it shut.

"What's wrong?"

"Max. He's changed since he started dating that girl from Spawnstertown."

Uh oh. Girls almost always spelled trouble, especially for a young Hellspawn who'd never dated before. "What does dating have to do with him telling you the Snits are sick?"

"He won't tell me how he knows and I think she's the reason why." Vernon leaned back in his chair. "He's never kept secrets from me."

"I wouldn't worry too much. He's an eighteen-year-old kid. Who knows what goes on inside that adolescent brain of his."

"That's what worries me. I *don't* know, and I should."

Henry disagreed. The boy needed his privacy, even from his father, as long as what he knew couldn't hurt him or anyone else. "Does it really matter *how* he found out?"

Vernon puffed out a weary sigh. "I have my team of mages working on a cure. In the meantime, all my Snit-possessed machines are locked in a warded room. They're not going anywhere."

Henry thought about Wanda's aunt and how close the Snit had come to killing her. "I can ask Wanda to come over and take care of them for you."

"No! I want to keep them alive as long as there's a chance they can be cured." Vernon glanced down at Henry's leg. "That doesn't look good."

"It doesn't feel good."

"I have a first aid kit in the kitchen. Let's have a look, and get you something to eat while we're in there."

Henry liked the sound of that. He was hungry enough to eat an entire cow, raw if he had to. But he'd settle for a couple of rare steaks.

On the way to the kitchen, they ran into Max in the hallway. The boy was dressed nattily in a vest and frock coat, his flannel slacks pressed to create a sharp crease down the front. The cuff broke at a perfect length above a pair of shiny black shoes sheathed in spats. Max was no fashion expert and it was obvious he hadn't dressed himself.

"Where'd you get the outfit?" Vernon asked him, his tone more accusing than inquisitive.

"Claire gave it to me."

Claire? The name piqued Henry's interest. Levi had a girlfriend named Claire, but it was a common name that could belong to any number of girls.

"So where are you off to in such fancy duds?" Henry asked, following it up with a chuckle. He didn't want the boy feeling self-conscious.

The look Max gave him was sharp enough to cut steel. "None of your business."

"Now hold it right there, mister," Vernon said in a stern voice he rarely used with Max. "You give your uncle some respect."

"Why?" Max's tone was surly. He turned around and started walking back the way he'd come. "He doesn't respect the Hellspawn, so why should I respect him?"

Henry stared after him, dumbfounded.

Vernon took a step toward his son. "Come back here and apologize—"

Henry grabbed Vernon's arm. "It's okay. Let him go." The words sounded familiar, but they didn't belong to Max. He spoke on behalf of someone else.

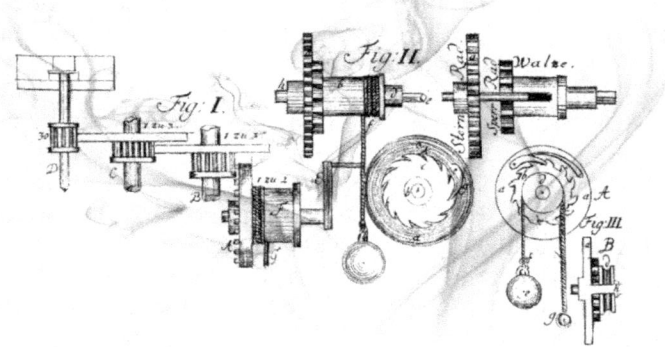

CHAPTER TWELVE

W anda sat in an uncomfortable wooden chair and watched her aunt sleep. The hospital room was stark and clean, and crowded with patients.

Alva's head was wrapped in so much gauze she could hardly move, which apparently was the point. Wanda hoped to take her home later that day, but the doctor had said they'd have to wait and see.

Henry had saved her aunt's life, and grateful didn't begin to describe how she felt about that. If not for him, Alva's burns would have been far more severe. She had mostly first and second degree burns on her face, and first degree burns on her arms where parts of her coat had burned away. Alva's only other injuries were bruises on her back and upper arms, where Henry had grabbed her to pull her from the car.

When Alva moaned, Wanda left her chair and rushed to her aunt's bedside. "Hi, Auntie. How you feelin'?"

"Crappy." Her voice sounded muffled through the bandage that covered most of her mouth. "And loopy."

"That would be the morphine."

Alva pointed at a cup and straw sitting on the table beside her. Wanda brought it to her, and angled the straw to her mouth so she could drink. "My mouth feels like a cotton farm in a drought."

Wanda swallowed the sudden lump that swelled inside her throat. "I'm sorry about what happened in the alley."

Alva tried to shake her head, but couldn't move it much. "Don't be silly. Wasn't your fault. I should have backed farther out of the alley, but I couldn't bear for you to face those things alone."

"I wasn't alone," Wanda reminded her. "Henry was there."

"You two make quite a team, you know."

Wanda felt her face warm and she turned away to stare out the window as the morning sun made a half-hearted attempt to lighten the room. Fog filled the air outside, just like always. Wanda had forgotten what color the sky was supposed to be.

"Henry and I work well together."

"You sweet on him, Wanda?" Alva asked.

She had to think about that for a second. "I like him very much. He makes me feel safe. And he has a good heart."

"You don't find that attractive?"

Wanda shrugged and gave it some thought. Were her feelings toward Henry romantic? Maybe a little, but she was so consumed by her mission that she couldn't afford any dalliances. She had to stay focused. "I feel... connected to Henry. It's as if we were destined to tackle this crisis together." Perhaps that's all it was. She shouldn't confuse destiny with romance.

Alva wheezed and Wanda asked, "You okay, Auntie? You need the nurse?"

"I'm fine, dear. I was just hoping... Well, never mind. I'm glad you found a good friend in Henry Paine."

Wanda smiled. "So am I."

"My eyes haven't been open but five minutes and I already feel sleepy again." Alva yawned, or tried to under all the gauze.

"I'm sure it's the medicine workin' on you." Wanda backed away from the bed. "Get some sleep. I'm gonna go down to the cafeteria for a cup of coffee." She stepped away from the privacy screen that surrounded Alva's bed. That's when she saw Henry filling the doorway. Her heart fluttered in surprise, thought it was not an unpleasant feeling. Heat flushed her face. "Hello, Henry."

His enormous hands dwarfed a bright bouquet of flowers. "How's she doing?"

"Could be worse." Wanda glanced at her aunt, who'd already drifted back to sleep. She joined Henry at the door and took the flowers. "Very gentlemanly of you. Aunt Alva will love 'em. I'll ask a nurse to put 'em in water for you."

She started down the hallway toward the nurses' station and Henry walked beside her. "How about you. Holding up all right?" he asked.

"Sure. Nothin' much gets to me these days. I'm just glad I didn't get taken in for questionin'—" She stopped and gazed up at him. "Henry, what happened after I left?"

"Just what you'd expect. Cops tried to arrest me."

"Tried?"

"Mystic got me out of there before anything ugly could happen."

She had to smile at that. "You love that demon cab of yours, don't you?"

"She's my best friend."

Best friend? It was a machine, for Heaven's sake. Wanda shook her head and started down the hall again. He matched her steps. That's when she noticed his limp. "You're keepin' secrets. Tell me what *really* happened."

"I just did."

"Then why are you limpin'?"

"Damn cop shot me in the leg with a brine gun."

She stopped walking to turn and stare at him. "You got a salt burn?"

He grimaced. "Yeah, on the back of my leg. But I made it to my nephew's without being followed and Vernon fixed me up. Fed me, too, but my stomach's growling again."

How he could afford to keep himself fed was beyond her. The man seemed to eat twenty-four hours a day. She clucked her tongue. "I'm headin' to the cafeteria. Want to join me? My treat."

He nodded and they continued down the hall, stopping at the nurse's station along the way to hand off Alva's flowers.

A number of people stood by a row of elevators. Wanda headed in that direction, but Henry said, "There's gotta be stairs in this place. How far is the cafeteria? China?"

She laughed. "It's on the first floor. And yes, there are stairs, but what about your leg?"

"I still have it, and it still works."

"Then follow me." She turned the corner and headed for the exit door to the stairwell. She tugged it open and voices mixed with laughter sifted up from the landing below. She closed the door.

"What's wrong?" Henry asked.

"There are people on the stairs."

"So?"

"They're talkin'." She opened the door a crack and leaned her head in to catch a few words.

"You sure are nosey."

"Hush." She listened for a few more seconds. "I'm a practiced eaves-dropper. You can learn all kinds of stuff by listenin' in on other people's conversations. You ought to try it some time."

Looking smug, he asked, "So what did you learn?"

"I'm not sure. Somethin' about Spawnstertown? And some guy named Jasper."

Henry stiffened and locked his jaw.

"You all right?"

"Yeah. Who's on the stairs and what do they look like?"

"I can't see 'em," she said, watching the corners of Henry's eyes tighten with anger. "I heard two voices, but there could be more than two people. Why are you interested all of a sudden?"

"I'll tell you later. I want to hear what they're saying."

"And you call *me* nosey."

He didn't even crack a smile. He apparently knew this Jasper guy and didn't like him much.

"You know who they're talkin' about?" she asked.

Henry gave her a sharp nod, then gestured for her to open the door. He mouthed, "Quietly."

They stepped out into the stairwell and Wanda let the door swing shut behind them with a faint snick. They stood and listened to the conversation going on below.

"The meeting's tomorrow night," said a man with a deep voice bordering on a growl.

"Yeah," said another man, who sounded more tenor than base. "This is what we've been waiting for. After a hundred and fifty years, it's a long time coming. You think Jasper will finally let us know his plans?"

"Not sure," said the growler. "I imagine he's gotta be careful what he says. If the wrong people find out what he's up to, there'll be Hell to pay."

Both men laughed. Obviously an inside joke.

Henry stepped to the edge of the landing and peered over the rail. He gazed down and a corner of his mouth lifted in a sneer. He looked at Wanda and mouthed, "Two hospital orderlies." He pulled up on his pointed ears and silently formed his lips around the name, "Ronald."

Wanda joined Henry at the rail to see who he meant. The one with unnaturally long ears must be Ronald, and Henry apparently knew him.

"Want to meet for a drink first?" Ronald asked the growler.

"Sounds good. Greaser's at eleven?"

"See you then."

Henry and Wanda waited a few minutes before making their way down the stairs. Just before reaching the last step to the next floor, Wanda asked Henry, "So are you goin'?"

"Going where?" The growler stepped out from behind the stairs. "You were right, Ronald. You did hear a door close."

Wanda's heart jumped. She and Henry hadn't breathed a word. No one could have heard them. No human, anyway.

Ronald smiled and his narrow-eyed gaze raked Henry up and down. "Well, if it isn't my old friend Henry Paine. Long time no see."

Henry nodded. "Ronald. I'd say it was good to see you, but I'd be lying."

Ronald's long ears had pointed tips and his nose was flat like a bat's. His scaly forehead protruded apelike above his eyes. Wanda imagined it was the Spawnster's exceptional hearing that had given them away. Ronald saw her interest and his smile widened. He tugged the lobe of one giant ear. "That's right, doll. I can hear a cat sneeze from two blocks away. Impressed?"

Wanda yawned. "Not particularly."

Ronald pressed his lips together in a straight line, then flashed a grin and grabbed her by the shoulders. He spun her around and pulled her hard against him, wrapping his arms around her chest to hold her close. He nuzzled her neck. "Yummy."

She didn't struggle. There was no point considering his grip was like iron, but she wasn't about to let him get away with anything. She watched Henry's face turn stony, his jaw so tight she worried he might crack a tooth.

"Let her go," Henry said.

The growler gripped Henry's arm, but not tight enough. Henry stepped back and locked gazes with the growling Spawnster, who rivaled Henry in size. But the growler was clumsy, his oversized feet like planks of wood, and his hands were hindered by the webbed flesh between his long fingers. The second Henry pinned him with a stare, the growler went stiff.

Ronald laughed. "That trick never gets old, Henry. But you'd better release my web-fingered friend or I'm going to test how sweet your sweetie really is." The Spawnster's tongue was long enough to wrap around Wanda's neck and slide along her chin. It felt slimy and smelled like garlic. She held back a gag.

She didn't want Henry to release his man, so it was up to her to make a move on lizard-boy. "How did you know what I like?" she asked Ronald.

"What?" He didn't sound so confident now.

"I enjoy bein' tasted." She snuggled against him, pressing her bottom into his groin. "You feel good. I bet *you* taste good, too."

His grip loosened and she turned in his arms so that she faced him, her forehead level with his chin. She smoothed her hands up his belly, sliding them over his chest until she reached his heart. Power surged through her skin, seeking the demon energy beneath her palms. Her single lock of green hair heated her scalp. Looking at Ronald's face, she asked, "How does that feel, lizard-boy?"

His skin had gone pale and he was making choking sounds, as if he couldn't breathe. "What are you doing?"

"Easin' your burden. It must be rough bein' only half a monster. So now you get to be half a man."

He groaned. "No. Please. Don't take away the best part of me." The light went out of his eyes and his expression became slack as drool dribbled down his chin. He sagged against her and she backed him toward the stairs, easing him down to sit on a step, her hand still on his chest.

Her fingers still glowing, she watched Ronald's face. The reptilian features began to fade. The scales on his forehead vanished and his ears shrank to a more normal size, the tips no longer pointed. His nose was a regular shape now and she imagined his tongue shrank, too, but she wasn't about to check.

Her skin tightened with transformation as scales itched across her own forehead and into her hairline. A prickling sensation at her temples told her she now had horns and she vaguely wondered what color they were this time.

Wanda lifted her hand from his chest and curled her fingers around the ball of red energy glowing in her palm. That's when her own features became human again. She held

Ronald's demon half in her hand, and without it, he was an ordinary human with an eggplant for a brain. Or a squash. Name your vegetable and he was it. She tightened her fist and smoke puffed between her fingers. The demon part of Ronald was dead.

She turned around to face Henry, who struggled to concentrate on his victim. He'd been watching her with Ronald, and though he couldn't have seen the changes to her face, he looked unnerved by what she'd done. Even so, he appeared no less determined to keep the growler in check.

"You didn't see Wanda or me in the stairwell," Henry told the web-fingered Spawnster. "You came out on the landing for a smoke and found an ordinary man in a catatonic stupor sitting on the stairs. He must be a patient who wandered away from his room. You have to call someone for help, but not until we're gone. Do you understand?"

"I understand," the growler said, his eyes glazed and vacant.

"Good. Now count backwards from one hundred. When you get to one, we'll be gone."

"One hundred, ninety-nine, ninety-eight..."

"Let's go." Henry rushed past Wanda and headed down the stairs. She followed close behind.

Once out on the street, Henry appeared angry, his eyes narrowed and gleaming. He stared at her and said, "You almost did the same thing to me when we first met."

How could she forget? The memory of it still haunted her. Ashamed, Wanda peered down at her feet. "Almost. But I didn't."

"And you never will." He backed away while throwing up his hands. "This isn't going to work, Wanda. I can't take the risk. Find yourself another partner."

CHAPTER THIRTEEN

Henry strode down the street away from the hospital, and away from her.

"Wait!" Panic squeezing her heart, Wanda ran after him. "Henry, I had to do it. I had no other choice!"

Henry didn't turn around. His long strides ate up a lot of pavement and she had to double-time her steps to keep up.

It was important she make him understand. "You told me you can only control one mind at a time, so I had to do *somethin'* about Ronald."

Henry said nothing.

"I got the impression you didn't like him, so why do you even care?"

Henry stopped. He glared down at her and said, "That's right, I didn't like him. He was a thief, a rapist, and a murderer. But *you* didn't know that. You only exorcised him because he was Hellspawn."

"You're wrong. I exorcised him to protect myself." She matched his glare. "It's not like you were in any position to help me."

He blinked. "Now you're blaming *me* for what you did?"

She shook her head. "Of course not. Killin' demons is what I do. I didn't *kill* Ronald. You saw him. His heart didn't stop and he's still breathin'—"

"But he might as well be dead." Henry folded his arms and threw his head back to stare up at the overcast sky. "What will happen to him now?"

"Does it matter that much to you?"

He jerked his gaze back to her. "He's a living being, Wanda, and now just a *human* being, without the part that made him whole. He'd be better off if you *had* killed him."

Wanda reached out to touch Henry's arm, but he jerked it away. "I've seen some of 'em get their minds back," she told him. "Not completely, but they became conscious, learned how to walk and talk again, how to feed themselves."

Henry's eyes widened. "You've done this a lot?"

She shrugged. "A few times. At first I thought my gift was a way to make Spawnsters human. I had a Hellspawn friend in high school who begged me to take her demon part away."

Henry's expression turned sympathetic, but he sounded wary. "What happened?"

"You just saw what happened."

He went quiet and stared down at the ground.

"But she got better after time. Her parents were so happy to have their little girl lookin' human again that they didn't care if she had forgotten how to talk or feed herself."

"Did she learn?"

Wanda nodded. "It took a few years, but yeah, she's almost normal now. But her memories from before are gone for good. She doesn't even remember me, and I was her best friend." Recalling what she'd done to Mary brought the guilt back, and also the pain of losing someone she loved. There would always be something missing in Mary, some spark of life and intelligence she'd had as a whole person: half demon, half human. Hellspawn.

His expression contrite, Henry said, "Look, Wanda, I didn't mean what I said about you and me. I over-reacted and I apologize."

She let a little smile tug at her mouth. "We're friends again?"

"Just keep your distance. I don't want you turning me into the vegetable special. I've grown attached to my scales."

"They look good on you."

"I know." He headed back up the street toward the hospital. "Now I'm hungrier than ever. Do they serve possum in the cafeteria?"

"Maybe." She walked alongside him, careful not to get too close. She didn't want to risk getting so close to losing him again.

Confrontation always gave him an appetite. Henry set his full tray down on the table, then glanced at Wanda's tray. The girl had a healthy appetite. She'd chosen two different kinds of sandwiches, a piece of strawberry cake, a brownie, and a hot cup of chicory. He looked her over, checking for bulging hips and thick legs, but the fabric of her long, split skirt was loose and flowing. Not a bulge in sight. The only tight garment on her was the leather corset that squeezed her torso into the shape of an hourglass.

"What are you lookin' at?" she asked as she took her seat at their table.

"I'm looking for your extra leg because the food on your tray has nowhere to go."

She patted her stomach. "Believe me, it goes somewhere. Exorcism makes me hungry."

Henry didn't get the possum he wanted, but the cafeteria had a lovely haggis with all his favorite organ meats drowned in a sea of peppery hot gravy. No salt. "I thought hospital food was supposed to be terrible."

"I wouldn't know." She took a bite of her sandwich and continued talking with her mouth full. "I've never had to stay in one. You?"

He shook his head and shoved a forkful of haggis in his mouth. Tasty. He swallowed and said, "About the question you asked before we were so rudely interrupted in the stairwell, the answer is no, I'm not going to the meeting."

Her mouth full of egg salad, Wanda asked, "Why not?"

"Because I can't let Jasper see me."

She wiped her mouth with a napkin. "You two have a history?"

"Unfortunately, yes. And if he sees me at this meeting, he won't disclose whatever mysterious big news he's planning to give his followers."

Her expression curious, she said, "Makes sense to me. So what kind of *followers* are you talkin' about?"

Henry dug into his food. He chewed a few thoughtful bites before saying, "I'm talking about Hellspawn followers. Or more accurately, Spawnster followers."

"I didn't know there was a difference."

Appearing thoughtful, he tilted his head one way, then the other. "A slight one. It's mostly about attitude. Spawnsters have this huge chip on their shoulders. They think the world owes them something because they're special. The chosen ones." He had to laugh at that.

"But you *are* special."

"That's nice of you to say, and even if it's true, a Spawnster defines being special as superior." He eyed Wanda's brownie. "You going to eat that?"

She dragged the plate with the brownie beyond his reach and he shrugged.

"So what are you saying?" she asked.

"I'm saying Spawnsters think they have a right to rule the world and humans should, I don't know, live on a deserted island somewhere." Actually, he knew the idea was to farm humans as food. Jasper had acquired a taste for human flesh, or long-pig as he called it, when he was homeless and starving. Henry would rather Wanda not know that when Ronald had called her yummy, he'd meant it. Literally.

"Tell me about this gang you used to belong to."

He nearly choked on his haggis. He gulped some water and cleared his throat. "My father —my human father—threw me out of the house when I started showing signs of being Hellspawn. I had nowhere to go, no friends, no family, so I lived on the streets of Brooklyn, eating out of trash cans and stealing dog food from people's yards."

Wanda wrinkled her nose. "It sickens me to think how many Hellspawn have been abandoned by their families. It was like that in Kentucky, too."

"Yeah, but the city's a lot tougher than a mining town. Hellspawn kids grouped together to survive, to protect themselves from humans who wanted us dead. Jasper saved my life."

She set down her sandwich. "How?"

The memory didn't hurt as much as it used to. It was true about time healing all wounds. Well, most of them. "A group of men tied me to a fence. They ripped off my shirt and started peeling the scales from my back. Claimed they were *curing* me."

Wanda held her hand over her mouth. "Oh, my God. They were torturing you?"

Oh, yeah. They sure as Hell were. "I'm none the worse for it. My scales grew back."

"Are you saying Jasper saved you from those hooligans?"

He eyed her brownie again and this time she pushed it toward him. "Thanks. Yeah, Jasper saved me." He chomped into the brownie. "He and his gang rushed in and, uh, taught the guys a lesson."

"What kind of lesson?"

"They killed them." Then roasted their bodies in fires they built inside some old steel drums by the railroad tracks. The gang ate well that night, but Henry went hungry. The very thought of eating people made him want to throw up.

Wanda shuddered. "That was harsh, don't you think?"

"I was in agony, my back was raw and bleeding, and at the time, I honestly didn't care what happened to them. So I stayed with Jasper and his Demon Lords after that. They were the only family I had back then."

"*Demon Lords?*"

"That's what they called themselves. We were together more than seventy five years, up until my human niece found me and asked me to rejoin the family." But that was a story for another time. Right now they had to decide what to do about Jasper's big meeting. "So as far as tonight goes..."

Wanda picked at her cake with her fork, and gazed up at him with questioning eyes. "I'm guessing Jasper disowned you when you left him for your real family. Your *human* family."

"You guessed right. He hates my guts. I don't visit Spawnstertown much, seeing as how he's the mayor."

"I see." She arched her eyebrows. "So I'll have to go to the meeting by myself."

Henry was about to protest, but the hard glint of determination in her eyes warned him to keep his mouth shut. Besides, she had a decent idea. She could get away with looking like a Spawnster by adding a few embellishments. "I'd like to object, for your own safety, but on second thought, Spawnsters should be more afraid of you than you are of them."

"I'm not afraid of anyone."

"Of course not." He cleared his throat. "In order to pass as one of us, you'll have to let your hair down. Literally. Show off that glowing green lock of yours, and rev it up a few watts. It should be bright enough to read by. We'll pretend you have other Spawnster features hidden beneath your clothing."

She looked down at herself. "Like what?"

"Oh, I don't know. Scales. A tail. An extra appendage or

two." He laughed. "Don't look so disgusted."

"I'm not disgusted. I'm just remembering one of my cousins."

"Oh." He'd forgotten she had Hellspawn relatives. "And as far as how you dress..."

She narrowed her eyes. "My clothes are just fine, thank you."

"No, they're not. You look too feminine and you'll be mistaken for one of Hell's Belles. Want everyone to think you're a whore?"

She leveled him with a glare.

"Then replace the corset with a man's vest and dress it up with lots of medals. I have some you can borrow. Wear trousers, the boots you have on are fine, and a driver's cap will work. That watch on your arm is great. Spawnsters love big watches, the more the better."

"What's with all the hardware?"

Country Spawnsters were so different from city born. "We, or I should say they, like to play up the connection to our demon kin who possess machines. City Spawnsters decorate themselves with machinery, like buckles, rivets, cogs, and clockworks, lots of leather, wire, cable, and wood. Think of it as Spawnster jewelry."

She tilted her chin. "Hey, I like that. It's a great look. I haven't seen much of it on the streets around here."

"And you won't." He stacked his empty dishes on the tray. "City Spawnsters stay mostly in Spawnstertown. They feel uncomfortable around humans."

"I don't understand. I see Hellspawn in the city all the time."

"You're mostly seeing the ones who feel accepted by society and were never discarded by their human families. Rejected Hellspawn have a completely different mindset and a lifestyle to match: alone and unwanted."

She nodded. "So they've banded together."

"That's right." He stood. "Go home and get some sleep. I'll pick you up at ten to take you to Spawnstertown, but we can't be seen together. Our knowing each other is a secret."

"Got it."

He thought he saw a flicker of fear cross her face, but it passed quicker than he could blink. "You sure you can do this?"

"Are you kidding?" She snorted as she scooted back her chair and stood from the table. "It's like second nature for me. I definitely can do this."

Back at her aunt's apartment, Wanda considered what she'd committed herself to. Could she do this? Spawnstertown? It sounded medieval. Heavy-metal-wearing Spawnsters all grouped together with chips large as the island of Manhattan on their shoulders. Oh, yeah. She could hardly wait.

She brushed out her long hair and gazed at her reflection in the full-length mirror mounted on her aunt's bedroom door. She wished Alva were here, but the doctor had said another day or two in the hospital would be best. Her aunt needed her rest and Alva wouldn't get a wink of sleep if she caught wind of what Wanda was up to.

Wanda turned sideways to see the long swath of green hair mingle with the blonde, the ends stopping just below the small of her back. She concentrated on her energy and the emerald strands glowed phosphorescent. It stood out, all right. But she couldn't keep it at high power for long periods of time. She'd have to temper it from medium to high. It did look impressive, though. And it would be a relief to express this secret part of herself without having to hide it for a change.

Her outfit looked Spawnster-chique. The tan canvas trousers had been no problem, but she'd had to do some digging to find a vest. Henry lent her some of his medals, which were ornamental pins he'd acquired over the years but never wore. She found a street vendor selling some amazing Spawnster jewelry, so she bought a new neck ring to replace the collar she usually wore. This one was wider and decorated with gears and shiny screws.

Alva's closet yielded a men's vest that fit tight enough around her sternum to push her breasts up and show some impressive cleavage. But she buttoned her blouse to her neck to cover it up. Heaven forbid she be mistaken for one of Hell's Belles. Good grief.

If she'd had a scale to stand on, it would have shown an extra five pounds added to her weight due to all the hardware. How did these people drag around so much metal? Her lungs felt constricted by the extra weight on her chest.

Wanda took some deep breaths and glanced at the clock on her aunt's nightstand. It was nine-fifty. Henry would arrive any minute.

Three sharp knocks sounded on the apartment door. He was early.

She opened the door, but it wasn't Henry. It was Mr. Sanchez from 301 down the hall.

"You have to help me," he said, eyes wild.

"What is it?" She stepped back to allow him inside.

"I know you're an exorcist."

"How do you know that?"

"It's all over the building." He began wringing his hands. "We know what you did to the demon that ate the ghost possessing Mrs. Stravinsky's sister."

Holy Moly. Gossip traveled faster than a steam locomotive around here.

"My cousin in Mexico is also an exorcist so I know how it works." Mr. Sanchez looked frantic, his hair frazzled and dark circles shadowing his eyes. "Come with me, please." He reached for her arm and she evaded him.

"Look, Mr. Sanchez, I'm about to go out. Can't this wait?"

He shook his head. "No. I worry for my family. It tries to hurt my family!"

Well, damn. Another rogue demon on the loose. "Okay," she said and let out a long breath. "What's it doing?"

"I show you." He led the way down the hall and as they got closer to his apartment door, she heard loud music, then shouting. What the Hell was going on in there?

"Hey!" Henry trotted down the hall toward them. "I was just coming to get you. Where are you off to?"

She gestured at her neighbor's retreating back. "My neighbor Mr. Sanchez has a demon problem."

"Wanda, we don't have time for this." Henry glanced at his watch. "We're not sure exactly when and where Jasper's meeting is. I don't want you to miss it."

When they arrived at Mr. Sanchez's door, she had to raise her voice to be heard over the noise coming from inside. "This won't take long."

Henry winced and covered his ears. "What?"

"If we don't stop what's goin' on, someone will get hurt." She stepped inside the apartment and the noise abruptly stopped. "What the Hell *was* that?"

Mr. Sanchez pointed at an enormous radio that dominated one side of the room. Wanda had never seen one that big. Its polished wood console shone with glossy varnish and it had an enormous tuning dial in the center. The speaker took up half the radio, which accounted for the head-splitting volume.

"Okay, the Snit's in there," Wanda said, nodding at the radio. "It's out of control, but I can't see how it's dangerous other than blowin' out someone's ear drums."

Mr. Sanchez stood in the doorway of his kitchen, his arm around his tiny Latino wife. Both his children, two little girls, clung to their mother's skirt. "We do not keep demons in our home."

"You do now," Henry said.

Mr. Sanchez looked annoyed. "It showed up early this morning and helped itself to our radio. I thought that if it knew it was not wanted, it would go away like they usually do. But this one refuses to leave."

That was true most of the time, but not lately. At least not with the Snits. "The demon operatin' your radio is sick, Mr. Sanchez. It's not in its right mind."

Henry lowered his head and absently scratched the scales on his neck. "My nephew told me about that. He has his mages working on a cure."

Well, it was good to know at least someone was trying to fix the Snit problem. Just the same, she'd feel safer if all the Snits were dead.

"Can you get rid of it?" Mr. Sanchez asked.

"On one condition," Wanda said.

Mr. Sanchez narrowed his eyes. "What's that?"

"You help me find that missin' box I asked you about." Wanda was never certain of Mr. Sanchez's innocence.

He ran his fingers through his hair. "Deal. Now will you take the demon away?"

"Sure." Wanda approached the benign-looking radio and reached out to touch it. A bright flash of light erupted from its dial, knocking Wanda to the other side of the room. She hit the wall and slumped to the floor, her skin tingling and her chest burning as the room faded to a black fog around her.

CHAPTER FOURTEEN

What the Hell? Henry ran to Wanda, who lay in a heap on Mr. Sanchez's floor. The little girls started screaming and Mrs. Sanchez made the sign of the cross over her chest.

"Mr. Sanchez, please take your family to another room until this is over." Henry checked Wanda's pulse. It beat strong and regular. "Wanda? Can you hear me?"

Wanda moaned and Henry saw smoke rising from the medals and other pins on her chest. "What happened?" she asked.

"You got zapped by a Snit." He held her by the shoulders to prop her up against the wall. "How do you feel?"

She rubbed her forehead, her green stripe of hair glowing so bright it forced Henry to squint. "Dizzy, but strangely energized."

"The metal on your vest is smoking." Yet the fabric wasn't scorched. Whatever had blasted from that radio wasn't an electrical charge. It was psychic energy, the same kind demons used to run the machines they possessed. "Can you stand?"

He helped her up off the floor. She staggered for a second before pushing him away. "I'm fine. Where's Mr. Sanchez?"

"I told him to take his family to another room."

She frowned at the radio. "The nerve of that thing."

The radio console began to shake.

"Oh, no you don't," she told it, and held out her arms as if to give it a hug. A blue misty energy shot up from the radio like a geyser, then angled toward one of Wanda's outstretched hands. She jerked as she caught it, made a fist, and squeezed. Smoke puffed out between her fingers.

Clapping her hands together as if ridding them of dirt,

she said, "All done. Now we can go." She marched out of the apartment without looking back.

"It's over, Mr. Sanchez," Henry called out. "You and your family are safe." He glanced at the demon-free radio before rushing out into the hall to follow Wanda down the stairs.

He waited inside Mystic while Wanda ran back up to her aunt's apartment for her hat and coat. It surprised Henry when Mystic opened the door for her. Wanda was taken aback as well. She slid onto the seat and said, "Awful considerate of you, Mystic. Thanks."

The radio dial spun. "*You... are... welcome.*"

Henry stepped on the accelerator and eased out into the flow of traffic. "I'm glad to see you two finally getting along."

Wanda gripped the dashboard, but she smiled while doing it. "I have a new appreciation for our lesser demon friends. There's much more to them than I thought."

"It's about time you saw the light."

She chuckled. "I wouldn't go that far, but there's a glimmer in the distance. Let's leave it at that."

He jerked a thumb over his shoulder. "So what happened back there?"

"A deranged demon decided to take me on. Big mistake, but I'm glad it tried. The jolt it gave me was a boost to my own power." She rolled her shoulders and tilted her head side to side, making her neck crack. "It feels like a caffeine buzz times fifty."

Good, Henry thought. The fact she felt stronger helped lessen his concerns over her being the only human in a tank full of surly Spawnsters.

"Based on what you asked your neighbor, I take it you suspect him of stealing the fifth Vox box."

"Mr. Sanchez? I honestly don't know." She lost her death grip on the dashboard and dropped her hands to her lap. "He was really offended when I accused him of knowin' where it was. Maybe too offended. Even if he doesn't have it, I bet he'll try findin' it for me now."

Henry waved at the front window as Mystic drove through the entrance to the underground section of New York City. "Welcome to Spawnstertown."

They crept the cab through the backstreets and alleys, careful to avoid the main drag. He'd surely be recognized, which wasn't necessarily a bad thing, but if Wanda was seen with him their plan would be screwed. He gave her a quick once-over and approved of her Spawnster get-up. She'd look like the real deal if she kept the wattage up on her emerald lock. Despite her unusual gift for exorcism, she was still a vulnerable human. If Jasper ever found out what Wanda was... Henry didn't want to think about what would happen.

The streets were dark as coal seams, and minimal light shown from windows in the old buildings that lined either side. Cracked concrete, missing bricks, rotted and splintered wood trim, and peeling paint that was little more than a long-ago memory. Spawnstertown used more horse-drawn cars than steam run, and the stench of manure was strong enough to make Henry's eyes water. He also smelled rotting garbage and other nasty odors that burned his nose hairs. Wanda didn't utter a single complaint.

He let her out of the cab in the alley behind the favorite Spawnster hangout called Greaser's. The joint was a dive, but its oils were potent. If you ordered enough drinks you'd get complimentary beef tripe jerky and fried pig chitterlings. Thinking about those treats made his mouth water.

"Do I have to drink... oil?" Wanda asked him, her face set in a grimace.

"Yeah. Sorry." Henry winked. "But you can dilute it with vinegar."

She rolled her eyes. "Can I order some lettuce to go with it?"

He shook his head.

"You comin' in?"

"Yep. We just can't arrive at the same time, or sit together. I'll watch from a close distance and follow you to wherever this meeting is supposed to take place. You gonna be okay alone?"

She nodded and slapped her open hand lightly on Mystic's hood. Backing away from the cab, she said, "See you inside."

Wanda held her breath while skirting around the garbage cans stacked up in the alley. How did the people here stand the smell? Their senses were different from those of humans. Considering their taste in food, she wasn't surprised.

Wanda stood in front of the building, glancing up and

down the quiet street dotted with traffic that was as much on foot as by horse. A steam car crept by, its occupants checking her out, grinning, laughing. Had she made a mistake? Had they seen through her disguise?

"Ma'am?" came a man's voice from behind her. She turned to stare up into the brutish face of an overweight Spawnster with little hair on his head and plenty on his face. He had black horns growing out from his temples. On second glance, they looked more like small thorny antlers. "Can I buy you a drink?"

He stood in the doorway of Greaser's, his goat-pupil eyes scanning her top to bottom. He grinned and stepped aside to usher her in. "I'm Emmett," he said.

Wanda blinked and swallowed her uncertainty. She had a part to play and she damn well better start playing it. With a smile deliberate and slow, she said, "I'm Wanda. Pleased to meet you."

"You're new in town. I can tell by the accent."

She started to mock a curtsy, but switched it to a bow. Less feminine. Heaven forbid she be mistaken for a whore. Thickening her accent even more, she said, "I'm from the South, relocatin' to the city. It's too borin' where I come from."

His grin broadened, showing long and pointy canines. "Then I think you'll like it here. Never a dull moment in Spawnstertown. What's your poison?"

Her stomach turned at the thought of oil pooling thick and warm at the bottom of it. "I'm partial to safflower."

He chuckled. "A lady's drink. Want cinnamon on top?"

Cinnamon? Yuck. "No, thanks. And make it a single shot, please. I don't drink much. Goes straight to my head." She smiled and gazed up at him with what she hoped was a sultry look. She didn't feel sultry, especially not with this guy.

It must have worked because his eyes began to glow red. "Can I take your coat?"

She slid her coat off and folded it over her arm. "I'll hang on to it, if you don't mind."

He guided her to a table that had seen better days. The top was pitted and stained, yet a thick coat of varnish made the wood glisten as though wet. She sat down on a black chair with a ripped seat cushion.

Wanda rested an elbow on the table and leaned forward, her chin cradled in the palm of one hand. "So tell me, Emmett, what's so great about Spawnstertown?"

"You name it, we got it," he said as he eased into the seat across from her. "Gambling, weapons, drugs, prostitution—"

"I have no use for whores."

"We got some handsome Spawnster bucks in the stable who'd be happy to tickle your fancy." He waggled his bushy eyebrows.

Heat flushed her face and she hoped it didn't show.

"Did I embarrass you?"

"Not at all. You excited me."

He growled deep in his throat. "I'll be right back with our drinks."

Wanda breathed out a long sigh. So far so good. But she still hadn't learned anything about this meeting she was supposed to attend.

A tall male Spawnster swaggered into the bar and Wanda's breathing hitched. It was the growler they'd seen at the hospital yesterday. Henry had erased his memory of their confrontation, but had it stuck? She was about to find out.

The growler sat at the bar with a smaller Spawnster, who had practically no demon features she could see. Without waiting for Emmett, she left their table and approached the bar.

Danger buzzed up her spine like a string of bees, but she had to test him. "I know I've seen you before." She watched the growler's eyes for any sign of recognition. "At the hospital yesterday."

He squinted at her. "No. I'd remember a chippy like you." His gaze lingered on the glowing stripe of green in her hair and he dipped his chin. "What was a Spawnster girl doing in a hospital?"

"Same as you, I suppose." She cocked a hip. "I hear humans pay serious dough for help from the likes of us and I was lookin' for a job."

Grinning, the growler said, "I'm an orderly. It's not glamorous work."

"Don't matter. All I want's their money." She spat on the floor. "If dumb were dirt, one human would cover 'bout half an acre."

The growler and his buddy laughed. "Hey, you're all right. What's your name?"

"Wanda. Yours?"

"Webster, on account of my hands." He waggled his webbed fingers at her. "And this is Clem."

She nodded at them both.

Webster looked over her shoulder and called out, "Emmett!"

Wanda turned to see the goat-eyed Spawnster, drinks in hand, swagger toward them. He didn't look happy. "Web, Clem. Uh, Wanda? Here's your drink."

"Thanks much, Emmett." She accepted the glass of clear, thick liquid and gave it a sniff. "Sorry. I forgot to ask for a vinegar chaser."

Emmett grabbed the drink back. "Women. Always waterin' down the good stuff."

"Take it easy, pal." Webster slid off his stool and loomed beside her.

Wanda held out both her hands to warn them off from each other. "It's just a drink. Never mind, I'll take it straight." She took the glass away from Emmett and gulped down the oil. Lord have mercy. She imagined her bowels loosening right then and there. "Let's get a table and all sit together." She tossed a glance at Clem, who had yet to say a word. "Including our silent friend here."

"I can talk," Clem said, though he hardly spoke above a whisper.

"He's a different sort," Webster explained. "An exorcist nearly got him last year in Florida. He's never been the same sense."

A nerve jumped in Wanda's right temple. "Really? What happened?"

"The exorcist broke up a bar fight to help a human tourist, and when Clem stuck his nose in, she sucked out some of his demon side." Webster thumped a webbed hand on Clem's shoulder and directed him to a table. All four of them sat and faced each other. "But Clem got her back, didn't you Clem?"

Clem nodded. "I dried her up."

Wanda shot him a questioning look.

Clem grinned and said, "I took her water away. She crumbled like a sand castle in the sun."

Webster laughed. "I was there and let me tell you, it was something to see. She got what she deserved, the self-righteous bitch."

Holy crap. Wanda sent a burst of energy to her skunk stripe to make it glow. She had to make these Spawnsters believe her ruse or she could end up as Clem's next mummy.

"That's some beacon you got there." Emmett reached out to touch her hair, but Webster batted his hand away.

Wanda caught sight of Henry from the corner of her eye. Her new "friends" were so focused on her they hadn't seen him come in. Henry kept his head down, his long hair drifting forward to cover half his face. He sat at the bar and ordered a drink. She hoped he was within hearing range.

"Fellas!" She slapped her hand on the table to get their attention. "Talk to me, okay? Convince me Spawnstertown is the place to be."

Emmett frowned. "What do you want to know?"

"Surprise me." She put on a thoughtful face. "What do you do for fun around here?"

"Conspire against humans," Clem said softly, his watery vacant eyes staring out the window.

Webster and Emmett looked suddenly wary, their eyes shifting to peruse the small crowd inside the bar. "That's supposed to be secret, Clem."

"Sorry." Clem stared down at his glass of oil.

Wanda touched his hand. "That's okay, Clem. I'm glad you said somethin'. That's just the kind of thing I'm lookin' to get into."

Clem gazed up at her. "Really?"

She smiled, feeling sorry for this simple guy whose wheel was turning even though his hamster was dead. "Yes, really. Is something going on?"

"Maybe." Emmett tossed a hasty glance at Webster.

"Are you serious about wanting to be part of something destined to change the world?" Webster asked.

"Hell, yes." Wanda's heart beat in her throat. This was it.

Webster winked at her. "Then come to the meeting tonight."

She leaned toward him. "I'd love to. When and where?"

Emmett grinned, his long teeth glinting in the light cast by an oil lamp hanging from the wall. "Midnight at the Aristocrat Hotel on the corner of Ninth and Elm. It's not a hotel anymore after Jasper Clark moved in and made it his own personal mansion. He's mayor of Spawnstertown. He owns everything."

Webster added, "Jasper's the go-to guy around here."

Wanda tried to look impressed. "Sounds great! Count me in."

Emmett's attention wandered to the bar's doorway, where a Hellspawn couple just entered. One was a big-headed Spawnster, who looked barely out of his teens, and on his arm clung a beautiful woman who would easily pass for human if not for the turquoise scales covering her bare arms. Her purple satin ball gown showed more cleavage than Wanda thought legal in the city. She wondered if this woman was one of the notorious Hell's Belles.

Emmett waved the couple over. "Hey, Max! Come join us. There's someone here you should meet."

By Max's grin, he apparently recognized the men Wanda was with, but the smile dropped quickly from his face. His attention focused on the bar behind her, and she turned to see what he was looking at.

"Uncle Henry?" Max called, his expression bewildered.

But all she saw was Henry's retreating back as he rushed toward the rear exit.

Wanda's surprise at his reaction wasn't an act.

Max showing up and recognizing these low-lives tipped her off that he might have a role in tonight's performance. So why hadn't Henry said anything to her about it? Maybe he was surprised, too.

She kept up her charade by standing and extending her hand. "Hello, Max. I'm Wanda."

Appearing unsettled, Max blinked as he shook her hand. "It's a pleasure." He pulled his woman closer and gazed at her with possessive pride. "This is my girlfriend, Claire."

Wanda would have thought them a mismatched pair if Claire hadn't worn such a besotted expression on her face. She glanced quickly at Wanda, flashed a smile, then settled her adoring gaze back on Max.

Beauty and the beast seated themselves at Wanda's table. Webster looked at Max and said, "That's the first time I've seen Henry here in twenty years."

Max shrugged. "He can stay away another twenty for all I care."

Now that was interesting. Animosity between family was

never a good sign. An uncomfortable silence fell over the group and Claire whispered something in Max's ear that made him blush. She began nibbling at his neck and Max squirmed.

Looking disgusted, Clem said, "Get a room."

Claire snuggled closer to Max and in a husky voice said, "I don't need a room to please my man."

"All right, that's enough." Webster averted his gaze from the couple. "You're making me jealous."

Claire giggled and Max's grin spread so wide his eyes nearly squeezed shut. "Claire, come on. I love you, too, but let's save it for later, okay?"

The lovely Spawnster woman mocked a pout and slouched in her seat, though mischief continued to dance in her eyes. When she focused her attention on Wanda, the exorcist's gut clenched at the secret she sensed the woman was keeping. Claire winked at her and smiled.

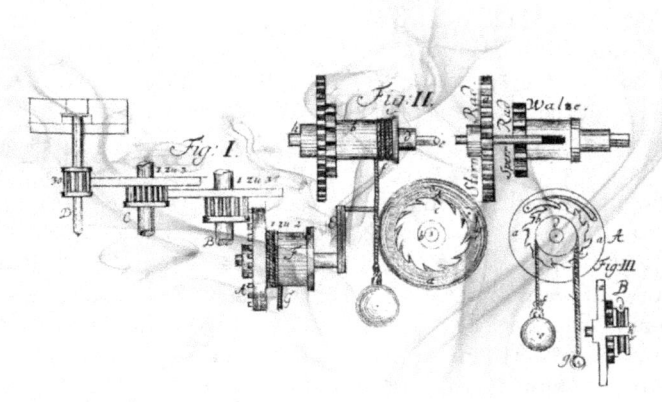

CHAPTER FIFTEEN

Jasper stood behind his podium and surveyed the gathering crowd. Quite a turnout, but he expected as much. The Revolution had been a hot topic among the Spawnster community for decades, and he was overjoyed with the opportunity to unveil some of the mystery surrounding his plan. The Demon Lords would soon have the fight they'd been longing for.

He recognized most of the faces, but there were a few new ones he'd have to get to know. He imagined some were from out of town, as news always spread quickly through the coast-to-coast Spawnster grapevine. New York City was at the heart of it all, but other cities in other states would eventually get on board. They'd have to. It was their destiny to become the dominating race. As for the rest of the world? The Great Earthquake had prevented most countries from keeping in touch, but that would change. He wanted a global revolution.

Jasper gazed out into the crowd to find the eager faces of young ones recently tossed from their homes just for being different from their human parents. These were his favorites because they were impressionable. Also in attendance were the newly converted: Spawnsters who'd enjoyed a brief acceptance among humans but were later rejected after outliving their human relatives. They had no family left. But Jasper offered them what they were missing; camaraderie and a sense of belonging among people just like themselves.

Max and Claire sat in the front row. Claire leaned against her new boyfriend, and he put his arm around her shoulders. Jasper wasn't sure how he felt about that. She belonged to *him*, not to that post-pubescent skagg who lived with the enemy. Granted, Max's conversion to being a true Spawnster was coming along nicely, but Max was still too attached to his adoptive father and grandmother. The boy had a gift and Jasper intended to exploit it for his own needs.

"Thank you all for coming," Jasper called out to the crowd. Voices continued to rumble among the gathering and quickly faded into silence. "And thank you for your patience. Many of you have been with me since the beginning, and though we continue to mourn our fallen brothers and sisters murdered by our human cousins, revenge is close at hand."

Appreciative murmurs hummed through the crowd.

"Vengeance, in fact, has provided some of the hors d'oeuvres on the back tables." Jasper pointed toward the back of the ballroom. Not everyone here would appreciate the irony, but some would enjoy the tasty spoils of war. "Please help yourselves after the meeting."

There was laughter from the ones who got it, and bewildered stares from those who did not.

"I realize some of you are new here, either to the city or the Demon Lords, but you learned of this assembly from those who trust you. This is not an open forum and your secrecy is critical. If the humans learn of our plans, they *will* try to stop us. Not that they'll succeed, but their efforts could slow us down. We've waited long enough to take our rightful place on this planet—at the top of the food chain. We were put here for a reason. We *are* the superior species!"

Clapping and cheers echoed against the ballroom walls and Jasper had to hold out his hands, palms down, to regain order. "Your natural instinct to survive has helped you keep your psychic abilities in check when you could. You know what happens when a human finds out what we can do."

"They try to kill us!" someone shouted from the back row.

Jasper nodded. "That's right! Even though it's difficult to kill Hellspawn, it's still done all the time, as well as maiming and torture. We're the freaks they're ashamed of and they'll do whatever they can to get rid of us." He knew that wasn't entirely true, but it was important they believe it. Most humans were intelligent enough to understand the value of Hellspawn, but the Spawnsters in this room didn't need to know that. Their ignorance was Jasper's bliss. Anyone not on his side would pay for their disloyalty with their lives.

A shiny green light pulsed within the sea of faces and Jasper peered among them to see where it came from. He was amazed that it shone from the hair of a beautiful blonde woman too human to sit with his followers. Yet the green lock of hair wasn't human at all, and couldn't possibly be a disguise. He touched his head, feeling the absence of feathers, and experienced an odd attraction to this stranger. Intuition told him she had a power in common with both him and Max.

He cleared his throat. "If you read the paper, you know about the Snit problem in the city. The lesser demons seem to have gone mad, and it's spreading." He hesitated for a heartbeat. "And I know why."

A chorus of voices rose in response. He had their attention.

"The Snits are sick and I'm responsible for making them that way." Jasper paused for effect, and his followers gazed at him with expectation in their eyes. "My cabinet of mages cursed them with a virus that only infects the Snits. I'm leaving the Imps alone for now. The Vox are too important to damage because they're the ones that will help us win this war."

"Why hurt the Snits?" asked a female Spawnster in one of the middle rows. "They're our kin. They help us."

"And they help humans." Jasper smiled. "It's not their fault they help the enemy, it's their nature. The virus, or curse, reverses their natural impulse to assist others, which causes them to harm instead. But that's not enough to make a noticeable dent in the human population. Our goal, my friends, is to take over this city, and then more cities after this one. When other Spawnsters hear about our victory, they'll join us and we'll become even stronger. But we need a special kind of army to succeed!"

"Is that how you'll use the Vox?" asked a bearded Spawnster from the back row.

Jasper shook his finger at him. "Let's not get ahead of ourselves. It's too early to share my next play in this fast moving game, but it will be soon. Bear with me. My success with the Snits proves how strategy can work to our advantage. I promise you victory with the next step. Be ready, but that's all I can tell you for now."

There was a collective groan of disappointment when Jasper stepped away from the podium. The group dispersed, the majority flocking to the back tables for their forbidden treats. He understood their appetite for the enemy. Jasper had already dined on the best parts.

Grabbing Max's arm as the boy stood to leave, Jasper asked him, "Do you know that woman?"

Max frowned. "Which one?"

Jasper pointed at the blonde decorated with more metal than his kitchen had knives. She was backing her way toward the door, and the expression on her face surprised him. She looked horrified.

"Oh, that one. She's a friend of Emmett and Webster. We met at Greaser's earlier."

If she had friends in Spawnstertown, why did she look frightened? "Introduce us."

Max nodded and detached himself from Claire to do what he was told. Jasper looked down his nose at the Belle who stared after Max with longing in her eyes. "Claire!" he snapped.

She jerked and glared up at him, her expression defiant.

"It won't last." His tone was soft, but his words had a steel edge to them. "I'll make sure of it."

Uncertainty flickered in Claire's black eyes before she moved her gaze away from his.

"Let me introduce you to the man of the hour," Max said proudly as he guided the lovely blonde by the elbow. "Wanda Snow, meet Jasper Clark."

The woman blinked, but when she gave him her full attention, there was a glint of iron in those vibrant blue eyes. He'd anticipated something more submissive there, but the sudden change was impressive. He squinted at her and asked, "New in town?"

"And not sure if I'm stayin'," she said, her voice an octave lower than he expected.

"I hope nothing I said tonight is scaring you off."

She sneered. "Dominance over humans? Nothin' scary about that. Happens every day, right?"

Disdain. He liked it. "Cheeky girl. Didn't you know sarcasm is the lowest form of wit?"

"Yet the dimwitted are the ones who don't get the joke."

Jasper laughed. "I appreciate a woman who speaks her mind. If you decide to stay in New York, will you get a job in the city?"

"Of course."

"Would you consider working for me?"

"That depends."

"On what?"

"On the kind of job you have in mind."

He nodded and gave Max a sideways glance, but the boy had already lost interest in the conversation. He had eyes only for Claire, and vice versa.

"I'll think of something," Jasper told Wanda. "I own most of the apartment buildings in Spawnstertown, so if you need a place to stay, I'll give you a good deal."

The corners of her lips curled up in a slow smile. "I might take you up on that. Thanks."

"Max." He nudged the boy with his elbow to get his attention. "Give Miss Snow a ride home. Use the Dolby Avenue car."

"Don't bother," Wanda said quickly. "I've already got a ride."

"I didn't know Webster or Emmett had a car."

She shrugged. "Not sure they do. That's why I'm takin' a cab."

Jasper knew of only one Spawnster-owned taxi service in the city and the traitorous Spawnster who owned it. The row of feathers on his spine ruffled at the thought of this lovely lady sitting in Henry Paine's cab. "Let me save you money on cab fare, okay? No strings."

Her face blanked for a second before brightening with a toothy smile. "Sure. Why not?"

He offered her his hand to shake. "Very nice to meet you, Wanda Snow."

She touched his fingers and a tingle of electricity sparked between them. Surprised, Jasper released her and she jerked as if bitten.

Heart thudding in his chest, he said, "Call me. Max will give you my card." Unnerved, Jasper stepped away and spun on his heel to exit the room.

Wanda sat in the back seat of Jasper's Dolby Avenue car and repeated in her mind: *oh shit oh shit oh shit oh shit...* That hadn't gone as planned. Did Henry think she'd ditched him? She hoped he had been watching when she left Jasper's mansion and that he was now following her home. The two of them had a lot to talk about, and soon. She glanced out the back window to search for Mystic's headlamps.

"Everything okay back there?" Max asked from the driver's seat. "You're awful quiet."

"Just tired," she told him. "It's way past my bedtime."

He chuckled. "My day's just beginning."

Lucky him.

So what the Hell was that between her and Jasper? Sparks actually flew when she touched his hand. His demon side felt stronger than most of the Hellspawn she knew, and she suspected the exorcist part of her was eager to take it away from him. She smiled to herself. Wouldn't the Demon Lord's gang leader be surprised to know who, and what, she really was?

The mayor of Spawnstertown was a decent-looking guy for a Spawnster. He didn't have many of the animal features she normally associated with Hellspawn. He appeared... avian. His bald scalp was tattooed with a colorful spiral design, he had a beakish nose that suited his narrow face, and there were gold pin feathers growing from his temples and brow line. She suspected from the coffee-colored hue of his skin that his human mother might have been either black or Hispanic. He was quite exotic looking.

"So what did you think of Jasper?" Max asked.

She forced a smile. "Nice guy. Very charismatic. And wow, what a plan, huh? I can't wait to get started."

"Same here." But Max's soft, flat voice didn't ring with enthusiasm. Maybe he wasn't as keen on the idea as he pretended.

Wanda thought about how fast Henry had rushed out of Greaser's when he saw Max and his girlfriend arrive. There was a story there and she was curious to know Max's side of it.

"Hey, Max? Can I ask you something?"

Max looked at Claire, who sat silently beside him. "I guess so. What is it?"

"Back at Greaser's, you called the man sitting at the bar Uncle Henry. He ran out of there like someone just sprayed him with salt water."

She couldn't see Max's face because he was driving, but she heard disappointment in his voice when he said, "Maybe he ran away out of shame."

"You don't sound too happy about that."

"I'm not." He exhaled a long breath. "Henry is disloyal to his people."

"What do you mean?"

"He sold out his Spawnster family for a human one. He turned in his friends to the cops, then abandoned them when they needed him."

"Wow," she said, not believing a word of it, though Max had no reason to lie. She knew Henry well enough by now to know he wasn't that kind of man. "That's serious."

"It is. And if it's all the same to you, I'd rather not talk about it."

Wanda sensed he actually *did* want to talk about it, just not with her. She'd like to change his mind, but it wouldn't happen tonight, especially not with his girlfriend sitting right beside him.

"I know it's none of my business, but if he's family—"

"You're right," Max said, his youthful voice tough as granite. "It's none of your business."

And he'd seemed so friendly a minute ago.

"This it?" he asked as he pulled up to the curb in front of her aunt's building.

"Yep. Thanks." She grabbed the door handle to let herself out and a white card was thrust in her face.

"Jasper's card," Max said. "He told me to give it to you."

Wanda grabbed it from him and stepped out onto the sidewalk. She haded toward the building.

Light footsteps tapped behind her and she turned around to see Claire following her up the walk. "Can I talk to you for a minute?"

Wanda shrugged.

Claire looked quickly over her shoulder at Max, who remained inside the car. She stood so her back was facing him. Her lovely face molded in a severe expression when she said to Wanda, "You're not one of us."

Throat tight, Wanda forced indignation into her voice when she said, "Yes, I am."

Light from the gas lamp by the building's entrance glinted in Claire's eyes. She shook her head slowly. "No, you're not. You're an exorcist."

Panic zinged across Wanda's skin and the polluted air suddenly became too thick to breathe. Her reaction must have been obvious because Claire placed a hand on her arm and hushed her. "Relax. It's okay."

Wanda's constricted chest eased and she inhaled deeply. "What gave me away?"

"I'm an intuitive. I sense lies. And you're too nice to be a Spawnster anyway." Claire smiled.

"You're not going to tell anyone?"

"Why would I do that?"

Wanda chuckled. "Maybe because having an exorcist among your ranks could spoil the whole take-over-the-city scheme."

"I hope it does."

This puzzled Wanda. "Aren't you and your boyfriend in on Jasper's coup?"

Claire shook her head and her face turned deadly serious. "Jasper is using Max and he'll hurt him bad if we don't do something to stop it."

   ⚅ ⚄

Henry parked Mystic down the block from Alva's building. He held a spyglass to his right eye and watched Wanda talk with Claire. What the Hell?

"I don't get it, Mystic." He refocused the glass and squinted, trying to read their lips. It was no use. "They've been chatting like a couple of school pals for at least five minutes. What's going on?"

"No... idea."

He sighed and tried not to worry. He'd waited in the shadows across the street from Jasper's mansion while his "old friend" gave his speech. When he saw Wanda walk out with Max and Claire, he about had a heart attack. It was bad enough that Max was there, but why did Wanda leave with him? Had they become buddies over drinks in Greaser's? Nah, Max wasn't the buddy type. The boy was an egghead who didn't have time for friends. At least he hadn't until he met Claire, the very same Claire who was dating Levi. He'd recognized her the moment he saw her in the bar. Max couldn't possibly have a clue what he'd gotten himself into.

"Claire's turning around and walking back to the steamer," Henry said to Mystic. "Now Wanda is entering the building."

He set the glass down in his lap. "I'm going up to her apartment and find out what happened."

"*Tell... Wanda... Hello... from... me.*"

Henry blinked. "Oh, I get it. Now you want on her good side so that she won't smoke you like she did those other demons." He patted the steering wheel. "Don't worry, my friend. You're safe with me."

He watched to make sure Max and Claire were out of sight before leaving the cab. Taking the stairs two at a time, he arrived at Wanda's door in less than a minute. She opened it the second he knocked.

"Come in," Wanda said, her voice tight with anxiety.

He stepped inside and she pushed the door shut behind him.

"Tell me everything," Henry said.

So she did.

"Jasper's responsible for the Snits being sick?" Henry asked. Recent events were starting to come together now.

"It's a curse that acts like a virus because it's contagious," Wanda said. "Jasper told us his cabinet of mages infected the Snits with a spell that reversed their instincts."

Brilliant, and evil as hell. "I checked on the Snits in my apartment yesterday and they've all left. Only the Imps stayed behind." And Mystic, of course, who wasn't infected because she was a Vox.

Wanda arched her eyebrows. "I guess your devoted servants aren't so devoted. Where'd they go?"

"They must have gone off to possess some innocent humans' machines so they could wreak havoc and endanger lives." He hoped she caught the sarcasm. Henry couldn't imagine his mild-tempered demons hurting anyone. "I assume the harmful effects of the curse are intended for humans only?"

"Jasper didn't say." She wheeled around to head for the kitchen. "Want anythin'? I'm gonna eat some bread to soak up the oil sloshin' in my belly."

His stomach rumbled. "Have any organ meat cold cuts?"

"No."

"Then never mind."

She emerged from the kitchen with a thick slab of dark bread. Cheeks bulging, she chewed before saying, "Please tell me Jasper wasn't serving human-burgers to his gang tonight."

Henry blew out a sigh and closed his eyes. It was bound to come out sooner or later.

Wanda gave her bread a disgusted look. "I think I'm going to be sick." She swallowed and eyed him with suspicion. "You don't—"

He held up a hand. "Never touch the stuff."

"Good to know. Does he really hate humans that much?"

"I'm not even sure it's hate anymore. Do you eat cows because you hate them?"

"Of course not. But they don't sit next to me on the subway or shop at Macy's. Cows are not my neighbors."

He grimaced. "Jasper's sick in the head."

She gazed up at the ceiling. "I got that. And it's infectious. You should have seen how the crowd hung on his every word. Your nephew was among 'em, you know."

His sudden nausea didn't come from thoughts of literal finger sandwiches, but from knowing Max had been lured into Jasper's Demon Lords. "So Max is stuck on Claire, huh?"

"Oh, yeah. And she's stuck on him."

"Impossible." He sat down in a side chair, resting his back against a needlepoint cushion stitched with the words *Home Sweet Home.* "Claire already has a beau."

"You don't say?" Wanda's tone was sardonic. She seated herself on the claw-footed sofa across from him.

"She's been dating my friend Levi for years."

"I'm pretty sure they broke up."

Henry chuckled. "Somehow I doubt Claire would leave a wealthy PT Subway baron for a whiz kid like my nephew. Which makes me wonder what the two of you were chatting about outside."

"Oh, that." She leaned back and crossed her legs. "Claire knows I'm an exorcist."

He clamped his jaw so tight he almost bit his tongue. Through his teeth, he asked, "She knows? How?"

"She's an intuitive and she sees people for who and what they really are. Don't worry. It's okay that she knows."

"How can it be okay? She'll tell Max, who'll tell his hero Jasper, and then Jasper's henchmen will come after *you*." Henry leaned forward with his forearms resting on his knees. Panic nibbled up his spine at the thought of Wanda in danger. He didn't know why he cared as much as he did because only a few weeks ago he wanted her out of his life for good. Now he couldn't imagine his life without her. "I didn't know you were suicidal."

She grinned. "I'm not. But I'm not worried because Claire is on our side."

Henry frowned. "You believe that?"

Her eyes gleamed with mischief. "You bet. Wanna know why? Because she's head-over-heels in love with your young nephew."

A woman-of-the-world like Claire? No way. She had to have an ulterior motive. "Even if that were true, which I doubt, what difference does it make?"

"She knows Jasper's up to no good, and that he's using Max. She doesn't want Max gettin' hurt so she'll do just about anythin' to keep him safe."

Henry's stomach clenched. "What's Jasper doing to Max?"

"Claire didn't say, there wasn't time. She didn't want Max to know what we were talkin' about. We set up a time to meet in private, here at my aunt's apartment." Her eyebrows tilted with worry. "I'm goin' to see if Alva can stay in the hospital a day or two longer. I don't want her involved in any of this."

Henry wished he knew Jasper's end game. His old friend was obviously using the Snits as a distraction from something bigger. A few humans maimed or killed in accidents didn't constitute a war. Jasper had bigger plans, and if those plans involved Vox demons, they could be in for some real trouble.

"Claire insisted you be there, too." Wanda tossed the last of the bread into her mouth. "She knows you and Max used to be close."

That hurt. Up until a week ago, Max had looked up to Henry. Then Jasper had to go and sink his talons into Max. The only way Henry could unsink them would be to convince Max that his hero was a tyrannical madman. If Max wouldn't listen to Henry, he'd surely listen to Claire.

"Wanda, have you ever had demons of your own?"

She scowled. "As in possessin' my machines? Absolutely not. My great grandmother's prophecy—"

"I know, I know. Your great grandmother said demon-possessed machines would destroy the world. But did she say how?"

Wanda looked uneasy. "No, but that shouldn't matter."

"I think it does. It'll take more than a few possessed lawnmowers and washing machines to annihilate this city.

What's coming is bigger than that."

Wanda nodded.

"So how about fighting fire with fire?"

She stood slowly and shook her head while saying, "I don't keep demons, Henry, I exorcise them, remember? That's why they hate me."

"Mystic doesn't hate you."

"Sure she does. She made that clear the moment we met."

"Maybe at first, but she's Vox, and she's smart. She figures things out. That's why I think we should try to get the Vox to help us."

Wanda stared at him. "You're insane."

He shook his head. "I've never been saner. The Vox can give us the edge we need to protect the city from Jasper."

"But if he was able to infect the Snits, what says he won't go after the Vox next?"

"Which is why we have to beat him to it."

Wanda squinted and stared off into the distance. "Cast a spell on the Vox. That could work."

Henry had no desire to manipulate lesser demons with magic that would take away their free will. That's what Jasper had done to the Snits and Henry would never sink so low. Instead of spells, Henry would use reason. "You still don't understand how sentient the lesser demons are."

"Oh, here we go again. They have *feelin's*, is that it?"

"You said yourself that you think Mystic hates you. If hate isn't a feeling, I don't know what is."

She lost the squint and looked sheepish now. "Maybe you've got a point."

"You know I do. Demons are emotional beings, even the Imps. And they have a natural attachment to humans. It's their nature."

"Then how do you propose to control the Vox?"

"I don't want to control them. I want them to choose to do the right thing."

Wanda raised both eyebrows and grinned. "I still think a spell would work better."

"I don't. Spells can be broken."

"True." She brightened. "Can we break the spell on the Snits?"

Henry smiled. "Possibly. And I know just the witch who can do it."

CHAPTER SIXTEEN

"I think you'll like my niece," Henry told Wanda as they walked up the granite steps to the front porch of his niece's house. A stone gargoyle stood sentry over a massive front door, and the knocker at the door's center looked like the head of a dragon. "Eunice is seventy-five years old, but she's a powerful witch. It's thanks to her that I have my family back."

Wanda's forehead crimped with a puzzled frown. "What do you mean?"

"She used an Imp and a location spell to find me." He smiled at the memory. "After being estranged from my relatives for over a hundred years, I'd given up on ever seeing members of my human family again."

Wanda gazed at him with pity in her eyes.

He chuckled and gave her a half-grin. "I'm over it. All parents were scared of their Hellspawn offspring after The Great Earthquake. They thought we'd been sent by the devil to take them to Hell. So I stayed away from them and accepted the Demon Lords as my new family."

"Until your niece came along to reclaim you."

"That's right." He folded his arms to keep out the cold. They were still standing outside the house and a winter wind blew through the street, making his scales clatter from the chill.

He reached up to tap the knocker, and a stream of smoke spewed from the dragonhead's nostrils. Annoyed by the knocker's hostility, he told it, "It's me, you stupid chunk of metal. What's wrong with you?"

The pewter head began to pulse with a red glow. It had never done that before. Henry grabbed the door latch, clutched the lever, and shoved the door hard with his shoulder. Wood splintered as it swung open on a groan of hinges.

Henry's temples pounded with adrenalin as he dragged Wanda behind him into the entry hall. "Eunice?" he called, certain something was wrong. Though an amazing witch, she was still human, and she had at least a dozen Snits and Imps possessing the machines in her house.

"Eunice!" he yelled.

Wanda gazed around her, eyes wide, her green lock of hair glowing. She held out hands that shimmered with power. "What's going on?"

"I don't know." The hall shone bright with light from several wall sconces, and the house felt calm and quiet. Even so, with all that had been going on lately, he had good reason to feel on edge.

"What on earth are you bellowing about?"

Henry spun around to face his elderly niece, who seemed to have appeared out of nowhere. He clutched his chest and panted as if he'd just run a marathon. "Eunice, you shouldn't sneak up on people."

"You're not people, you're family. And I can do whatever I want." When she spotted Wanda, her mouth puckered in a sly smile and her forehead tripled its aged ridges. "Well, my word. You got yourself a girl."

Henry blew out an audible breath. "I don't have a girl. This is, uh, she's..." What was Wanda? She was no longer an enemy, and not just a friend. Partner? That sounded *so* wrong. "This is Wanda Snow, an acquaintance of mine."

"How do you do, dear?" Eunice tilted her head. "What a lovely lock of green hair. You must give me your hairdresser's name. I wouldn't mind some colorful accents myself." She patted her bun of silver hair.

Wanda touched her own head. "This is my hair's natural color. I don't have a hairdresser."

"Remarkable." Eunice gave Wanda the once-over. "I thought everyone in New York had a hairdresser."

Henry sniffed the air for alcohol. His niece was known to take a nip now and again, but there was no obvious sign she'd been drinking. He did smell sulfur though, a sure indication of spell-casting.

"Eunice, what's the matter with your door knocker?" Henry knew an Imp possessed the knocker and he wondered if it had somehow gotten infected like the Snits.

"There's nothing wrong with Draegor. I just added a few new effects to frighten off the riff-raff. I hate door-to-door salesmen."

For crying out loud. Henry tightened his jaw. "I thought something bad had happened to you."

She looked confused. "Why?"

"You know why. Vernon must have told you about the city's Snit problem."

"Oh, that." She quickly dismissed him and turned her attention to Wanda. "Can I get you anything, dear? A cup of tea? A brandy? Or do you prefer oil?"

Wanda's face paled and she fingered her green lock of hair. "Nothin' for me, thank you. And the only oil I like is on my salad. I'm human."

Eunice squinted at her. "Mostly, but not completely."

Henry glared down at his niece. "You're being rude, Eunice."

"I'm being honest. There's a difference." She punched Henry's arm. "Stop being such a bully."

He inhaled deeply and pinched the bridge of his nose to stall an approaching headache. "Can we please sit down and talk?"

Eunice covered her chest with a thin wrinkled hand. "Certainly. Where are my manners? Uncle Henry, show your lady friend into the den. I'll join you after I get myself a refreshment."

He knew what kind of refreshment she was going for and it would do no good to stop her. She'd just help herself to the liquor cabinet the moment his back was turned anyway.

Eunice started down the hall, then stopped and held up one finger as if she'd forgotten something. "By the way, Wanda, I know you're an exorcist. The Imps told me. I have a freezer full of misbehaving Snits in the kitchen at the back of the house. Would you be a dear and take care of them for me?" She winked and walked away.

Henry stared, open-mouthed, at his niece's receding back. "Eunice!" he called, but she ignored him. "Did they hurt you?" Still no response.

Wanda tugged on his sleeve and when he looked at her, he saw her lips pressed together in a restrained smile.

"It's not funny." He stomped down the hall toward the den. "Something bad could have happened to her."

"Are you kiddin' me?" Wanda trailed after him. "I'm surprised she didn't exorcise those demons herself."

"Believe me, she's tried on other occasions, but she doesn't have that type of power." Irritated as he was, he couldn't help being proud of his niece. Eunice was one of a kind.

He parted a pair of sliding wood doors and stood aside to let Wanda in ahead of him. She stopped and gazed into the enormous room. "Oh, my."

"What?"

"It's beautiful." She strode in slowly, her head turning one way and then the other, as if taking it all in. He watched her gaze linger on the heavy walnut furniture, the massive Persian rug covering the hardwood floor, and the Regency-style sconces mounted on dark-paneled walls. "I'm impressed," she said. "Someone's got money."

Henry thought about that and supposed she was right. Money hadn't been an issue for him in so long that he forgot he had as much as he did. But that would change soon if Vernon couldn't get his demonetics business back on track. Henry was his primary investor and he'd given his nephew almost everything he had short of liquidating his landholdings. "I had this house built for Eunice. Her fiancé had been trampled to death by a horse the year before she found me, and she had a toddler, my nephew Vernon, to take care of. She was an unmarried mother, dirt poor, and living in a shabby apartment on Canal Street. Building her this house was the least I could do."

"I'm surprised you don't live here, too."

"I do, sometimes. But usually I prefer my apartment. I need my own space."

"This house looks plenty spacious to me."

"It's big, but size and space don't necessarily mean the same thing." He considered all the people Eunice had invited to live with her over the years, most of them distant family members who hated Hellspawn. They had refused to acknowledge Henry's existence, so he'd stayed away. Those cousins of cousins were all dead and buried now, but their resentment hung in the air like a bad smell. He moved back into the house a few days ago just to avoid the cops, who may or may not still be looking for him. Better safe than incarcerated.

Eunice glided into the room, the hem of her orange silk dressing gown dragging on the floor behind her. She frowned when her gaze landed on the cold fireplace. Hugging herself with an exaggerated shiver, she said, "It's terribly chilly in here. How about some heat for this big cold room?" She thrust out one hand and a large spark flew from her fingers. It landed on the kindling piled beneath some logs in the hearth and the wood erupted into flames as if doused with kerosene.

Wanda blinked and Henry sighed. His niece could be such a show-off.

"So are those nasty Snits gone from my freezer?" Eunice asked.

Wanda cleared her throat and gave Henry a pleading look. "Not yet."

"In a minute, Eunice," Henry said. "Can we talk first?"

"Of course." She settled herself on a Marquise chair and rested her feet on the matching footstool. The years had been good to Eunice. When it came to queenly living, she was a natural. "What did you want to discuss?"

"The Snits," Wanda said. "Henry tells me you're a powerful witch. Can you reverse the virus spell that's making them sick?"

"They've been bewitched?" Eunice asked.

Henry nodded. "My old pal Jasper made it happen. He's up to no good."

Eunice snorted. "That's nothing new."

"It's more serious this time." He knew Eunice was familiar with the hawk-faced Spawnster who'd made it a habit to give Henry grief every few years. "He wants to take over the city."

Eunice laughed. "With Snits?"

"We think he's using them as a distraction," Wanda said. "He has something bigger in store, but we don't know what it is."

Eunice's brow knitted in thought. "I can try breaking the spell, but I can't promise it will work. The ingredients for a reverse enchantment might be difficult to come by."

"I doubt there's an ingredient I can't find," Wanda said. "My aunt's a witch, and half the tenants in her apartment building are magic users of some kind. One or two of them owe me a favor."

Henry thought of the grateful Mr. Sanchez and nodded.

Eunice looked suddenly sad. "I might have to sacrifice an Imp or two."

Henry swallowed and glanced at Wanda, who appeared unfazed. She still doubted the sentience of lesser demons. For Hellspawn, sacrificing an Imp would be like killing a kitten to a human. "There must be another way."

Eunice scowled. "Possibly. I'll also need bait to fool the Snit into accepting the enchantment. And the bait I need is hard to find."

"What kind of bait are you talking about?" Wanda asked.

"Ghosts."

Henry nodded. Snits, Vox and Imps were all attracted to ghosts and would munch on them like candy.

"I'll coat the ghosts with a counter-enchantment that should cure the Snits," Eunice said. "I'll need to examine one of the infected Snits to come up with an antidote."

Henry thought about what Eunice was saying. "Can you cure them all?"

"I'll try to heal as many as possible, but Wanda may have to kill the rest."

Wanda closed her eyes. "How many are we talking about?"

"Total? A thousand are here in the city, more or less." Eunice smiled sweetly. "At last count, anyway."

"How many Vox are in the city?" Henry asked.

"A little over two hundred. The Vox are much cagier than the Snits. They're also picky about who they serve, whether it be human or Hellspawn." Eunice peered at Henry through curious eyes. "Why are you asking about Vox?"

"I want to try and get the Vox on our side before Jasper gets to them first."

Eunice looked thoughtful again. "I could create a spell that would—"

"No more spells." He wondered about the fate of the poor Snits, many of which would be executed through no fault of their own. The Vox didn't deserve the same end. They were caring, intelligent, compassionate... Like his Mystic.

Wanda sat on Eunice's footstool to face her. "You must be very proud of your uncle's skill for summoning demons."

Eunice looked bewildered. "Who, Uncle Henry? He can't summon demons, though Vernon believes he does. Henry's friend Levi is the Bringer, but he'd rather no one knew about his special talent. Don't tell him I told you. I only know because I made Henry tell me. I don't like secrets."

Wanda squinted up at Henry. "But I thought it was you who summoned them from The Source. You're the Bringer."

He remembered her calling him that when they first met. "Well, yeah. I bring them to Vernon for his inventions. So?"

She looked unsettled, and her face pinched with confusion. "I've been going about this all wrong. My grandmother told me I'd work with the Bringer to save the city from demon-possessed machines."

Henry had to chuckle at the thought of Levi working with *anyone*, let alone a human. "The lesser demons are fond of me, but that's as far as it goes. Sorry."

She stood and backed toward the door. "I have to leave. Henry, please take me home."

"What about my Snits?" Eunice asked, her voice pitched an octave too high. "You have to exorcise them before you go."

Ignoring her, Wanda began to pace. "How could I have been so wrong? The demons' thoughts told me you were the one. You're the Bringer."

Amused as well as uneasy now, Henry shook his head. "I've never summoned much more than my breakfast when it comes to demons. What's the big deal?"

"The big deal, Henry, is that it's my destiny to save this city."

"And I'm helping you."

"Not anymore." Wanda stormed from the den and marched down the hall toward the front door.

"What about my Snits?" Eunice called out.

"Later." Henry chased after Wanda and reached the door before she did. "Just wait a minute. I'll drive you home. I'll even take you to see Levi, who hates humans, by the way. He's not as bad as Jasper, but I doubt he'd lift a finger to save the humans in this city."

"He has to. My great grandmother said—"

"Your great grandmother said some things that don't make much sense." He blocked her advance to the door. "Listen to me. Everything you've told me about this so-called prophecy is like a fortune cookie. It could mean anything for anyone, anytime, anywhere. There are a few holes in your old granny's prediction."

Wanda ran her hand through her long hair and absently wrapped the pulsing green stripe around her finger. "But you're not the Bringer."

He shrugged. "Maybe I am, maybe I'm not. It's not like I've ever tried to summon a demon from The Source. Who says I can't?"

She blinked at him. "The city's demons did tell me it was you."

"Check again and see what they say."

She touched the metal band around her neck. "It hurts my head to listen."

Henry had resisted the idea of having his destiny joined with hers, but now he *wanted* to help her. It surprised him to realize the fate of this city mattered to him as much as the fate of his demon kin.

He feigned a look of indifference when he said, "So what's a little pain? I thought knowing the truth meant something to you." He hoped she took that as a challenge.

Wanda narrowed her eyes and clenched her jaw as she unlatched the band from around her neck. Sucking in a breath, she squeezed her eyelids shut. She actually looked injured and Henry almost grabbed her neckband to clasp it back in place. But she gulped in a breath and said, "I'm okay, Henry. I just need a minute."

"Is she listening to them now?" Eunice peeked around the corner like a naughty child afraid of getting sent to her room. "What are they saying?"

Henry hushed her and stared hard at Wanda. He was fascinated by what the woman would endure to protect her species. Would he do the same? Of course he would. Not all Hellspawn were jackasses like Jasper and his Demon Lords.

"The Snits. They're hurtin' bad. The virus causes 'em pain if they refuse to turn against humans." Her breathing came hard and fast, and she licked her lips before adding, "I wish they'd kept their feelin's to themselves." Her eyes flashed open, glazed and red. "They *want* me to kill them. They'd rather die than harm the folks they're meant to serve."

Henry's throat constricted and his chest tightened with a breaking heart. How could Jasper not know the agony he caused his demon kin? The idiot had no compassion.

"And what about the Bringer?" Henry asked.

"Their thoughts about that haven't changed." She looked at him, her face pale, violet shadows darkening the hollows beneath her blue eyes. "It's still you."

He wasn't sure how he felt about that, but if it helped save innocent demons and humans, he'd do whatever had to be done.

"Will you trust me?" Henry asked her.

She re-clasped her neckband. "I want to, but I need proof."

The only way he could prove it to her was to summon a demon from Hell, and the gateway inside Levi's tunnel was the only one he knew of. If she wanted to see Henry perform, she'd have to come with him, and he didn't think Levi would allow a human in his home.

"So are you going to exorcise my Snits or not?" Eunice asked sharply.

Wanda nodded. "Lead me to 'em."

Eunice led the way to a service area at the back of the house, where there was a laundry room and a pantry big enough for a king-sized bed. She gestured to the closed door of a giant walk-in freezer. "They hate the cold, so I figured the freezer would keep them in line. With the addition of a warding spell, it seems to be working."

"They went in there of their own free will?" Wanda asked.

Looking sheepish, Eunice said, "I conjured a ghost. It's just an illusion, not the real thing, but it held itself together long enough to lure the Snits inside."

"Doesn't a Snit run your freezer?" Henry asked.

"No. Plain old garden-variety electricity. I only use the demons for the fancy contraptions Vernon gives me. Like my hair braider, massage chair, manicure and pedicure machine, mending machine, and my popcorn popper, just to name a few."

Henry frowned at the thought of what a rogue Snit would do with his niece's hair, like strangle her with it, or the massage chair could squeeze the life out of her.

"How many are in there?" Wanda asked, her voice barely above a whisper.

"About a dozen," Eunice said.

Wanda whistled. "I'll be busier than a cat coverin' crap on a marble floor."

"Eunice, I don't think Wanda can take on a dozen Snits

all at once." He remembered their scuffle with the rickshaws in Chinatown. She'd had only six to deal with then, and one of them got away.

Wanda's stripe of hair began to glow like neon. "After the zap I got from Mr. Sanchez's radio, my power is stronger than it's ever been. I can pull this off if you help me."

"Help you how?"

"You can kind of herd 'em, you know? Just let two or three by at a time."

He didn't feel all that confident he could hold back a dozen demons. Plus they were already loose of whatever machines they had possessed, so it would be hard to corral their misty energy.

"Wanda, you said they *want* to die, isn't that right?" he asked.

"Yes, but their instinct to survive is strong. They won't give up without a fight."

Henry cracked his knuckles, then glanced at his niece. "Go to your room."

Eunice raised her eyebrows. "I beg your pardon?"

"I want you safe from whatever happens here. Just stay in your room for now. Please?"

She scowled. "Fine. But save one of them for me. I'll need to analyze it to figure out a counter spell for the virus."

"What should I save it in?" Henry asked.

Eunice grabbed a bear-shaped cookie jar from the pantry. "Put it in here."

Wanda plucked a few strands of green hair from her glowing lock. "Tie these to the lid."

He wrapped the hair around the ear-shaped handles on the jar's lid. The teddy bear's smile seemed to mock him as he held it out toward the freezer door. "Beat it, Eunice," he told his niece, and she shuffled quickly down the hall toward the other end of the house. "Okay, Wanda. Open the freezer door."

CHAPTER SEVENTEEN

"Do you see them?" Jasper asked Max, who wore the helmet fashioned of wires and cables wrapped in feathers. "How many are there?"

Max squinted as if watching something at a great distance. "Thirteen hundred and fifty-two infected Snits in the city."

"How many have we lost?"

"Eight are dead, and two have returned to The Source."

Not bad. But the deaths concerned him. It could mean an exorcist was in town. "What killed them?"

Frowning, Max shook his head. "I can't see what did it, only a black space where they used to be. It's gray where the Snits have returned to The Source."

"Was an exorcist responsible?"

Max blinked and turned his head to face Jasper, though his eyes were rolled back so far that only the whites showed. "I can only see demons, nothing else." He slipped the headgear off and his eyes rolled forward, the golden irises focused on Jasper's face. He grinned. "Your plan is working. All the surviving Snits are infected."

Jasper clasped his hands behind his back. "I'm concerned about the dead Snits and what killed them."

Shoulders hunched with a shrug, Max said, "This virus you created could have lethal side effects."

"This is the first time we've used it so I imagine anything's possible." Jasper frowned with a sudden thought. "Would the Snits kill each other?"

"It's rare, but it's been known to happen. The lesser demons are nonviolent by nature, especially with each other. There's a chance the virus makes them hostile toward more than just humans. Come to think of it, one tried to kill me in my father's lab."

"Are you sure it wasn't acting in self-defense?"

"I'd done nothing to provoke it. The attack was sudden and unexpected."

Which meant the Snits *would* turn on Hellspawn and that was a disturbing thought. Jasper's plan could backfire. He needed to meet with his mages as soon as possible.

Jasper took the headgear from Max and strode across the ballroom to the exit. The likelihood of there being an exorcist in town disturbed him most of all.

⚙ ⚙

Wanda grabbed the freezer door's handle and gave it a twist. Her muscles tensed, the power inside her building as it reached out to detect the demon energy it wanted to destroy. But it felt somehow different this time. Strong, but empty. Like what it searched for wasn't completely there.

Henry crouched in front of the door as it opened, his arms out to his sides with elbows bent as if to greet what came out of the freezer with a hug. "I'm ready," he said.

When she pulled open the door, a cloud of icy fog billowed out, but no demons. The snakes of misty blue energy Wanda expected never emerged. "I don't feel anythin'."

Henry straightened his legs but didn't lower his arms. "What do you mean?"

"I mean there's nothin' in there." Wanda's gaze fell to the floor of the freezer, where several blue puddles oozed toward the open door. "Wait. That's them. The Snits have... liquefied?"

Henry knelt on the floor for a closer look. "They're more like glops of syrup. I'll bet it's the low temperature inside the freezer that did this to them."

That made sense to Wanda. All demons had a strong aversion to cold, which is why no one ever encountered one in the Arctic or northern-most parts of the world. She watched the puddles struggle to rise, and as the warm air hit them, they began to steam. "We better close the freezer door before they thaw."

"Let me get one into this jar first." Henry scooped up a slippery lump of sludge. It stayed intact inside the jar and left no residue behind. "It's the consistency of pudding, only slimier." He pulled a face.

Wanda flexed her fingers, repulsed by the idea of touching the gooey mess. She sensed the Snits couldn't be killed in their liquid state. The low temperature in the freezer kept them safe from her, but now they were immobile and powerless.

Henry must have been thinking the same thing because he grinned as he capped the cookie jar and closed the freezer door. "The Snits won't have to die."

"What if they thaw out?" Wanda asked.

"We just make sure they don't."

Sounded reasonable. "So how do you propose we freeze every Snit in the city?"

His grin faltered. "A blizzard?"

Like that would ever happen. The temperatures around the world had steadily risen since The Great Earthquake and freezing temperatures were rare except in the far North. Wet snow flurries were the most New Yorkers could hope for.

Henry sent an Imp pinwheel to fetch his niece, then led Wanda to the fabulous den she hadn't stopped thinking about. If she had a den like this she'd never leave it, but she would add a few feminine touches. The room needed flowers to liven it up, and that dark paneling had to go. The walls should be painted something soft, like pale yellow to attract more light and chase away the shadows. And floral pillows would be a nice accent to the stiff, formal furniture...

Henry cleared his throat. "Did you hear what I just said?"

She blinked. "Sorry, no. My mind was elsewhere."

"So I gathered." He motioned for her to sit on one of the velvet salon chairs positioned to either side of the fireplace. There was no ash in the hearth and no other wood in sight. Magic logs? Or was it magic fire that gave warmth but didn't burn?

"Mission accomplished?" Eunice asked as she made her entrance and returned to her favorite chair. She propped her slippered feet on the footrest. "No more Snits to worry about?"

"Your idea to use the freezer to hold them was brilliant, Eunice," Henry said. "It liquefied them and made them powerless."

The wrinkles on Eunice's forehead became more pronounced as her eyes widened. "They're dead?"

"No, just in an altered state that's made them sluggish.

They're still very much alive," Wanda said. "If we could freeze all the Snits in the city, our problem would be solved."

"I don't think the city's Snits will all fit in my walk-in freezer," Eunice said.

"Of course not," Henry told her. "We have to come up with something else."

"The key is to heal all the Snits we can at the same time," Wanda said. She sucked in her bottom lip and bit down lightly as she thought it through. "A public area in the center of the city. Someplace that would attract the attention of a lot of Snits all at once."

"You mean like Central Park?" Eunice asked.

Wanda shook her head. "Too wide open. It needs to be a place that's active with machines and people."

"Times Square?" Henry suggested.

Wanda slapped her knee. "Perfect!"

Henry seemed to catch on to her line of thinking. "That's where we can release the ghosts baited with antidote and offer an all-you-can-eat demon buffet."

Looking thoughtful, Eunice added, "Imps and Vox will likely join in the feast. I'll have to make sure my potion affects Snits only."

"We have our plan so let's get started." Henry studied his niece. "Are you busy, Eunice?"

She blinked and brought a hand to her chest, fingers splayed. "I'm hosting a tea for the Ladies' Auxiliary on Tuesday, I'm chairing the annual Hellspawn Sanctuary for Indigent Youth Benefit, and it's my turn to hold the monthly meeting for Manhattan's Witch Council here at the house. I'm a very busy woman."

Wanda saw Henry's head tilt, his eyes round and pleading.

Eunice sighed and threw up her hands. "Okay, fine. Just remember I'm over seventy-five years old and don't have the energy I used to."

"Bullshit." Henry grinned and Eunice grinned back.

Eunice stood and clapped her hands. "Scram, you two. I've got work to do. Now go get me some ghosts."

Henry parked Mystic outside the cemetery gate. "I know your favorite treat is ghost tartar, Mystic, but please ignore any tasty specters that might happen by. I need them."

Mystic was silent for a few seconds, then her radio's tuner spun like a roulette wheel. "*May... I... eat... just... one? Please?*"

Vernon sat in the passenger seat next to Henry. He chuckled and said, "No demon can stop at just one."

"*I... can.*"

"Sorry, Mystic. Another time." Henry gazed out at the dark cemetery with tombstones sticking up from the ground like jagged teeth. A light fog rolled over a blanket of brown grass, the blades shorn to stubble. It would be green again come spring, but winter frost had leached the lawn of most of its color. The cold protected the resident ghosts from hungry demons, so Henry expected to find a few hanging around the headstones.

"Ready?" Henry asked Vernon.

Vernon lifted an etched cube of glass the size of a shoebox from a carton on the back seat. "Ready."

Both men emerged from the cab, and Henry gave Mystic one last warning to leave the ghosts alone. He grabbed the carton that held two-dozen ghost traps and joined Vernon at the gate.

His nephew lifted a slender lock pick from his pocket and sprung the fist-sized padlock, releasing the heavy chain. It fell away and clinked against a metal post. The iron gate swung open with a creak of hinges and they stepped through into the land of the dead.

"I remember how scared you were of ghosts when you were a kid," Henry said.

"Who says I'm not still scared?" But Vernon laughed and held a trap up to a lighted lamppost, the filigree on the brass bottom glistening in the light. "My mother wrote down an incantation that I etched in the glass on all four sides. It will attract the ghosts, then keep them contained once they're trapped."

"Look for headstones dated this year, mainly fall and winter," Henry said.

Vernon gave Henry a puzzled look. "What difference does it make?"

"New ghosts are easily tricked for one thing. And for another, any ghosts that were around during warmer months have probably become demon chow by now."

"Ah." Vernon nodded. "Is there an area of the cemetery we should look in first?"

"We can start anywhere." Henry wasn't familiar with this graveyard because he didn't know anyone buried here. When Hellspawn died, they left no ghost behind. Every dead human had a ghost, but no one knew for sure whether it was an actual soul or the shell of a life force that refused to accept it no longer had a body. Henry suspected it was the latter.

"Ghosts are harmless," Henry said. For the most part. They could be dangerous when possessing a body, like what happened to the Hebeite. But that was extremely rare.

Vernon grinned as if he knew better. He shrugged. "My mother used to tell me stories about the nasty ones that can cause physical harm to people. Their energy is so angry that it manifests as a tangible force, even to the point of looking solid."

Henry had never heard such stories. "Maybe Eunice was telling you scary bedtime tales to keep you in line."

"Very funny." Vernon switched on an electric tube lamp and directed it toward the narrow cement path ahead. The beam highlighted clouds of fog that billowed over the dead lawn and curled around headstones like finely spun cotton. "The ghosts my mother told me about were the specters of murderers, rapists, terrorists, and all manner of evil humans. Their character didn't die with their bodies. The way my mother told it, they got even worse."

"Is that so?" Henry chuckled, but the scales stood up on his spine. It was still a pile of horseshit. A ghost couldn't do much unless it possessed a body. If gods or goddesses weren't involved, ghosts had absolutely no power. Besides, looking solid and actually *being* solid were two different things.

"Might as well start setting traps," Henry said. He placed the box on the ground and took a few out. "Did you bring an extra tube lamp?"

Vernon tossed him one and he switched it on. Henry walked among the headstones, shining the light on names and dates that went back decades. He found one that was only a few weeks old and bent to place a ghost trap beside it. He slid back the lid and hooked it to a spring that would close it automatically once the ghost was inside.

He grimaced as he set the trap. Ghosts were disgusting.

They were refuse, spirit garbage that had no purpose but to satisfy a demon's appetite. It repulsed him to think how a demon could eat one of the filthy things. At least the ghosts they caught would be put to good use.

After they set all the traps, Vernon joined Henry under a thick oak tree with gangly, leafless branches. The air smelled musty, like damp earth and old dust. Henry glanced down the hill and saw Mystic, her headlamps dark, her engine silent. She was probably sleeping.

He heard a distinct snapping sound in the distance.

"Caught one," Vernon said.

Another snap, then another.

Henry grinned. "The ghosts are biting tonight." He sauntered over to collect the traps. As he retrieved one with a smoky blue essence that swirled like fog thick as gravy, he glanced at the ghost's headstone. It said it belonged to Sara Ann Taylor, beloved daughter of John and Astor Taylor. The girl had only been ten years old when she died. Henry experienced a sick feeling in his stomach.

"What's wrong?" Vernon asked.

"This ghost." Henry held up the trap and his skin crawled with chill bumps. "It came from a ten-year-old child."

"A child that's dead, Uncle Henry." Vernon, always the pragmatic scientist, pointed at the glowing trap in Henry's hand. "That's not a child, it's a ghost. It's not alive anymore."

Henry sighed. His nephew was right, but he still felt uneasy. He retrieved two more traps, making sure not to read the headstones' inscription this time, and placed them in the box.

There was a succession of several snaps and Vernon held up his fists and cheered victory to the night. At this rate, they'd be home within the hour. Henry thought it a bit odd to have trapped so many ghosts this quickly, but this was his first ghost hunt. Except they weren't really hunting. More like shooting fish in a barrel.

A glowing figure of a man hovered above a headstone about fifty yards away.

"Hey, take a look at that." Henry studied the apparition dressed in baggy pants and a torn jacket. "Did you set a trap on that side?"

Vernon swallowed loudly. "No."

"I'm taking an empty trap over there to catch it," Henry said.

Vernon grabbed his arm. "Don't. Leave it alone. I think we have enough."

Henry smiled. So his nephew hadn't lost his fear of ghosts after all. "Well, what luck. It's heading our way."

Vernon directed his tube lamp at the approaching specter, the ghost's fluid movements cutting a swath through the fog. It didn't walk, it floated. And it was finally near enough for Henry to make out a few details.

The male ghost appeared to have died in his late forties or early fifties. Henry couldn't make out what color its hair was since the body was transparent. It looked as though it was made of glass because Henry could see right through it. The ghost's naked chest was splattered with some kind of dark paint.

Vernon picked up the box of filled traps. "I have a bad feeling about that one. We really should let it go."

Henry grabbed an empty trap from one of the graves and held it out to the ghost. "Here, ghosty, ghosty, ghosty."

"Don't tease it like that."

"Why not?" Henry grinned. "It's not a person, it's a thing. It's not alive, Vernon. You said so yourself." He squinted at the ghostly form as it approached. It gripped something in one of its see-through hands. "What's it holding? Looks like an ax."

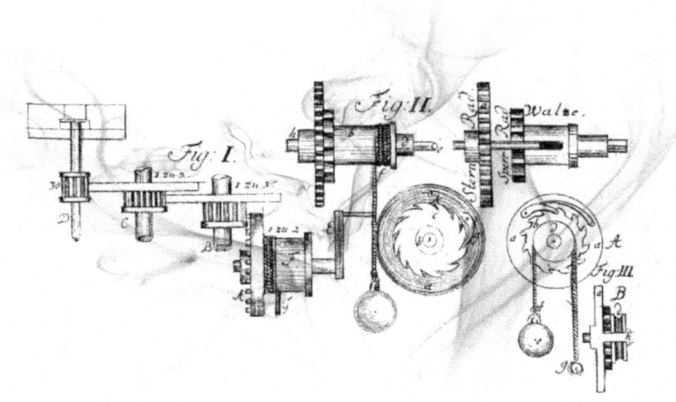

CHAPTER EIGHTEEN

"I recognize that guy. I remember seeing a photo of him in the newspaper," Vernon said, his voice pitched low. "He murdered his entire family, chopped them up into little pieces. Cops peppered him with bullets before he finally went down. Killed him on the spot."

"Sounds like a real nut case." Henry stepped forward with the ghost trap in his hand, but Vernon tugged him back. Henry jerked his head around to look at him. "What?"

"It's one of those ghosts my mother told me about." Vernon stepped backward, dragging Henry along with him. "It's carrying a weapon, probably the same ax he used to kill his wife and kids."

Eunice had really put the scare into this boy, who was far too old at fifty-plus to still believe in fairy tales. Henry jerked his arm free. "Close your eyes if you don't want to watch."

"I'm serious. That ghost is bad news."

"What was his name when he was alive?"

Vernon paused before saying, "Alfonso Soriano. The article called him a crazy alcoholic." He heaved in a quick breath. "Look at his eyes. They're wild!"

Henry could see that. The ghost's eyes appeared huge and enraged, its brow furrowed. Henry glanced at the weapon in Alfonso's transparent hand and saw that it was as ghostly as the ghost itself.

"Vernon, the ax isn't even solid. Relax." He stepped up to the ghost that had stopped only a few feet from them. It held up its ax as if to defend itself, but its expression had turned curious. Henry held out the trap. "Looky here, Alf. Know what's inside? More members of your family. Go on in and hack away, son. Let it all out."

"Uncle Henry!"

"Hush." Henry waggled the trap at the ghost. "Come on. You know you want to."

The thing drew back its arm and swung the ax down on the trap, which shattered in a shower of shimmering pieces.

Henry frowned. "How the Hell did that happen?"

Vernon stepped behind the oak tree, using the trunk as a shield. "I don't know, but I say we make a run for it."

If the ax-that-wasn't-there could smash a ghost trap, it could probably do serious damage to skin and bone. Henry held up his hand. "Peace, okay? We'll leave you alone. Just go about your business and have a nice... death." He started down the hill, motioning for Vernon to follow.

The ghost swung its ax again, and the blade sliced right through the sleeve of Henry's coat. It also sliced his arm and the pain seared him like a salt burn. Henry hissed through his teeth. "Vernon, run. Fast!"

Vernon was quick as smoke, kicking up clods of dead grass as he made tracks down the hill toward the cab. The carton of ghost traps in his arms clattered like discordant wind chimes. Mystic's headlamps flicked on and her engine started. She hadn't been sleeping, she'd been watching.

The ghost took another swing and Henry was ready this time. He leaned back, the ax blade missing his neck by inches.

"Look, pal. I never did anything to you. Take a hike." Henry felt his eyes heat up and his will push forward. "I'm warning you."

Alfonso what's-his-name paid no attention and lunged at him again. Henry danced backwards and sideways to evade the blade. He focused on controlling the ghost, but there was no mind inside it to manipulate. It was like Eunice had told Vernon: Angry energy, and powerful. But no match for a hungry demon.

"Mystic!" Henry called. "Come and get it!"

A line of green mist shot out of the cab and flew up the hill toward him. The ghost continued its furious mission to cleave Henry in two, oblivious to the Vox demon speeding toward it. Within seconds, the snake of demon energy twined around the specter and squeezed. The ghost's eyes widened and its mouth grew round in an O of surprise. It began to shrink and fade as

Mystic devoured her meal. Then it was gone.

"Thanks," Henry told her.

She sparkled, coiled around Henry as if giving him a hug, then shot back down the hill and out the cemetery gate.

When Henry arrived at the cab, he found Vernon huddled in the back seat, his face pale as the fine, misty snow just starting to fall. "Is it gone?"

"Yes, compliments of Mystic." Henry rubbed his hand affectionately over the cab's dashboard. "She might have saved our lives tonight."

Mystic cycled through radio stations until she came up with just the right word. "*Burp.*"

"Rude," Henry told her, but smiled when he said it. "We have what we need now. The rest is up to Eunice."

A twinge of pain made Henry jerk the arm the ghost's ax had sliced. It should have healed by now. Sliding back the sleeve of his torn coat, he saw welts covering his arm from wrist to elbow. "Uh oh."

"What's wrong?" Vernon asked.

"Nothing." Henry tugged his sleeve back into place. It was nothing a hot shower and a meal wouldn't cure. "We better get going."

⚭ ⚭

"Good job, Levi," Jasper said to the man crouched at his feet. He pushed Levi's masked head down to the fiery glow coming up through a hole in the ground. "That wasn't so hard, was it?"

Levi gasped for air as steam rose from his back. A Spawnster with rat-like features stood over him, a brine gun aimed at Levi's spine.

A ceramic ashtray levitated from a nearby table and flew toward Jasper's head, but Jasper ducked before it could make contact. The gun delivered a spurt of saltwater to Levi's back. He groaned, but didn't scream from the pain he must have been feeling. Jasper admired his tenacity.

"Nice try." Jasper tapped Levi with his foot. "It would be so much easier, and less painful, if you had agreed to cooperate without such a fuss."

"Fuck you," Levi said.

"Thanks, but I'd rather Claire do it, if it's all the same

to you." Jasper tilted his head toward the dark-haired beauty standing in the shadows of Levi's subway tunnel home. "Isn't that right, dear?"

Claire hid her face and edged toward the exit. The ratty Spawnster grabbed her arm and yanked her back.

Jasper clucked his tongue. "Claire, sweetheart, you're not going anywhere. Now you know what will happen if you think about betraying me." She'd been acting too aloof lately and that spelled trouble. Claire needed to know her place. She belonged to Jasper and always would.

The girl's hair fell forward to cover most of her face, but there was no disguising the venom in her eyes as she glowered at him. He thought she looked adorable.

"How many is that, Raul?" Jasper asked the ratty Spawnster.

"Fifty-one." Raul held up a gallon-sized glass jar etched with cuneiform script. The Vox demons inside pulsed with a phosphorescent green glow. Jasper had no idea what the writing said, but his mages assured him the incantation would keep the demons in hibernation until he was ready to wake them up.

"Levi, come now. Fifty-one? That's hardly worth the effort." Jasper stepped around Levi, who trembled with obvious pain. It shouldn't have gone this far. All Levi had to do was follow instructions. How difficult could it be? "You're obviously missing some. Use your Spawnster mojo. Bring me more!"

Levi coughed and bloody drool dribbled from his mouth onto the dirt floor. "I... can't."

"Why not?"

"They're not willing, and I can't force..."

Jasper nodded at Raul, who shot Levi with another dose of saltwater. This time Levi collapsed to the ground and didn't move.

Jasper let out an irritated sigh and paced in front of the fallen Hellspawn. If Jasper had the power to Bring, he would have forced hundreds of demons from that hole. Demons always followed his orders. They were powerless to resist. Unfortunately, they had to already be on Earth's surface for his power of persuasion to work. Which is why he needed a Bringer, and Levi was the only Spawnster he knew with that kind of power.

Claire stared at him from the shadows, a look of rage and hate distorting her pretty face. She had lovely white teeth, but not so lovely when she snarled.

"Get over it, Claire. Your ex-lover will recover just fine. If you want your new beau to remain healthy, remember what you witnessed here today. Do we understand each other?"

She continued to stare, her body shaking as if chilled. Then she smiled.

Jasper saw the malice in that smile, but he didn't care. "That's better. It's good to see you've come to your senses. Now remember what I told you."

Her voice barely above a whisper, she said, "I'll never forget."

⚅ ⚄

Wanda sat at Alva's kitchen table drinking coffee with Henry, who had just told her about his ghost hunt with Vernon.

"So where is Claire?" Henry asked, a plate of pickled chili peppers in front of him.

Starting to worry, Wanda checked her watch. "She should have been here an hour ago." Frowning, she watched Henry scratch his arm for the hundredth time. "You better stop that or it'll get infected."

"What will get infected?"

"Whatever it is you're scratchin'."

He dropped his hand to the table and grabbed a pepper to pop in his mouth.

"What's wrong with you?" she asked. Spawnsters weren't prone to itching. They healed so fast their wounds never got the chance to itch. "Are you... sick?"

Henry scowled. "No. It's just a rash."

"A salt rash?" Now that would make sense. If he got salt on his skin, it would definitely burn and itch. "How'd it happen?"

He shook his head. "No salt. It was a ghost."

"Excuse me?"

"A ghost attacked me."

"Ghosts don't attack people."

"I didn't think so either, but this one did." He started to scratch again and Wanda grabbed his hand to make him stop. "The ghost turned into something almost solid. Vernon recognized it as an ax murderer from an article he'd read in the newspaper."

Angry spirit energy. Of course. She'd heard of it but never

saw it in action. "The ghost touched you?"

"It cut me with its ax."

"Don't be ridiculous. If it wasn't solid, there's no way it could—"

"It did, okay? It cut me with a ghost ax and gave me a salt rash. End of story."

"I'm sure your niece has a potion or ointment that will make it go away."

He hung his head and gave his arm another scratch.

"You didn't tell her, did you?"

"No."

Pride goeth before a fall. Stubborn Spawnster. Wanda held out her hand. "Let me see."

"No."

"Henry, my aunt's a witch. She's got all kinds of herbal remedies in her pantry." Except that Alva wasn't here to tell her which one to use.

Though Alva's burns were healing nicely, she had to spend at least one more night in the hospital. Wanda planned to live somewhere else temporarily so that her aunt wouldn't get mixed up in Wanda's troubles again. She'd been thinking about Jasper's offer of a place to stay in Spawnstertown. The idea had merit. While living there, she might get the inside scoop on the scheme Jasper was hatching, but... It was a huge risk.

Wanda reached for Henry's injured arm. "Let me have a look."

He jerked away at the same time a knock sounded at the door. Jumping up from the table, he said, "I'll get it."

His long legs covered the distance between dining room and living room in four strides. He opened the door. "Where the Hell have you been?"

Claire stepped inside, and she didn't look happy. She looked furious. "Hell is exactly where I've been." Throwing her coat on a chair, she stalked over to the dining room table and glared down at Wanda. "I want him dead."

Wanda's heart tripped over itself. "You want *who* dead?"

"Jasper." Staring through brimming tears, Claire said, "He almost killed Levi."

That got Henry's attention. "What?"

Wanda rushed to the kitchen to get a decanter of olive oil from the icebox. She brought it and three glasses back to the table, then returned to the kitchen for a bottle of scotch. She needed a drink just as much as they did.

Claire gulped down half a glass of oil before saying, "He forced Levi to Bring over fifty Vox demons through Hell's Gate."

Henry slammed his meaty fist on the table. "I was afraid that would happen. Jasper got to them first."

"But there must be more Vox down there, right?" Wanda looked hopefully at Henry, remembering what he'd said about never having tried to Bring demons from The Source. There was a chance he could do it and he'd said he would try.

She shifted her gaze to Claire. "Why only fifty?"

"Levi said those were the only ones willing to come. He didn't say why." Eyes filling again, she took another gulp of oil. "I wouldn't be surprised if Levi had warned the Vox to stay away. Even though Jasper tortured him horribly..." She brought her fist to her mouth. Cheeks shiny with tears, she said, "Unbelievable. The pain! Saltwater soaked his back, ate through his skin, and the blood—"

Henry growled and his upper lip peeled back in a snarl. "I'll kill Jasper myself."

Was Wanda the only sane one in the room? "People, get a grip, okay? There's a war brewin'. We need to strategize a defense and an offense. Jasper's got a jump on us so now we move forward with the plan we made yesterday." She explained to Claire what their plan was.

Claire blew her nose and dried her eyes, nodding at everything Wanda said. "And the antidote for the virus?" Claire poured herself another glass of oil, while Wanda helped herself to more scotch.

"My niece analyzed one of the infected Snits and she's certain she can reverse the spell." Henry studied Claire. "I'm worried about Max. What's his part in all this?"

Claire leaned back in her chair, her empty oil glass clutched firmly in one hand. She tapped it with one perfectly manicured fingernail. "Jasper makes Max wear some kind of helmet he created with feathers from his own head. It's creepy."

So that's why Jasper was bald when Wanda met him. "What does the helmet do?"

"It's an amplifier. It strengthens the psychic signal Max gets when he communicates with the lesser demons." Claire blinked and her thin brows tilted with worry. "He's been staying in contact with the Snits, but he has no influence over them. He knows there are thirteen hundred and fifty-two in the city, eight have died, and two have returned to The Source."

That was damn accurate information. Wanda had no idea how many demons sent her their thoughts. "How does Max know eight of them are dead?"

"He knew by their absence."

A jolt of concern shot through Wanda. "Does he know how they died?"

Claire shook her head before locking her eyes with Wanda's. "But Jasper suspects there's an exorcist in town."

Crap. It was bound to come out at some point, but Wanda had hoped for more time. As long as her identity remained secret she'd be safe to do what she had to: kill demons to save the city.

Henry looked worried, too. "We can't let him find out about Wanda. Which means Max can't know about her either."

Claire nodded.

"What happened between you and Levi?" Henry asked Claire. "I thought you two were an item."

Claire didn't appear one bit guilty to Wanda, who now had to question the Spawnster woman's loyalties. Perhaps it was her species that made her come off as less caring than she actually was.

"We were more like intimate strangers than lovers," Claire said. "Jasper got us together so that I could..." Her voice trailed off and she began twisting her napkin.

"What did he want you to do, Claire?" Henry asked, but Wanda saw the answer in his eyes. He already knew.

"My job was to let Jasper know every time you went to Levi for more demons." Tearing off pieces of napkin and still not looking up from the table, Claire murmured, "I was his spy." Her gaze flicked up to meet his. "I'm sorry, Henry. He threatened to torture me. I didn't think I had a choice."

Henry blinked once, slowly, before saying in a soft voice, "I know Jasper. He always makes good on his threats. You made the only choice you could."

Wanda's heart went out to Claire. How awful to be enslaved to a mad man. But Claire's coming here proved she was done taking his crap. "If we're to beat Jasper, we need to put the next part of our plan into action," Wanda said, then directed her question at Henry. "Remember what you promised?"

He looked confused before recognition brightened his eyes. "Wanda, I can't prove I'm a Bringer without Hell's Gate. I'm sure Jasper has it heavily guarded."

"Not to worry," she said with a smile. "There's more than one way to The Source and it's inside this building."

His mouth curved into a slow grin. "Why didn't you tell me this before?"

Wanda shrugged, but it felt good to finally trust him enough to share such an important secret. Claire, on the other hand, she wasn't as sure about. She'd be keeping an eye on the Hellspawn woman.

Claire glanced between Wanda and Henry, her lips tilted up in a sly smile.

Henry asked, "What's so funny?"

Eyes twinkling, Claire lifted both eyebrows. "How long have you two been together?"

"We're not *together*," Henry and Wanda said in unison.

"Are you sure? I have a way of sensing these things, but..." Claire held up both hands in surrender. "My mistake."

Wanda and Henry shared a sidelong look before jerking their gazes elsewhere. Wanda had no clue how Henry felt about her, but she could admit to having a physical attraction to him. And so what if she did? It's not like she had ever acted on it. They started out hating each other and were finally getting to know each other. By no means did that make them "together."

Henry *harrumphed* and stood to get his coat. "Wanda, show me this Hell hole of yours."

All three of them slipped their coats on and headed for the door. When Henry opened it, a disheveled man stood just outside with his fist raised as if preparing to knock. His glasses were broken and he wore a gray coat smudged with dirt, parts of it torn and scorched. One corner of his mouth looked swollen and blood caked his split lower lip.

"Vernon?" Henry asked, his voice tinged with worry and surprise. "What happened to you?"

"They..." The man named Vernon heaved a breath as if in pain and wrapped both arms around his middle. "They broke in. Stole my machines. And all my Vox demons... are gone."

CHAPTER NINETEEN

Eunice felt a flutter of excitement while putting the finishing touches on her potion. She lit another candle on her worktable. "Oh, Sylvester, these old eyes of mine aren't nearly as sharp as they used to be."

The clockwork cat twitched its tail of wooden beads that waggled from a wooden rump. "Meow," it said, activating the voice box Vernon had placed inside its chest at Eunice's request. She wanted a companion she could talk to, and preferably one that would talk back. This was the best her son could do with what he had to work with.

She absently stroked the mechanical cat's metal back. Not as comforting as the real thing, but at least she didn't have to mess with a litter box. And fur had to be brushed. She simply wiped Sylvester down with a dry cloth when he got dusty.

She added a pinch of brimstone to the boiling concoction in the beaker and turned up the Bunsen burner's flame. "I think it needs more Hippopotamus weed, don't you?" she asked her cat. "And lion's bane. The animalistic elements will help ground the Snit and boost its immune system."

Sylvester meowed again and began to rumble, which had been Vernon's rendition of a purr. The Imp that animated the mechanical cat might be dumb, but it was affectionate and had become a dear friend for over forty years.

"Let's try it, shall we?" She drew some of the potion into an eyedropper and lifted a lid to one of the ghost traps. "Here you go," she told the ghost inside. The potion changed the swirling blue mist to a rather unattractive brown smoke. "Oh, dear. Not so appetizing now, is it? I need to change one or two ingredients to make the ghost retain its yummy blueness. A Snit may not eat a yucky-looking ghost. You demons can be so finicky."

Sylvester arched its back.

"That's exactly what I mean. This ghost isn't for you, anyway. You stay away from these traps, you hear?"

The clockwork cat meowed softly, then curled up on the table and nestled its nose of metal screws under its beaded tail.

"Good kitty," Eunice said, and stroked its back again.

A loud crash sounded somewhere at the front of the house. Eunice jumped, and so did Sylvester. "Someone's here."

Footsteps thundered on the floor above her basement workshop. Yep, someone had definitely broken in. She should have made Draegor's flaming breath more powerful, but there was only so much a witch could do with a doorknocker.

She grabbed the cat off the worktable and backed up to the wall, her elbow searching for the lever that would open the door to a hidden tunnel under the house. Thinking he might need to escape through it someday, Henry had installed the door while building the house. Their hate-filled relatives had constantly threatened Henry with a saltwater bath. Eunice never should have invited those awful people to live with her in the first place. Sylvester was, and always would be, the best company.

The door above her rattled. She bet it was one of Jasper's goons. That nasty old gang of Demon Lords had always treated Uncle Henry badly, and it wasn't a stretch to think they'd come after her to get to him. They'd tried it before. She would never let them. Having three-quarters of a century's worth of mileage on her bones gave her good reason not to go down without a fight.

"Hey, you old bag!" called a gruff voice from behind the door at the top of the stairs. There came a hard bang, then the sound of splintering wood. "If I break my shoulder trying to get in, I swear I'll break your neck."

Eunice shoved her back against the wall, her elbow slamming against the lever, but it didn't budge. The thing was rusted in place.

"One, two, three!" There was a final bang, and then heavy footfalls pounded down the stairs toward her.

"Oh, Sylvester!" She held the cat close to her chest as her confidence fled like water down a drain. "I'm afraid our goose is cooked."

"Tell me what happened," Henry said to his nephew as he ushered him inside Wanda's apartment. Jasper probably wanted *more* than Vernon's Vox demons. Jasper must feel confident about taking over the city, and Henry's attempts at helping folks with their crazed Snit demons had made Henry an inconvenience. Abusing his family to get at him was Jasper's style.

Vernon wobbled on his feet. Wanda clamped onto one of Vernon's arms while Henry took the other, and they led him to Alva's sofa. Henry helped his nephew take off his coat and the battered man sagged onto the cushions.

"My life's work destroyed. My inventions stolen and my building torched." Tears welled in Vernon's reddened eyes. "I'll have to start all over again."

"That bastard." Henry didn't have to ask who was involved. He didn't need names. All of Spawnstertown would pay for this; every mean-spirited, human-eating, murderous Hellspawn criminal—

"Henry!" Wanda grabbed him by the shoulders to give him a hard shake. "You're scratchin' your arm again and now it's bleedin'. Stop!"

Henry still wore his coat and the sleeve was soaked with blood. He blinked, fire roaring behind his eyes, and it wasn't his will trying to break through that was causing it. He had a fever.

"You're sweatin'." Wanda pulled him gently down to the couch beside his nephew. "You're really sick. Would you just show me your arm—"

He turned away from her and stared at Vernon. A murderous rage built inside him and his scales rose like hackles on an angry dog. Someone had hurt his nephew! His blood boiled, and not just with fever. His fury was unlike anything he'd ever experienced.

"What's she doing here?" Vernon glared at Claire, who still stood by the open door. "I bet she's the cause of all this. She took my Max away and turned him against me! Thanks to her, Max is in cahoots with hooligans out to destroy me!"

"Vernon, right?" Wanda asked, while granting him a gentle smile. "Vernon, Claire loves your son. She's trying to protect him from those hooligans."

Vernon frowned at Wanda and gave Henry a questioning look. "Who is this woman?"

Ignoring Vernon, Henry swallowed, his mouth dry as a dust storm. He had to get something to drink. He eased off the couch and stumbled toward the kitchen, but dizziness overtook him and he fell to his knees before he got there.

Claire rushed over to help him to his feet. "Henry, are you okay?" she asked.

"He's sick," Wanda said. "He got cut by a ghost—"

"I remember." Vernon seemed to forget his own injuries as he scooted to the edge of the sofa, his eyes glassy with anxiety. "I was there. I saw it happen." He heaved himself off the couch and staggered over to Henry.

Henry tried to focus on his nephew, but the image was blurry and washed out. Instead of Vernon he saw a woman and two small children cowering in the corner of the apartment. They looked terrified, their eyes wide and their mouths open with silent screams that brought about a strange excitement in Henry. He wanted to see them bleed, smell their blood, and watch their eyes become vacant while life seeped out of their mutilated bodies. He wanted...

The hallucination faded and he saw Vernon, Wanda and Claire staring down at him with concern scrawled on their faces.

Henry's heart raced and he sucked in a choked breath. "That ghost imprinted a memory on me, gave me its diseased anger." He scratched at his arm, trying to rake the skin off, to peel away the sickness that wanted to drive him insane.

Henry dragged himself up from the floor and stumbled the rest of the way to the kitchen. He grabbed a butcher knife off the counter.

"So what do you think?" Jasper asked Max as he led him into the ballroom. He wanted his young friend to feel at ease. "Comfortable enough for you?"

Max stared, open-mouthed, at two reclining bergere chairs upholstered in red brocade velvet. One had a sculpted wooden frame shaped for a body just his size. It even made room for Max's tail. "Is this for me?"

Jasper nodded. "And the other one is for me."

Max tilted his head like a dog that's heard a puzzling sound.

Jasper chuckled and draped a fatherly arm across Max's shoulders. "I can't let you do this alone, can I? I'll be here to support you on the big day, when we let our weapons loose on the city."

Now Max looked curious. "What weapons?"

Jasper ushered him to his chair and Max eased himself into it with a sigh. He stretched, appearing very comfortable, which is just what Jasper wanted.

"I'll show you." Jasper approached a paneled screen beside the recliners. He folded it back.

A cylindrical machine stood about four and a half feet tall and balanced on a pair of thick hydraulic legs. It had six arms with three joints each, and they ended in pincer-like claws. The machine's riveted body sported a variety of nozzles and gun barrels, some recessed into its "body," and some protruding like extra appendages. It had no head, but the top was like a plate-shaped lid with a spyglass protruding up from its center. A couple of light bulbs sprouted from the lid, with coils and wires strung between them, and the entire contraption was braided with cord and wire cable.

"What *is* that thing?" Max asked, his voice just above a whisper. He tensed and leaned forward as if to bolt. "I've never seen anything like it, not even in my father's lab."

"It's remarkable, isn't it? I call it a Demonized Robotic Device, or Robot for short." And Jasper was very proud that it didn't look humanoid aside from its bipedal legs. He'd considered adding wheels, but if he had, it couldn't climb stairs.

"I'm guessing there's a Vox demon inside," Max said.

"And you'd be right." Jasper focused on the robot, mentally sending it a command. The lights on top of its dinner-plate head winked on and sparks tripped across the coiled wire between them. Steam puffed from a pipe on its back and it clacked its pincers.

Max frowned. "It looks dangerous."

"That's because it *is* dangerous." Jasper gave it another command and a dozen gun barrels sprouted from its middle. They spun in a circle and bullets sprayed from the barrels in a single direction, splintering wood and shattering tile on one narrow section of wall.

When the smoke cleared, Max stared at the ruined wall. His lips parted to speak, but no sound left his mouth for a few long seconds. "That thing could kill somebody."

Jasper grinned. "That's the idea."

Max eased off the recliner and stood. "How many of these did you make?"

"About a hundred and fifty, but we only have enough Vox to power little more than half."

Shaking his head, Max said, "I had no idea..."

"Really?" Still grinning, Jasper asked, "You had no idea I could pull off my genius plan?"

Max cleared his throat. "This thing's a killer, Mr. Clark. You can't murder innocent humans. It's... wrong."

Amazed at the boy's naiveté, Jasper laughed. "Max, my boy, how did you think I planned to overpower the humans in this city? Ask them to surrender while wooing them with tea and cookies?"

"Of course not!" Max tried to sound indignant, but his voice broke. "I figured we could all come to an agreement, like a truce. Put equality laws in place and ensure Hellspawn would be protected from murderous bigots."

Jasper laughed even harder, a full-throated laugh that came from his belly and made his throat ache. "Politics? Diplomacy? Oh, Max, you're priceless. Equality indeed. There's nothing equal between the humans and us. They're cattle and should be treated as such." He pointed to himself and said, "We're the superior species. Why do you think The Healing created us to begin with? World domination is our destiny. I thought you understood that."

Max stood a little straighter. "I won't help you commit genocide."

The smile slid from Jasper's face. "I'm afraid you have no choice."

Now the young man's over-sized head turned red, his brows furrowed in a disapproving frown. "You can't make me do anything I don't want to do."

"You're mistaken, son." Jasper snapped his fingers and two large Spawnsters, one with rat-like features and the other more lionesque with horns, entered the ballroom carrying two machines that looked like giant typewriters.

Max pointed at them, his finger shaking. "Those are my

father's inventions! They're his D-Mail machines."

"Is that what they're called?" Jasper motioned the two men to set the machines down. "Fascinating. Your father has made some amazing creations."

The boy looked frightened, as well he should. "How do you know about my father's creations?"

"Because they're mine now." He turned to his goons, hands on hips, and demanded, "Report."

"The entire building is probably ash and rubble by now," the ratty Spawnster said.

"And Vernon Paine?" Jasper asked.

Ratman shrugged. "Didn't see him come out. I assume he went down with his ship."

"No!" Max yelled, and lunged for Jasper, but the lionman grabbed him, picked him up, and slammed him into the reclined chair. Max was undeterred. "Where's my father? I demand to see him. Now!"

"He's dead," Jasper said, enjoying the taste of the word on his tongue. "And your grandmother is next on my list."

Max's eyes filled with tears, but he did well at holding them back. He even held his tongue. What could he say? His entire family was gone. Well, almost gone. Two down, one to go. Henry wasn't much longer for this world if Jasper had his way.

Jasper stepped over to the recliner and leaned over Max. "Son, your daddy's dead, and I won't hesitate to kill your grandma, too, if you don't do exactly what I say."

"Excuse me, sir?" Ratman said.

"What is it?" Jasper despised interruption, especially during such a special moment as this.

"My brother hasn't come back from Eunice Paine's house. And he hasn't called."

Max breathed deeply and his lips moved with an oath too quiet for Jasper to hear.

CHAPTER TWENTY

Wanda followed Henry into the kitchen. When he grabbed the knife off the counter, he turned to stare at her with such hostility he didn't look like himself anymore. He'd gone completely mad.

"Put the knife down, Henry," Wanda said calmly, though she felt anything *but* calm. Panic swelled inside her like pent up steam inside an engine. A scream crawled up her throat but she swallowed it down. "Your arm is still bleedin'. If you let me help you I can make it stop."

He gave her an exaggerated smile, his mouth spreading wide and his sharp canines looking more like fangs than teeth. "I'm fine." He waved the knife back and forth through the air as if in play, but Wanda knew better. Holding out his bleeding arm, he said, "Want to see it, Wanda? Come closer and I'll show it to you."

Who was this man? Certainly not the same Henry she'd grown to care about and admire over the past few weeks. His sudden change in personality reminded her of her great-grandmother who'd also gone crazy, except that she'd killed *herself* and not someone else. Henry had murder in his eyes.

Claire and Vernon stood beside her, so she asked them, "What should we do?"

"I'll call my mother," Vernon said. "She's a witch. She'll know how to help him." He ran to the candlestick phone on the hutch in the dining room.

"I've seen this before," Claire said in a small voice. "But it happened to a human. A ghost rumored to have stabbed a prostitute to death haunted the hotel room I was in with a client. The ghost cut the man with its ghost knife and he went crazy."

"How did it end?" Wanda didn't take her eyes off Henry, who continued to stare at her with eerie intensity.

"He threw himself out the window." Claire inhaled deeply before adding, "We were fifteen stories up."

Fear clawed its way up Wanda's spine.

"My mother's not answering," Vernon said, and there was a note of hysteria in his voice. "What if the same goons who burned down my building went after my mother?"

Sweet, elderly Eunice? Henry appeared to have heard what Vernon said because his eyes lost their murderous glint. "No. Not my niece. If they hurt her..." A light seemed to spark in his eyes as if he finally understood something. "It's the sickness the ghost gave me that's making me this way. I can't help Eunice if I'm sick." He turned to face the counter and pushed up his sleeve, laying his scratched and bloody arm on the shiny white surface. He lifted the knife blade.

Horrified, Wanda yelled, "Henry! You can't cut off your arm."

"It's okay," he said. "It'll grow back. I think."

Wanda couldn't let him do it. She had to call Alva at the hospital, find out if she had a potion in the pantry that could fix whatever the ghost had done to him. "Stop, Henry. I mean it."

He held the blade higher, poised to strike his own flesh.

There was only one thing left for Wanda to do. She rushed up behind him and wrapped her arms around his chest, pressing her hand firmly over his heart. Power surged through her, her vibrant stripe of hair pulsing against her scalp, and she began drawing out the demon half of his soul.

Henry sucked in a breath. "Do it," he whispered. "If it will stop what's happening to me, please do it."

Wanda struggled to hold steady and drew out just enough of his demon soul to stop him from hurting himself. She clamped her jaw in concentration, the muscles in her neck coiled so tight she was afraid they might snap. Her ears rang with the power trying to force its way through her. *Must maintain control.* It took every ounce of force she had to resist her natural compulsion to extract his demon side completely.

Eyes watering, she turned her head to glance at Vernon and barely managed to speak. "Vernon, call the hospital. Ask for Alva Snow. She's my aunt... a patient there. She's a witch like your mother and might be able to help. Hurry."

Vernon blinked, but asked no questions. He ran back to the phone and dialed.

Claire's eyebrows lifted to practically reach her hairline. "Wanda, are you exorcising him?"

Wanda gritted her teeth. "Sort of."

Narrowing her eyes, Claire asked, "Can that kill him?"

Wanda shook her head, feeling Henry sag against the counter. "No, but I'm not sure... how long I can... hold back."

Her temples began to itch. Her forehead felt scratchy. The features of her face would shift if she didn't stop what she was doing.

Henry moaned. Wanda hated hurting him like this. It had to be agony, but the alternative was unthinkable. She couldn't let him chop off his own arm. Or what if he suddenly turned the knife on *her*?

"I have your aunt on the phone," Vernon said. "She says it's ghost sickness and that she never heard of a case involving a Spawnster. The remedy for human infection is all she knows."

"Fine." Wanda's hand covering Henry's heart throbbed in time with his beating pulse. "What's the remedy?"

There was a pause while Vernon listened to Alva on the other end. "She says she has a batch already made and it's in the pantry. The bottle's labeled."

Wanda was hit by an overwhelming sense of relief. "Claire? Would you, please?"

Claire rushed to the walk-in pantry.

Vernon said, "Wait a minute." He listened and closed his eyes, a look of defeat washing the color from his face. "Alva says it contains a lot of salt."

"I don't care," Henry said in a raspy voice. Wanda was surprised he was still coherent. "Just give it to me."

Claire emerged from the pantry with a bright blue bottle in her hand. She approached Wanda, who said, "Pour it over Henry's arm."

"Sorry, Henry." Claire yanked out the cork stopper and held the bottle over his arm. The flesh was bumpy with bloody blisters that burst as they watched. Claire hesitated.

"What are you waitin' for?" Wanda asked.

"The salt. It will burn him."

Henry gasped. "It can't possibly hurt any more than it already does."

Claire sprinkled the bottle's contents over Henry's infected skin.

Smoke rose from his arm and his body began to shake.

"What's happenin'?" Wanda tightened her hold on Henry as he convulsed. The odor of camphor and rotten fish permeated the tiny kitchen.

Claire stepped back and pressed her hand to her nose. "I can't see his arm. There's too much smoke."

Henry dropped the knife and it clattered to the floor. Her arm still wrapped around him, Wanda stared at his neck, watching his scales fade. She had to release her hold on him. If she didn't, he'd become human with half a soul, and half a brain. Not only had he become a dear friend, and possibly more if she was forced to consider it, he was the only one who could help her. She couldn't keep the prophecy from coming true without him. *Must hold back... Stay focused...*

"I told Alva about the smell, and she says it sounds right," Vernon said. "Can you tell if it's working?"

Wanda peered around Henry's bulk to stare at his arm. The smoke had cleared, but the skin was still bloody. "It looks bad."

Claire stepped forward to see for herself. "I don't see any blisters. It looks like only a salt burn now."

Vernon said something into the phone then nodded at Wanda, who took a chance and let Henry go.

He heaved in a breath and staggered before dropping to the floor.

Claire and Wanda grabbed his arms to keep him from falling on his face, and Wanda smiled when she saw the scales on his neck had come back. But what about his sanity?

"Henry?" Wanda asked as gently as she could, though her voice was still tight with tension.

He panted as if having just run a dozen blocks. No answer. *Please let him be okay.* She tried again. "Henry?"

The kitchen had become so quiet Wanda thought sure she heard the beating hearts of everyone in the room. Then Henry's stomach growled.

"Getting turned into a psychopath sure makes a Spawnster hungry. What does a guy have to do to get a sandwich around here?"

Vernon slapped him playfully on the back and Claire opened the door to the icebox. Wanda threw her arms around Henry and hugged him tight.

"Whoa," he said, his muscles tensing at her touch. "What was that for?"

She swallowed the emotion clogging her throat and shoved away from him before slapping him hard on the shoulder. "Don't you ever do that to me again!" Still shaking after nearly sucking half his soul away, she stomped off to her room so he wouldn't see her cry.

🜃 🜄

Eunice prayed her old ticker would keep on ticking as adrenalin sang through her veins. The lever at her back still hadn't budged and Jasper's thug was plodding down the stairs toward her.

Sylvester leapt from her arms.

She lunged to grab him, but she wasn't fast enough. The clockwork cat scuttled across the floor on its wood and cable legs, the visible gears on its sides spinning to make it move. It sprang for the stairs and landed on the step just below her invader. The Spawnster's heel slid across the cat's metal back and kept on going, both his feet leaving the stairs while gravity forced him to tumble backward. His head thumped against every step on the way down. There was a loud pop like a snapping tree branch just before he collapsed at the bottom.

Dear, oh, dear. Eunice choked in a breath, thankful to her cat for saving her from the brute, but she didn't feel like celebrating. Not yet. Hellspawn were quick to recuperate... only this one didn't move.

She stepped carefully to where the fallen Spawnster lay. The cat jumped up on him, and Eunice gasped, but the man remained still. Crouching down with a crackling of joints unused to bending, she touched his wrist to check for a pulse. Nothing. The ratman was dead.

"Goodness me, Sylvester," Eunice said to her mechanical pet. "Poor thing must have broken his neck when he fell." She stood and nudged the body with her foot just to be sure.

Taking a calming breath, she returned to her workbench to finish her potion. One Spawnster had come after her, which meant there would probably be more.

"Where'd she go?" Henry asked Claire when Wanda fled from the room. He'd never seen the exorcist behave like that. She was acting like such a... girl. "Was it something I said?"

"More like something you did," Claire said.

"It's not my fault I got cut by a ghost. How could I know it would affect me that way?" He flashed back to those horrible homicidal feelings he'd had and it made him sick. He'd never experienced so much rage.

Claire shook her head. "Men. You're all thick-headed scalawags."

"I beg your pardon?" Henry had to wonder who Claire considered the victim here. It sure wasn't Wanda.

Plunking down a loaf of bread and a jar of mustard, Claire said, "Make your own sandwich."

"I'm not hungry anymore." Actually, he was, but now wasn't the time to stuff his face. Especially when he remembered what Vernon had said. *Eunice.* "Have you reached your mother yet?" Henry asked him.

Vernon was just returning the cone-shaped receiver to its cradle. His split lip had swelled to twice its normal size and his chin was purple. He winced as he told Henry, "Her phone's still out. I'm worried."

"Me, too." Henry eyed Vernon up and down. "You all right?"

His nephew huffed out a breath. "Fair. Just a couple of bruised ribs after having half my building fall on me, but other than that I'm fine."

A scientist trying to be a tough guy. It wasn't a good look on his studious nephew. Henry motioned for him to follow him out of the apartment. "We need to go check on your mother."

Claire gave Henry a withering look.

"What is it with you?" he asked her.

She cocked a hip and crossed her arms. "Scalawag."

He rolled his eyes and kept going, out the door and down the hall.

"Can the prostitute be trusted?" Vernon asked him as they walked side by side down the stairs.

"I think so." Henry *hoped* so. "She seems very attached to

Max. She's risking a lot to help him."

"What kind of danger is he in?"

"If you knew Jasper like I do, you wouldn't need to ask." Henry led the way outside and opened Mystic's door for Vernon, who groaned while easing onto the front seat.

Henry wondered about Jasper's plans for Max. His old friend had a talent for commanding the lesser demons, but he couldn't control the minds of Spawnsters or humans, unless you counted his charismatic talent for brainwashing. Pushing minds was Henry's bailiwick, not Jasper's.

So how did any of this affect Max? Jasper had started collecting Vox for a reason, probably to hurt humans in some way. His scheme must be far more clever than the spell that turned the docile Snits into homicidal maniacs. Whatever it was obviously demanded Max's ability to train demons, and his communication skills. But Max would never agree to being an instrument of destruction. Could he be forced to follow Jasper's orders? Possibly. Henry had to get him away from Jasper.

They pulled up in front of Eunice's house. None of the lights were on, including the porch light, which she always kept burning.

"Vernon, you're in no shape to confront an intruder. Stay here."

"No." Vernon climbed out of the cab with some effort. "And don't even try your mind control on me. I'd never forgive you if you did."

Damn him for knowing the right button to push. Henry growled under his breath and said, "Fine. Just stay behind me."

Vernon nodded and followed him up the steps to the front door.

Draegor, the doorknocker, was gone. Not completely gone, but most of him. He'd been ripped off the door and now lay in pieces on the stone floor of the porch. The knocker wasn't breathing smoke anymore so Henry could only assume the Imp inside was no longer there.

The door itself had a busted lock and stood ajar.

Henry led the way into the dark house and nearly tripped over his niece's clockwork cat. It scurried for the basement stairs so he and Vernon followed.

Halfway down they heard Eunice humming an old church hymn.

"Mother?" Vernon called, and passed Henry on his way down the stairs.

A ratty-looking Hellspawn lay in a heap on the basement floor. He looked an unhealthy color and from the angle of the man's head, he appeared to have broken his neck.

"Vernon, sweetheart! I'm so relieved you—" The welcoming smile dropped from Eunice's face. "What happened to you?"

"Did that Spawnster hurt you?" Vernon asked, giving her a hug instead of answering her question. "I tried calling, but you didn't answer. I was worried."

"That big guy must have cut my phone line." She flipped her hand like it was no big deal and frowned up at her son. "Your lip is swollen."

"My building burned down." Vernon stared down at his feet.

Eunice gaped at him, her face pale.

"But he's okay, see?" Henry said. "And so are you, apparently. Who's the rat Spawnster?"

"He was sent to get me," Eunice said, still staring at her son. "Jasper is responsible for this, isn't he?"

Henry nodded. "We make him nervous, and that's a good thing. It means we're on to something and he knows it."

Eunice blinked. "Where's your girl?"

"Girl? What girl?" Vernon asked, turning to squint at Henry.

Henry blew air through his nose. "Eunice, I don't have a girl. I told you that."

"You mean Wanda?" Vernon's mouth tilted in a half-grin. "I had no idea you were seeing her that way. How long's it been since you had a date? Ten years?"

"I don't remember." He rubbed his eyes. It hadn't been that long, had it? "Anyway, we're not dating. We're partners."

"Sounds serious," Vernon said.

"It's not. It's business. Look, forget about Wanda." Henry wished he could forget, but he hadn't stopped thinking about how upset Wanda had been when she ran from the kitchen. He felt bad about that, but couldn't dwell on the emotional tirades of females. He turned his attention to the ratman instead and nudged him with his foot. "What's the scoop on this guy?"

Eunice told them what had happened.

"You're lucky he was clumsy," Henry said.

She bent down to pet her mechanical cat. "I have Sylvester to thank for that. If not for him, I wouldn't be standing here right now." Her gaze jumped to the box of ghost traps, which were glowing. "Would you look at that?"

"What?" Henry focused on the ghost traps and saw the blue smoke inside them brighten with intensity. "Isn't that what ghosts do?"

"They only glow when agitated." Eunice crouched beside the box, her knee joints making an audible creak, and lifted out one of the glass containers. She looked at Henry. "Is there something you haven't told me?"

He frowned. "Why?"

She narrowed her eyes. "Something that happened in the cemetery?" Her gaze dragged down to the ripped sleeve of his coat, the fabric stiff with dried blood. "What happened?"

After he gave her the gory details, including his episode in Wanda's kitchen, she said, "You're marked forever now."

"What does that even mean?" he asked.

"Anyone who survives the sickness carries the Ghost Scar." She jerked a nod at his arm. "You've got one."

The implications of such a mark were disconcerting. "So?"

She slipped the trap back in the box. "The nasty ghost energies will be attracted to you from now on. They'll want to be near you, to touch you." She shook her head. "Have Mystic with you at all times, if you can. She'll get rid of them for you."

"What if she doesn't?"

Eunice shrugged. "You'll get cut or bitten, and then you'll get the sickness again. It's curable as long as you have the antidote close at hand."

Damn. More salt burns.

She went to a wooden chest in the corner of the basement and opened the lid. After digging around inside, she pulled out a small leather pouch tied to a leather string. "I'll put an Imp in this pouch that I want you to keep around your neck at all times. Even while you're sleeping."

Henry hated wearing anything around his neck. That's why he never wore a tie. "Do I have to?"

"Only if you don't want to become an insane psychopathic killer." Eunice stepped toward a brightly burning wall sconce. "You can have this Imp," she said, gesturing at the lamp. "Call it out for me, please? And direct it here." She opened the pouch.

Henry focused his will on the Imp, letting it know what he wanted it to do without making it an order. The sconce light faded to darkness, then an orange wisp of energy streamed to the pouch in Eunice's hand.

She closed the drawstring, said a few words in a language Henry didn't understand, and tiny sparks flickered out the top of the pouch. She handed the necklace to Henry. "Put it on before you attract trouble."

He arched one eyebrow and slipped the necklace over his head, tucking the pouch beneath his shirt. His neck was already starting to itch.

"Don't fidget," Eunice told him.

He kind of liked it when she fussed over him, though he pretended not to. He hadn't had much mothering when he was a child.

"Pull back your sleeve so I can put some salve on that salt burn."

Heavy footsteps tromped across the floor above them.

"Oh, my," Eunice said. "Here comes another one."

Henry immediately went to the hidden door that led to the secret tunnel beneath the house. "We'll go out this way."

"Wait!" Eunice wrung her hands and Sylvester raised himself on his hind legs to be picked up. She obliged, stroking the clockwork cat with nervous fingers. "My potion for the Snits. The ghost traps. We can't leave them here!"

"We'll take them with us." Vernon lifted the box of traps.

A voice called out from the doorway upstairs. "Brewster? Are you down there?"

All three of them glanced at the Spawnster on the floor. Eunice handed Sylvester to Henry and gathered her notes off the worktable to stuff them into a canvas bag. Shaking her head, she clucked her tongue. "Where are we going?"

"I know just the place." Henry pushed at the lever on the door. It was stuck.

"I was about to tell you," Eunice whispered. "The door's rusted shut."

CHAPTER TWENTY-ONE

Henry heard a second voice echo down to them from the top of the stairs. "I've looked in every room and they're all empty. Where's your brother?"

"Must be in the basement," said whoever had called out for Brewster. "There's nowhere else he could go."

If there'd been only the one, Henry could have controlled his mind. But there were two of them, which meant he and his family were trapped.

"Eunice, do you have any oil down here?" Henry asked his niece.

"Uncle Henry, I'm surprised at you," she whispered. "Drinking at a time like this."

"No, you old bat," he said, though not without affection. "The oil is for loosening up this rusty lever."

Eunice gave him an exasperated look and went to a dusty old shelf covered in cobwebs. She retrieved a burgundy-colored bottle and handed it to Henry. "Castor oil. This stuff will loosen *anything*."

Henry handed the clockwork cat to Eunice and focused on the door. He uncorked the castor oil to dribble it over the rusty lever. Giving it a twist, he carefully jiggled until the door popped loose from its frame.

"Did you hear that?" asked one of the voices on the stairs.

"I told you he was down there." The stairs creaked beneath heavy feet.

Henry opened the door, its hinges complaining loudly, and the three of them rushed across the threshold. His arms filled with the box of traps, Vernon shoved the door closed with his back. Henry slid a heavy plank of wood through a pair of slats to bar the entrance. A heavy weight landed against the door from the other side.

A fist banged on the door. "What did you do to my brother?"

Eunice said, "I—"

Henry shushed her, though he knew it was too dark for her to see the finger he held to his lips. The front of his shirt began to glow.

"The Imp from the lamp," Eunice said.

Henry motioned for them to follow as he headed through the tunnel, and he held out the pouch from around his neck to guide the way. The pounding continued behind them as they raced through the dark cavern beneath the house. Vernon had nudged his mother in front of him, and one of Eunice's small hands grabbed onto the back of Henry's coat. Her breathing already sounded labored and that made him worry.

"Will the door hold?" Vernon asked, now in full voice since they were no longer hiding.

"It will until they find something to chop through it," Henry said, grinding his teeth and cursing himself for not making the passageway more secure.

He remembered the tunnel's path like he knew the streets of New York City. A turn was coming up soon, and that's where he'd stowed candles, extra food, and a few items of clothing. They couldn't stop for long. The two Spawnsters behind them would be on their tails any minute.

This tunnel fed into another that was part of the subway maintenance tunnels under the city. It would lead them directly to Levi's place. If Jasper had left only one guard with Levi, Henry could force the guard's mind into leaving them alone, then make him forget they were ever there.

He saw the turn coming up. Finally. "We're almost at a place we can stop," Henry said over his shoulder.

"That's lovely, Uncle Henry," Eunice said, her thin voice breathless. "I'm afraid I can't keep up this pace much longer."

But when they arrived at the bend in the passageway, they could go no further. A copper wall barred their way. What the Hell? It looked exactly like the one Levi used to close his place off from the subway.

"I hope I'm doing the right thing," Wanda said to Claire, who sat beside her in the back seat of the cab. They hadn't taken Mystic but rode in another steam car from Henry's taxi service. They were on their way to Spawnstertown. Wanda had left a note for her aunt, which she knew would be shared with Henry. It didn't say precisely where she was going, but she felt confident Henry would find her. Wanda banked on it.

"Don't worry," Claire told her. "Spawnstertown isn't such a bad place, and you'll like my apartment. Jasper made sure I had the best of everything." She smoothed her hands over the front of her coat as if to straighten invisible wrinkles. "Of course, that was before Max and I got together. Now Jasper is jealous."

And probably pissy as Hell, but Wanda didn't say it out loud. She didn't need to. "You think I can win Jasper over?"

Claire grinned. "Absolutely. I saw how he looked at you the other night. Jasper's smitten, and maybe a bit intimidated by you."

"Intimidated?" Wanda hadn't picked up on that. "How so?"

"He can't figure you out," Claire said. "You're a challenge, Wanda. An enigma. I saw the spark that flickered between you two when your hands touched."

Wanda remembered and it made her uncomfortable. "The exorcist in me wants to take away his demon half. And it wants it bad."

"I figured that's what must have happened. It's what tipped me off to what you are."

"And Jasper still doesn't know?"

Claire shook her head. "He probably thinks it was a sexual spark between you. Fireworks of passion." She giggled and shook her head. "His arrogance will get the best of him some day."

We could only hope.

Wanda worried about her aunt, who'd be coming home to an empty apartment. She'd wanted to call Henry and ask him to pick up Alva, but she had no way to reach him. She wasn't even sure where he was.

"Wanda, your aunt will be just fine," Claire told her and gave her a friendly pat on the arm. "One of Henry's guys can pick her up and drop her off. Then we'll call her from my place so that you'll know she's okay."

"Maybe Alva should stay in the hospital another day."

"The doctor said she was ready to come home now, right?" Claire gave her a long look. "She must be going nuts in that place."

"I'm sure you're right." Wanda sighed. Though she felt guilty for leaving, she knew it was best to stay clear of her aunt's apartment. Things were getting dangerous for all of them. There was no telling what Jasper would do next.

The cab drove down a steep hill and into the cave-like bowels of Spawnstertown. They left the bleak light of early morning and entered the dim, night-like atmosphere of the underground city. The buildings had loose bricks and peeling paint, and shingles lay scattered in the street. Streetlamps flickered as if running low on fuel. Huddled forms wearing long dark cloaks or coats lurked on street corners and in shop doorways. Such a dismal place.

"Turn left down this alley," Claire told the driver.

The alley was narrow and even darker than the streets. Small animals scurried over the ground between dumpsters and Wanda assumed they were exceptionally large rats, but considering this was Spawnstertown, they could have been anything.

The taxi stopped beside a lowered set of stairs from a fire escape. This building appeared in a better state of repair than most of the others she'd seen. A glowing lamp illuminated freshly mortared bricks and a clean layer of red paint on the metal stairs.

"Home sweet home," Claire announced, hesitating a moment before climbing from the cab.

Wanda didn't move right away. She sensed from her new friend that something was off. "Everything okay?"

Claire smiled. "Of course! Hey, I'm excited to show you my place." She gave the cab driver a sultry look. "I just have to settle up with our driver, if you know what I mean."

Wanda really hoped she didn't know. Especially not in public. Though the inky darkness would hide anything and everything the two might do.

The driver was human, middle-aged, grizzled but plain. He hadn't shaved in a while and his rheumy eyes looked as if they'd missed a few nights' sleep. Claire touched his arm resting just outside the window, then leaned in and bent forward as if to give him a kiss. That's what he must have thought, too, because his red eyes brightened and he tilted his head before parting his thin, dry lips.

"Uh, Claire? Do you really think—"

Claire grabbed the man's head and gave it a hard jerk. The crack of breaking bones echoed against the building, the noise ricocheting through the alley in a chorus of loud snaps.

Sickened with shock, Wanda was speechless. She couldn't even summon up a scream.

Claire pushed the dead driver over and opened the cab door so she could shove him onto the passenger seat. She speared Wanda with a hard look. "I know what you're thinking, and you're wrong."

Claire reached inside the driver's coat pocket and pulled out a folded sheet of paper. After opening it, she quickly scanned the message inside. "I knew it. This is Jasper's handwriting. The driver was one of his spies."

Wanda's heart beat into her throat, cutting off her breath. "How did you—"

"I told you. I see through people for who they really are. No one can lie to me." She sat behind the wheel and thrust a set of keys out the window at Wanda. "Take them. The big one will let you inside my apartment. It's on the top floor, facing the alley. The fire escape will take you right to the back door."

"But where are you going?"

"I have to get rid of the body." She gave Wanda a lopsided grin. "Can you tell I've done this before? I had to kill him, Wanda. He would have told Jasper what you are, and who your aunt is."

"Without the driver to tell him, Henry won't know how to find me."

"He'll read the note you left for your aunt. Don't worry. He'll find you." Claire faced forward and stomped the accelerator, causing the cab's tires to spin on the damp asphalt. Wanda watched until the cab turned a corner and disappeared from sight.

Mouth dry as dust in a mummy's pocket, she hoped Claire had more than oil in her liquor cabinet. Wanda needed a drink, the stiffer the better.

⚙ ⚙

"What's that wall doing there?" Vernon asked.

Henry shook his head. "Wish I knew. Levi has a wall just like it outside his home in the tunnels, but that's at least a mile away from here." He pulled back both sleeves to uncover the glyphs tattooed on his arms. The back of his right arm had a thick, ropey scar caused by the salt in Alva's potion. He was lucky the ghost hadn't cut through his tattoos or they'd really be stuck.

"If Levi put this up himself, the spell he tattooed on my arms should get us in." He held his breath and laid both arms against the copper surface. It softened instantly and relief flushed through him like adrenalin. "It's working. I'll stand here while the two of you pass by me to go through this door."

"Uncle Henry, dear," Eunice said, her voice patronizing. "I think you snorted a bit too much grave dirt at the cemetery."

"Trust me, okay?" He nodded at the wall. "Just walk through. Nothing to it."

"What's on the other side?" Vernon asked.

Good question. Henry wasn't sure. He imagined the tunnel continued as he remembered, but what if Levi had set a trap for trespassers? No. Levi knew this section of tunnel was close to the house Henry had built for his niece and nephew. Levi also knew about the escape route. So why hadn't he told Henry about this barrier?

An echo of footsteps sounded in the distance behind them. "Jasper's goons got through the door," Henry said. "We don't have time to debate this. Walk on through. It'll be fine."

Henry held his breath as Vernon and Eunice closed their eyes and walked directly through the wall. Without hesitating, he followed.

The tunnel continued, just as he believed it would. There were no guards, no sudden drops into nothingness, no additional barriers. No traps. At least not yet.

All of them breathed heavily as they swiveled to take in their surroundings.

Eunice chuckled. "Would you look at that?"

They all turned in the direction she pointed to see a coal car sitting on a track with a clockwork mule harnessed to the front.

"I think Levi's been expecting me," Henry said, though how his friend could possibly know his current situation was a total mystery. He couldn't have. This track and car had been here for years. Layers of dust caked both the mule and the car, which had rusty wheels. Cobwebs covered the car's seats like layers of lace, and a rat leapt over the side to scurry down the track.

"Can I sit in front?" Eunice asked, sounding like an eager child at an amusement park. She shuffled closer to the car.

"Mother, we don't know if it's safe," Vernon said.

Henry eyed the rig and its lifeless mule. "It's safe, not that it matters. That mule is a lifeless piece of junk."

Just as he said it, orange lights blinked on inside the mule's wooden head and shone from its eyes. Its metal ears turned as if to listen, and its steel muzzle opened to emit a tinny bray.

Vernon smiled and stepped up to the mechanical creature. "What a marvel. I should have thought of this one myself! Where do you think Levi got it?"

Henry shrugged. "He used to tinker with this stuff back in the day. A hobby, really. I never thought any of his machines actually worked."

The mule lifted each wood and metal leg, the knees bending with a loud creak. It clopped in place a few times before braying again.

"It seems to be working okay with an Imp at the helm." Henry climbed into the front of the car. "All aboard!"

Eunice climbed into the seat behind Henry, and Vernon nestled in beside her. The Imp in Henry's necklace continued to glow and was now joined by a bright light on top of the mule's head.

"Where will it take us?" Eunice asked.

"Probably Levi's place." Henry knew that's what his old friend would have designed it to do. Regardless, it was on a track so didn't have a choice of destination.

The mule headed forward at a steady trot, the car behind it creeping along with creaks and groans.

"It's not very fast," Vernon said. "Can you speed it up?"

The mule must have heard him because the gears on its sides spun faster and its trotting picked up speed.

Eunice's clockwork cat meowed. "Sylvester is nervous," she said.

Henry glanced over his shoulder at the mechanical cat, noticing its tense posture. It looked ready to spring from the car.

"I don't think it's an Imp possessing this machine," Henry said, feeling increasingly uneasy. The glow from the mule's eyes turned from orange to blue. He'd never known a demon to disguise its color, but no demon had ever been cursed with a virus before. "The demon inside this thing is a Snit."

He heard Vernon gasp from behind him. "We should stop and get out."

"I think it's too late for that," Eunice said as the mule's trot turned into a gallop. "Vernon, why did you have to say anything about going faster?"

The tracks clattered like rapid gunfire as the cart sped through the tunnel. Henry was forced back in his seat, and he struggled to lean forward and grip the reins of the mechanical beast more tightly. He marveled at how the car could remain on the rickety old track as the mule raced around each turn.

"Were you able to coat any ghosts with the antidote yet?" Henry had to shout to be heard. He shot Eunice a quick glance. "Did you?"

She nodded, her eyes squinted against the wind caused by the speed hurling them over the tracks. "Just one. It turned brown, though. I was afraid the Snits wouldn't eat it."

"Oh, they'll eat it." Henry gazed ahead at the dark tunnel. Where would the track end? Nothing looked familiar anymore. "Demons aren't picky when it comes to ghosts."

Henry peeled up a strip of metal that rimmed the top edge of the car and yanked it free. "Hand me the trap with that brown ghost in it," he yelled over his shoulder.

Vernon handed him the trap with a swirling mass of smoke the color of tobacco. Henry bent the end of the metal strip and hooked it through the latch closing the trap. He gave the end a hard twist to keep the hook secure. Using the strip like a fishing pole, he held it in front of him, stretching his arms to dangle the trap high above and a little behind the mule's head.

The mechanical beast slowed to a fast trot. A very fast trot.

But it didn't stop. Its head tilted back so that it could focus on the swaying trap.

"The track ends up ahead!" Vernon shouted, his arm thrust stiffly over Henry's shoulder as he pointed.

Sure enough, the darkness beyond was where the track ended and a wall began. The end of the line.

Henry yanked back the reigns. The mule continued its forward journey, paying no attention to what was, or wasn't, ahead. Henry held the trap higher. The mule lengthened its neck to snap at it with steel jaws hinged by springs and cable. Henry lifted the trap so high out of reach that the mule finally did stop, rearing up on its hind legs and tilting sideways. It lost its balance and crashed down on its back, sending wires and gears tumbling across the rocky ground.

The brick wall ahead stood less than ten feet away.

The mule kicked its wooden legs and brayed, snapping its jaws at the air. It appeared to be having a tantrum. Henry hated to waste the ghost on just one Snit when dozens could feed off it and be cured of the virus. The metal strip, which was rusted with age, snapped in two. The ghost trap dropped to the ground and shattered. A stream of blue mist spun out of the mule's eye socket and wrapped itself around the ugly brown ghost.

"At least now we'll see if your antidote works," Henry said.

Eunice nodded and watched intently, her brows knitted and lips pursed in concentration.

After it devoured the ghost, the Snit hovered, unmoving, above the clockwork mule.

"So is it cured?" Vernon asked his mother.

"Call it to you, Uncle Henry," Eunice said.

Henry focused his will on the Snit, asking it gently to come to him. If it was still infected, it would try to resist like the others had done. This one didn't. It floated lazily toward him and caressed his legs, twining there like a snake wrapped around a tree.

"You have your answer." Eunice smiled, her eyes twinkling with pride.

"How nice," Henry said, not hiding his sarcasm. "Now what do I do with it?"

"Bring it with you," said a voice from the shadows. A figure in a wheelchair rolled out into the dimly lit tunnel. It was Levi and he held up a crystal decanter. "Can I offer anyone a drink?"

CHAPTER TWENTY-TWO

W anda stood in Claire's living room and eyed the luxuri-
ous furnishings that seemed so out of place in run-down
Spawnstertown. She was especially impressed by the
French iron daybed that dominated the center of the room.
Upholstered in delicate French ticking, the bed's iron scroll-
work had more detail than some museum pieces she had seen.
But it didn't look very comfortable.

She went to the window and stared down at the ugly alley
below. When would Claire be back? And how did she plan to
dispose of the driver's body? The image of her breaking the
man's neck flashed through Wanda's mind and she shuddered.
Claire was a lot stronger than she looked. Wanda made a
mental note never to cross her.

She stepped into the kitchen, afraid to open the icebox
for fear of what she'd find. But when she finally did, she saw
a bottle of red wine on the top shelf. There was also cheese, a
bowl of grapes, and a few horrid items that might be considered
food if you were Hellspawn. Was that jar filled with rat tails or
worms? She grabbed the grapes and cheese, then slammed the
icebox door shut before she saw anything else.

The bejeweled telephone on a marble table jangled. Why
not answer? She wasn't hiding from anyone, and in fact wanted
people to know where she was. The caller might be Henry.

She snatched up the receiver. "Hello?"

The caller hesitated before saying, "You're not Claire."

"She stepped out for a few minutes. Would you like to
leave a message?"

"I recognize your voice," said the man on the other end,
and she thought she recognized him as well. His voice sounded

low and silky, charming and dangerous. "We met a few days ago at a town meeting. You don't live here in town. Or do you?"

"At the moment I do," she said, knowing without a doubt she was talking to Jasper. "You must be Mayor Clark."

"And you must be Wanda Snow." He chuckled. "I've been waiting for your call."

"I lost your card," she lied. "But Claire told me she knew you, so I figured I could get your number from her."

"I'm pleased you're in town. May I give you the grand tour?"

Wanda swallowed, her throat scratchy as though lined with sandpaper. This was what she wanted, right? She focused on sounding cheerful. "I'd love that."

"Terrific." She heard the rustle of paper. "How about dinner and a play? Tomorrow is opening night for a new show at the Brimstone Theater. Are you free?"

She heaved a silent breath and prayed Henry would find her before then. "When can you pick me up?"

"Why didn't you tell me about this?" Henry asked Levi, kicking the dead mule in the head. "That thing almost killed us."

Levi's leather mask hid his expression, but there was a smile in his voice. "I set up the car and mule as soon as you told me about the escape route you added to your house. I had hoped you'd never need to use it, but I wanted you to have it just in case."

"That Snit was infected," Henry said. "Has it been inside the mule all this time?"

The masked man shook his head. "I have no idea where it came from. The mule was an empty machine when I put it there forty-some-odd years ago."

Henry gazed down at the blue ribbon of demon smoke curled around his leg.

"I see you found a cure for the virus," Levi said.

"Actually, it was *me* who found the cure." Eunice stepped out of the coal car with Sylvester in her arms. She gave Henry a glacial stare and smiled at Levi. "My uncle has no manners. I'm Henry's niece, Eunice Paine, and this is my son, Vernon." She tugged on Vernon's sleeve and he climbed from the car, wincing as he did.

Henry worried he might have bruised more than just his ribs.

"Your reputation precedes you, Ms. Paine," Levi said with a nod. "You must be an incredible witch to have come up with a potion to cure our demon kin." He tilted slightly forward in his chair, imitating a bow. "Thank you."

"They're not all cured yet, but we have a plan." Henry tossed a wave at Levi's chair. "What's all this?"

"Jasper's minion poured so much salt water on my back that it ate through my spinal cord." He grabbed a leg, lifted it a few inches, then let it flop limply to the side. "I can't walk, but it's temporary."

Henry's scales stiffened with rage. Jasper had gone way too far this time. "Claire told us what happened, that you were forced to call up Vox through Hell's Gate."

The twin holes in Levi's mask showed bright eyes focused on Eunice and Vernon. Levi had always been guarded about his ability to summon demons and never wanted Vernon or any human to know what he could do. "It wasn't easy," Levi said. "They didn't want to rise."

Frowning, Henry asked, "I thought Jasper would have a guard holding you prisoner."

"He did." Levi chuckled. "But he underestimated me by thinking I was too crippled to cause trouble. He was wrong."

Henry liked the sound of that. "What did you do?"

Using his hands to roll the chair backwards, he then snapped his fingers and an orange glow circled the spoked wheels to propel him forward. "Come and I'll show you."

The three of them followed Levi through an arched doorway cut into the stone tunnel wall. A thick wooden door opened automatically at their approach.

"Just a minute." Levi wheeled himself over to block the hallway that Henry knew led to Hell's Gate. "Don't take this the wrong way, Ms. Paine. Vernon. But there are... secrets here that I want to keep that way."

"What about Henry?" Vernon asked, his voice pitched high with dejection.

"I need his help." Levi shrugged. "And Henry knows all my secrets anyway."

True enough. The less his niece and nephew knew, the better for them. No one Henry cared about was safe, at least not while Jasper had the power to hurt them.

Levi showed Eunice and Vernon to the copper exit door at the other end of the hallway.

"Take a cab to Alva's apartment. I'll catch up with you later," Henry told them.

Eunice's eyebrows raised in bewilderment. "Can't we just return home?"

"It isn't safe for you there," Henry said. "Not yet, but it will be. I promise."

Now Vernon looked puzzled. "Why Alva's?"

"Because Alva's a witch and she'll have what Eunice needs to make more antidote." Henry looked at Eunice and said, "We'll head to Times Square tomorrow. Once we release the ghosts, there won't be an infected Snit left in the whole city."

Eunice reached up to give him a hug, and while her mouth was close to his ear, she whispered, "Be careful."

He wrapped his arms around her and whispered back, "I will."

Eunice clutched her clockwork cat and slung the canvas bag over her shoulder. Vernon, with his box of ghost traps, looped his arm around his mother's waist and the two of them vanished through the copper door.

Levi exhaled loudly. "It's a good thing those ghosts are gone. I'm not sure how Hell's Gate would have responded to such an easy meal."

Henry hadn't thought of that. "What is it you want to show me?"

"I think you'll like this."

Henry followed Levi to the center of the tunnel. Hell's Gate glowed with red and amber light that flickered like flames. Though The Source was a hot place, it wasn't a fiery inferno ruled by devils wielding pitchforks. The Gate did look hungry though, and Henry could see why. A large morsel of living Hellspawn hung suspended upside down above the Gate with nothing but air to hold him up. It was the guard Jasper had left to watch Levi.

Henry clucked his tongue and said to the guard, "You should know better than to mess with a Spawnster with telekinetic powers."

The guard dangled helplessly from an invisible rope made with Levi's will. The monkey-faced Spawnster struggled to free his hands from behind his back. "Go bull yourself."

"Looks like you're the one who got bulled." Henry grinned and looked at Levi. "What do you plan to do with him?"

"That's where you come in." Levi sounded grim. "I need you to wipe his mind clean of everything that happened after he did this." Levi swept a hand down his body to his lifeless legs.

Henry blinked. "This the guy who tortured you?"

"I had no choice," the monkey-man said, not sounding a bit sorry. "You have no idea what Jasper—"

"Shut up." Henry's scales rattled with anger and the ones between his shoulders strained against his shirt. He felt the fabric tear. "How could you do something like this to your own kind?"

The Spawnster didn't answer.

Henry wanted to clear the Spawnster's mind of *everything*, but his conscience would never let him go that far. Even so, his eyes burned as he prepared to shove the monkey-man's mind.

Levi grabbed his shoulder and pointed at the wall.

"What?" Henry asked.

"Incredible. I've never seen anything like it," Levi said in a hushed voice.

Henry squinted at the wispy shapes emerging through the solid dirt side of the tunnel. Ghosts. Two of them, each dressed in rags, their blue-gray skin completely transparent. Each ghost held a knife blade poised to strike.

"Oh, no." They were coming after him, just like Eunice had said they would. "Levi, there's no time to explain now, but I had the ghost sickness."

Levi nodded. "And now the demented specters are after you. I've only heard of humans being afflicted. How in the world did you—"

One of the ghosts rushed at Levi. The shock of attack must have broken his concentration because when he jerked his chair back to evade the ghost's blade, he lost his telekinetic hold on the guard.

As if released by a giant hand, the guard dropped. He plummeted headfirst through Hell's Gate, his terrified scream echoing into silence.

The Snit that had latched itself around Henry's leg released him so fast that his skin burned from the friction. The Imp inside the pouch around his neck spewed out in a bright orange stream. The Snit devoured one of the ghosts within seconds. Henry's Imp and the one in Levi's chair chewed up the other one until barely a wisp of ghostly essence remained.

Henry ran to the Gate's edge and peered down through the gaping hole. He saw nothing but flickers of fiery light that winked a few times before blanking into darkness. The Spawnster must have landed somewhere down there. He just didn't know how far.

Regardless of how much Henry despised the Spawnster who'd hurt his friend, he hadn't wanted him dead. "We can't leave him down there."

"I know *you* can't," Levi said quietly. "But I can."

Eunice and Vernon stood side by side in front of Alva's apartment door. Eunice didn't want to go in, and when Vernon lifted his fist to knock, she grabbed his arm to stop him.

He frowned. "What's wrong?"

"We know next to nothing about this woman." Eunice stroked Sylvester and the mechanical cat rumbled its motorized purr, which helped keep her calm. "Strangers make me nervous. What if she doesn't like cats?"

"Mother, she's not really a stranger if Henry knows her," Vernon said, his voice tight with frustration. "And she's Wanda's aunt."

Eunice blinked. She liked Wanda. The young woman was the breath of fresh air Henry needed in his life. And she had grit. Eunice admired a woman with grit. She nudged Vernon away from the door and knocked on it herself.

When the door opened, Eunice was taken aback by the woman's shiny red face spotted with bandages on her chin and forehead. She knew Alva had been in the hospital, but she hadn't known the details of her injuries. The poor dear.

Eunice glanced at Vernon to check his reaction and was surprised by the expression of awe on his face. She knew her son well enough to know he found this woman attractive.

Alva's gaze flicked between her and Vernon. Her blonde hair was pulled back from her face and if not for the burns, she'd be pretty for a middle-aged woman. Though she could stand to lose a few pounds.

"May I help you?" Alva asked.

Vernon smiled and his cheeks turned a blotchy red. "Henry Paine told us to come here. This is my mother—"

Alva's face brightened. "Of course! You must be Eunice. And Vernon? We talked on the phone." When he nodded, she grabbed the lapels of her robe to tug it closer to her chest. "I must be a sight. Please come in." She ushered them inside. "Henry just now called to tell me you were coming."

"Is Henry all right?" Eunice asked as she settled on Alva's sofa that was worn but comfortable. The pillows helped hide patches of faded upholstery. "I was a trifle concerned when we left him."

Alva winced. "Physically, he's aces. But he had a brief run-in with a couple of nasty ghosts."

Eunice pressed her fingers to her mouth. "Oh, my. I was afraid that might happen."

Giving Eunice a reassuring pat on the hand, Alva said, "Not to worry. A couple of demons took care of the ghosts before they could hurt anyone." She went on to tell them what had happened to the guard. "Henry's on his way here now."

"What did they end up doing with the guard?" Eunice asked.

Alva shrugged. "From what Henry said, the guy's a goner. They couldn't get him out."

What a shame. But when messing with a Spawnster more powerful than himself, what did the guard expect? It was Levi she worried about most. All alone in that dank tunnel, paralyzed, no family to help him...

Vernon hadn't taken his eyes off Alva. The woman was starting to look uncomfortable. Eunice cleared her throat. "You must still be exhausted after your accident. How about I make us all some tea?"

"Great idea," Alva said. "I'll help."

"Can I do anything?" Vernon asked, brows arched high above eyes that shone with earnest.

"No, dear," Eunice told him. "Just sit and read a magazine or something. How do your ribs feel?"

"Okay," he said, rubbing the sides of his chest.

"You relax. Alva and I will take care of making the tea."

Once she was in the kitchen with Alva, she said, "I have to apologize for my son. He's usually not so... obvious. He likes you."

Alva's face reddened more than it already was. She touched her hair and gave Eunice an embarrassed smile. "I can't imagine why. He doesn't even know me."

"No, but you did talk him through a precarious situation with our uncle, *and* you had the cure for Henry's ghost sickness. He's beholden to you for that."

Alva opened the cupboard and took down three teacups with matching saucers. "The teapot's on the stove."

Eunice filled the pot with water from the tap. Sylvester scurried in from the living room and rubbed against Eunice's legs.

"Is there a demon in that?" Alva stared down at the clockwork cat, the corners of her lips turned down in a look of disgust. She might be okay with cats, but it was apparent she had no love for demons.

"It's just an Imp," Eunice said, feeling defensive. She crouched down to pet Sylvester and the mechanical cat purred with pleasure.

Alva cleared her throat. "I, uh. I'm not comfortable having demons in my home."

"Oh?" Eunice gathered her cat in her arms and held him close. She had actually liked Alva a minute ago. "Sylvester is sweet and gentle. He'd never hurt anyone."

Scowling, Alva said, "But he's a demon."

"There's nothing wrong with demons."

Alva crossed her arms in a pose of defiance. Her voice raised a couple decibels when she said, "The Snits are trying to kill people. I'd say there's a lot wrong with *that.*"

Eunice had grown up with demons all around her, including the one that operated her pram when she was a baby. She'd not tolerate bigotry, especially toward her beloved pet. Through gritted teeth, she said, "Demons help us all. The Healing gave them to us as gifts, to ease our burden of loss after The Great Earthquake."

Alva dropped the tea ball she'd been preparing and a mess of black and green flakes burst onto the counter. Eyes hard as glass, she glared at Eunice. "Demons are *not* gifts, they're a menace. Part of a grand plan The Source is putting into action as we speak. The demons intend to destroy this city and everyone in it, and they—"

"What's going on in here?" Vernon stood in the doorway, hands on hips. He narrowed his eyes at them both. "What are you arguing about?"

Eunice stomped out of the kitchen. "We're leaving. Grab the traps, Vernon."

"What about the antidote?" Vernon asked.

"We'll find somewhere else to make it. This, this..." She flung up her free hand in exasperation. "This *witch* isn't even on our side."

Sounding indignant, Alva said, "I *am* on your side. I want to cure the demon vermin as much as anyone. It's the only way to keep people safe."

Eunice stopped in the kitchen doorway to stare back at Alva. "Really? And then what?"

Alva squared her shoulders. Her gaze wavered between Vernon and Eunice. "Then they can be exorcised to prevent this from ever happening again."

"But it's not their fault!" Eunice clung fiercely to Sylvester, whose gears rattled as if in fear. She'd never let any harm come to her beloved cat. "You can't blame all of them for one tyrant's act of terrorism."

"It's not about blame." Alva's voice had lowered to just above a whisper as she wiped the tea from the counter. "It's about the natural order of things, and how demons should return to what they were before The Great Earthquake."

Flabbergasted by Alva's narrow-minded view, Eunice could think of nothing more to say. Nothing polite, anyway. The demons had always been her friends. Sylvester, a lowly Imp, had saved her life! How could anyone want to see these amazing beings banished from the face of the Earth? The natural order, as Alva had called it, began the day The Healing Waters changed everyone's life for the better.

"I wondered why no one was answering the door," said a deep voice from outside the kitchen. Henry rounded the corner to stand next to Vernon. "What's all the yelling about? You'll scare my friend away."

Vernon's face relaxed. He appeared relieved by the distraction. "What friend?"

The squeak of turning wheels preceded the chair that rolled up behind Henry.

"This one," Levi said.

CHAPTER TWENTY-THREE

Henry placed a comforting hand on Levi's shoulder. "I couldn't leave him behind knowing Jasper would return. Who knows what that sadistic bastard would do to him next? He's caused enough damage."

"I hope you don't mind that I came along, Ms. Snow," Levi said to Alva. "I'll understand if you want me to leave. It was Henry's idea." He glanced up at Henry. "Perhaps I should go. I'm out of place in your world, Henry. I belong underground with the rest of the moles."

"You're not a mole. You're staying." Henry wanted his friend to feel comfortable here. He turned to his niece, who looked agitated. She had a death grip on that clockwork cat of hers. "What in the world is going on?"

Alva wiped her hands on a tea towel. "Nothing to worry about, Henry. Your niece and I were having a slight disagreement."

"*Slight?*" Eunice's nostrils flared. "Wanting to rid the world of demons is not slight. It's huge. Exorcising demons from their home here is the most unnatural thing I've ever heard."

"Hold on," Henry said, coming up behind Eunice to place his enormous hands on her thin shoulders. "Don't get worked up or you'll give yourself a stroke."

Eunice's mouth gaped like a dying fish before she said, "But she—"

"I don't care what Alva said. We're running out of time and we all have the same goal, don't we?" It figured that Wanda's aunt would share her niece's opinions about demons. They'd simply have to agree to disagree for now. "We have a job to do." Eunice's taught muscles relaxed beneath his hands. "Can we get past our differences to get it done?"

Alva wrinkled her nose at the mechanical cat. "Henry, that thing—"

"Is alive. It's Eunice's pet. Would you deny an old woman her dearest companion?"

Eunice gasped. "I'm not an old—"

Henry glared at her and frowned.

Looking contrite, Eunice licked her lips. "I am quite attached to my precious Sylvester. I don't know how I'd manage without him."

Alva closed her eyes and sighed. "All right. It can stay. But keep an eye on it. I don't want it getting out of that cat and possessing something in my home. Is that clear?"

Henry sympathized with his niece and he could sense Eunice fuming inside, but she nodded and attempted to smile, managing only a grimace instead.

The tea-making forgotten, both women began gathering the tools and ingredients they'd need to brew the Snit antidote. Henry saw that once involved in their craft, both seemed to forget their argument. He hoped it would stay that way, but he wasn't counting on it.

Watching the women work, he realized someone was missing.

"Where's Wanda?" he asked.

"She's staying with one of her girlfriends," Alva said. "She left me a note."

Henry thought it odd that Wanda would disappear with a friend considering these dire circumstances. Now wasn't the time for a girl's night out and slumber parties. "Did she mention the friend's name?"

"Yeah. Claire somebody."

"Claire Beauchamp?"

Alva nodded, slipped the note from her robe pocket and handed it to Henry.

Dear Aunt Alva,

I'll be staying with my friend Claire Beauchamp for a few days. With all that's happened lately, I'm afraid that if I continue to live with you, I'll only put you in danger. Don't worry, I'll be fine. Claire understands what's going on. Please let Henry know I'll be underground.

Love, Wanda

"The underground part didn't make sense to me, but I figured you'd know what she meant," Alva said. "Do you?"

Henry nodded. He didn't want to upset Alva by telling her Wanda was in Spawnstertown and smack dab in the middle of Jasper's web. Wanda obviously wanted Henry to find her without upsetting her aunt.

While Vernon helped the two women in the kitchen, and Levi lounged in the corner of the living room with an issue of *Harper's New Monthly* magazine, Henry called his cab company to see if they'd given Wanda a ride. Sure enough, dispatch had a record of two women being picked up at Alva's building a few hours earlier, but the driver never returned to the garage.

"Did he call in after dropping off his fare?" Henry asked his dispatcher.

"No. But George is new, so he's still figuring things out. I can track him down with an Imp if you want."

Henry had more important things to worry about than an MIA driver. "Forget it. He's bound to show up. And when he does, fire him."

"Will do, boss." The dispatcher ended the call.

"It's ready." Eunice emerged from the kitchen with a tiny blue bottle in her hands. "I don't want to waste a ghost on a sample, but we need to try it. We need a Snit."

Alva entered the dining room wiping her hands on her apron. "I know where we can get one," she said.

Henry eyed her with interest, remembering what Wanda had told him the other night. There was a fissure leading to The Source right here in this building. "In the basement here?"

Alva nodded.

Eunice, who was several inches shorter than Alva, looked up at the woman in surprise. "Well, I'll be."

"It's why I moved into this building," Alva said. "My grandmother's prophecy predicted we'd need access to The Source to stop the uprising."

"What uprising?" Vernon asked.

"The one that's going on right now," Levi said from behind his magazine. He lowered it and faced them all. "It's supposed to be a secret. Jasper aims to take over the city, and he'll use our demon kin to get the job done."

Henry glanced down at his watch. It was late afternoon and all of them were exhausted. They needed to rest before they went loopy and stopped thinking straight. But first they had to make sure they had an antidote that worked. "Curing the Snits is our first step toward stopping Jasper. Once we know they're no longer a danger, we can go after Jasper."

Vernon studied Levi and said, "Claire told us you were forced to call Vox through Hell's Gate."

Levi shifted uncomfortably in his wheelchair. "Since my life is no longer private, I can respond to that with an unequivocal yes."

"Do you know why?" Henry asked.

Shaking his masked head, Levi said, "Jasper didn't say. But whatever it is requires a lot of them. I called up fifty-one, and it still wasn't enough."

What the Hell was Jasper doing? That's exactly what Wanda was trying to find out. And Henry had to help her.

"The antidote?" Eunice held up the bottle. "We need to test this batch."

"I'd offer my services, but I'm still regaining my strength." Levi patted his thighs and shrugged.

Someone had to *bring* a Snit up from The Source. "I'll do it. I'll summon the Snit," Henry said.

Levi chuckled. "Really? I never knew that was one of your abilities."

"Me neither, but I want to give it a try." He had to know if the thoughts Wanda had picked up from the city's demons were true.

"If anyone could do it, Henry, it would be you." Levi wheeled his chair closer. "You're one of the oldest Hellspawn in the city, as am I, and our powers increase with age. I wouldn't be surprised if Bringing is a latent talent of yours. My telekinesis didn't show up until a decade ago."

Jasper was also one of the first Hellspawn born after The Great Earthquake. What new abilities did he have now?

"Come with me," Henry said to Levi. "For moral support. Having an expert around wouldn't hurt."

Levi shook his head. "There's nothing I can do to help you. Bringing is an instinct that isn't taught or learned. Either you have it, or you don't."

Point taken. Better to learn his limitations in a test run now rather than later when he might really need the ability.

Henry led Eunice and Alva to the basement. Alva showed

him the fissure leading to The Source. When he moved the plywood aside, the hole beneath glowed with familiar red and amber light.

Henry clapped his hands together. "Okay, so the plan is to call up a Snit. Then what?"

Eunice glanced around the basement cluttered with boxes and odd bits of stored furniture. She stepped over to a pile of stuffed toys and tugged out a large doll. It was an old porcelain effigy with matted red hair and glass eyes that rolled up in its head when you tilted the body back. The eyelids were stuck open. Its dirty white face leered above a blue frock edged in torn and dirty lace. A hideous thing, but based on its worn condition, someone had loved it once.

Eunice handed Henry the doll. "Put it in this."

The humanoid features of the toy gave him the creeps. "If I'm successful."

"You will be," Alva said, her lips curving up at the corners. "My niece wouldn't say you're a Bringer if you couldn't do the job."

He sucked in a breath and knelt beside the hole in the basement floor, holding out his hands to feel its heat. How should he start? He waggled his fingers over the hole and made a mental command for a Snit to come to him. Nothing happened. "It's not working."

"Then you're doing it wrong," Eunice said.

Maybe he was. He remembered back to all the spontaneous times he'd called a lesser demon, like the one inside the insane oven that wanted to burn down the building. It was even bonded, yet he'd encouraged it to obey. Then there was the Snit in Trudy's kitchen that had skewered him with a butcher knife, but it came to him the second he willed it to. Same with the one inside Levi's Mule in the tunnel. He'd always figured the demons' attraction was due to his fondness for them, and they liked him back. Perhaps there was more to it than that.

Henry concentrated, sending his will into the fissure, directing it down, farther and farther, searching for the demon energy he wanted. It felt good to pour his intent through his point of origin, his heredity, his roots. The demon he sought was like a part of him. And that's when he felt the tug.

He saw nothing, smelled and heard nothing, but his brain buzzed with recognition. The Snit recognized him back and followed the line of his will up from the Earth's core. It rose quickly, its presence more distinct the closer it came to the surface. "I've got one," Henry whispered.

Then it was there, curling around his hand like a fat blue tail, warm and real and humming with energy.

"You did it," Eunice said on an exhaled breath.

"Yep." He could easily accept this new skill. He felt born to it, and probably was. "Now for the real test."

He guided the Snit to the doll and willed it to possess the mangy-looking thing. It was reluctant at first, then slid right in.

"How fast does the virus work?" Alva asked.

"Wish I knew." Henry nodded at the doll. "If it's infected, it would know, and reading a demon's thoughts is not my forté. I'm only a guide."

They didn't have to wait long for an answer.

The doll's blue glass eyes glowed and the expression on its face changed from docile to furious within seconds.

Henry crouched, ready to dart and snatch the Snit from its vessel. "Eunice, have the antidote ready~"

The doll ran. It had an awkward gait with its hinged legs under the rag of a dress, but it moved fast. It held its little arms out in front of it, the porcelain fingers jutting from its hands like tiny daggers.

Eunice unstopped the bottle as the doll rushed at her. Aiming the bottle at the doll's face, she tossed the contents. And missed.

"Get out of the way!" Henry lunged for the doll, but it sped off in the opposite direction. He landed on a stack of boxes that burst beneath his weight, their contents spewing in all directions. More toys. Balls, marbles, building blocks, and small wooden animals rolled and tumbled across the basement floor. A box of pick-up sticks cracked open, spilling the sharp jackstraws at the doll's feet.

The deranged Snit scooped up a stick, wedging it between its stiff thumb and forefinger. The doll cocked back its arm and aimed the jackstraw at Eunice.

Like a javelin thrower, the thing extended one leg and leaned forward, the stick poised over its narrow shoulder. But before it let the stick go, Alva splashed the doll with liquid from a glass beaker. The doll dropped the stick and toppled onto its side, legs kicking. Then it went still.

"You didn't trust I could do it myself." Eunice glared at Alva.

"That's not true," Alva told her, voice cool. "I only wanted to be prepared in case something went wrong."

"And it's a good thing you were." Henry stared down at the broken doll as the wispy Snit unfurled snake-like from the toy's eyes. He frowned at it, wondering what to do with it now.

Alva shook her head. "It's too bad Wanda's not here to snuff it out."

Eunice's glare was smoldering now. "How could you of all people be racist?"

Alva's eyes went round with shock. "I'm not racist!"

Eunice took a step closer to Alva, hands on hips. "How dare you want to end the life of an innocent demon."

Alva snorted a laugh. "There was nothing innocent about it. It tried to kill you!"

"It couldn't help itself." The older woman's voice grew thick with indignation. "It was sick. And if it hadn't been for us, it would still be safe in its home at The Source."

"Which is where our problems started." Now Alva sounded angry.

"Ladies, please," Henry said, their shrill voices giving him a headache. He scrunched his eyes shut to ward off the pain. "Don't be petty."

"Petty?" Eunice pressed her lips together before adding, "These demons are your cousins, Uncle Henry. How could you call this discussion petty?"

"It's not a discussion, it's an argument. And we don't have time for it. Settle your differences later." He stared down at the Snit that had curled up in his hands. It was a victim without choices, and he didn't see the need for a death sentence. Crouching beside the hole in the basement floor, he allowed the Snit to uncurl from his fingers and watched it vanish into the flicker of lights below.

Anxiety clung to Henry like a shroud as the cab driver pulled his car to the curb behind Mystic in front of his niece's house. Relief at seeing she was still parked where Henry had left her calmed his frazzled nerves.

The driver turned to glance at him in the back seat. "Will

we see you at the garage today, Henry?"

"I'm afraid not, Duffy," Henry said. "I'm working on a special project and it's not finished yet. I'll be back next week. Everything going okay with me gone?"

Duffy nodded. "No complaints, but George hasn't come back to work. He's not at home, either." His gaze flicked to the masked man sitting beside his boss. "Can I help you get the wheelchair from the back?"

"No thanks, I got it." Henry climbed from the cab and popped the trunk. "I hope you don't mind staying at my apartment in the city for a few days, Levi."

"Not at all." Levi looked out the window at Henry. "I appreciate the hospitality."

Henry helped his friend into the chair and waved goodbye to Duffy. The cab blew out a puff of steam from a pipe in the back as it rolled down the street.

"How are the legs?" Henry asked.

Levi shrugged. "They tingle a little. If it hadn't been salt that severed my spinal cord, I'd be whole by now." He wheeled himself in front of Henry and headed for Mystic, but paused in front of Eunice's house. "You sure we shouldn't go inside and check things out?"

"Nah." Henry pushed the chair forward. "I don't want Eunice staying in her house right now anyway, so there's no point. And if someone's inside waiting for me, I'd rather not give him the satisfaction."

"You could take him."

"True." Henry grinned. "But why waste my time? I want to get you settled in at my place, grab some shut-eye and then head over to Spawnstertown."

"To look for that exorcist you told me about?"

He grunted. "I'm sure she can take care of herself, but I want to know what she's doing. I'm nosey, and she's dangerous. She can suck out the demon-half of a Hellspawn faster than you can say *Peter Piper picked a peck of pickled jalapeno peppers.*"

"Doesn't sound like someone I'd want to know." The sneer in Levi's voice was obvious.

Henry would have said the same thing a few weeks ago, but he didn't think of her that way anymore. Wanda was a good egg. Mostly. And despite what he'd just told Levi about her ability to take care of herself, he still worried about her.

But lord help him if he barged in and foiled whatever hair-brained scheme she had concocted. He'd have to be subtle when checking up on her.

He rolled Levi's chair to the back of Mystic. Something about the little demon inside his cab felt off. The car looked the same, there were no new dents or scrapes, just a couple of bullet holes compliments of the cops from a few nights ago. Mystic still had all her tires, but an odd silence surrounded her. She was so still, so... vacant.

"Oh, no," Henry said on an exhaled breath. "Mystic?" He rushed to the driver's side door and yanked it open. Nothing. He sat inside and started the ignition. The engine turned, compressed steam pushing pistons and spinning flywheels, making a pleasant hum. But the radio was dark and lifeless. He switched it on and manually turned the tuner dial to pick up a variety of stations. Mystic didn't jump in to snatch the words she wanted to speak. She was quiet because she wasn't there.

Henry gritted his teeth and swore an oath to The Source that whoever stole his best friend would pay dearly. That "whoever" was none other than Jasper Clark. Jasper had probably shanghaied every Vox demon he could lay his hands on and Mystic was no exception.

"What's going on?" Levi asked. "I need a hand getting out of this chair."

Biting back his rage, Henry forced himself to stay calm as he dutifully helped Levi into the backseat. He folded the chair and slid it into the trunk.

"You're being very quiet, Henry." His friend's tone carried genuine concern. Henry wasn't used to such sincerity from a cynic. "Isn't this your demon-possessed cab?"

"It *was*." Henry buckled himself in behind the steering wheel, his hands shaking with suppressed fury. "But it appears she's been kidnapped."

Levi sounded matter-of-fact when he said, "You'll get her back."

"Damn right I will." Henry put the cab in gear and peeled out into the deserted, fog-shrouded street.

CHAPTER TWENTY-FOUR

"Comfortable?" Jasper asked Max.

Max didn't respond. Jasper heard the boy's teeth grind and saw the muscles in his jaw flexing. Max's eyes were covered with a blindfold to discourage visual distractions so that he could focus his psychic energy on his task. Leather straps secured his arms and legs to the reclined chair. Max wasn't going anywhere.

"How's the training coming along?" Jasper didn't expect an answer to this question, but he knew it would irritate Max and that amused him. Having control over someone made him feel more powerful than he already was. It made him feel like a god. "They certainly look ready to take on the world. What do you think?"

Silence. Jasper smiled and gazed affectionately at his shiny metal army. What an amazing group of robots, each one possessed by a Vox demon. A cloud of steam hovered above his militia of two-legged machines as their pipes puffed and their pistons pumped. Yet they made barely a whisper of sound.

"You stole Mystic from my uncle," Max said quietly, but with a hard edge Jasper had never heard from him before.

"Is that what he calls his demon?" Jasper chuckled. "I'm amazed you were able to single out one Vox among the hundred standing here. You truly are talented."

"Mystic isn't a soldier." The young man's voice softened when he added, "She's too gentle to be a killer."

Now Jasper laughed from his belly. "A Vox can be anything you want it to be, Max. You should know that better than anyone. Besides, your uncle won't miss his pet."

Max frowned above his blindfold. "Of course he will. He's—"

"Dead." Jasper couldn't keep the smirk off his face. Too bad Max wasn't able to see it despite the lie he'd just told. Henry would soon be joining his true father in Hell if Jasper had his way, and he always had his way. "Your dear Uncle Henry is no longer among the living."

"You're lying." Max pressed his lips so tightly together they turned almost white.

"Am I?" Jasper circled the recliner while looking down at the young Spawnster. "Do you really think your uncle would give up his best friend without a fight to the death?"

Max's chin quivered.

"I don't know why you're so upset," Jasper said. "He wasn't your *real* uncle. Just like your father isn't your *real* father, or your grandmother isn't your *real*—"

"She better be all right!" Max's voice cracked on the last word. "I only agreed to help you because you threatened to hurt her if I didn't."

"But she's not your *real* grandmother, Max. Why do you care?"

Max made a strangled noise in his throat and his mouth turned down sharply at the corners. It looked like he was trying hard not to cry. Jasper loved it.

"As I understand from your adoption records, your *real* grandmother died soon after your pretend father murdered your *real* mother." Jasper sighed deeply. "But he's dead, too, isn't he? He killed himself after rubbing out your mom. You were all that was left following your family's slaughterfest." He clucked his tongue. "Poor little Maxie."

"Shut up!"

Jasper laughed and gave Max a playful slap on the leg. What did Claire ever see in this ridiculous boy? "Okay, that's enough fun for now. It's time to get down to business. I have an important date tonight with that pretty blonde Spawnster girl and I don't want to be late."

"She looks like a human," Max said, obviously hoping the insult would annoy Jasper. It didn't.

Without a word, Jasper lay back on the twin recliner next to Max. He refused to agree with the boy, though Wanda really did have more striking human features than demon ones. He didn't mind, not really. It was her stripe of pulsing green hair that made him shiver, and in a good way. The literal spark between them when they first met was proof of her desire. They were meant to be together.

Jasper closed his eyes. He cleared his mind and focused on joining his consciousness with Max. His feathers, a major component of Max's headgear, made the connection between them practically automatic. Once Jasper enforced his mental commands to the robots through Max, the hard part was over. For him, anyway. But for Max? His work had just begun.

His thoughts twined around Max's will as he directed them at the Vox demons inside the robots. Jasper mentally gave his instructions and the minute he did, Max lost all ability to control his own actions. Jasper was in control now. And the best part? He didn't have to stick around to keep it that way. He was free to go. Max was not.

Jasper opened his eyes and sat up to see his metal army disband, each machine marching off in a different direction, all of them heading for different parts of the city above. Excellent. They'd stealthily move through the shadows while getting into position on street corners, retracting their legs to disguise themselves as garbage cans. When Jasper gave the command, the city, and all its surviving inhabitants, would be his.

Jasper slipped his pocket-watch from his vest pocket and checked the time. He had a few hours before his date with the lovely blonde Wanda. His stomach twitched and that made him smile. He felt like a schoolboy with his first crush.

Looking down at Max's reclined form, he shook his head at the drool seeping from the corner of the young Spawnster's mouth. Claire should see her boyfriend now. Jasper would give her a call and invite her over.

Eunice was exhausted. She hadn't slept well at Alva's apartment last night. She'd stayed in Wanda's room, while Vernon took the couch. But when she ventured out to the kitchen in the middle of the night for a glass of something to help her sleep, the couch had been empty. And strange noises were coming from Alva's bedroom. That woman had a squeaky mattress.

After that, Eunice didn't sleep at all, not even after downing a brimming glass of brandy. So not only was she tired, she was also hungover. And extremely cranky. If she never saw that Alva woman again, the rest of her life would be happy.

Eunice plucked the receiver from a candlestick phone and listened for a dial tone. It was time for Henry to come pick her up.

The phone rang more than a half dozen times before Henry answered. "What?" he said, his tone sharp.

"Were you sleeping?"

There was a pause and then, "Yeah. I was up late last night and Levi snores. Loud."

"I know it's early, but I can't stay here a minute longer."

Henry's exhale sounded like a gale-force wind. "Can't you two at least *try* to get along?"

"You don't understand," she told him. "That woman... That woman is corrupting my son."

Henry chuckled. "It's about time."

Eunice snorted. "Maybe so, but I'd rather he not be with *her*. I want you to come get me now."

"Is the antidote ready?"

"We made two gallons and I baited every single ghost we have. The Snits don't stand a chance."

"That's great, Eunice. Good job."

Aside from being grumpy, Henry didn't sound like himself. The sadness in his voice tore at her heart. "Is something wrong?"

"It's Mystic. She's gone."

"That's impossible. Are you sure?"

"The cab is empty, Eunice. Jasper's rounding up every Vox demon he can find, and he kidnapped Mystic."

"Bastard."

"He sure is." Henry paused for a split second before saying, "Hang tight. I'm on my way." The line went dead.

"Try calling Mystic again," Henry said to Levi. Henry's hands clutched Mystic's steering wheel, but it wasn't really Mystic's anymore. The cab was nothing more than a run-of-the-mill steam car now. An empty machine sHell. He stomped down his anger and said one more time, "Please. Try."

Levi's mask turned to face the cab's front window. Cars whooshed by, clouds of steam wafting behind them like clotted mist. People streamed down the sidewalks on both sides, young and old, short and tall, men and women, all of them dressed in wool scarves and hats. An ordinary winter's day in the city, but not for Henry. Not without Mystic.

Levi tilted his head back and stared up at the canvas underside of the cab's roof. "I *have* tried, Henry. We both have. We've been trying to summon Mystic since last night. If she hears us, she's either refusing our call, or she's trapped. There's nothing more we can do."

Damn. "Could Jasper have bonded her to him?"

"Perhaps. That's precisely what *you* should have done. She'd still be with you if you had."

"I'm not a slaver, Levi," Henry said bitterly, though he now regretted allowing her absolute freedom for her own good. "I believe in free will."

"This from a Hellspawn who can control the will of others."

Henry raised an eyebrow. "Ironic, isn't it?"

"Indeed."

Halfway to Alva's to pick up Eunice, they found themselves stuck in traffic in the middle of Manhattan. It seemed like everyone was out and about, even small children, all of whom wore gas masks. A high degree of air pollution from the ubiquitous steam generators had made the fog especially dense this morning.

The rare sight of kids on the sidewalk made Henry wonder if today was a holiday. Decorations glittered on street corners and tiny lights in shop windows twinkled through the foggy gloom. So it *was* a holiday, or a preparation for one. The city teemed with people who juggled bags and packages while going about their business. From the ribbons and colorful paper poking from the sacks, Henry surmised a gift-giving ritual.

"Levi, is today a holiday?"

Levi nodded. "I believe it's getting close to what the humans call *Christmas.*"

Henry vaguely recalled the holiday as a child, but neither Eunice nor Vernon had ever practiced the custom. He drove slowly past four people wearing green and red scarves, all of them grouped tightly together as they sang through the cloth masks that covered their mouths. The muffled song was beautifully harmonized and had something to do with a king named Wenceslas, who feasted on Stephen. Had humans practiced cannibalism in the past?

Henry turned up the heat, annoyed and then saddened

that he had to bother. Mystic had always known when he was cold and she had kept the cab's temperature perfect at all times.

When they arrived at Alva's apartment building, Eunice was outside waiting for them. She grabbed her canvas bag off the frozen concrete and shuffled toward the cab, her nose red and her lips almost blue.

Henry met her halfway. "Eunice, you'll catch your death. Give me that." He grabbed her bag and helped her into the back seat, then gestured at the box of ghost traps and the two gallon-sized jugs beside it. "Did you carry all this down the stairs by yourself?"

She nodded, teeth chattering.

"Vernon didn't offer to help you?"

"He was busy so I didn't tell him I was leaving. I left him a note."

It wasn't like Vernon to ignore his mother. Henry shook his head and loaded the Snit-curing paraphernalia into the trunk.

Eunice and Levi exchanged pleasant greetings, and the threesome headed for Manhattan's Times Square. Henry turned up the cab's heater again and watched color return to his niece's gaunt cheeks. Her eyes were ringed in violet and he could tell she'd had a rough night. All three of them could use some coffee.

He drove down a side street where he knew of a small delicatessen known for its rich espresso and spicy possum turnovers. He had just steered the cab around the corner when the door of a butcher shop flew open and a group of people came running out, waving their hands and screaming. They looked terrified, as if chased by something...

"Uh oh," Henry murmured, slowing the cab to park at the curb. "We may have another Snit problem. Either that or there's a very strange stick-up going on in broad daylight."

"We could make this a dry run for Times Square," Eunice said.

"I'd rather not waste a ghost if it's only one or two Snits." Henry waved his hand and added, "Who knows what's going on in there. I'll run inside to check it out. You two stay here."

"I'm coming with you." Eunice held up an atomizer bottle the shape and size of a small tangerine. "I poured some potion in this, just in case."

Levi grabbed a pair of crutches from the back seat. "My legs still tingle, but I can walk a little. I'm right behind you."

Henry knew better than to waste time arguing with either of them. He didn't anticipate much trouble, especially now that they had the antidote. Starting the cure here was as good a place as any. He just wished Wanda were here to lend her expertise.

The last customer disappeared down the street as Henry grasped the handle to the butcher shop's door. It opened with a creak of rusty hinges. All was quiet inside.

He held the door open for Eunice. "Looks like the party's over, whatever it was." Levi hobbled in behind her and all three stood to gape at the empty shop.

A rustle of paper came from behind the counter.

"Hello?" Henry called. "Someone there?"

A package wrapped in blood-stained butcher paper popped onto the counter, followed by another, then another. They levitated and assembled themselves into a life-size jigsaw puzzle of a headless cow.

Eunice backed towards the door.

"Toss me the potion," Henry told her.

Eyes round and brows raised in awe, she threw the atomizer bottle at Henry. It bounced off his shoulder and clattered to the floor, then skittered beneath the counter.

Henry dove for it before it could roll out of reach. He stretched his fingers, but they didn't quite touch the bottle.

He glanced back at Levi, whose eyes were glowing through the eyeholes in his mask. He was either trying to pull the Snit out of the sliced-up carcass, or to manipulate it telepathically. Either way, it wasn't working. The jigsaw cow ambled out from behind the counter and reared up on hind legs composed of two large rump roasts, some tip steaks, round steaks, and two shanks.

Levi used one of his crutches to swipe the puzzle of legs out from under the patchwork beast. It worked, and the packages tumbled to the floor. A stream of blue mist snaked up from the pile of wrapped beef.

Henry almost dislocated his shoulder while stretching to snag the rubber bulb of the atomizer. He yanked the bottle toward him and aimed the nozzle at the Snit, spraying it with antidote. The demon hovered for a few seconds before drifting toward Levi.

"Hello, my friend," Levi told it, opening his coat to expose an inside pocket. "Feel better? Come now, in you go."

The wisp of blue twirled like a funnel cloud and disappeared inside Levi's pocket.

Relieved to have the Snit contained, Henry stood and brushed off his coat. "Eunice, are you all right?"

She lingered in the doorway, eyes blinking, and cleared her throat. "I'm fine." She walked over to help Henry swat the dust bunnies from his coat. "That was exciting."

Without warning, the storefront window imploded. A metal cylinder landed on the floor and rolled toward Henry's feet. *What the Hell?* On reflex, he crouched down to pick it up. Levi slapped his hand away with the foot of his crutch. He shoved both Henry and Eunice as hard as he could and both went sprawling.

"It's a bomb. Take cover!" Levi raised the cylinder as if to throw it, but appeared to change his mind when he clutched it to his chest and threw himself on the ground, covering the bomb with his body.

"No!" Henry lunged for his friend but was blown backward by the explosion.

A glass display case burst like crystal fireworks as Henry rolled over to shield his niece from the rain of shattered glass. Black smoke billowed around them and the smell of gunpowder and burned meat permeated the air.

"Levi!" Henry coughed and sat up, waving his hands to clear the air. "Where are you?"

Eunice struggled to a sitting position and made a choking sound. She pointed a shaky finger. "There."

Levi's severed masked head lay on the floor ten feet away.

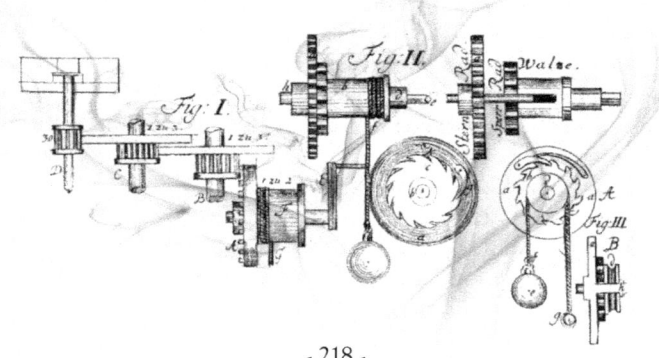

CHAPTER TWENTY-FIVE

"I don't know about this, Claire," Wanda said, concern for her new friend making her uneasy. Not only was she afraid for Claire's safety, but she was the only person Wanda knew, and liked, in Spawnstertown. "What if you don't come back?"

Claire stood in front of the gilded mirror in the bathroom and applied the last of her make-up. The black lipstick made her face appear pale as flour. She flicked her hand at the air. "I'm not worried about Jasper." She blotted her lips on a tissue and puckered her mouth at her reflection "I've known him for years. He'd never hurt me unless I asked him to." She winked at Wanda and gave her a wicked smile.

Wanda sighed. She had a date with Mayor Jasper Clark that very night, so there was a good chance he'd be too preoccupied with his evening plans to make trouble for Claire. Except that Wanda honestly didn't know what the man was capable of. "Claire, please don't go. Tell him you're sick. Or better yet, tell him I'm jealous."

"Are you?"

Wanda scowled. "Hell no."

Claire chuckled. "Maybe you should be. He may be an asshole, but he's a fabulous lover. Have you ever had sex with a Hellspawn?"

Holding her hand to her throat, Wanda choked on the wine she'd just sipped. "Can't say I've had the pleasure."

"You mean Henry hasn't popped your Spawnster cherry?"

Now that was plain vulgar. "How many times do I have to tell you there's nothin' goin' on between Henry and me?" Heat rushed to her face and she lowered her head to hide the blush.

Claire tsked. "You're fooling yourself if you believe that. You two are like a couple of firecrackers with slow-burning fuses. I see the truth in people, remember?" She pinned up half her long black hair into a simple but sophisticated chignon, letting the rest fall in soft waves across her shoulders. The delicate line of turquoise scales on her forehead glistened like jewels beneath the overhead lamp. "How do I look?"

"Gorgeous."

Claire appraised herself in the mirror. "I do, don't I?" It wasn't a question.

"You're just goin' to check on Max, right? Make sure he's okay? Then you're comin' straight back here."

"That's the plan."

"And what if he's *not* okay?"

The smile left Claire's lips and she looked away from her reflection. "Then I'll have to help him."

"You can't do it alone. Wait until tonight after Henry gets here." If he ever does. Wanda was starting to have her doubts.

Claire switched off the bathroom lamp. "Don't worry about me, worry about yourself. And about how you and Henry are going to take down the most powerful Spawnster in New York City."

Jasper may have political connections and criminal clout, but he was no match for an exorcist. His days of long-pig cuisine and racketeering were over. "Don't forget what I am," she said.

Claire turned black eyes on Wanda, her face cold. "Let's hope Jasper never finds out what you are."

An icy shudder coursed through Wanda and she swallowed.

Grabbing a tasseled silk wrap from a hook on the wall, Claire stepped to the door. Her look was funereal chic today, though dark colors seemed her usual style. Wanda wondered if the widow persona wasn't symbolic of what lay ahead. "I'll probably be home before you leave on your date," she told Wanda, a sly smile tugging up the corners of her lips. "But if not, it means Max and I are making up for lost time." Her grin widened and she was out the door.

Jasper sat at the bar and Claire stood behind it, mixing a drink for herself while preparing a fresh one for him. Neither had spoken a word to each other since she set foot inside his home. He was curious to see how long it took for her to ask about Max. So far she'd kept a calm demeanor, though he noticed her hands tremble as she poured a mixture of coconut oil and peanut oil into two cocktail glasses. She floated a cucumber slice on top of each and handed him one.

"You're so quiet today," Jasper said, infusing his tone with as much sincerity as he could muster. "Aren't you even interested in how Max is doing?"

Her eyebrows lifted to create two perfect arches above her almond-shaped eyes. She fluttered her lashes while gazing down at her drink. "You said you had a special job for him. It's going well?"

Jasper grinned and cocked his head. "It most certainly is. He's performing admirably."

Her eyes flashed. "Then let him leave with me."

It was so much fun seeing her riled. "He's not finished yet. I'm sure he'd love to see you, though."

She studied him and frowned. Jasper hadn't lied to her, yet he saw mistrust in her eyes. Such an intuitive girl.

He offered her his arm. "I'll take you to him. He's in the ballroom."

"Training the Vox?"

He looked at her askance. "What do you know about it?"

She shrugged. "Not much. He told me only what *he* knew. It's been days since we last spoke." Her fingers tightened on Jasper's arm.

"Everything is going as planned and he's none the worse for it. Promise. You'll see."

Jasper kept his focus on her as they turned the corner of the hallway and entered the old ballroom. He watched her forehead crease as her gaze settled on Max's reclined form in the middle of the room. Her slender throat convulsed when she swallowed, and her lovely chest heaved with quickened breaths. The boy wasn't dead, and he looked perfectly fine on the outside. But he was in a coma, and Claire sensed it immediately.

"You son of a bitch," she whispered.

Jasper couldn't decide if today was the best day of his life, or if the best day had been when he killed his sadistic human brother and ate him for supper. Tough choice. "I thought it only fair you see Max before his mind is gone for good."

Claire's breathing hitched and she looked up at Jasper with pleading eyes. "Please, you have to stop this. Max is an innocent man and a fellow demon who would never hurt anyone. He means more to me than..."

Icy rage shot through Jasper's stone-cold heart. "He means more to you than I ever did."

She tried to jerk her hand from his arm, but he grabbed it and held her still. "Claire, I have more to offer you now than ever before. Thanks to your friend Max, the city will be mine in a matter of hours. It can be yours, too, if you join me."

She stared at Max and stretched her hand toward him. "I need to go to him. Please!"

"Say your goodbyes," he told her gently.

Jasper released her and she ran to Max's side. His body was still as death, yet the feathered headgear he wore vibrated with psychic energy. His large head had paled within the last couple of hours, and his mouth was slack, drool pooling in the corners and dribbling down his chin. He wouldn't last much longer, but it would be long enough to see Jasper's plan through to the end.

Claire knelt and hugged Max's limp body and ran her fingers down the side of his ashen face. She tugged a black handkerchief from the sleeve of her dress and mopped at his wet chin. Then she kissed his cheek.

Such a saccharine gesture. Jasper wanted to throw up.

"I'll do anything you want. Just let Max go."

"Claire, you don't understand—"

"Anything!" she shouted, the word echoing against the walls of the room. "I know things," she added, in a much quieter voice. "Things that could help you."

Scowling, Jasper thought about that for a second. What could she possibly know that would be of any benefit to him? "I'm listening."

"There's someone new in the city." She spoke so softly that he had to lean in close to hear. "Someone who could hurt you."

He laughed. "Impossible. With all the protection I have, I'm practically invincible. You of all people should know that."

Without looking at him, she said, "This is no ordinary someone."

His curiosity was piqued. "What's so special about this person?"

Now she did look at him, her expression so bleak it made his neck tingle as though touched by frozen fingers. "She's an exorcist."

Henry knew cop cars and fire trucks would arrive any minute. The butcher shop had caught fire minutes after the explosion and he had to get Eunice out of there. So he scooped her up in his arms and ran.

Once outside, he found the cab's trunk popped open and empty of their traps and jugs. That didn't surprise him much. Compared to the grenade, this particular shock factor rated only five on a scale of one to ten.

After tucking Eunice into the front seat, he fastened her seatbelt. There was blood on her blouse. "You're hurt."

She hardly seemed to notice. "The explosion. How did it happen?"

"Pipe bomb." He jogged around to the driver's side and got in. "We were obviously followed. Whoever threw that bomb must have stolen our ghost traps and jugs of antidote."

"Levi knew what would happen." She sounded wistful. "He saved our lives."

Henry drove the cab through an alley across the street and stopped. A cop steamer skid to a halt in front of the flaming butcher shop. A fire engine with bells clanging wasn't far behind. One of the cops climbed from the steamer and crouched low to the ground with his gun drawn. Henry recognized him immediately. It was Officer Ned, the bad penny who always showed up at the worst of times. He had absolutely no doubt the slimy cop was on Jasper's payroll. He may even have been the one who threw the bomb.

"How bad are you hurt?" Henry asked Eunice.

She clutched her upper arm, blood showing between her fingers. "I might need stitches."

She needed medical care, but he didn't know any doctors. He recalled the nurse named Julia he had met the night Trudy's rogue Snit gored him with a butcher knife. "I'm taking you to an apartment on Park Avenue. I know someone there who can fix you up."

"I feel awful about Levi," Eunice said. "We shouldn't have left him back there."

"We had no choice." The image of Levi's head branded itself in Henry's mind. Though Hellspawn were impermeable to fire, their bodies burned like kindling once they had no demon soul to protect them. Cremation was a fitting burial for his faithful old friend. May Levi's soul be welcomed for eternity by The Source.

When they arrived at the building on Park Avenue, Eunice said, "I'll need to make more antidote now."

"Want me to take you back to Alva's? She has the ingredients you need and I'm sure she'll help you mix up a batch." But without ghosts for bait, how would they disperse the cure?

Eunice pursed her lips and blew out a puff of air. "I don't need Alva. I have a better idea. Remember Stan Chin?"

"That fireworks guy in Chinatown?" Henry knew the old man was also a sorcerer, the same one who had made the redwood boxes to hold the Vox he got from Levi. "What can he do?"

"He'll have what I need to make the antidote, but the bomb that destroyed the butcher shop got me thinking about something else. I know a better way to spread the cure to the Snits."

Henry was open to anything at this point. "As long as you know what you're doing."

"I do. No need to wait for me. Where are you off to now?"

"Spawnstertown. To find Wanda."

"You be careful." She leaned across the seat to give him a peck on the cheek. "I worry about you."

Henry escorted Eunice up to Gerald and Julia's apartment. The second Julia set eyes on Eunice's arm, she ushered the elderly woman inside to tend to her wounds. Julia nodded politely at Henry's explanation of what had happened, though it was clear her main concern was for her patient. Eunice was in good hands.

Henry returned to his cab, which felt more like an empty tomb without Mystic. He waited to be sure no one had followed him this time.

Jasper's criminal activities had never concerned Henry in the past because he believed it none of his business. Now he realized it *was* his business, always had been, but he'd been too preoccupied with himself and his family to notice. Then Wanda came along and forced him to pay attention to the world outside the small corner he lived in. Henry cared about the people in this city, both human *and* Hellspawn. It was about time he did something more for them than drive a cab and provide demons to automate their machines.

Seeing the coast was clear, Henry fired up the cab and headed for Spawnstertown. He had to find Wanda before she tried taking on a monster who would just as soon eat her as take her out to dinner. Henry wouldn't be surprised if Wanda accepted such an invitation just to get close enough to suck out Jasper's demon soul. But would she get away with it? Maybe, maybe not. He had to stop her before she did something that would get her killed. According to the note she'd left for her aunt, Wanda was staying with Claire, and Henry didn't know where that was. But he'd find out from the bartender at Greaser's.

He parked the cab in the alley behind the bar. The place was packed, which meant he'd be spotted and the news of his presence reported to Jasper. Fine by him. It was about time for a showdown.

"Hey, Henry," the bartender said when Henry slid onto a stool at the bar. "What'll it be?"

Henry yanked his hat down over his eyes. "Evening, Clyde. What infusions you got?"

Clyde, who had avian features that included a large wattle dangling beneath his chin, swept his hand at a shelf lined with bottles. "Today I got dill, cilantro, habanera pepper, garlic, curry, and horseradish. Oh, and a grapefruit infusion that's popular with the ladies."

"Hit me with a double habanera."

Henry downed the drink in one gulp and gestured for another. "I'm lookin' for a Belle."

Clyde grinned and his beak-like nose twitched when he winked. "Been wonderin' when you'd be piss-proud enough to come lookin' for Miss Laycock."

Damn, the man was crude. Henry tried to look amused and waggled his eyebrows. "You know it, friend. I'm not looking for any ordinary Belle. The laycock I want goes by the name of Claire. Know her?"

The bartender frowned and started wiping down the bar with a wet rag. "She ain't for sale."

Henry chuckled. Jasper had his hooks into everyone in this

town. "I don't want to buy her, just use her for a while. Come on, Clyde. Spill the beans."

The birdman didn't look up.

"There's a nice tip in it for you." Henry slapped a bill on the table that likely matched Clyde's daily till. "What do you say?"

Clyde grabbed the bill with the rag and pulled it toward him. His eyes shifted to look left and right before he said, "Balderdash Row, number five. Top floor."

Henry grinned and tapped the bar with his knuckles. "Appreciate it." He headed off to find Wanda and get her out of there. The two of them would come back to Spawnstertown when they had a concrete plan to take care of old Jasper.

He left the cab in the alley and ventured out on foot, remembering Balderdash was only a few blocks down the street from Greaser's. He kept his collar high to cover the parts of his face not already hidden by his hat and hair. He turned the corner to see a long, shiny black steamer parked at the curb. The passenger door opened and a bald Spawnster climbed out to stand on the crumbling sidewalk.

Jasper. Henry hardly recognized him without his plumage. His head looked like a plucked chicken with a tattoo.

Henry ducked behind a garbage can. He tried to ignore the stench of spoiled fish and discarded offal that clung in slimy clumps to the can's side.

Jasper looked in the steamer's window and said something, then turned and walked to the apartment building's entrance.

Shit. Had he come to take Claire out? If so, where was Max? Minutes later, Jasper emerged from the building with Wanda on his arm.

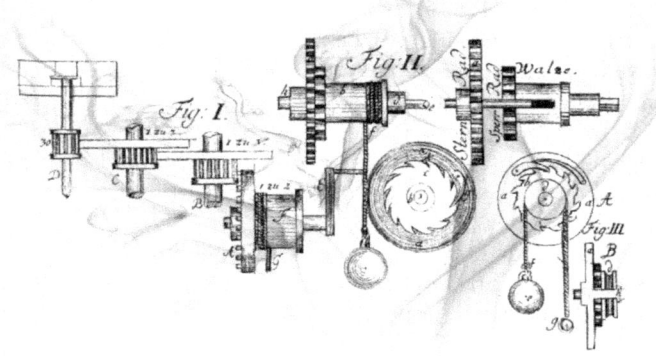

CHAPTER TWENTY-SIX

"**B**eautiful car," Wanda said as she settled herself on the cool leather seat. Claire had told her she could borrow any dress she wanted and Wanda had chosen a red velvet gown with a low-cut bodice that showed an impressive amount of cleavage. She fanned out the skirt and tugged it down over her black satin shoes with large gold buckles that glinted from beneath the lace hem. "It's quite luxurious."

Jasper eased in beside her. "I'm glad you like it."

She frowned at him, thinking he sounded much colder than he had when they spoke on the phone yesterday. "I've been looking forward to our date tonight."

"Is that right?" He slid a sideways glance her way, then leaned forward to open a cupboard door that folded down into a wet bar. It held a carafe of oil and some glasses. "Care for a drink?"

"No, thanks. I'm a bit flushed already. Claire keeps her oil cabinet well-stocked."

"I stock it for her." He gulped down his drink and poured himself another. "I buy her everything she wants."

What an odd thing to say. How did he expect her to respond? Good for you? Or, will you be *my* sugar daddy now?

"Have you found a job yet?" he asked.

"I applied at the hospital," she lied. "File clerk. I'm good at administrative tasks."

"I could use a good file clerk myself. I'll offer you more money, too. What do you say?"

"Wow, thanks!" She bit her lower lip, realizing how fake she sounded. Now she had to cover it up. "I'm sorry. I must sound ungrateful, but the fact is, I hate workin'. I'd much rather go shoppin', get my nails done, and spend the day readin' gossip magazines. But a girl's gotta make a livin' somehow."

Jasper's thin-lipped smile looked reptilian. What seemed handsome when they first met had morphed into something monstrous. "I can make that happen for you, Wanda. A beautiful woman deserves to be pampered. I'd happily pay you a salary just for the pleasure of your company."

That was disgusting. She wasn't a whore. "What are you saying?"

He leaned back deeper in the seat while sipping his oil and ignored her question. She pretended not to notice and glanced out the window behind him to see the neon sign on a theater marquee.

She jerked her chin at the window. "Isn't that the play you want to take me to?"

"I've made other plans."

Panic squeezed her heart. "What kind of plans?"

"It's a surprise."

Her dry mouth made it difficult to swallow. "I don't care much for surprises."

Jasper turned to look at her, his eyes like frozen orbs of amber. He sighed. "You're no fun. If you must know, I'm hosting a party in your honor."

Her smile didn't come easily, but she had to keep up her facade. "That's sweet of you, but you shouldn't have."

His eyebrows lifted. "Why not? It's my way of welcoming a new *Spawnster* to our fair town beneath the city." He put too much emphasis on the word Spawnster. Did he know who she was? The only person in this town who knew the truth about her...

"Will Claire be at the party?" Wanda asked.

"Of course. She's your best friend, so she was the first one I invited."

He *did* know. Dammit, he knew what she was and he was playing her. Two could play at his game.

"I think I'll enjoy this little party of yours." If he only knew how true that was. His timing couldn't have been better. She'd soon have the pleasure of relieving Jasper of his demon side. "I'm so excited I'm getting butterflies."

He looked startled at first, but recovered quickly. "That makes two of us."

She scooted closer to him and he mashed himself into the passenger door, as if trying to put as much space between them as he could. It made her smug. "Are you okay?" she asked him.

Jasper leaned forward and whispered something to his driver, then turned to her and said, "I'm very well, thank you. I hope you're hungry because I've planned a special buffet just for you."

Her stomach knotted as nausea climbed up her throat. A buffet. Yeah, she'd seen the kind of food he served at his buffets and would rather starve.

She should get it over with right now. It would be easy to pounce on him, cover his chest with her hand, and suck out half his soul. But she was alone, the car was moving, and she had to consider what the driver might do. It was best she wait until the two of them were alone; Jasper wouldn't know what hit him.

The car pulled up in front of an enormous building painted black to match the forever-night sky. Some of its windows were lit, like golden eyes shining from a panther's face, and its foreboding presence leached away the confidence she'd felt only seconds ago.

Jasper took her hand to help her from the car, and before she could nestle up against him in a pretense of snuggling, the driver inserted himself between them.

Wanda gave him a shocked look. "Excuse me?"

The big Spawnster sneered down at her, his reptilian features emphasized by his scowl. She could take him as well as Jasper, but exorcising two at once would be a challenge. If she wasn't fast enough, one or the other could—

"Xander, why don't you impress the young lady with one of your tricks?" Jasper bent forward to look at her from around Xander's thick chest. He winked.

"Sure boss." The hulking lizardman held out one hand, spread his fingers, then squeezed them into a fist.

Though it appeared he gripped only air, it happened to be the air from Wanda's lungs. Unable to breathe, she grabbed her throat and glared up at him. Was this how her life would end? Suffocation by one of Jasper's toadies? The big bad mayor didn't even have the balls to do the job himself.

"Enough!" Jasper ordered, and Xander opened his hand.

Wanda gulped in precious air and coughed.

"I think we understand each other, yes?" Jasper asked.

She closed her eyes and nodded, though her desire to steal the bastard's soul was ten times stronger now.

Jasper glowered at her. "Only a fool would try to trick me, especially in my own town."

Xander still stood between them, and he grabbed her by the elbow as the three of them walked abreast toward the mansion's entrance.

Jasper said, "Did you really think you could take me on so easily?"

Yes, she really did, but she said nothing. She'd been abandoned by Henry and betrayed by Claire, and was nowhere near giving up. She'd do whatever she had to and damn the consequences.

Wanda had been in his mansion before, but now it was without the crowd of Jasper's followers. The foyer of the mayor's home appeared massive. Black and white tile gleamed beneath their feet and a crystal chandelier sparkled above their heads. A number of oil paintings in gold frames hung on creamy walls that smelled of fresh paint. Black velvet drapes covered windows tall as the vaulted ceiling. It lacked the classic beauty of Eunice's home but was no less a palace.

Xander spun her around and grabbed both her arms to hold them behind her back.

"Hey!" She struggled against him, but he squeezed her wrists tightly together so she couldn't move. The scratchy fibers of a rope scraped her flesh.

"Insurance," Jasper explained, and jerked a glance at Xander. "Leave us. She's helpless now."

Gritting her teeth, she tried to think how else she could touch his heart, but her hands were her tools. Without them, she was useless.

Jasper held her elbow, his touch surprisingly gentle, and guided her down a long hallway. She knew it led to the ballroom where he'd held his meeting last week, and it was the perfect place for a party. What would tonight's guests say when they saw her trussed up like a pig for slaughter? Her veins flooded with ice water. Was she the dinner guest, or the dinner?

But when they entered the huge room, there were only two occupants, and both lay supine on reclining chairs in the center of the room. She tried to control her fast breathing as she noticed one was Henry's nephew, Max, and he wore a strange contraption on his head. He didn't see her because he was blind-folded. Beside him lay her new friend and betrayer, Claire Beauchamp.

"What have you done?" Wanda's voice sounded so soft she wasn't sure she'd actually said anything. But she must have because he answered her.

"I did what I had to."

Her feet were unwilling to move so he pushed her toward the room's center. "Max is doing an important job for me right now. He's deeply engrossed in his task so don't be offended if he ignores you."

A job? The boy was comatose. "That's not work. He looks half-dead."

Jasper shrugged. "He'll be the other half by tomorrow."

She couldn't despise Jasper more than she did at that moment. Narrowing her eyes at Claire, her heart softened when she saw the Hellspawn girl was no better off than Max. But she was conscious, her glassy eyes rolling back in their sockets as something liquid dripped onto her forehead from above. Wanda looked up at the source. Not a leaky roof, but a bag suspended from the ceiling. Each drop that touched Claire's skin left a blister that burst and bled, then healed, only to be blistered again by the next drop. Saltwater.

Jasper must have tortured Claire into revealing Wanda was an exorcist. Had he promised her Max's freedom in exchange? "Jasper, why are you being so cruel to her?"

His thin lips tightened with a grin. "I'm surprised you care."

"Of course I care. She betrayed me to save the man she loves. I can hardly blame her for that."

The smile faded. "I gave her everything she wanted, but she chose this bubble-headed Spawnster over me."

Jasper had a serious god complex and he needed to get over himself. Wanda would like nothing better than to help him do just that. But she couldn't with her hands tied behind her back.

"You want to stop her pain?" Jasper asked.

"Me?" She scowled up at the bag of salt water. "If I could reach it, yeah, I'd stop it."

He deftly unlatched the tin collar from around her neck and she was powerless to stop him.

"Wait." Her ears started ringing. "Stop!"

The band slid away from her skin and she braced herself for a rush of chaotic demon thoughts. She held her breath and watched Jasper's grin spread even wider.

"So it's true that exorcists are plagued by the random thoughts of demons." He twirled her band around his index finger. "Tin keeps the voices out."

Her head began to pound, her mind pulsing with the cacophonous roar of thoughts from hundreds of Imps and Snits, and dozens of Vox throughout the city. But they weren't as loud down here as they were on the streets above. A layer of earth muffled the thunder. She could tolerate it. "You're a mad man."

He brought his lips to her ear and whispered, "*Madness is badness of spirit, when one seeks profit from all sources.* Aristotle."

She gritted her teeth against the dull throb inside her head. He intended to torture her for his own pleasure.

"Now that your necklace is out of the way..." Cold steel slid against her throat, followed by stinging pain. Something warm dribbled down her neck. "You have a choice. Exorcise Claire's demon side, or become the main course for my dinner party."

"You'll kill me no matter what I choose," Wanda said, trying to sound brave and failing. Her voice cracked on every other word.

He nuzzled her ear. "No, I won't. I need you, Wanda. You can be the perfect weapon against any Spawnster who dares disobey me. You'll make a wonderful negotiating tool when I try to convince any reluctant Hellspawn to follow me."

Loosening the rope that bound her wrists, he said, "You know what to do. Make Claire an example of what my followers can expect if they screw up."

Her hands free, Wanda flexed her fingers and worked the circulation back into her wrists. Jasper held the knife more firmly to her throat and she again felt the sting of its blade. "I may not kill you, but I can come close and make you suffer in the process. Now do it," he said. "Make Claire human."

Hand shaking and temples pounding, she was almost too dizzy to stand. His hand gripped her arm to hold her up and she hovered her fingers over Claire's chest. She felt the familiar pull as power rushed through her, its intention to take away Claire's demon soul. The blade of Jasper's knife cut deeper.

She pressed her hand against Claire's beating heart.

⚝ ⚝

"Stan, leave some room in that rocket for my potion," Eunice told her sorcerer friend as he packed the rockets with gunpowder. She knew a way to distribute the Snit antidote that would make it spread farther than the ghosts could have done.

"Must shoot high into sky," Stan Chin explained in choppy English. "Need plenty powder for big bang. More is better."

"Not if there isn't enough antidote to explode along with it." Her theory was to salt the sky with potion so that it would rain over the entire city. All Snits would be affected and immediately cured. "That's the last of it," she said, and emptied a jug in one of Stan's rockets.

He bundled up the rockets in boxes and called in his apprentices from the front of his shop. Three Asian Spawnsters stepped into the room, their stocky bodies filling what little space there was.

"Where will you set them off?" Eunice asked.

Stan pointed up. "On roof of shop."

As his helpers grabbed up the loaded rockets, there came a discordance of excited voices out on the street followed by rapid gunfire and more yelling.

Eunice rushed to the plate glass window at the front of the shop. Outside, crowds of people scurried in all directions. They ran away from something, but she couldn't see what.

A haze of smoke mixed with fog and an overpowering stench of kerosene and gunpowder clung to the air. She peered through the dark at several blinking lights that bobbed like balls bounced on the air. When the objects got close enough, she could make out cylindrical machines, each one propelled by two mechanical legs.

"Robots?" Eunice whispered. The shouts and screams from outside drowned out her voice. Where had they come from? The machines looked like something Vernon would make, except these were weapons with a dozen or more smoking gun muzzles extended from their cylindrical bodies. Vernon had no interest in violence. Whoever had created these things did.

Stan Chin darted to her side and clutched her elbow. "Come, Eunice. We must leave. Machines come this way."

"But what about the rockets?" She knew her job wasn't

done yet. More gunfire exploded in the distance, meaning more robots. Jasper's plan, it had to be. He must have sent them, but how did the things know what to do? "Where are the stairs to the roof?" Eunice asked.

"On roof we expose ourselves. Get shot. Not safe."

"Possessed," Eunice said.

Stan stared at her, mouth agape. "What?"

She should have realized it at once. "The machines. I'm sure it's Vox demons that are operating them." Which is why Jasper had collected them, but Vox were compassionate demons and too smart to blindly follow a madman. Someone, or something, was controlling them.

The shop's front door splintered as gunfire pelted the wood. The door drooped from its hinges and one of the robots marched inside. "Surrender!" came a synthesized voice from inside the machine. "Surrender!"

Eunice looked beyond it to a crowd of people being herded toward the middle of the street by other machines.

"Hands up. Will shoot." Clacks and grinding gears sounded from inside the metal body. It was hard to believe people would obey these things, but the robots had a compelling argument. She saw a woman trudge through the street, her body bowed beneath a limping man whose drooping leg left a trail of blood behind. These robots meant business.

"What is this?" Eunice asked the machine.

"Surrender! Hands up. Will shoot."

The recorded commands were obviously the extent of its vocabulary.

Stan pulled at her. "We go outside with others. Not get shot."

She backed up to a store shelf stacked high with brightly colored boxes.

"Will shoot," the robot repeated.

All she needed was a spark. The explosive fireworks were in the back room, but Stan kept the less volatile trinkets here in front. Sparklers, spinners, flyers, poppers, snakes and colored smoke bombs ought to do the job.

Eunice threw up her hands. "I surrender."

Her gaze swiveled to the doorway, where two of Stan's apprentices stood poised to run. "Go," she told them, and they sped down the hall toward the stairs.

The robot swiveled a hundred and eighty degrees, its gun barrels sliding out to point where the men had vanished.

Eunice swept her hand across a shelf and scattered boxes of fireworks in every direction. The robot redirected its aim and fired.

She lunged for the doorway to follow Stan's retreating back and felt a burning sting on her shoulder. Stan was no fool. He knew gunfire in a room filled with fireworks was the last place he should be.

Popping firecrackers and screaming whistle-rockets rivaled the rapid fire of bullets from the robot. Though focused on the stairs ahead, her peripheral vision picked up flurries of colored flashes and the noise of ignited fireworks shrieked in her ears. That should distract the Vox for the short time they needed.

Her old legs were fueled by adrenalin as she scampered up the steps, tripping every so often as she made her way to the roof. The frigid air outside cooled the burns on her arms and legs. She arrived to find Stan and his helpers arranging the rockets to point up at the sky. They lit the wicks.

Eunice stared out across the city and spotted pockets of bedlam similar to what was happening here in Chinatown. The robots were spread throughout Manhattan, and two streets over she witnessed them rounding up people like cattle. It looked like the end of the world.

A sudden flurry of crackles and sparks followed her rockets as they shot up into the evening sky. Once they reached several hundred feet the rockets burst open and lit the black heavens with a shower of brilliantly colored lights.

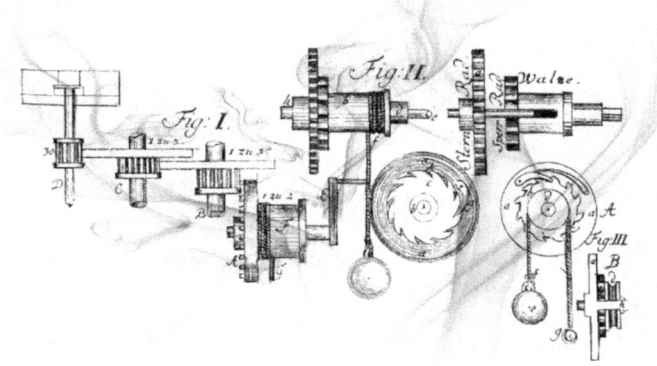

CHAPTER TWENTY-SEVEN

The antidote from Eunice's potion floated down from the sky in a cloud of purple mist so fine it sifted into the fog. The smoke billowing out of the shop below blended with smoke from the robots' guns. It was eerily quiet on the street. Too quiet. Eunice wondered if the explosions had blown out her eardrums.

"Eunice?" Stan asked.

Her ears were fine. "What is it, Stan?"

"I think it is over."

Looking down on the crowd below, she saw people disperse from tight clusters. Some scampered off into the shadows, while others meandered in the street. They appeared disoriented. The injured either limped or were dragged to safety by friends and neighbors. The robots themselves stood like metal sculptures, lights no longer blinking, hydraulic legs no longer pumping.

"Machines dead?" Stan asked.

"It appears so." Eunice heard the sirens of fire trucks and police cars shrieking in the distance. The end of the world had been postponed.

Her sorcerer friend pointed down at the street and exclaimed something in Chinese she didn't understand.

"Well, I'll be damned." Eunice stared, eyes so wide they hurt.

Green tendrils of mist rose from the robot corpses. Vox. They were abandoning their hosts. What had called them out? The demon mist lifted and seemed to dissipate in the fog, though Eunice knew they were intact. Dispersion was a demon's perfect camouflage.

Then she saw what she'd been hoping for. Masses of blue

Snit energy swirled out of buildings, sewer grates, and horse buggies. They hovered above the people, their movements hesitant, before whooshing around them as though concerned. No one seemed to know how to react after the recent trouble with Snit demons, so the people ran away in every direction. Blue demon mists rose into the sky and disappeared within the fog along with their Vox cousins.

"Where are you, Henry?" Eunice wondered aloud. She could only pray her uncle was safe.

Henry sneaked into the ballroom behind Jasper and Wanda, then hid behind a tall cluster of potted plants. Gazing through the spiny branches, he watched Jasper remove Wanda's neckband, untie her hands, then hold a knife to her throat. He couldn't hear what was said, but he could now see that Jasper was forcing Wanda to do something to Claire.

Myriad emotions hit Henry all at once. He experienced fear for his nephew strapped to a chair, confusion at seeing Claire tied down beside him with Wanda's hand on her breast, and worry that Jasper would slice open Wanda's slim, white neck. Worst of all was his blind fury aimed at the evil Hellspawn responsible for it all.

He clenched his teeth to stay quiet, hoping his shaking body wouldn't vibrate the floor hard enough to give him away. He'd made it past Xander because he and the bully had a little chat in the foyer. Once in control of the Spawnster's mind, Henry had ordered Xander to drive Jasper's fancy car off the pier. Had he cautioned him to get out of the car first? Damned if he could remember.

Claire screamed.

All Henry needed was a split second of eye contact to force Jasper under his control. He took fast, stealthy steps toward his enemy, his boots making barely a whisper of sound. It was a trick Jasper himself had taught him back in their gang days.

His old friend must have sensed him coming because he quickly sliced his blade across Wanda's throat. She fell on top of Claire, dark blood gushing from a gaping wound in her neck.

Henry roared, his feet beating their way across the floor the way his fists wanted to beat Jasper's head in. His rage blinded him to reason, and emotion took him over, possessing him like a demon would possess a machine. He couldn't take his eyes off Wanda's long waves of blonde hair stained red with her blood. How had he allowed this to happen? If only he'd arrived sooner, kept her away from that maniac.

Jasper averted his gaze from Henry's to prevent having his mind taken over. He didn't stand a chance.

Jasper spun around to run but slipped on Wanda's blood. He fell to the floor, cracking his bald head on the shiny tile that glistened with so much red. He lay unmoving, but Henry knew his stillness wouldn't last for long.

Maybe Henry could still save Wanda. Save his nephew. Maybe even save Claire, but one look at the Belle told him that Wanda had done her job: exorcised Claire's demon soul. Though still a dark haired, porcelain-skinned beauty, something was missing. Claire's demon features had vanished.

Should he grab Jasper and break the man's neck? Or should he see what he could do for Wanda first? He tossed a glance at Max and couldn't tell what state the boy was in, though he was too still to be healthy. Something was very wrong.

Jasper stirred.

Wanda moaned.

She had lost so much blood that it would be a miracle if she lived, but Henry had hope. He reached out to touch her just as Jasper leapt to his feet and tried again to run. This time Henry clotheslined him, stopping him mid-lunge, but Jasper wheeled his arm back and swung a powerful uppercut to Henry's jaw.

The blow made Henry almost lose his balance, but he held tight to Jasper's arm and remained upright. Jasper whipped around his other hand, the one holding the knife. He sunk its blade deep into Henry's side, just below his rib cage.

All the starch left Henry's legs as his knees buckled. He fell hard, his body landing in a splash of blood that was now a mix of both his and Wanda's. He'd heal, but not fast enough. Jasper was sure to get away this time.

But the mayor of Spawnstertown appeared to have a sudden change in plans. He didn't avoid Henry's gaze, possibly because he knew Henry was in too much pain to concentrate. Henry was paralyzed with agony, physical and otherwise. Guilt and grief ruled his inner world.

Jasper smiled, the expression more malicious than happy. "Our final showdown." He grabbed the hilt of the knife protruding from Henry's side and yanked it free. Henry yelled in pain so intense he could hardly breathe. Hellspawn were difficult to kill, but not impossible. And nobody knew how to murder his own kind better than Jasper.

"You've been good at staying out of my way all these years," Jasper told him. "When did you suddenly grow a spine? Or did you take the one Levi had before I salted him.."

"You cowardly son-of-a—" Henry grunted and grabbed his side. Something warm and slimy touched his fingers. Blood, yes, but something more. His guts burned. He was turning inside out.

"Careful there," Jasper said, rolling the knife over and between his fingers. "Gut wounds don't heal as fast as the superficial ones."

"What do you want from me?" Henry asked, his voice low and dangerous.

"Not much. Your loyalty would be nice, but I'll settle for compliance." He knelt on the floor beside Henry. "You're one of the first Hellspawn born of the Healing Waters, just like me. We're stronger than the Spawnsters who are younger than we are by decades. You and I are among the few Demon Lord centurions left."

"I'll never follow you again."

"Ah, come on. It'll be like old times, Henry. We'd be a team, a force to be reckoned with. The young ones will obey anything we tell them."

Henry blinked sweat from his eyes. "And if they don't?"

Jasper shrugged. "They face the consequences."

Henry shook his head and bared his throat. "Just do it, Jasper. I'm sick of listening to you talk."

"But I'm not sick of listening to you, my friend." He wiped Henry's blood from the blade with a handkerchief. "Just answer one thing for me."

Henry only glared.

Jasper must have taken his silence for a yes because he went ahead and asked, "Why is it you never interfered before?"

Not sure how to answer, Henry said only, "I never had a reason."

"It's unfortunate you decided to don your hat of virtue now. Not that it matters because this city is mine anyway. I own it and everything in it, including you."

Henry's insides were cooling, healing. If he kept Jasper talking, which shouldn't be too hard, he'd soon be strong enough to take control. "You don't own me."

Both of Jasper's feathered eyebrows lifted. "Sure I do. I can kill you, or keep you alive. It's my choice."

"I'll never do anything you say."

Jasper hesitated. "If I threaten to hurt the people you love, you'll do *everything* I say."

Henry's heart jumped. "My niece. My nephews. They're all I have."

Jasper yawned and positioned the knife against his shoulder like a violin, his other hand sawing across it with an invisible bow. "How touching. It's because of them all this happened, you know."

The man was delusional. "They've done nothing to you."

"True enough, but they *did* do something to *you*." Jasper waved his knife in Henry's face. "You centered your entire life around those humans. They're the ones who own you, my friend."

It was true he'd devoted his life to Eunice and Vernon, and then to Max when he joined the family. But it wasn't their fault. It was his. Henry had made the choice to put them first, and to hell with everything else, including Jasper. Henry never had any desire to re-associate himself with his old life, so much so that he had turned a blind eye and let Jasper literally get away with murder. He could have tried to stop him, but chose not to. A mistake he was about to rectify.

Henry's eyes grew warm, the heat of his core rising to summon his power. He directed his will at Jasper.

Jasper's face went slack and he tried to turn his head, but his eyes stared hard into Henry's. There was recognition in them. He realized too late that he was now Henry's puppet.

Henry wouldn't take complete control. He wanted Jasper to remember being outwitted and overpowered. A taste of his own medicine was just what the mayor of Spawnstertown needed, and Henry would be sure to make it a very bitter pill. "Stand up."

Jasper stood, and Henry struggled to his feet while clutching his side, which was still in the process of healing. Glaring at Jasper, he thought of all the humiliating things he could make him do. Force him to apologize to his gang, release his human slaves, confess his criminal dealings to the police. His prison term would be a long one, but only if another inmate didn't end it for him sooner.

A bloody hand reached out from Claire's recliner, but it wasn't Claire's. The hand belonged to Wanda. It grabbed hold of Jasper, tugging him close, the fingers glowing as they fanned over his chest.

Shocked she still lived, Henry peered at Wanda's face and understood why she hadn't breathed her last. The exorcist's forehead was covered in scales, her pupils elongated like a cat's, and tiny horns protruded from her temples. Her nostrils flared like an angry bull. She'd taken Claire's demon as her own so that she could heal herself.

Jasper's jaw dropped once he realized what was happening. Wanda's hand shimmered with power as she siphoned Jasper's demon soul through his icy heart.

"Please." Jasper gasped and tried in vain to pull Wanda's hand away. "Don't do it."

But Wanda didn't listen.

Henry could easily guess what she was feeling because her face had molded into an expression of pure hatred.

"You. You tried to kill me," Wanda whispered, her hand steady on Jasper's chest. Her breathing sounded labored, as if she struggled to draw breath. "You *were* a monster, but no more. I've cured you."

The colorful pattern on Jasper's head started to fade and his feathery eyebrows became ordinary black bristles of hair. His amber eyes darkened to a chocolate brown, his beaked nose shrank, and his lower lip plumped as if in a pout. He no longer looked like himself. He looked... human.

Henry's attention returned to Max, who lay still as death on the recliner. But something had changed. His headgear had lost the feathers Henry knew had come from Jasper's head. That was how he'd been controlling Max. Without Jasper's demon soul, the link between them had broken. Max was free.

The man who was once Jasper Clark slid to the floor. His ordinary brown eyes inside his ordinary human face gazed up at nothing, his wits cut in half since he was now a shadow of his former self. Maybe Jasper would become a better person as a human, though Henry doubted that was possible.

Wanda groaned. Henry grabbed her to keep her from

sliding off the recliner and taking Claire with her. The exorcist made a fist around the red lump of swirling energy she'd taken from Jasper. With a single squeeze, the demon soul was snuffed into smoke.

"Wanda," Henry said gently. "What happened to you?"

When she didn't answer, he pulled back her hair to see the wound on her neck. Her skin looked as if painted in blood so thick it had cracked like dried plaster. The gash was completely healed, leaving no scar in its place.

Wanda's hand moved back to Claire's chest and rested over her heart. The Belle's human eyes were like Jasper's: unfocused and unblinking.

"There's nothing left in her for you to take," Henry said.

"Not taking." Wanda was panting now, and her hand shook. "Giving."

Her fingers glowed the same as they had with Jasper, only this time the features on her victim's face were changing back to what they had been, scales and all. Claire gasped in a breath so deep it forced her back to arch, and when she coughed her body shook from head to toe.

"You brought her back." Henry couldn't believe what he'd just seen. He'd always thought an exorcism was permanent. "I didn't know you could—"

"Neither did I," Wanda said, her sapphire eyes drooping closed before her body collapsed onto Claire.

Henry took Wanda by the shoulders and eased her up. He checked her pulse, which was weak but definitely there.

"I saw it all," Claire said, voice hoarse and tinged with awe. "I was inside Wanda, watching her take Jasper's demon away. Then she put mine back. She—" With a shudder, Claire said, "She saved my life."

As well as her own. Quick thinking under pressure was Wanda all the way. "Are you strong enough to stand?" he asked Claire, who blinked up at him and nodded. He used Jasper's knife to cut away her bonds. "Then help me get her out of here."

Claire glanced beside her. "Max!" She slid off her recliner, wobbling on unsteady feet. She pressed the side of her head against his chest and smiled. "He's alive."

Henry grabbed Wanda's neckband from the floor and refastened it around her neck. He gathered her into his arms and lifted her from the recliner. An unfamiliar sensation stung his eyes and he wondered if he'd somehow gotten salt in them. His heart ached almost as much as his wounded side, yet his joy at having Wanda back filled him with relief. It struck him that she meant far more to him than he felt comfortable with, but it wasn't a bad feeling. It actually felt very, very good. He hugged her close and ran his dry lips over her stripe of green hair that dimly pulsed with power.

He cleared his throat and blinked. "Claire, are you strong enough to carry Max?"

Max was small for a Hellspawn, but he matched Claire in height. Even so, she pulled Max's limp body to a bowed sitting position, then tucked her shoulder into his middle and lifted. With a grunt, she stood with Max hanging like a sack of grain across her back. She jerked her head toward a doorway. "That's the fastest way out."

They lugged their burdens to the exit, but a tall Spawnster appeared in the doorway to bar their way. It was Webster, one of the two guys Henry and Wanda had encountered at the hospital two weeks ago.

Webster scowled as he looked between Claire and Henry. "Claire, what are you doing? Where's Jasper?"

Claire's eyes narrowed and she jerked her thumb behind her to where the human version of Jasper lay. "We were attacked by one of Jasper's human slaves."

Webster peered past her to the catatonic figure on the floor. "Okay, but where's Jasper?"

"He took a ride with Xander." Henry dug inside himself for his power and held it ready. If he didn't need to use it, he wouldn't have to tax his waning strength, but if he did...

Brows tilted in concern, Webster tipped his chin at Wanda. "Is she hurt bad?"

"Healed," Henry said. "But she fainted. Hates humans."

Webster still looked skeptical. "Speaking of humans, I came over to tell the boss his army of robots fizzled out and the humans they rounded up all got away. It was real sudden, too. Happened about fifteen minutes ago."

Robots? An army of them? So that had been Jasper's plan. Jasper must have controlled this robot army through Max and when Jasper lost his demon soul, he also lost his power. *And* his army.

"Wait a second." Webster peeked around Claire to see Max's face. "That's Max! He was linked to the bots. And you released him? No wonder the machines failed."

Henry locked his gaze with Webster's. "There's a human on the floor in there. He needs medical attention. You have to call an ambulance."

"Yes, an ambulance," Webster droned, his vacant gaze staring at nothing.

Claire piped up, "Have him call the chef from the kitchen instead. Fresh meat. It would serve Jasper right."

"Don't think it didn't cross my mind," Henry said, but the thought of Jasper getting fricasseed was too disgusting to consider no matter how much his old friend deserved it. Putting him on the Spawnstertown menu would only drag Henry down to Jasper's level and he was better than that.

"Repeat to me what you're going to do," Henry ordered.

"Call an ambulance for the human," Webster said.

"Good." Henry blew out a relieved breath. "You never saw us. Jasper let Max go home to his family. Got that?"

Webster nodded.

Claire glanced back into the room. "Bastard."

"Who will never hurt you, or anyone else, ever again." Henry stepped away from the stupefied Webster and readjusted his hold on Wanda's sleeping form. "Now let's get these two home."

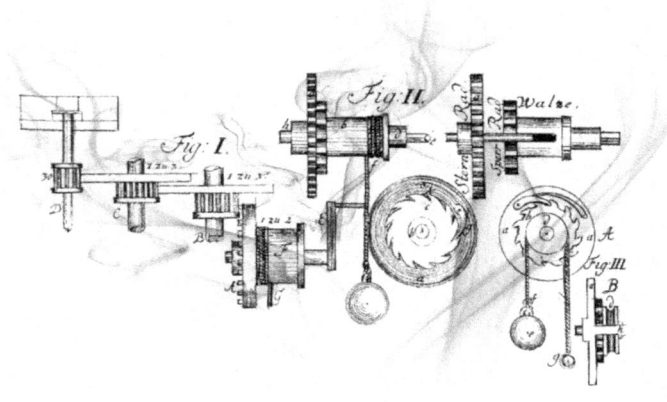

CHAPTER TWENTY-EIGHT

Max lay in bed in his room at Eunice's house. Henry watched from the doorway while Claire held his hand and told him something that made him laugh. It was so good to see Max acting like his old self again.

"How are *you* doing?" Eunice asked as she walked up behind Henry. She gave him a friendly pat on the back. "All healed up?"

Henry touched his side. "Mostly. It's been a whole week, but Jasper stabbed me deep. I'm positive his knife was salted."

"Oh, dear." She laid a small, warm hand on his arm. "Anything I can do to make you feel better? I have a pantry full of potions and salves."

He shook his head and gazed down at his elderly niece. Her plucky demeanor and quick action had saved her life last week. Had saved them all. The story she'd told him of her harrowing experience in Chinatown still made his hair stand on end. He couldn't fathom how she'd survived it. The bruise on her forehead had faded to a yellowish green and her burned arms and legs were healing beneath their bandages. One look at her would make most people take her for an old granny who spent her days knitting and listening to soap operas on the radio. They'd be *so* wrong.

"The least I can do is make you a cup of tea." Eunice threaded her arm through his and led him down the hall toward the parlor.

The front door opened and Vernon walked in, looking happier than Henry had seen him in weeks. He was covered head to toe in ash and soot, and the pockets of his canvas trench coat were torn. Eyes bright with excitement, he said, "I found something."

He'd been searching the ruins of his lab all week, looking for anything salvageable. So far he'd found nothing but a charred strongbox containing a few thousand dollars, and a melted silver coffee pot.

"Don't keep us in suspense," Eunice said, shooing her son off the foyer rug so that soot sifted onto the tile instead. "What did you find?"

Vernon lifted a dirty gunnysack and reached inside to pull out a redwood cube of wood. It was one of the Vox boxes Henry had delivered to him last month. "I found all four," Vernon said and handed one to Henry.

Seeing the boxes brought Henry a twinge of remorse over the lost fifth box, as though he'd failed his nephew. He turned over the box Vernon had given him and found his thumbprint branded on one side. The box hadn't burned. The blessed wood that had made it was even stronger than he first thought. "What if these are the only Vox left in the city?"

"Henry, they're not gone for good. They're just... laying low for now," Eunice said.

"How can you be sure?" Henry thought about Mystic and how empty he felt without her. There'd been a hole in his heart since the day Jasper had taken her away from him. The grieving process was ongoing.

"I'm *not* sure." Eunice looked thoughtful. "After The Great Earthquake, the demons came to us for a reason. It makes no sense for them to abandon us now, not when they still have work to do."

"They were never our slaves," Henry said.

"No, but they were our friends and loyal servants. By *choice*."

That was until Jasper tried to take control and ruin things for everyone, demons included. Now that Henry's old friend was a human vegetable void of any influence, negative or otherwise, there was a chance the city's Hellspawn could finally assimilate into human society. If minds opened to the mutual benefit of working together, Hellspawn would not only be tolerated but accepted as well. Henry believed that was the grand design all along. However, he had to wonder if Jasper's interference had queered the deal for them all.

"The newspaper is reporting demon activity in other parts

of the country as unchanged," Eunice said. "New York seems to be the only city affected."

And it appeared that an invisible bulletin had circulated to every demon on the planet telling them to stay away from New York City. Henry couldn't blame them.

The doorbell rang.

"It's become Grand Central Station around here," Eunice muttered.

Vernon opened the door and there stood Wanda Snow.

Henry hadn't seen or talked to her all week. She'd been traumatized after taking on Claire's demon soul and her recovery from the experience was slow. He only knew this after calling Wanda repeatedly and her Aunt Alva intercepting each call to speak on her behalf.

"Hello, Wanda" He'd wanted his greeting to sound warm and welcoming, though his voice came across chilly to his own ears. He was miffed at having been ignored all week. Eunice gave him a reproving look. "What brings you here?" he asked.

Wanda's mouth widened with a toothy smile, her enormous blue eyes twinkling with suppressed news. "I couldn't wait to give you this."

Henry frowned. "Give me what?"

She retrieved the Vox box from her coat pocket. The fifth one.

Puzzled, Henry asked, "I thought it was gone forever. Where did you find it?"

"Remember when Mr. Sanchez asked what he could do for me after I exorcised the Snit from his radio?"

Henry nodded.

"I told him he could find this box, and he did. You'll never guess where it was."

It was as though the entire house held its breath, but it was only Henry.

Wanda chuckled. "It was in the sandbox behind my aunt's apartment building. One of the little boys in the building, I think it was the Browns' son, used it for a toy army fort he was building."

Henry shook his head. "I'll be damned."

"We were just talking about whether or not to release the Vox from their boxes," Eunice said.

"I'm concerned these might disappear like the others,"

Henry told Wanda, hope clinging to the boxes in his hand. If these were all that were left, he couldn't give them up. They might never replace Mystic, but they would help ease his grief over losing her.

"Have you heard anything?" Eunice asked, nodding at the collar around Wanda's neck.

Her face fell and she shook her head. "The Vox and Snits are either gone or figured out a way to block me. The Imps, on the other hand, are chattier than ever, but only with each other. I think the Imps are enjoying being the center of attention for a change."

Sylvester the clockwork cat trotted over to rub against Eunice's ankles. She picked him up and held him close, stroking his metal back. Letting him nuzzle her cheek, she said, "He's been more clingy lately."

"How's Max?" Wanda asked.

"Getting stronger every day," Vernon said. "How about your aunt?" He slid his mother a sideways glance and she glowered at him. Eunice wasn't happy about Vernon's romantic involvement with Alva Snow.

"Alva's doin' great," Wanda told him. "Her burns are completely healed."

The mention of Max sparked a sudden thought in Henry, so he said, "Speaking of Max, he's the expert when it comes to training demons, right?"

"That's right." Vernon studied him, one eyebrow raised. "What are you thinking?"

"If he's strong enough, maybe he can instruct these Vox to find their fellows."

"What you really mean is look for Mystic," Vernon said.

Henry blinked. "Yes, but we want the others to come back too, don't we?"

"It's worth a try." Wanda sidled up beside Henry and pressed herself close to his side. She lifted her face to look at him, her pleading eyes giving her a look of vulnerability he wasn't used to seeing. It was as if she wanted him to forgive her, though she'd done nothing to forgive.

He snaked an arm around her waist and pulled her closer, and she relaxed against him with a relieved sigh. Perhaps she had missed him, too.

"All we can do is ask," Vernon said, and led the way down

the hall to Max's room.

Henry followed Vernon in to see Max, while Eunice and Wanda stayed just beyond the doorway. Claire sat in a ladder-back chair beside Max's bed, her turquoise-scaled fingers stroking Max's hand. The room wasn't big enough to fit everyone.

Henry cleared his throat and held out one of the boxes, explaining what it was and what he'd like Max to do. "So what do you think?"

Max glanced at Claire, who only shrugged. He addressed Henry when he asked, "You want Mystic back, is that it?"

"Just tell me if you can do this."

"How about releasing only one Vox for now, as an experiment?" Max said. "I'm not sure I'm strong enough to direct five at once. A week ago I was responsible for training over fifty demons, and it taxed my power pretty good. I'm still not completely recharged."

"I understand," Henry said, conscious of the young man's anxiety. "And if you'd rather wait a few more days, that's fine."

Max grinned, his big head cocked at an amused angle. "Uncle Henry, you saved my life. Both you and Wanda. The least I can do is help you get Mystic back."

Claire peered beyond Henry at the two women still standing in the hall. "Hey, Wanda."

Wanda waved.

Henry wondered if the two women had talked since the incident, and if there were any hard feelings between them. Betrayal was a tough pill to swallow.

He cleared his throat again and held up the box Wanda had returned. "Let's try it." He placed his thumb over the print he'd made with his own blood. The gesture brought back sudden memories of Levi and all they'd been through together, especially toward the end. He dearly missed his friend.

Henry focused his will on the box and recalled the words Levi had taught him for the reverse bonding spell. Pressing his thumb tightly over the print, he said, "Bound no longer, I set your spirit free."

The wooden lid slid back on its own and a thick green mist poured slowly from the box. It rose toward the ceiling and hovered, as if to study the strange creatures that gazed up at it with expectant looks on their faces.

Max's eyes turned cherry-red as his power flowed to the demon. The green mass of energy held still, as if listening, and after a few seconds, it streamed toward the window and vanished.

Max exhaled a loud breath. "That wasn't so hard." But a sheen of sweat covered his face. "Uncle Henry, there's no way of knowing how long this will take, or even if the demon will be successful. I wish I could be more encouraging."

Henry smiled. "That's okay, Max. I appreciate the effort. I was afraid Mystic might be gone for good, but you've given me hope. I appreciate that."

Claire dabbed Max's damp forehead with a handkerchief. "Max needs to rest now," she told them.

"Of course." Henry turned to leave.

"Grandma?" Max called.

Eunice stepped into the room. "What is it, dear?"

"Is there any leftover haggis from yesterday?" He ducked his head and peered up at her through long dark lashes.

His grandmother smiled. "Of course. I'll warm it up for you right now." Eunice strode off to the kitchen.

"Can I talk to you for a second?" Wanda asked Henry.

He nodded. "Do you need a ride home?"

"Please."

She appeared more demure than her usual brassy self, and Henry wasn't sure what to make of it. He imagined her near-death experience might have altered her perspective on things, and he understood how it could. Though truth be told, he wanted his old Wanda back.

They stood in the foyer, toe-to-toe. Their connection felt awkward to Henry. He'd had very few human friends in his life and wasn't always sure how to act with Wanda. It helped that a few drops of demon blood ran through her veins because it gave them something in common. He was a demon, or at least half of one, and she was an exorcist. Not much of a match.

"Look," she started, then stopped to lick her lips. "I know I'm the one who got you involved in all this, and I'm sorry."

"Don't be. It was the kick in the ass I needed."

"What do you mean?"

"If not for you, I'd never have known how far Jasper had taken his criminal operations. You opened my eyes to what I should have been paying attention to all along. I thank you for that."

"Oh." This seemed to surprise her. She paused before saying, "Then maybe you'll be open to the proposition I'm about to make."

He wasn't sure he liked where this conversation was going. "What kind of proposition?"

"A partnership, you and me. We both know there's more meat on this bone."

"The prophecy thing?"

She nodded. "I could really use your help. We make a good team."

Uncertainty made him wince. "I'd say we already managed to nip your granny's prophecy in the bud."

"I'm not so sure about that."

He knew she was right, but saying it out loud would make it real. If only he could savor their victory a while longer before launching into another take-down mission.

"Admit it," Wanda said. "You feel it too. I can see it on your face."

"I don't know that I feel it so much as know it. I've been around for more than a hundred and fifty years, Wanda. There's always trouble brewing among the Spawnsters in this city. It's how it's always been, and how I suspect it will always be."

"We can control it."

He huffed. "*Control* it? You're kidding, right?"

A fire lit in her eyes and her green stripe of hair started to glow. Much better. His old Wanda was back.

"I think we can do anythin' we're determined to do, Henry Paine. Don't give up before we have a chance to get started. Are you turnin' that bristly cheek of yours again?"

She knew how to get to him, but she wouldn't goad him into a fight this time. "No ma'am."

Her eyes softened and she stuck out her hand. "Then let's shake on it. Partners?"

What was he getting himself into? His involvement so far had nearly cost him the lives of what little family he had left. Was it worth the risk?

"Stop thinkin' so hard," she said. "I see smoke comin' out of your ears."

His gut told him it was the right thing to do. Protect the city, and he'd protect his family. He grabbed Wanda's hand

and gave it a hard shake. "Partners."

She yanked her hand free and flexed her fingers. "Ow."

They left the house together, walking side by side toward the yellow steam car that used to be Mystic. Just seeing the empty shell that once housed his friend made Henry's breathing hitch. Where had she gone? Why hadn't she come back?

"I'm real sorry about Mystic, Henry," Wanda said as she reached her arm around his waist. "That bastard had no right to take her from you."

Henry draped an arm over her shoulder. "I never thought I'd hear such sentiment coming from an exorcist."

"I've got feelin's. I've lost a few pets over the years and it's heartbreakin'. I understand what you're goin' through."

"She was more than a pet, Wanda. Mystic was my friend."

She said only, "I'm your friend, too. You can *always* count on me."

He gave her a searching look, seeking something he wasn't quite sure about. The word friend sounded so detached. He liked to think their relationship was something more. "I appreciate that. Thank you."

They both climbed inside the cab, Henry on the driver's side, Wanda on the other, and just as he reached for the ignition, the engine started by itself. The lights on the dashboard sprang to life and the radio dial spun the same way it used to.

Henry clasped the steering wheel. "Where the Hell have you been?"

"*Around*," came a radio voice-bite through the Victrola horn. "*Here... and there...*"

A lump formed in Henry's chest. "I thought I'd lost you."

"*Scared*," Mystic said. "*All... fine... now?*"

"Yes, it's fine now. I'm just happy you came home."

"*Me... too.*"

"So am I," Wanda said.

The cab had nothing to say at first, and then, "*You... still... here?*"

Wanda rolled her eyes. "I thought you and I understood each other. Why don't you like me?"

Mystic was silent.

Henry said, "Never mind. I'm just so... I can't express how..." His voice cracked so he cleared his throat before saying, "I only want things to be the way they were before."

"You know that can never happen," Wanda told him, her soothing voice like a balm for his battered soul. "The world is changin' and we have to change with it."

"You... are... right," Mystic said.

"It's nice to see we finally agree on somethin'," Wanda said, a surprised lilt to her voice. "Thank you."

"You... are... welcome."

Henry steered Mystic onto the street, overjoyed at having his best friend back, but he had a feeling of trepidation over what lay ahead. Like Wanda had said: *There's still meat on that bone.* He glanced at the exorcist, whose determined eyes were fixed on him. It was comforting to know she had his back, and that she would never let him down.

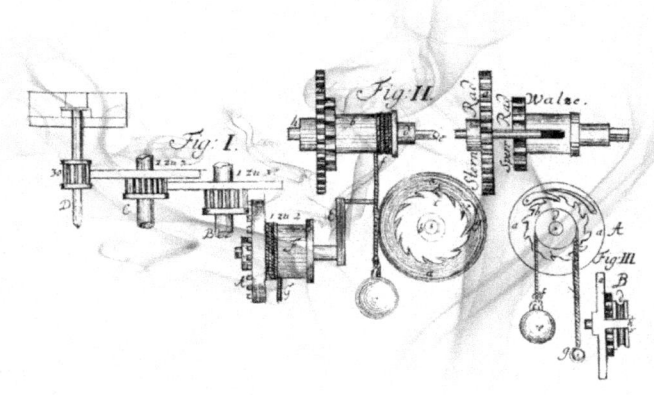

If you enjoyed this book, please consider
giving it a review on Amazon.com, BarnesandNoble.com,
Goodreads, your own personal blog, or any website
that welcomes reader reviews.

Thank you for reading!

http://www.karenduvallauthor.com/
http://www.karenduvall.blogspot.com
https://twitter.com/KarenDuvall
http://www.facebook.com/Karen.Duvall.Author

Karen Duvall was born in L.A., California and grew up in Hilo, Hawaii. She now lives in the Pacific Northwest with her husband and four incredibly spoiled pets. Karen is represented by Elizabeth Winick Rubenstein of the McIntosh & Otis Literary Agency. Her Knight's Curse series was published by Harlequin Luna in 2011 and 2012, and her post apocalyptic novella, Sun Storm, appeared in Luna's 'Til The World Ends anthology in 2013. Karen is also a professional graphic designer who designs book covers and book interiors for self-published authors, and creates original 3D graphics for computer gaming. Demon Fare is the first book in her Spawnstertown Chronicles.

www.ingramcontent.com/pod-product-compliance
Lightning Source LLC
Chambersburg PA
CBHW060130130626
46556CB00006B/2290